'At times Burke's writing and atmosphere remind one of William Faulkner; at other moments Raymond Carver. I cannot think of much higher praise that can be accorded a novel'
Marcel Berlins, *The Times* Metro

'Resounds with poetry and rage. Sometimes it seems the only Americans fighting the death penalty are crime writers'
Independent

'Although the novel's tone is elegiac and aches with an excruciating sense of despair, it's Robicheaux's humanity which shines a light through the gloom and invests the book with a life-affirming quality. *Purple Cane Road* is undoubtedly Burke's best novel yet, an ambitious work which blurs the boundaries between so-called "serious" literature and crime fiction'
Crime Time

'This is prose that cuts straight to the heart, summoning a wonderful parade of damaged humanity in its wake'
Maxim Jakubowski, *Guardian*

'It is difficult to think of new superlatives to describe *Purple Cane Road* . . . [it] is written in a language which, at once sharp yet poetic, can handle with nonchalant skill anything from extreme violence to languorous ease. But this must be the best of the series . . . the final pages have an emotional impact which lifts the novel far above its genre'
T. J. Binyon, *Evening Standard*

'A thrilling piece of fiction, at once exciting and elegiac . . . In *Purple Cane Road* he writes with a depth of feeling that is rare in the mystery genre'
Observer

'I can think of no other writer today who captures the American South with such eloquence and sympathy'
Susanna Yager, *Sunday Telegraph*

James Lee Burke is the author of twenty-six novels, including sixteen featuring Detective Dave Robicheaux, and two volumes of short stories. *The Lost Get-Back Boogie* was nominated for a Pulitzer Prize; *Black Cherry Blues* won the Edgar Award in 1989; and *Cimarron Rose*, Burke's first novel featuring Billy Bob Holland, won the 1997 Edgar Award. In 1998 *Sunset Limited* won the CWA Macallan Gold Dagger for Fiction. James Lee Burke divides his time between Missoula, Montana and New Iberia, Louisiana. Visit his website at www.jamesleeburke.com.

By James Lee Burke

DAVE ROBICHEAUX NOVELS

The Neon Rain
Heaven's Prisoners
Black Cherry Blues
A Morning for Flamingos
A Stained White Radiance
In the Electric Mist with Confederate Dead
Dixie City Jam
Burning Angel
Cadillac Jukebox
Sunset Limited
Purple Cane Road
Jolie Blon's Bounce
Last Car to Elysian Fields
Crusader's Cross
Pegasus Descending
The Tin Roof Blowdown

BILLY BOB HOLLAND NOVELS

Cimarron Rose
Heartwood
Bitterroot
In the Moon of Red Ponies

OTHER FICTION

Half of Paradise
To the Bright and Shining Sun
Lay Down My Sword and Shield
Two for Texas
The Lost Get-Back Boogie
The Convict and Other Stories
White Doves at Morning
Jesus Out to Sea

JAMES LEE BURKE
PURPLE CANE ROAD

PHOENIX

A PHOENIX PAPERBACK

First published in Great Britain in 2000
by Orion
This paperback edition published in 2001
by Orion

Reissued 2005
by Phoenix,
an imprint of Orion Books Ltd,
Orion House, 5 Upper St Martin's Lane,
London WC2H 9EA

An Hachette Livre UK company

A CIP catalogue record for this book
is available from the British Library.

Printed and bound in Great Britain by
Clays Ltd, St Ives plc

The Orion Publishing Group's policy is to use papers that
are natural, renewable and recyclable products and
made from wood grown in sustainable forests. The logging
and manufacturing processes are expected to conform to
the environmental regulations of the country of origin.

www.orionbooks.co.uk

For old-time University of Missouri pals
Harold Frisbee and Jerry Hood

chapter one

Years ago, in state documents, Vachel Carmouche was always referred to as the electrician, never as the executioner. That was back in the days when the electric chair was sometimes housed at Angola. At other times it traveled, along with its own generators, on a flatbed semitruck from parish prison to parish prison. Vachel Carmouche did the state's work. He was good at it.

In New Iberia we knew his real occupation but pretended we did not. He lived by himself, up Bayou Teche, in a tin-roofed, paintless cypress house that stayed in the deep shade of oak trees. He planted no flowers in his yard and seldom raked it, but he always drove a new car and washed and polished it religiously.

Early each morning we'd see him in a cafe on East Main, sitting by himself at the counter, in his pressed gray or khaki clothes and cloth cap, his eyes studying other customers in the mirror, his slight overbite paused above his coffee cup, as though he were waiting to speak, although he rarely engaged others in conversation.

When he caught you looking at him, he smiled quickly, his sun-browned face threading with hundreds of lines, but his smile did not go with the expression in his eyes.

Vachel Carmouche was a bachelor. If he had lady

friends, we were not aware of them. He came infrequently to Provost's Bar and Pool Room and would sit at my table or next to me at the bar, indicating in a vague way that we were both law officers and hence shared a common experience.

That was when I was in uniform at NOPD and was still enamored with Jim Beam straight up and a long-neck Jax on the side.

One night he found me at a table by myself at Provost's and sat down without being asked, a white bowl of okra gumbo in his hands. A veterinarian and a grocery store owner I had been drinking with came out of the men's room and glanced at the table, then went to the bar and ordered beer there and drank with their backs to us.

'Being a cop is a trade-off, isn't it?' Vachel said.

'Sir?' I said.

'You don't have to call me "sir" . . . You spend a lot of time alone?'

'Not so much.'

'I think it goes with the job. I was a state trooper once.' His eyes, which were as gray as his starched shirt, drifted to the shot glass in front of me and the rings my beer mug had left on the tabletop. 'A drinking man goes home to a lot of echoes. The way a stone sounds in a dry well. No offense meant, Mr Robicheaux. Can I buy you a round?'

The acreage next to Vachel Carmouche was owned by the Labiche family, descendants of what had been known as free people of color before the Civil War. The patriarch of the family had been a French-educated mulatto named Jubal Labiche who owned a brick factory on the bayou south of New Iberia. He both owned and rented slaves and worked them unmercifully and supplied much of the brick for the homes of his fellow slave owners up and down the Teche.

The columned house he built south of the St Martin Parish line did not contain the Italian marble or Spanish ironwork of the sugar growers whose wealth was far greater than his own and whose way of life he sought to emulate. But he planted live oaks along the drives and hung his balconies and veranda with flowers; his slaves kept his pecan and peach orchards and produce fields broom-sweep clean. Although he was not invited into the homes of whites, they respected him as a businessman and taskmaster and treated him with courtesy on the street. That was almost enough for Jubal Labiche. Almost. He sent his children North to be educated, in hopes they would marry up, across the color line, that the high-yellow stain that limited his ambition would eventually bleach out of the Labiche family's skin.

Unfortunately for him, when the federals came up the Teche in April of 1863 they thought him every bit the equal of his white neighbors. In democratic fashion they freed his slaves, burned his fields and barns and corn-cribs, tore the ventilated shutters off his windows for litters to carry their wounded, and chopped up his imported furniture and piano for firewood.

Twenty-five years ago the last adult members of the Labiche family to bear the name, a husband and a wife, filled themselves with whiskey and sleeping pills, tied plastic bags over their heads, and died in a parked car behind a Houston pickup bar. Both were procurers. Both had been federal witnesses against a New York crime family.

They left behind identical twin daughters, aged five years, named Letty and Passion Labiche.

The girls' eyes were blue, their hair the color of smoke, streaked with dark gold, as though it had been painted there with a brush. An aunt, who was addicted to morphine and claimed to be a *traiture*, or juju woman, was assigned guardianship by the state. Often Vachel Carmouche volunteered to baby-sit the girls, or walk them out to the road to wait for the Head Start bus that took them to the preschool program in New Iberia.

We did not give his attentions to the girls much thought. Perhaps good came out of bad, we told ourselves, and there was an area in Carmouche's soul that had not been disfigured by the deeds he performed with the machines he oiled and cleaned by hand and transported from jail to jail. Perhaps his kindness toward children was his attempt at redemption.

Besides, their welfare was the business of the state, wasn't it?

In fourth grade one of the twins, Passion, told her teacher of a recurrent nightmare and the pain she awoke with in the morning.

The teacher took Passion to Charity Hospital in Lafayette, but the physician said the abrasions could have been caused by the child playing on the seesaw in City Park.

When the girls were about twelve I saw them with Vachel Carmouche on a summer night out at Veazey's ice cream store on West Main. They wore identical checkered sundresses and different-colored ribbons in their hair. They sat in Carmouche's truck, close to the door, a lackluster deadness in their eyes, their mouths turned down at the corners, while he talked out the window to a black man in bib overalls.

'I've been patient with you, boy. You got the money you had coming. You calling me a liar?' he said.

'No, suh, I ain't doing that.'

'Then good night to you,' he said. When one of the girls said something, he popped her lightly on the cheek and started his truck.

I walked across the shell parking area and stood by his window.

'Excuse me, but what gives you the right to hit someone else's child in the face?' I asked.

4

'I think you misperceived what happened,' he replied.

'Step out of your truck, please.'

'My cotton-pickin' foot. You're out of your jurisdiction, Mr Robicheaux. You got liquor on your breath, too.'

He backed his truck out from under the oak trees and drove away.

I went to Provost's and drank for three hours at the bar and watched the pool games and the old men playing bouree and dominoes under the wood-bladed fans. The warm air smelled of talcum and dried perspiration and the green sawdust on the floor.

'Have any locals pulled in Vachel Carmouche?' I asked the bartender.

'Go home, Dave,' he said.

I drove north along Bayou Teche to Carmouche's home. The house was dark, but next door the porch and living room lights were on at the Labiche house. I pulled into the Labiche driveway and walked across the yard toward the brick steps. The ground was sunken, moldy with pecan husks and dotted with palmettos, the white paint on the house stained with smoke from stubble fires in the cane fields. My face felt warm and dilated with alcohol, my ears humming with sound that had no origin.

Vachel Carmouche opened the front door and stepped out into the light. I could see the twins and the aunt peering out the door behind him.

'I think you're abusing those children,' I said.

'You're an object of pity and ridicule, Mr Robicheaux,' he replied.

'Step out here in the yard.'

His face was shadowed, his body haloed with humidity in the light behind him.

'I'm armed,' he said when I approached him.

I struck his face with my open hand, his whiskers

scraping like grit against my skin, his mouth streaking my palm with his saliva.

He touched his upper lip, which had broken against his overbite, and looked at the blood on his fingers.

'You come here with vomit on your breath and stink in your clothes and judge me?' he said. 'You sit in the Red Hat House and watch while I put men to death, then condemn me because I try to care for orphan children? You're a hypocrite, Mr Robicheaux. Be gone, sir.'

He went inside and closed the door behind him and turned off the porch light. My face felt small and tight, like the skin on an apple, in the heated darkness.

I returned to New Orleans and my problems with pari-mutuel windows and a dark-haired, milk-skinned wife from Martinique who went home with men from the Garden District while I was passed out in a houseboat on Lake Pontchartrain, the downdraft of U.S. Army helicopters flattening a plain of elephant grass in my dreams.

I heard stories about the Labiche girls: their troubles with narcotics; the bikers and college boys and sexual adventurers who drifted in and out of their lives; their minor roles in a movie that was shot outside Lafayette; the R&B record Letty cut in prison that made the charts for two or three weeks.

When I bottomed out I often included the girls in my prayers and regretted deeply that I had been a drunk when perhaps I could have made a difference in their lives. Once I dreamed of them cowering in a bed, waiting for a man's footsteps outside their door and a hand that would quietly twist the knob in the jamb. But in daylight I convinced myself that my failure was only a small contributing factor in the tragedy of their lives, that my guilty feelings were simply another symptom of alcoholic grandiosity.

Vachel Carmouche's undoing came aborning from his

long-suppressed desire for publicity and recognition. On a vacation in Australia he was interviewed by a television journalist about his vocation as a state executioner.

Carmouche sneered at his victims.

'They try to act macho when they come into the room. But I can see the sheen of fear in their eyes,' he said.

He lamented the fact that electrocution was an inadequate punishment for the type of men he had put to death.

'It's too quick. They should suffer. Just like the people they killed,' he said.

The journalist was too numb to ask a follow-up question.

The tape was picked up by the BBC, then aired in the United States. Vachel Carmouche lost his job. His sin lay not in his deeds but in his visibility.

He boarded up his house and disappeared for many years, where to, we never knew. Then he returned one spring evening eight years ago, pried the plywood off his windows, and hacked the weeds out of his yard with a sickle while the radio played on his gallery and a pork roast smoked on his barbecue pit. A black girl of about twelve sat on the edge of the gallery, her bare feet in the dust, idly turning the crank on an ice cream maker.

After sunset he went inside and ate dinner at his kitchen table, a bottle of refrigerated wine uncapped by his plate. A hand tapped on the back door, and he rose from his chair and pushed open the screen.

A moment later he was crawling across the linoleum while a mattock tore into his spine and rib cage, his neck and scalp, exposing vertebrae, piercing kidneys and lungs, blinding him in one eye.

Letty Labiche was arrested naked in her backyard, where she was burning a robe and work shoes in a trash barrel and washing Vachel Carmouche's blood off her body and out of her hair with a garden hose.

7

For the next eight years she would use every means possible to avoid the day she would be moved to the Death House at Angola Penitentiary and be strapped down on a table where a medical technician, perhaps even a physician, would inject her with drugs that sealed her eyes and congealed the muscles in her face and shut down her respiratory system, causing her to die inside her own skin with no sign of discomfort being transmitted to the spectators.

I had witnessed two electrocutions at Angola. They sickened and repelled me, even though I was involved in the arrest and prosecution of both men. But neither affected me the way Letty Labiche's fate would.

chapter two

Clete Purcel still had his private investigator's office in the Quarter, down on St Ann, and ate breakfast every morning in the Cafe du Monde across from Jackson Square. That's where I found him, the third Saturday in April, at a shady outdoor table, a cup of coffee and hot milk and pile of powdered beignets on a plate in front of him.

He wore a blue silk shirt with huge red flowers on it, a porkpie hat, and Roman sandals and beige slacks. His coat was folded over an empty chair, the handkerchief pocket torn loose from the stitching. He had sandy hair that he combed straight back and a round Irish face and green eyes that always had a beam in them. His arms had the girth and hardness of fire plugs, the skin dry and scaling from the sunburn that never quite turned into a tan.

At one time he was probably the best homicide investigator NOPD ever had. Now he ran down bail skips in the projects for Nig Rosewater and Wee Willie Bimstine.

'So I'm hooking up Little Face Dautrieve when her pimp comes out of the closet with a shank and almost cuts my nipple off,' he said. 'I paid three hundred bucks for that suit two weeks ago.'

'Where's the pimp?' I asked.

'I'll let you know when I find him.'

'Tell me again about Little Face.'

'What's to tell? She's got clippings about Letty Labiche all over her living room. I ask her if she's morbid and she goes, "No, I'm from New Iberia." So I go, "Being on death row makes people celebrities in New Iberia?" She says, "Brush your teeth more often, Fat Man, and change your deodorant while you're at it." '

He put a beignet in his mouth and looked at me while he chewed.

'What's she down on?' I asked.

'Prostitution and possession. She says the vice cop who busted her got her to lay him first, then he planted some rock in her purse. He says he'll make the possession charge go away if she'll provide regular boom-boom for him and a department liaison guy.'

'I thought the department had been cleaned up.'

'Right,' Clete said. He wiped his mouth with a paper napkin and picked up his coat. 'Come on, I'll drop this at the tailor's and take you out to the project.'

'You said you hooked her up.'

'I called Nig and got her some slack . . . Don't get the wrong idea, mon. Her pimp is Zipper Clum. Little Face stays on the street, he'll be back around.'

We parked under a tree at the welfare project and walked across a dirt playground toward the two-story brick apartment building with green window trim and small green wood porches where Little Face Dautrieve lived. We passed a screen window and Clete fanned the air in front of his face. He stared through the screen, then banged on the frame with his fist.

'Lose the pipe and open the front door,' he said.

'Anything for you, Fat Man. But don't get on my

bat'room scale again. You done broke all the springs,' a voice said from inside.

'My next job is going to be at the zoo. I can't take this anymore,' Clete said when we were on the front porch.

Little Face pushed open the door and held it while we walked inside. She wore cut-off blue jeans and a white T-shirt and had very dark skin and lustrous, thick hair that she wore on her shoulders. Her eyes were no bigger than dimes.

'This is Dave Robicheaux. He's a homicide detective in Iberia Parish,' Clete said. 'He's a friend of Letty Labiche.'

She tilted up her profile and pursed her lips and brushed back her hair with her fingers. She had on heels, and her rump and the backs of her thighs were taut against her shorts.

'How about flexing your brain instead of your stuff for a change?' Clete said.

'What he want wit' me?' she said.

'Why would you keep all those newspaper clippings about Letty?' I asked.

'They for Zipper,' she replied.

'You know how Zipper got his name? He carved all over a girl's face with a razor blade,' Clete said to her.

'We still love you, Fat Man. Everybody down here do,' she said.

'I hate this job,' Clete said.

I placed my hands lightly on the tops of Little Face's arms. For a moment the cocaine glaze went out of her eyes.

'Letty Labiche is probably going to be executed. A lot of people think that shouldn't happen. Do you know something that can help her?' I said.

Her mouth was small and red, and she puckered her lips uncertainly, her eyes starting to water now. She pulled out of my grasp and turned away.

'I got an allergy. It makes me sneeze all the time,' she said.

The mantel over the small fireplace was decorated with blue and red glass candle containers. I stooped down and picked up a burned newspaper photo of Letty from the hearth. Her image looked like it was trapped inside a charcoal-stained transparency. A puff of wind blew through the door, and the newspaper broke into ash that rose in the chimney like gray moths.

'You been working some juju, Little Face?' I asked.

' 'Cause I sell out of my pants don't mean I'm stupid and superstitious.' Then she said to Clete, 'You better go, Fat Man. Take your friend wit' you, too. You ain't funny no more.'

Sunday morning I went to Mass with my wife, Bootsie, and my adopted daughter, Alafair, then I drove out to the Labiche home on the bayou.

Passion Labiche was raking pecan leaves in the back-yard and burning them in a rusty barrel. She wore men's shoes and work pants and a rumpled cotton shirt tied under her breasts. She heard my footsteps behind her and grinned at me over her shoulder. Her olive skin was freckled, her back muscular from years of field work. In looking at the brightness of her face, you would not think she grieved daily on the plight of her sister. But grieve she did, and I believed few people knew to what degree.

She dropped a rake-load of wet leaves and pecan husks on the fire, and the smoke curled out of the barrel in thick curds like damp sulfur burning. She fanned her face with a magazine.

'I found a twenty-year-old hooker in New Orleans who seems to have a big emotional investment in your sister's case. Her name's Little Face Dautrieve. She's originally from New Iberia,' I said.

'I don't guess I know her,' she said.

'How about a pimp named Zipper Clum?'

'Oh, yes. You forget Zipper about as easy as face warts,' she said, and made a clicking sound and started raking again.

'Where do you know him from?' I said.

'My parents were in the life. Zipper Clum's been at it a long time.' Then her eyes seemed to go empty as though she were looking at a thought in the center of her mind. 'What'd you find out from this black girl?'

'Nothing.'

She nodded, her eyes still translucent, empty of anything I could read. Then she said, 'The lawyers say we still got a chance with the Supreme Court. I wake up in the morning and think maybe it's all gonna be okay. We'll get a new trial, a new jury, the kind you see on television, full of people who turn abused women loose. Then I fix coffee and the day's full of spiders.'

I stared at her back while she raked. She stopped and turned around.

'Something wrong?' she said.

'I didn't mention Little Face Dautrieve was black,' I said.

She removed a strand of hair from the corner of her mouth. Her skin looked dry and cool inside the smoke from the fire, her hands resting on the rake, her shoulders erect.

'What are the odds she work for Zipper and she white?' she said.

When I didn't reply her eyes wandered out into the yard.

'I'll stay in touch,' I said finally.

'You bet, good-looking man, you.'

I operated a boat-rental and bait business on the bayou down toward Avery Island, south of New Iberia. The house my father had built of cypress sat up on a slope above the dirt road, its wide gallery and rusted corrugated roof shaded by live-oak and pecan trees. The beds were planted with roses, impatiens, hydrangeas, and hibiscus, and we had a horse lot for Alafair's Appaloosa and a rabbit hutch and a duck pond at the foot of the backyard. From the gallery we could look down through the tree trunks in the yard to the dock and concrete boat ramp and the bait shop and the swamp on the far side. At sunset I pulled back the awning on the guy wires that ran above the dock and turned on the string of overhead lights and you could see the bream feeding on the insects around the pilings and the water hyacinths that grew in islands among the cypress knees. Every night the sky over the Gulf danced with heat lightning, white sheets of it that rippled silently through hundreds of miles of thunderheads in the wink of an eye.

I loved the place where I lived and the house my father had built and notched and grooved and pegged with his hands, and I loved the people I lived with in the house.

Sunday night Bootsie and I ate supper on the picnic table under the mimosa tree in the backyard. The wind was balmy and smelled of salt and fish spawning, and the moon was up and I could see the young sugarcane blowing in my neighbor's field.

Bootsie set out a tray of deviled eggs and sliced ham and onions and tomatoes on the table and poured two glasses full of crushed ice and sun tea and put sprigs of mint in them. Her hair was the color of honey and she had cut it so it was short and thick on the back of her neck. She had the most lovely complexion of any woman I had ever known. It had the pinkness of a rose petal when the rose first opens into light, and a faint flush came into her cheeks and throat when she made love or when she was angry.

'You saw Passion Labiche today?' she asked.

'Yeah. It bothered me a little bit, too,' I said.

'Why?'

'A hooker in New Orleans, a bail skip Clete ran down, had saved all these clippings about Letty. I asked Passion if she knew her. She said she didn't, but then she slipped and referred to the girl as being black. Why would she want to lie?'

'Maybe she was just making an assumption.'

'People of color usually make derogatory assumptions about their own race?' I said.

'All right, smart,' she said.

'Sorry.'

She hit the top of my hand with her spoon. Just then the phone rang in the kitchen.

I went inside and picked it up.

'I got the word on Zipper Clum. He's going to be in a fuck pad in Baton Rouge about two hours from now. Out towards where Highland Road runs into the highway . . . You there?' Clete said.

'Yeah. I'm just a little tired.'

'I thought you wanted the gen on those news clippings.'

'Can we nail this guy another time?'

'The Zip's a moving target,' he said.

I put my army-issue .45 that I had brought home from Vietnam on the seat of my truck and took the four-lane to Lafayette, then caught I-10 across the Atchafalaya Basin. The wind came up and it started to rain, dimpling the bays on each side of the causeway. The islands of willows and flooded cypress were in early leaf, whipping in the wind, and there was a hard chop in the bays that broke against the pilings of abandoned oil platforms. I crossed the Atchafalaya River, which had swollen over its banks into the woods, then the wetlands began to fall behind me and I was driving through pasture and farmland again and up ahead I could see the bridge across the Mississippi and the night glow of Baton Rouge against the sky.

I drove through the city, then east on Highland, out into the country again, and turned on a shell road that led back into a grove of trees. I saw Clete's maroon Cadillac parked by a white cinder-block apartment building whose windows were nailed over with plywood. A second car, a new Buick with tinted windows, was parked next to a cluster of untrimmed banana trees. A light burned behind the plywood on the second floor of the building, and another light was turned on inside a shed that had been built over the stairwell on the roof.

I clipped my holster on my belt and got out of the truck and walked toward the front entrance. It had stopped raining now, and the wind puffed the trees over my head. The dark blue paint of the Buick was luminous with the rainwater that had beaded into drops as big as quarters on the wax.

I heard feet scraping on the roof, then a man's voice yell out and a sound like a heavy weight crashing through tree limbs.

I slipped the .45 out of its holster and went to the side of the building and looked up toward the roof. I saw Clete Purcel lean over the half-wall that bordered the roof, stare at something down below, then disappear.

I went in the front door and climbed the stairs to a hallway that was littered with garbage and broken plaster. Only one room was lighted. The door was open and a video camera on a tripod was propped up by a bed with a red satin sheet on it.

I went up another stairwell to the roof. I stepped out on the gravel and tar surface and saw Clete grab a black man by his belt and the back of his collar and run him toward the wall, then fling him, arms churning, into a treetop down below.

'What are you doing?' I said incredulously.

'They were gang-banging a pair of sixteen-year-old girls down there and filming it. Zipper and his pals have gone into the movie business,' Clete said. He wore a blue-black .38 in a nylon and leather shoulder holster. A flat-sided sap stuck out of his back pocket. 'Right, Zip?'

He kicked the sole of a mulatto who was handcuffed by one wrist to a fire-escape rung. The mulatto's eyes were turquoise, the irises ringed with a frosted discoloration. A puckered, concentric gray scar was burned into one cheek. His hair was almost white, straight, like a Caucasian's, cut short, his body as taut and shiny as wrapped plastic, his arms scrolled with jailhouse art.

'Robicheaux?' he said, focusing on my face.

'Why's Little Face Dautrieve collecting news articles on Letty Labiche?' I asked.

'Her brains are in her ass. That's where they suppose to be. Say, your man here kind of out of control. How 'bout a little intervention?'

'I don't have much influence with him,' I said.

'It's your flight time, Zipper. I'm not sure I can hit that tree again, though,' Clete said. He pulled his revolver from his shoulder holster and threw it to me, then leaned down and unlocked the cuff on Zipper's wrist and jerked him to his feet.

'Look over the side, Zipper. It's going to break all your sticks, guaranteed. Last chance, my man,' Clete said.

Zipper took a breath and raised both hands in front of him, as though placating an unteachable adversary.

'I tole you, Little Face got her own groove. I don't know why she do what she do,' he said.

'Wrong answer, shithead,' Clete said, and hooked one hand under Zipper's belt and clenched the other tightly on the back of his neck.

Zipper's face twisted toward mine, the rictus of his mouth filled with gold and silver, his breath a fog of funk and decayed shrimp.

'Robicheaux, your mama's name was Mae . . . Wait, it was Guillory before she married. That was the name she went by . . . Mae Guillory. But she was your mama,' he said.

'What?' I said.

He wet his lips uncertainly.

'She dealt cards and still hooked a little bit. Behind a club in Lafourche Parish. This was maybe 1966 or '67,' he said.

Clete's eyes were fixed on my face. 'You're in a dangerous area, sperm breath,' he said to Zipper.

'They held her down in a mud puddle. They drowned her,' Zipper said.

'They drowned my . . . Say that again,' I said, my left hand reaching for his shirt, my right lifting Clete's .38 toward his face.

'These cops were on a pad. For the Giacanos. She saw them kill somebody. They held her down in the mud, then rolled her into the bayou,' Zipper said.

Then Clete was between me and Zipper Clum, shoving me in the chest, pushing away the gun in my hand as though it were attached to a spring. 'Look at me, Streak! Get out of it! Don't make me clock you, noble mon . . . Hey, that's it. We're copacetic here, yes indeedy. Nothing rattles the Bobbsey Twins from Homicide.'

chapter three

My father was an enormous, black-haired, illiterate Cajun whose saloon brawls were not only a terrifying experience for his adversaries but beautiful to watch. He would back against a wall in Provost's or Slick's or Mulate's and take on all comers, his hamlike fists crashing against the heads of his opponents, while cops and bouncers tried to nail him with pool cues and chairs and batons before he destroyed the entire bar. Blood would well out of his scalp and glisten in his beard and wild, curly hair; the more his adversaries hit him, the more he would grin and beckon the brave and incautious into range of his fists.

That was the Aldous Robicheaux people saw publicly, fighting, his shirt and striped overalls ripped off his back, his wrists handcuffed behind him while a half dozen cops escorted him to a police car. They never saw what my father and mother did to each other at home before my father went to the saloon to find a surrogate for the enemy he couldn't deal with inside his own breast.

My mother was a plump, attractive woman who worked for thirty cents an hour in a laundry that employed mostly Negro women. She loved to dress up and wear her lavender pillbox hat, one with a stiff white net on it, and go to dance halls and crawfish boils and the *fais-dodo* in Breaux Bridge. While my father was in the parish prison, other men came to our house, and two of them offered my mother access to what she thought was a much better world than the one she shared with my father.

Hank was a soldier stationed at Fort Polk, a tall, sun-browned man with a red, welted scar from Omaha Beach on his shoulder who told my mother he belonged to the stagehands union in Hollywood. In the morning he would go into the bathroom when my mother was already in there, and I would hear them laughing through the door. Then he would stay in there a long time by himself, filling the room with steam. When I went in to bathe before school, no warm water was left in the tank, and he would tell me to heat a pan on the stove and wash with a rag at the kitchen sink.

'Mama wants me to take a whole bath,' I said one morning.

'Suit yourself, kid. Scrub out the tub when you get finished. I don't like sitting in somebody else's dirt,' he replied.

He smelled of testosterone and shaving cream and the cigarette he kept balanced on the lavatory while he combed Lucky Tiger into his hair in front of the mirror, a towel wrapped around his hips. He saw me watching him in the mirror and he turned and cocked his fists like a prizefighter's.

He and my mother boarded the Sunset Limited in 1946 and went out to Hollywood. On the platform she hugged me against her and kept patting me on the head and back as though her hands could convey meaning her words could not.

'I'm gonna send for you. I promise, Davy. You gonna see movie stars and swim in the ocean and go on roller-coaster rides out over the water, you. It ain't like here, no. It don't never rain and people got all the money they want,' she said.

When she returned to New Iberia on the bus, the ticket purchased with money my father had to wire a priest, she showed me postcards of Angel's Flight and Grauman's Chinese Theater and the beach at Malibu, as though these were magic places that had defined her experience in California rather than a garage apartment by a downtown freeway where Hank had left her one morning with the icebox empty and the rent unpaid.

But it was a thin, small-boned bouree dealer named Mack who took her away from us permanently. He owned a car and wore a fedora and two-tone shoes and had a moustache that looked like it had been drawn above his lip with grease pencil. I hated Mack more than any of the others. He feared my father and was cruel in the way all cowards are. He knew how to inflict injury deep into the bone, and he always had an explanation to mask the nature of his real agenda, like a man who tickles a child incessantly and says he means no harm.

My calico cat gave birth to her litter in the barn, but Mack found them before I did. He put them in a paper sack and weighted the sack with a rock and sank it in the coulee, pushing me away with his palm, then raising a cautionary finger at my face.

'Don't touch me again, no, 'cause I'm gonna hit you,' he said. 'Them kittens gonna grow up and kill the chicks, just like their mama been doin'. You gonna buy more chickens, you? You gonna put food on the table, you?'

He and my mother drove away one summer's day in a rooster tail of dust to Morgan City, where Mack got her a job at a beer garden. I didn't see her again until many years later, when I was in high school and I went to a roadhouse on the Breaux Bridge Highway with some other boys. It was a ramshackle gambling and pickup place, where the patrons fought over whores with bottles and knives in the parking lot. She was dancing with a drunk by the jukebox, her stomach pressed into his loins. Her face was tilted up into his, as though she were intrigued by his words. Then she saw me looking at her from the bar, saw my hand lift from my side to wave at her, and she smiled back at me briefly, her eyes shiny and indolent with alcohol, a vague recognition swimming into her face and disappearing as quickly as it came.

I never saw her again.

Monday morning the sheriff called me into his office. He wore a striped, black suit with a purple-and-white-striped snap-button shirt and a hand-tooled belt and half-topped boots. The windowsill behind his head was lined with potted plants that glowed in the thinly slatted light through the blinds. He had run a dry-cleaning business before he was elected sheriff and was probably more Rotarian than lawman; but he had been in the First Marine Division at the Chosin Reservoir and no one questioned his level of integrity or courage or the dues he had paid and never spoke about (except, to my knowledge, on one occasion, when he'd had a coronary and thought he was dying and he told me of pink airbursts high above the snow on the hills and Chinese bugles blowing in the darkness and winds that could swell fingers into purple balloons).

His stomach hung over his belt and his cheeks were often flushed from hypertension, but his erect posture, either sitting or standing, always gave him the appearance of a much greater level of health than he actually possessed.

'I just got off the phone with the East Baton Rouge sheriff's office,' he said, looking down at a yellow legal pad by his elbow. 'They say a couple of black lowlifes were thrown off a roof east of town last night.'

'Oh?'

'One of them has a broken arm, the other a concussion. The only reason they're alive is they crashed through the top of an oak tree.'

I nodded, as though unsure of his larger meaning.

'The two lowlifes say Clete Purcel is the guy who made them airborne. You know anything about this?' the sheriff said.

'Clete's methods are direct sometimes.'

'What's most interesting is one of them took down the license number of your truck.' The sheriff's eyes dropped to his legal pad. 'Let's see, I jotted down a quote from the East Baton Rouge sheriff. "Who told your homicide investigator he could come into my parish with an animal like Clete Purcel and do business with a baseball bat?" I didn't quite have an answer for him.'

'You remember my mother?' I asked.

'Sure,' he replied, his eyes shifting off mine, going empty now.

'A pimp named Zipper Clum was on that roof. He told me he saw my mother killed. Back in 1966 or '67. He wasn't sure of the year. It wasn't an important moment in his career.'

The sheriff leaned back in his chair and lowered his eyes and rubbed the cleft in his chin with two fingers.

'I'd like to believe you trusted me enough to tell me that up front,' he said.

'People like Zipper Clum lie a lot. He claims two cops drowned her in a mud puddle. They shot somebody and put a throw-down on the corpse. My mother saw it. At least that's what Clum says.'

He tore the top page off his legal pad and crumpled it up slowly and dropped it in the wastebasket.

'You want some help on this?' he asked.

'I'm not sure.'

'Ernest Hemingway said chasing the past is a bum way to live your life,' the sheriff said.

'He also said he never took his own advice.'

The sheriff rose from his swivel chair and began watering his plants with a hand-painted teakettle. I closed the door softly behind me.

I took a vacation day Friday and drove back to New Orleans and parked my truck on the edge of the Quarter and walked through Jackson Square and Pirates Alley, past the deep green, shaded garden behind St Louis Cathedral, and down St Ann to Clete Purcel's office.

The building was tan stucco and contained an arched foyer and flagstone courtyard planted with banana trees. An 'Out to Lunch' sign hung in the downstairs window. I went through the foyer and up the stairs to the second floor, where Clete lived in a one-bedroom apartment with a balcony that gave onto the street. The ironwork on the balcony was overgrown with bougainvillea, and in the evening Clete put on a pair of blue, baggy, knee-length boxing trunks and pumped barbells out there under a potted palm like a friendly elephant.

'You really want to 'front this vice cop over Little Face Dautrieve?' he asked. He had unwrapped two fried-oyster po'boy sandwiches, and he set them on the table with two cardboard containers of dirty rice.

'No, I want to find out why she has this personal involvement with Letty Labiche.'

He sat down at the table and hung a napkin like a bib from his shirt collar. He studied my face.

'Will you stop looking at me like that?' I said.

'I can hear your wheels turning, big mon. When you can't get it to go your way, you find the worst guy on the block and put your finger in his eye.'

'I'm the one who does that?'

'Yeah, I think that's fair to say.' He chewed a mouthful of oysters and bread and sliced tomatoes and lettuce, a suppressed smile at the corner of his mouth.

I started to speak, but Clete put down his sandwich and wiped his mouth and his eyes went flat. 'Dave, this vice cop is a real prick. Besides, a lot of guys at NOPD still think we're the shit that wouldn't flush.'

'So who cares if we rumple their threads?' I said.

He blew out his breath and slipped his seersucker coat over his shoulder holster and put on his porkpie hat and waited for me by the door.

We went down to First District Headquarters on North Rampart, not far from the Iberville Welfare Project, but the detective we were looking for, a man named Ritter, had gone to Mississippi to pick up a prisoner. Clete's face was dark, his neck red, when we came back outside.

'I thought you'd be relieved,' I said.

He bit a hangnail off his thumb.

'You see the way those guys were looking at me in there? I don't get used to that,' he replied.

'Blow 'em off.'

'They were down on you because you were honest. They were down on me because they thought I was dirty. What a bunch.'

We got in my truck. A drop of perspiration ran out of the lining of his hat into his eye. His skin looked hot and flushed, and I could smell his odor from inside his coat.

'You said Little Face was supposed to come across for both Ritter and a liaison guy. Who's the liaison guy?' I said.

'A political fuck named Jim Gable. He's an insider at City Hall. He was in uniform at NOPD before we came along.'

'A City Hall insider is extorting sexual favors from a street hooker?'

'This guy's had his Johnson out for thirty years. You want to brace him?'

'You up for it?' I asked.

25

Clete thought about it. 'He's on vacation, over at his home in Lafourche Parish.' Clete pressed his palms together and twisted them back and forth, the calluses scraping audibly. 'Yeah, I'm up for it,' he said.

We drove out of the city, south, to Bayou Lafourche, then followed the state highway almost to Timbalier Bay and the Gulf of Mexico. We turned down a dirt road through farmland and clusters of paintless cabins and clearings in the sugarcane that were filled with tin-roofed sheds and farm equipment. It was late afternoon now, and the wind had kicked up and the cane was blowing in the fields. Clouds moved across the sun and I could smell rain and salt in the air and the odor of dead animals in the ditches. Off in the distance, silhouetted against the dull shimmer of the bay, was a three-story coffee-colored, purple-tiled house surrounded by palm trees.

'How's a cop own a house like that?' I asked.

'It's easy if you marry an alcoholic with heart disease in her family,' Clete said. 'Stop up at that grocery. I'm going to have a beer and shot. This guy turns my stomach.'

'How about easing up, Clete?'

I pulled into the grocery store and he got out without answering and went inside. The store was weathered gray, the nail holes leaking rust, the wide gallery sagging on cinder blocks. Next to it was an abandoned dance hall, the Montgomery Ward brick peeled away in strips, the old red and white Jax sign perforated with bird shot.

Behind the nightclub was a row of cabins that looked like ancient slave quarters. The wind was blowing harder now, flecked with rain, and dust lifted in clouds out of the fields.

Clete came out of the store with a half pint of bourbon in a paper bag and an open can of beer. He took a hit out of the bottle, finished the beer, and put the bottle under the front seat.

'I called Gable. He says to come on down,' Clete said. 'Something wrong?'

'This place . . . It's like I was here before.'

'That's because it's a shithole where whitey got rich while a lot of peons did the grunt work. Like where you grew up.'

When I ignored his cynicism, his eyes crinkled at the corners and he sprayed his mouth with breath freshener. 'Wait till you meet Jim Gable. Then tell me he's not a special kind of guy,' he said.

The light had faded from the sky and rain slanted across the flood lamps that were anchored high in the palm trees when we pulled through the iron gates into Jim Gable's drive. He opened the side door onto the porte cochere, grinning with a gap-toothed smile, a man dressed in white slacks and a blue-striped sports coat. His head was too large for his narrow shoulders.

He shook my hand warmly.

'I've heard a great deal about you, Mr Robicheaux. You had quite a war record, I understand,' he said.

'Clete did. I was over there before it got hot,' I replied.

'I was in the National Guard. We didn't get called up. But I admire the people who served over there,' he said, holding the door open for us.

The inside of the house was softly lit, the windows hung with red velvet curtains; the rooms contained the most beautiful oak and cypress woodwork I had ever seen. We walked through a library and a hallway lined with bookshelves into a thickly carpeted living room with high French doors and a cathedral ceiling. Through a side door I saw a woman with a perfectly white, death-like face lying in a tester bed. Her hair was yellow and it

27

fanned out on the pillow from her head like seaweed floating from a stone. Gable pulled the door shut.

'My wife's not well. Y'all care for a whiskey and soda?' he said from the bar, where he tonged cubes of ice into a highball glass. His hair was metallic gray, thick and shiny, and parted sharply on the side.

'Not for me,' I said. Clete shook his head.

'What can I help y'all with?' Gable asked.

'A pimp named Zipper Clum is throwing your name around,' I said.

'Really?'

'He says you and a vice cop in the First District have an interest in a prostitute named Little Face Dautrieve,' I said.

'An interest?'

'Zipper says she gets into the sack with you guys or she goes down on a possession charge,' I said.

Gable's eyes were full of irony. 'One of my men held Zipper's face down on an electric hot plate. That was fifteen or twenty years ago. I fired the man who did it. Zipper forgets that,' Gable said. He drank from his glass and lit a thin cigar with a gold lighter. 'You drove over from New Iberia to check on corruption in the New Orleans Police Department, Mr Robicheaux?'

'I think the prostitute has information that might be helpful in the case of Letty Labiche,' I said.

He nodded, his eyes unfocused with half-formed thoughts.

'I hear Labiche is born again,' he said.

'That's the word,' I said.

'It's funny how that happens on death row. As far as I'm concerned, Letty Labiche doesn't deserve to die by lethal injection. She killed a lawman. I think she should be put to death in the electric chair, and not all at once, either,' he said.

Clete looked at me, then at the door.

'A lot of people think different,' I said.

'Fortunately it's not my obligation to argue with them,' Gable replied. 'On another subject, would you care to look at my collection of ordnance?' He was grinning again now, his callousness or meanness of spirit or whatever moral vacuity that seemed to define him once more hidden in the smiling mask that he wore like ceramic.

'Another time,' I said.

But he wasn't listening. He pushed open two oak doors with big brass handles on them. The inside of the room was filled with glass gun cases, the walls hung with both historical and modern weapons. One mahogany rack alone contained eight AK-47 rifles. On a table under it was a huge glass jar, the kind used in old-time drugstores, filled with a yellow fluid. Gable tapped on the lid with his fingernail so the object inside vibrated slightly and moved against the glass.

I felt a spasm constrict the lining of my stomach.

'That's a V.C. head. My cousin brought it back. He was in the Phoenix Program,' Gable said.

'We've got all we need here,' Clete said to me.

'Have I offended you?' Gable asked.

'Not us. I wish you'd made it over there, Jim. It was your kind of place,' Clete said.

Clete and I both turned to go and almost collided with Gable's wife. She wore a white silk robe and silver slippers and supported herself on a cane with a rubber-stoppered tripod on it. Her rouged cheeks and lipstick made me think of cosmetics applied in a desperate fashion to a papier-mache doll. Her yellow hair was like wisps of corn silk. When she smoothed it back, lifting it coyly into place, her temples pulsed with tiny blue veins.

'Have you invited the gentlemen for a late supper?' she asked her husband.

'They're just here on business, Cora. They're leaving now,' Gable replied.

'I apologize for not coming out to welcome you. I didn't realize you were here,' she said.

'That's quite all right,' I said.

'You mustn't pay attention to Jim's war souvenirs. They were given to him or he purchased them. He's a gentle man by nature,' she said.

'Yes, ma'am,' I said.

She placed her hand in mine. It had no more weight or density than a bird's wing.

'We'd love to see you again, sir,' she said. Her fingers tightened on mine, her eyes more than earnest.

The sky was dark and streaked with rain when Clete and I went back outside. The air smelled of ozone and schooled-up fish out in the bay. Lightning leaped from the horizon to the top of the sky, and I looked out at the pale green color of the sugarcane blowing in the wind and at the crossroads in the distance where we had stopped at the general store next to the abandoned nightclub with the cabins in back, and I remembered when I had been there before.

'My mother ran off with a man named Mack when I was a little boy,' I said to Clete. 'She came back for me once and we stayed in one of those cabins behind the nightclub.'

'Let it go, Streak,' he said.

'My father was in jail. Mack dealt cards at that club. My mother was a waitress there.'

'That was a long time before she died, big mon. Don't hurt yourself like this.'

We had backed out almost to the front gate. I stopped the truck and walked to the front door in the rain and knocked loudly on the door.

Jim Gable opened it with a turkey drumstick wrapped in a paper napkin in his hand. He was grinning.

'You forgot something?' he said.

'You're from Lafourche Parish, Mr Gable?'

'I grew up right down this road.'

'My mother's name was Mae Guillory. I think she was murdered somewhere close by. Zipper says it was around '66 or '67. Did you know a woman named Mae Guillory?'

His face transformed itself into the smiling, disingenuous countenance that all dishonest people know how to affect, the light in his eyes deliberately unfocused, the lips parted solicitously.

'Why, no, I don't think I ever knew anyone by that name. Mae? No, I'm sure of it,' he replied.

I got back into the truck and backed into the road and headed toward the crossroads.

Clete reached under the seat and removed his half pint bottle of whiskey and unscrewed the cap with one thumb, his eyes on the sugarcane and the rain ditches that swept past both sides of the truck. He took a sip from the bottle and put a Lucky Strike in his mouth.

'How about eighty-sixing the booze while we're driving?' I said.

'Gable knows something about your mother's death?' he said.

'Put it in the bank,' I said.

chapter four

On Monday I drove to the women's prison at St Gabriel, ten miles south of Baton Rouge, and waited for a female guard to walk Letty Labiche from a lockdown unit to an interview room. While I waited a television crew and a male and female journalist from a Christian cable channel were packing up their equipment.

'You interviewed Letty?' I asked the woman.

'Oh, yes. Her story's a tragic one. But it's a beautiful one, too,' she replied. She was middle-aged, blond and attractive, her hard, compact body dressed in a pink suit.

'Beautiful?' I said.

'For a Christian, yes, it's a story of forgiveness and hope.' Her face lifted into mine, her blue eyes charged with meaning.

I looked at the floor and said nothing until she and the other journalist and their crew were gone.

When Letty came into the room with the female guard she was wearing prison denims and handcuffs. The guard was as broad as an ax handle, pink-complected, with chestnut hair, and arms like an Irish washerwoman. She turned the key in the handcuff locks and rubbed Letty's wrists.

'I got them a little tight. You gonna be okay here, hon?' she said.

'I'm fine, Thelma,' Letty said.

I could not tell the difference between Letty and her twin sister, except for a rose with green leaves tattooed on her neck. They had the same skin, the same smoke-colored, wavy, gold-streaked hair, even the same power-ful, physical presence. She sat down with me at a wood table, her back straight, her hands folded in front of her.

'You're going to be on cable television, huh?' I said.

'Yes, it's pretty exciting,' she said.

But she caught the look in my eyes.

'You don't approve?' she said.

'Whatever works for you is the right thing to do, Letty.'

'I think they're good people. They been kind to me, Dave. Their show goes out to millions of homes.'

Then I saw the consuming nature of her fear, her willingness to believe that exploitative charlatans could change her fate or really cared what happened to her, the dread and angst that congealed like a cold vapor around her heart when she awoke each morning, one day closer to the injection table at Angola. How much time was left? Six weeks? No, it was five weeks and four days now.

I remembered a film clip that showed Letty at a religious service in the prison chapel, rising from her knees in front of the cross, her clasped hands extended high above her head in a histrionic portrayal of prayer. It was almost embarrassing to watch. But I had learned long ago that unless you've had your own ticket punched in the Garden of Gethsemane, you shouldn't judge those whose fate it is to visit there.

'What can you tell me about a black woman named Little Face Dautrieve?' I asked.

'Tell you?'

'You know her, don't you?'

'The name's not real familiar,' she said.

'Why do you and Passion refuse to confide in me?' I said.

She looked at the tops of her big-boned hands. 'The information you're after won't help. Leave it alone,' she said.

One hand opened and closed nervously on the table-top. Her palm was gold, shiny with moisture, her nails trimmed close to the cuticle. I took her fingers in mine.

'You all right?' I asked.

'Sure.'

But she wasn't. I could see her pulse beating in her neck, the white discoloration on the rim of her nostrils. She swallowed dryly when she looked back into my face, her eyes working hard to retain the light that the reborn seemed to wear as their logo.

'No one has to be brave all the time. It's all right to be afraid,' I said.

'No, it's not. Not if you have faith.'

There was nothing for it. I said good-bye and walked outside into the world of wind and green lawns and sunlight on the skin and trees bending against the sky. It wasn't an experience I took for granted.

When I got home that evening Clete Purcel was leaning on the rail at the end of my dock, eating from a paper sack filled with hog cracklings, brushing the crumbs off his hands into the bayou. The sun was red behind the oaks and pecan trees in my yard, and the swamp was full of shadows and carrion birds drifting above the tops of the dead cypress.

I walked down the dock and leaned against the rail next to him.

'The moon's rising. You want to try some surface lures?' I said.

'I got a call from Zipper Clum today. He says a shitload of heat just came down on his head and we're responsible for it.' He pulled a crackling out of the sack and inserted it in his mouth with his thumb and forefinger.

'Gable sicced some cops on him?'

'They rousted him and put him in a holding cell with a bunch of Aryan Brotherhood types. Zipper left a couple of teeth on the cement.'

'Tell him to give us something and we'll help him.'

'The guy's a bottom-feeder, Dave. His enemy's his mouth. He shoots it off, but he doesn't have anything to give up.'

'Life's rough.'

'Yeah, that's what I told him.' Clete tore the tab on a beer can and leaned his elbows on the handrail. The wind rippled the bamboo and willow trees along the bayou's edge. 'Zipper thinks he might get popped. I say good riddance, but I don't like to be the guy who set him up. Look, the guy's conwise. If he's wetting his pants, it's for a reason. Are you listening to me?'

'Yeah,' I said abstractly.

'You stuck a broom up Jim Gable's ass. He plans to be head of the state police. You remember that black family that got wiped out with shotguns about ten years back? Out by the Desire Project? The husband was snitching off some narcs and they wasted him and his wife and kid. I heard Gable ordered the clip on the husband and it got out of control.'

'Let me tell Bootsie I'm home and we'll put a boat in the water,' I said.

Clete finished his cracklings and wadded up the sack and popped it with the flat of his hand into a trash barrel.

'I've always wondered what it was like to have a conversation with a wood post,' he said.

At that time the governor of the state was a six-foot-six populist by the name of Belmont Pugh. He had grown up

35

in a family of sharecroppers in a small town on the Mississippi River north of Baton Rouge, feckless, illiterate people who sold pecans off the tailgates of pickup trucks and pulled corn and picked cotton for a living and were generally referred to as poor white trash. But even though the Pughs had occupied a stratum below that of Negroes in their community, they had never been drawn to the Ku Klux Klan, nor were they known to have ever been resentful and mean-spirited toward people of color.

I had known Belmont through his cousin Dixie Lee Pugh at SLI when we were all students there during the late 1950s. Dixie Lee went on to become the most famous white blues singer of his generation, second only to Elvis as a rock 'n' roll star. Belmont learned to play piano in the same Negro juke joint that Dixie Lee did, but he got hit with a bolt of religion and turned to preaching as a career rather than music. He exorcised demons and handled snakes and drank poisons in front of electrified rural congregations all over Louisiana. He baptized Negroes and poor whites by immersion in bayous so thick with mud they could clog a sewer main, while cottonmouth moccasins and alligators with hooded eyes watched from among the lily pads.

But the donations he received from church people were small ones and he made his living by selling detergent, brooms, and scrub brushes out of his automobile. Occasionally he would stop by New Iberia and ask me to have lunch with him at Provost's Bar. He had attended college only one year, but he was proud of what he called his 'self-betterment program.' He read a library book thirty minutes before breakfast each morning and thirty minutes before going to bed. He learned one new word from a thesaurus each day, and to improve what he called his 'intellectual thinking skills,' he did his business math in his head. He performed one good deed a day for somebody else, and, in his words, 'as a man on his way up, one good deed for my own self.'

To save money he slept in his car, ate fifty-cent lunches in poolrooms, and sometimes bathed and shaved with a garden hose behind a church house fifteen minutes before his sermon.

Then Belmont discovered the carnival world of Louisiana politics, in the way a mental patient might wander into a theme park for the insane and realize that life held more promise than he had ever dreamed.

Newspeople called Belmont the most mesmerizing southern orator since Huey Long.

During his run for his second term as governor, the opposition spread rumors that Belmont was not only a drunk but that his mulatto mistress, whom he had stashed over in Vicksburg, had borne him twins. *Time* magazine said he was finished. Fundamentalist preachers, once his colleagues, denounced him from every pulpit in the state. Belmont appeared on a nationally telecast religious show and tried to rinse his sins in public. His contrition was a flop.

He held a July Fourth political rally and barbecue in Baton Rouge. The beer, the corn on the cob, the chicken, and the links were free, paid for, some said, by casino interests in Chicago and Las Vegas. Belmont climbed up onto a flatbed truck while his string band belted out 'The Orange Blossom Special.' He played harmonica into the microphone, his face reddening, sweat leaking out of his Stetson hat. When the song ended, the applause was no more than a ripple, while the audience waited to hear what Belmont Pugh had to say about his misdeeds.

He wore shined oxblood cowboy boots, a white suit, a blue shirt, and a flowered necktie. He was too tall to speak comfortably into the microphone, and he removed it from the stand and held it in his huge hand.

His face was solemn, his voice unctuous.

'I know y'all heered a lot of stories about your governor,' he said. 'I won't try to fool you. They grieve me deeply. I'm talking heartfelt pain.'

He paused, taking a breath. Then his knees bent slightly, as though he were gathering a huge volume of air in his lower parts.

'But I'm here to tell y'all right now . . . That *any*time, *any*where, *any*body . . .' He shook his head from side to side for emphasis, his voice wadding in his throat as though he were about to strangle on his own emotions. 'I mean *anybody* sets a trap for Belmont Pugh with whiskey and women . . .' His body was squatted now, his face breaking into a grin as wide as an ax blade. 'Then by God they'll catch him every time!' he shouted.

The audience went wild.

The price of domestic oil rose the same week and the economy bloomed. Belmont was re-elected by a landslide.

Late the next afternoon I looked through the screen window of the bait shop and saw Belmont's black Chrysler park by the boat ramp and Belmont walk down the dock toward the shop. His aides had started to follow him but he waved them off with his Stetson hat, then began slapping the hat against his thigh, as though pounding dust off his clothes. His brow was furrowed, his eyes deep in his face. He blew out his breath and punched and shaped the crown of his hat with his fist and fitted it back on his head just before entering the shop, his easy smile back in place.

Fifteen minutes later we were a mile down the bayou, the outboard pulled into a cove of cypress and willow trees. Belmont sat on the bow and flipped his lure toward the edge of the lily pads and retrieved it slowly through the dark water. He had a lean face and long teeth and pale eyes and graying hair that hung over his ears. His

Stetson, which he wore virtually everywhere, was shapeless and stained with sweat and wrapped with a silver cord around the crown.

'You a student of Scripture, Dave?' he asked.

'Not really.'

'The Old Testament says Moses killed maybe two hundred people when he come down off Mount Sinai with the Ten Commandments still smoking in his hands. God had just talked to him from the burning bush, but Moses saw fit to put them people to death.'

'I'm not following you, Belmont.'

'I've signed death warrants on a half dozen men. Every one of them was a vicious killer and to my mind deserved no mercy. But I'm sorely troubled by the case of this Labiche woman.'

I lay my rod across the gunnels of the boat. 'Why?' I asked.

'*Why?* She's a woman, for God's sakes.'

'That's it?'

He fanned a mosquito out of his face.

'No, that's not it. The minister at my church knows her and says her conversion's the real thing. That maybe she's one of them who's been chosen to carry the light of God. I got enough on my conscience without going up to judgment with that woman's death on me.'

'I know a way out.'

'How?'

'Refuse to execute anyone. Cut yourself loose from the whole business.'

He threw his rod and reel against the trunk of a cypress and watched it sink through a floating curtain of algae.

'Send me a bill for that, will you?' he said.

'You can bet on it,' I replied.

'Dave, I'm the governor of the damn state. I cain't stand up in front of an auditorium full of police officers and tell them I won't sign a death warrant 'cause I'm afraid I'll go to hell.'

'Is there another reason?'

He turned his face into the shadows for a moment. He rubbed the curls on the back of his neck.

'Some people say I might have a shot at vice president. It ain't a time to be soft on criminals, particularly one who's chopped up an ex-state trooper.'

'I don't know what to tell you,' I said, trying to conceal the disappointment in my voice.

He beat at the air with both hands. 'I'm gonna call the Mosquito Control down here and bomb this whole place,' he said. 'Lord God Almighty, I thought liquor and women's thighs were an addiction. Son, they don't hold a candle to ambition.'

The next morning a young black woman walked through the front door of the Iberia Parish Sheriff's Department and down the hall to my office and tapped on the glass with one ringed finger. She wore a lavender shirt and white blouse and lavender pumps, and carried a baby in diapers on her shoulder.

'Little Face?' I said when I opened the door.

'I'm moving back here. Out at my auntie's place in the quarters at Loreauville. I got to tell you something,' she said, and walked past me and sat down before I could reply.

'What's up?' I said.

'Zipper Clum is what's up. He say he gonna do you and Fat Man both.'

'Clete Purcel is "Fat Man"?'

'Fat Man shamed him, slapped his face up on that roof, throwed his pimp friends crashing down through a tree. I ax Zipper why he want to hurt you. He say you tole some people Zipper was snitching them off.'

'Which people?'

She rolled her eyes. 'Zipper's gonna tell me that? He's scared. Somebody done tole him he better clean up his own mess or Zipper ain't gonna be working his street corners no more. Anybody who can scare Zipper Clum is people I wouldn't want on my case.'

She shifted her baby to her other shoulder.

'You're an intelligent lady, Little Face.'

'That's why I'm on welfare and living with my auntie in the quarters.'

'The day Vachel Carmouche was killed a black girl of about twelve was turning an ice cream crank on his gallery. That was eight years ago. You're twenty, aren't you?'

'You been thinking too much. You ought to go jogging with Fat Man, hep him lose weight, find something useful for you to do so you don't tire out your brain all the time.'

'What happened inside Vachel Carmouche's house that night? Why won't you tell me?'

'He wanted to live real bad, that's what happened. But he didn't find no mercy 'cause he didn't deserve none. You ax me, a man like that don't find no mercy in the next world, either.'

'You saw him killed, didn't you?'

'Mine to know.'

'Did he molest you? Is that why Letty came to Carmouche's back door that night?'

Her small face seemed to cloud with thought.

'I got to come up wit' a name for you. Maybe an Indian one, something like "Man Who's Always Axing Questions and Don't Listen." That's probably too long, though, huh? I'll work on it.'

'That's real wit,' I said.

'It ain't your grief, Sad Man. Stay out of it before you do real damage to somebody. About Zipper? Some snakes rattle before they bite. Zipper don't. He's

41

left-handed. So he's gonna be doing something wit' his right hand, waving it around in the air, taking things in and out of his pockets. You gonna be watching that hand while he's grinning and talking. Then his left hand gonna come at you just like a snake's head. Pow, pow, pow. I ain't lyin', Sad Man.'

'If Vachel Carmouche molested you, we'd have corroborating evidence that he molested Letty and Passion,' I said.

'I got to feed my baby now. Tell Fat Man what I said. It won't be no fun if he ain't around no more,' she said.

She rose from her chair and hefted her baby higher on her shoulder and walked back out the door, her face oblivious to the cops in the hall whose eyes cut sideways at her figure.

Connie Deshotel was the attorney general of Louisiana. Newspaper accounts about her career always mentioned her blue-collar background and the fact she had attended night school at the University of New Orleans while working days as a patrolwoman. She graduated in the upper five per cent of her law class at LSU. She never married, and instead became one of those for whom civil service is an endless ladder into higher and higher levels of success.

I had met her only once, but when I called her office in Baton Rouge Wednesday afternoon she agreed to see me the next day. Like her boss, Belmont Pugh, Connie Deshotel was known as an egalitarian. Or at least that was the image she worked hard to convey.

Olive-skinned, with metallic-colored hair that had been burned blond on the ends by the sun, she was dressed in a gray suit with a silver angel pinned on her lapel. When I entered her office, her legs were crossed and her hand was poised with a pen above a document on her desk, like a figure in a painting who emanates a sense of control, repose, and activity at the same time.

But unlike Belmont Pugh, the sharecropper populist who was so untraveled and naive he believed the national party would put a bumbling peckerwood on its ticket, Connie Deshotel's eyes took your inventory, openly, with no apology for the invasion of your person and the fact you were being considered as a possible adversary.

'We met once, years ago, during Mardi Gras,' she said.

My gaze shifted off hers. 'Yeah, I was still with NOPD. You were in the city administration,' I said.

She touched a mole at the corner of her mouth with a fingertip.

'I was drunk. I was escorted out of a meeting you were chairing,' I said.

She smiled faintly, but her eyes hazed over, as though I were already disappearing as a serious event in her day.

'What can I do for you, Detective Robicheaux? That's your grade, *detective*, right?' she asked.

'Yeah. An informant told me two cops on a pad for the Giacanos killed a woman in Lafourche Parish in 1966 or '67. Her maiden name was Mae Guillory.'

'Which department were they with?'

'He didn't know.'

'Did you find a record of the crime?'

'None.'

'How about the body?'

'To my knowledge, none was ever found.'

'Missing person reports?'

'There's no paperwork on this at all, Ms Deshotel.'

She put down her pen and sat forward in her swivel chair. She looked into space.

'I'll call the authorities in Lafourche Parish. It sounds like a blind alley, though. Who's the informant?'

'A pimp in New Orleans.'

'Why's he coming forward now?'

43

'A friend of mine was going to throw him off a roof.'

'Ah, it's becoming a little more clear now. Is this friend Clete Purcel?'

'You know Clete?'

'Oh, yes. You might say there's a real groundswell for revocation of his P.I. license. In fact, I have his file right here.' She opened a desk drawer and removed a manila folder filled with police reports, a thickly folded printout from the National Crime Information Center, and what looked like letters of complaint from all over the state. 'Let's see, he shot and killed a government witness, stole a concrete mixer and filled a man's convertible with cement, and destroyed a half-million-dollar home on Lake Pontchartrain with an earth grader. He also slim-jimmed Bobby Earl's car at the Southern Yacht Club and urinated on the seats and dashboard. You say he's been throwing people off of roofs recently?'

'Maybe I misspoke on that,' I said.

She glanced at her watch.

'I'm sorry. I'm late for a luncheon. Give me your card and I'll call you with any information I can find,' she said.

'That's good of you,' I said.

'What was the victim's name again?'

'Mae Guillory was her maiden name. Her married name was Robicheaux.'

'Are you related?'

'She was my mother. So I'll be hanging around on this one, Ms Deshotel.'

The inquisitory beam came back in her eyes, as though the earlier judgment she had passed on me had suddenly been set in abeyance.

chapter five

As a little boy Zipper Clum tap-danced for coins on the sidewalks in the French Quarter. The heavy, clip-on taps he wore on his shoes clicked and rattled on the cement and echoed off the old buildings as though he were in a sound chamber. He only knew two steps in the routine, but his clicking feet made him part of the scene, part of the music coming from the nightclubs and strip joints, not just a raggedy black street hustler whose mother turned tricks in Jane's Alley.

Later on, Zipper Clum came to fancy himself a jazz drummer. He took his first fall in Lake Charles, a one-bit in the Calcasieu Parish Prison, before the civil rights era, when the Negroes were kept in a separate section, away from the crackers, who were up on the top floor. That was all right with Zipper, though. It was cooler downstairs, particularly when it rained and the wind blew across the lake. He didn't like crackers, anyway, and at night he could hear the music from the juke joint on Ryan Street and groove on the crash of drums and the wail of horns and saxophones.

His fall partner was a junkie drummer who had sat in with the Platters and Smiley Lewis. Zipper was awed by the fact that a rag-nose loser with infected hype punctures on his arms could turn two drumsticks into a white blur on top of a set of traps.

In the jail the junkie created two makeshift drumsticks from the wood on a discarded window shade and showed Zipper everything he knew. There was only one problem: Zipper had desire but only marginal talent.

He feigned musical confidence with noise and aggressiveness. He sat in with bands on Airline Highway and crashed the cymbals and bass drum and slapped the traps with the wire brushes. But he was an imitator, a fraud, and the musicians around him knew it.

He envied and despised them for their gift. He was secretly pleased when crack hit New Orleans like a hurricane in 1981. Zipper was clean, living on his ladies, pumping iron and drinking liquid protein and running five miles a day while his pipehead musician friends were huffing rock and melting their brains.

But he still loved to pretend. On Saturday mornings he sat in the back of his cousin's lawn-mower shop off Magazine and plugged in a cassette of Krupa or Jo Jones or Louie Bellson on his boom box, simultaneously recording himself on a blank tape while he flailed at his set of drums.

Witnesses later said the white man who parked a pickup truck out front wore Levi's low on his hips, without a belt, a tight-fitting white T-shirt, cowboy boots, and combed his hair like a 1950s greaser. One witness said he was a teenager; two others described him as a man in his thirties. But when they talked to the police artist, they all agreed he had white skin, a mouth like a girl's, and that he looked harmless. He smiled and said hello to an elderly woman who was sitting under an awning, fanning herself.

The bell tinkled over the front door and Zipper turned down the boom box and shouted from the back, 'My cousin's next door.'

But some crackers just don't listen.

'Hey, don't come around that counter, man,' Zipper said. 'Say, you not hearing me or something? The man who own this store ain't here right now.'

'Sorry.'

'Yeah, just stay out there in front. Everything gonna be cool.'

'When's he gonna be back?'

'Maybe two or three minutes, like the sign on the door say.'

'You play drums?'

There was a pause. 'What you want in here, cracker?' Zipper asked.

'Your cousin's got a big tab with Jimmy Fig. He's got to pay the vig to the Fig.'

Zipper got up from the stool he was sitting on and walked to the service counter. The counter was lined with secondhand garden tools that had been wire-brushed on a machine, sharpened, oiled, and repainted.

'Jimmy Fig don't lend money. He sells cooze,' Zipper said.

'If you say so. I just go where they tell me.'

'Don't grin at me, man.'

'No problem.'

'Hey, take your hand out where I can see it,' Zipper said.

'I delivered the message. I'm going now. Have a good day.'

'No, I want to show you something. This is a twenty-dollar gold piece. Bet you fifty dollars I can roll it across the top of my fingers three times without dropping it. I lose, I put in the gold piece, too. Damn, I just dropped it. You on, my man?'

'Fifty dollars? Without touching it with the other hand?'

'You got it, bo.'

'You give me the gold piece, too?'

'My word's solid, bo. Ask anybody about Zipper Clum.'

'All right, there's my fifty bucks. This isn't a hustle, is it?'

Zipper smiled to himself and began working the gold piece across the tops of his fingers, the edges of the coin tucking into the crevices of skin and flipping over like magic. At the same time his left hand moved under the counter, where his cousin had nailed a leather holster containing a .38 revolver. Zipper felt his palm curve around the checkered wood handles and the smooth taper of the steel.

'Oops, I dropped it again. I done made you rich, cracker,' he said, and slipped the .38 from the leather.

It was a good plan. It had always worked before, hadn't it? What was wrong?

His mind could not assimilate what had just happened. The gold piece had dropped off the tops of his fingers and bounced on the counter and rolled dryly across the wood. But the cracker had not been watching the coin. He had just stood there with that stupid grin on his face, that same, arrogant, denigrating white grin Zipper had seen all his life, the one that told him he was a dancing monkey, the unwanted child of a Jane's Alley whore.

He wanted to snap off a big one, right in the cracker's mouth, and blow the back of his head out like an exploding muskmelon.

But something was wrong in a way he couldn't focus on, like a dream that should illuminate all the dark corners of your consciousness but in daylight eludes your memory. His left hand wouldn't function. The coldness of the steel, the checkering on the grips had separated themselves from his palm. One side of him was lighter than the other, and he was off balance, as though the floor had tilted under his feet. He closed his eyes and saw the scene take place again, watching it now through a red skein on the backs of his eyelids, the cracker lifting a machete off the counter, one his cousin had honed on an emery wheel, swinging it across Zipper's forearm, chopping through tendon and bone like a butcher's cleaver.

Zipper stared down at the .38 and his severed arm and the fingers that now seemed to be trying to gather up the gold twenty-dollar piece from the countertop. Zipper's boom box was playing Louie Prima's 'Sing, Sing, Sing,' and he remembered a little boy on Bourbon Street stooping in mid-dance to catch the coins that bounced out of the cigar box by his feet and rolled across the sidewalk.

'It was supposed to be a clean hit. That's the way I work. So it's on you,' the cracker said, and came quickly behind the counter and shoved Zipper to the floor.

The cracker pulled back the slide on a .25 automatic and bent over and pulled the trigger, straddling Zipper, his cowboy boots stenciling the floor with Zipper's blood. But the gun clicked and did not fire.

The cracker ejected the shell, then aimed the muzzle an inch from Zipper's forehead and shielded his face with one hand to avoid the splatter.

'You the trail back to Robicheaux's mama. You got a mouth like a girl. You got blue eyes. You got skin like milk. You never done no outside work. You six feet tall. Boy, you one badass motherfucker,' Zipper said.

'You got that last part right,' the cracker said.

It was funny how loud a .25 was. A couple of pops and you couldn't hear for an hour. The shooter recovered his empty brass and the ejected dud from the floor, pulled off his T-shirt, which was now splattered with blood, wiped off the machete's handle, and walked to his truck with his shirt wadded up in his hand.

Then something bothered him. What was it? He went back inside and kicked the boom box on the floor and smashed its guts out with his boot heel. Still, something wasn't right. Why had the pimp started taking his inventory? A mouth like a girl's? What was that stuff about somebody's mama? Maybe the pimp was a latent fudge packer. There was a lot of weirdness around these days. Well, that's the way the toilet flushed sometimes.

The old woman outside, who was deaf, waved to him as he twisted the steering wheel of his truck, a pocket comb in his teeth, and turned into the traffic.

chapter six

Monday morning an old-time NOPD homicide investigator named Dana Magelli sat down in my office and
played the recording tape that had been recovered from
the destroyed boom box at the murder scene off Magazine Street. Magelli had dark, close-clipped hair and dark
skin and wore a neat mustache and still played an
aggressive handball game three days a week at the New
Orleans Athletic Club. Photos from the crime scene and a
composite sketch of the shooter were spread on top of my
desk.

'Why would Zipper call the hitter the trail back to
your mother?' he asked.

'Zipper says "Robicheaux" on the tape. He doesn't
mention a first name. Why do you connect the tape to
me?' I replied.

'You and Clete Purcel were at First District asking
questions about him.'

'He told me he saw two cops kill my mother back in
the sixties.'

'I see,' Magelli said, his eyes going flat. 'Which leads
you to conclude what?'

'That maybe the guys who did it put the hitter on
Zipper Clum.'

'Who might these guys be?'

'Search me,' I said, my eyes not quite meeting his.

He wore a beige sports jacket and tan slacks. He leaned forward in his chair and rested his elbows on my desk.

'You're a good cop, Dave. You always were. You got a rotten deal. A lot of guys would like to see you reinstated in the department,' he said.

'How about Purcel?'

'Purcel was a wrong cop.'

'The whole department was wrong,' I said.

'It's not that way now. Maybe a few guys are still dirty, but the new chief has either suspended or put most of the real slimebags in jail.'

'What's your point, Dana?'

'You'd better not be squaring a personal beef on your own in Orleans Parish.'

'I guess you never know how it's going to shake out,' I said.

'Bad answer from a guy with your mileage,' he said.

'Find my old jacket and put a letter in it,' I said.

But he wasn't listening now. 'We've run the shooter through the computer system every way we could,' he said. 'Nothing. He's got the look of a genuine sociopath, but if there's paperwork on him anywhere, we can't find it.'

'I think he's a new guy, just starting out, making his bones with somebody,' I said. 'He was personally upset he couldn't make a clean hit. But he was still doing everything right until he went back to smash the boom box. He knew he was leaving something behind, but his head was on the full-tilt boogie and he couldn't think his way through the problem. So he tore up the boom box but he left us the tape. He's an ambitious, new player on the block who doesn't quite have ice water in his veins yet.'

Magelli rubbed his chin with two fingers.

'I had a Tulane linguist listen to the tape,' Magelli said. 'He says the accent is Upper South, Tennessee or Kentucky, reasonably educated, at least for the kind of dirt bags we usually pull in. You think he's mobbed-up?'

'No,' I said.

'Why not?'

'Because he talks about paying "the vig to the Fig." Everybody in the life knows Jimmy Figorelli is a pimp, not a shylock.'

Magelli smiled.

'Come back to work for us,' he said.

'Take Purcel, too. You get two for one.'

'You wouldn't come if we did, would you?'

I took my eyes off his to change the subject. 'There's another possibility in this case,' I said. 'It was Zipper Clum's perception the hitter was sent by the people who killed my mother. That doesn't make it so. A lot of people would enjoy breaking champagne bottles on Zipper's headstone.'

'Zipper was a ruthless bucket of shit. But he was the smartest pimp I ever met. He knew who paid his killer. You know it, too,' Magelli said. He cocked his finger at me like a pistol as he went out the door.

Just as I was going into Victor's on Main Street for lunch, Clete Purcel's maroon Cadillac pulled to the curb, his salt-water fishing rods sticking out of the back windows. He'd bought the Cadillac, the only type of car he ever drove, for eight hundred dollars from a mortician who had bought it off the family of a mobbed-up suicide victim. The steel-jacketed .357 round had exited through the Cadillac's roof, and Clete had filed down the jagged metal and filled the hole with body solder and sanded it smooth and sprayed it with gray primer so the roof looked like it had been powdered from the explosion of a large firecracker.

'What are you doing here?' I asked.

'I had to get out of New Orleans for a while. This homicide guy Magelli was bugging me yesterday about Zipper Clum getting popped. Like I have knowledge about every crime committed in Orleans and Jefferson parishes,' Clete said.

'You usually do.'

'Thanks. Let's get something to go and eat in the park. I want to have a talk with you, big mon.'

'About what?'

'I'll tell you in the park.'

We ordered two Styrofoam containers of fried catfish and coleslaw and dirty rice and drove across the drawbridge that spanned Bayou Teche at Burke Street. The bayou was dented with rain rings. Clete parked the Cadillac by one of the picnic shelters under the oaks in City Park, and we sat under the tin roof in the rain and warm breeze and ate lunch. Inside all of Clete's outrageous behavior was the secular priest, always determined to bail his friend out of trouble, no matter how unwanted his help was. I waited for the sermon to begin.

'Will you either say it or stop looking at me like that?' I said finally.

'This homicide hotshot, Magelli? He's heard you've been moving the furniture around about your mother's death. He thinks you might just do a number on somebody.'

'Who cares what he thinks?'

'I think he's right on. You're going to coast along, not saying anything, stonewalling people, then when you think you've found out enough, you're going to blow up their shit.'

'Maybe you're right.'

'It's not your style, noble mon. That's why I'm going to be in town for a little while. I was out at Passion Labiche's place early this morning.'

'What for?'

'Because I'm not sure the hit on Zipper Clum is related to your mother's death. These political fucks in Baton Rouge want Letty Labiche executed, body in the ground, case closed, so they can get back full-time to the trough. You keep turning over rocks, starting with sticking a gun in Zipper Clum's mouth up on that roof.'

'Me?'

'So I helped a little bit. That Passion Labiche is one hot-ass-looking broad, isn't she? Is she involved with anybody?'

'Why don't you give some thought to the way you talk about women?'

'It was a compliment. Anyway, you're right, she's hiding something. Which makes no sense. What do she and her sister have to lose at this point?'

I shook my head.

'I think we should start with the hitter, the cracker on the tape,' I said.

'I got a question for you. Jack Abbott, this mainline con a writer got out of the Utah Pen some years back? Where'd he go after he knifed a waiter to death in New York?'

'Morgan City.'

'What can I say? Great minds think alike. I already put in a couple of calls,' Clete said, grinning while he wiped food off his mouth.

But I didn't have great faith in finding the killer of Zipper Clum in Morgan City, even though it was known as a place for a man on the run to disappear among the army of blue-collar laborers who worked out of there on fishing vessels and offshore drilling rigs. Clete had not heard the tape on which Zipper had said his killer had never done outside work and had skin like milk. I also believed Clete was more interested in monitoring me than the investigation into my mother's death. He came to the sheriff's department at quitting time, expecting to drive down together to Morgan City.

'I can't go today,' I said.

'Why not?' he asked.

'Commitments at home.'

'Yeah?' He was standing in the middle of my office, his porkpie hat slanted down on his head, his stomach hanging over his belt, an unlit Lucky Strike in his mouth. He tossed the cigarette end over end into the wastebasket. 'I refuse to light one of these things ever again. Why are you giving me this bullshit, Streak?'

'Come have dinner with us.'

'No, I'm meeting this retired jigger an hour from now. You coming or not?'

'A bank jigger?'

'More serious. He was the lookout man for a couple of hit teams working out of Miami and New Orleans.'

'Not interested.'

'Where do you think we're supposed to get information from, the library?'

When I didn't reply, he said, 'Dave, if you want me out of town, just say so.'

'Let's talk about it tomorrow.'

'*You* talk about it. I'm meeting the jigger. You don't want to hear what I find out, no problem.'

After he closed the door behind him, his heat and anger remained like a visible presence in the room's silence.

That evening Alafair, Bootsie, and I were eating supper in the kitchen when we heard a heavy car on the gravel in the driveway. Alafair got up from the table and peered out the window. She was in high school now and seemed to have no memory anymore of the civil war in El Salvador that had brought her here as an illegal refugee, nor of the day I pulled her from the submerged wreckage of an airplane out on the salt. Her Indian-black hair was tied up on her head with a blue bandanna, and from the back, when she raised up on the balls of her feet to see better through the blinds, her body looked like that of a woman ten years her senior.

'It's somebody in a limousine, with a chauffeur. She's rolling down the window. It's an old woman, Dave,' she said.

I went out the back door and walked around the side of the house to the limousine. It was white, with charcoal-tinted windows, and the chauffeur wore a black suit and cap and tie and white shirt. Oddly, his face was turned away, as though he did not want me to see it.

Through the limousine's open back window I saw Jim Gable's wife, in a white dress and gloves, drinking sparkling burgundy from a crystal glass with a long stem. The late sun's glow through the trees gave her skin a rosy tone it did not naturally possess, and her mouth was soft, full of wrinkles, when she smiled at me. What was her name? Corrine? Colinda?

'Micah, open the door so Mr Robicheaux can get in,' she said to the chauffeur.

He stepped out of the driver's seat and opened the back, his face still averted. When I was inside, on the rolled leather seat, he walked down toward the dock just as a flight of snow egrets flew across the water, their wings pink in the sunset.

'How you do, Miss Cora?' I said.

'I couldn't stand staying another day alone while Jim's in the city. So I got Micah to drive me on a little tour of your lovely area. Join me in a glass of burgundy, Mr Robicheaux,' she said.

I realized, listening to her voice, that her Deep South accent came and went arbitrarily, even though her eyes, which were violet, never seemed to vary in their level of warmth and sincerity.

'No, thanks. Would you like to come in and have a bite to eat?' I replied.

'I'm afraid I've intruded. I do that sometimes. Lack of an audience, that sort of thing.' She watched my face to see if I had inferred a second meaning. Obviously I had not.

'Audience?' I said, confused.

'It's a vanity of mine. I assume everyone on the planet spends time thinking about old movies.' She opened a scrapbook and turned several pages that were thick and stiff with glued news articles and black-and-white photographs. She turned another page, and I looked down at a stunning color photograph of a woman with long blond hair in a black nightgown, reclining seductively on a divan with one arm behind her head. Her eyes were violet, her lipsticked mouth waiting to be kissed.

'You're Cora Perez. You were a movie star. I saw you in a film with Paul Muni,' I said.

'That was at the end of Paul's career. He was such a wonderful man to work with. He knew how nervous and unsure I was, and he used to bring a flower to me each morning at the set,' she said.

'It's an honor to know you, Miss Cora,' I said, still unsure of the reason for her visit. My eyes drifted to the kitchen window, where Alafair's and Bootsie's silhouettes were visible at the table.

'I mustn't keep you,' she said, and touched me lightly on the back of the hand. 'Sometimes I just need someone to reassure me I'm not indeed of diminished capacity.'

'Pardon?'

'I'm being declared as such by the court. It's not flattering, of course. But perhaps they're right. How does one accused of being mentally impaired prove she is not mentally impaired? It's like trying to prove a negative.'

'I don't think you're impaired at all, Miss Cora. You strike me as a remarkable person.'

'Why, you're obviously a man of great wisdom, Mr Robicheaux.'

I thought she would say more and explain her presence or whatever need it was that hovered around the edges of her sentences, but she didn't. I shook hands with her and got back out of the car, which the chauffeur took as his signal to walk back up from the dock. He fixed his cap down on his forehead and pretended he was studying the details of the dirt road and trees and canebrakes on either side of him as he approached the limousine.

'Try not to stare at Micah. He has a deformity of the face. Jim calls him "Cyclops," even though I don't allow him to do it in my presence,' Miss Cora said.

Just as she finished speaking Micah tilted his chin into the light and I saw the nodulous skin growth that covered the right side of his face, like a strawberry-colored skein that had hardened and pinched the eye shut, tightening the cheek so that the teeth on the right side of the lip were exposed.

I pulled my eyes away and looked deliberately through the back window into Miss Cora's face.

'Good-bye, Miss Cora,' I said.

'Come see me. Please do. You impress me greatly, sir,' she replied.

I went back inside the house and sat down at the table with Alafair and Bootsie.

'Who was that?' Bootsie asked.

'Her stage name was Cora Perez. She was pretty big stuff in Hollywood back in the late forties and early fifties,' I said.

'I remember her. Where'd you meet her?' Bootsie said.

'Clete and I had to run down some character by the

name of Jim Gable. Clete says Gable married her for her money when he knew she had cancer.'

Bootsie looked down at her plate and picked up her fork. Her hair was the color of honey and it moved in the breeze through the window.

'Did I say something wrong?' I asked.

'No, not at all,' she replied. She put a very small piece of food in her mouth with the tip of her fork and kept her eyes on her plate.

That night, in bed, Bootsie rested her arm across her forehead and looked up at the ceiling. The moon was rising in the east and the revolving blades of the window fan marbled her body with shadows. I put my hand on her shoulder and she rolled toward me and rested her head under my chin. I raised her slip on her thigh and felt the tapered smoothness of her skin. But her hands were folded together and she didn't respond as she normally did.

'What's the problem, Boots?' I asked.

'This Jim Gable you were talking about? Was he a policeman in New Orleans at one time?' she said.

'He still is. A liaison wheel with the mayor's office.'

'I used to know him,' she said.

'Oh?'

'After my second husband was killed.'

She didn't continue. She seldom spoke of her earlier marriages. Her first husband had been an oil field helicopter pilot who crashed offshore, but the second one had been Ralph Giacano, nephew of Didi Gee, a gangster who held his enemies' hands down in an aquarium filled with piranha and who some people believe was mixed up in the assassination of President Kennedy. The nephew, Ralph, was not only a degenerate gambler who bankrupted Bootsie, but he also tried to take the Colombians over the hurdles and was shotgunned to death, along with his mistress, in the parking lot of Hialeah racetrack.

'What about Jim Gable?' I asked.

'He came to the house a lot after Ralph was killed. He was part of a special unit that was assigned to watch the Mob. We started seeing each other . . . No, that's not an honest way to put it. We had an affair.'

Her knees were drawn up against me, her body motionless. I could feel her breath on my chest.

'I see,' I said.

'I don't like hiding things from you.'

'It was all a long time ago,' I replied. I tried to keep my voice neutral and ignore the tight feeling in my face and the needles in my throat.

'Does Jim Gable bother you because Clete says he's an opportunist?' she asked.

'He keeps the head of a Vietnamese soldier in a jar of chemicals. He said he'd like to see Letty Labiche electrocuted in stages. I think he lied about his knowledge of my mother's death,' I said.

Bootsie lay very quiet in the dark, then rolled away from me and stared up at the ceiling. She sat on the side of the bed with her back to me for a long time. I started to touch her with my hand, but she reached behind her and picked up her pillow and went into the living room.

chapter seven

The next afternoon, just before quitting time, Clete came into my office.

'The jigger's name is Steve Andropolis. He worked for the Giacanos and did freelance stuff in Miami when it was an open city. You remember him?' he said.

'Vaguely.'

'I had the wrong address last night. He agreed to show up again tonight. The guy's a shitbag, Streak, but he's a gold mine of information.'

'Why's he want to help us?'

'He's into Wee Willie Bimstine for four large. I got him a one-month extension with no vig.'

'It sounds good, Cletus,' I said.

He smiled and put a breath mint on his tongue.

We drove south to Morgan City as the evening cooled and the clouds over the Gulf turned a deeper red in the sunset. The man named Steve Andropolis was waiting for us in the back of a diner set on pilings by the water's edge. A half-empty green beer bottle and a white plate filled with fried shrimp tails sat in front of him. The hard, rounded surfaces of his face reminded me of an old baseball. He wore a new golf cap and a bright yellow golf shirt and gray slacks and tan loafers, as though affecting the appearance of a Florida retiree, but he had big-knuckled hands, a faded blue tattoo of a nude girl on his forearm, and close-set, pig's eyes that took the inventory of everyone in the diner.

When Clete introduced me, I didn't take his hand. He let his hand remain in the air a moment, then parted his lips slightly and wiped at something on the corner of his mouth.

'I know you?' he said.

'From a long time ago. You had a DWI and the court sent you to a twelve-step program in the Quarter. You stole two-hundred dollars from the group's treasury.'

Andropolis turned to Clete. 'What's the deal?' he asked.

'There's no problem here, Steve. We just want to know what you've heard about this guy who did Zipper Clum,' Clete said.

'His name's Johnny Remeta. He's out of Michigan. They say he's got a lot of talent,' Andropolis said.

'A lot of talent?' I said.

'Is there an echo in here?' Andropolis said.

'This doesn't fit, Steve. The guy we're looking for is a hillbilly,' Clete said.

'You wanted to know who was the new kid in town, I told you. He's done hits for the greaseballs out on the coast, maybe a couple of pops in Houston. He don't have a sheet, either,' Andropolis said.

'Where is he?' Clete asked.

'A guy who blows heads? He ain't like other people. He does the whack, gets his ashes hauled, and visits Disneyland.'

Andropolis' eyes kept returning to my face as he spoke.

'Why's he looking at me like that?' he asked Clete.

'Streak's just being attentive. Right, Dave?' Clete said, and gave me a deliberate look.

'Right,' I said.

'Y'all want to know anything else?' Andropolis asked.

'I think I remember some other things about you, Steve. Weren't you in the Witness Protection Program? What happened on that deal?' I said.

'What do you mean "what happened"?'

'You were one of the guys who gave up Didi Gee. But you're obviously not a federally protected witness anymore.'

'Because that tub of guts had his insides eaten out by the Big C. I heard the mortuary had to stuff his fat ass into a piano crate,' he replied.

'You go way back with the Giacano family?' I asked.

'Yeah, I knew Didi when he used to carry a blood-stained baseball bat in the backseat of his convertible.'

'Ever hear about a couple of cops on a pad snuffing a woman in Lafourche Parish back in the sixties?' I asked.

His eyes cut sideways out the window. He seemed to study the swirls of color in the sky. The sun was almost down now, and small waves from a passing tugboat rippled back over the mudflat under the diner's pilings.

'Yeah, I remember that. A whore?' he said.

'Yeah, Zipper said the same thing. They killed a whore,' I said, my face expressionless, the skin tight against the bone, my hands folded one on top of the other.

'She had something on them. That's all I remember,' he said.

'No names?' I said.

'No, I don't know anything else about it.'

'But you're sure she was a whore? That's what you called her, right?' I said.

'You got some trouble with that word?' he asked.

'No, not really,' I said, and took my eyes off his and scratched a place on my forehead.

He raised a finger to the counterman to order a beer for himself, then said, 'I got to take a drain.'

Clete leaned forward in the booth.

'Quit baiting the guy,' he said.

'He knows more,' I said.

'He's a gumball. You get what you see. Be thankful. We got the name of the shooter.'

'Excuse me,' I said, and followed Steve Andropolis into the men's room and shot the dead bolt behind me. The room was small, the air fetid and warm, with a wood enclosure around the toilet. I reached under my seersucker coat and slipped my .45 from its clip-on holster. I pulled back the slide and released it, chambering the top round on the magazine.

I stood back from the door on the toilet enclosure and kicked it open. Andropolis had been tucking his shirt into his trousers when the door hit him in the back and knocked him off balance against the wall. He tried to push the door back into my face, but I stomped it again, harder this time, ripping the top hinge and screws loose, pinning him in a half-crumpled position against the toilet bowl. I held on to the side of the stall with my left hand and drove my shoe through the door, again and again, splintering plywood into his face.

Then I flung the door off him and pointed the .45 at his mouth. A twelve-inch strip of desiccated wood was affixed to his cheek with three rusty nails.

'I wanted to apologize to you, Steve. I lied out there. I *was* bothered by the word "whore." When a subhuman sack of shit calls my dead mother a whore, that bothers me. Does that make sense to you, Steve?'

He closed his eyes painfully and pulled loose the splintered board that was nailed to his cheek.

'I've heard about you, you crazy sonofabitch. What do I know about your mother? I'm a spotter. I never capped anybody in my life.'

'You tell me who killed her, Steve, or your brainpan is going to be emptied into that toilet bowl in ten seconds.'

He began getting to his feet, blood draining in a long streak from his cheek.

'Fuck you, Zeke,' he said, and drove his fist into my scrotum.

My knees buckled, and a wave of pain rose like a gray, red-veined balloon out of my loins, took all the air from my lungs, and spread into my hands. I fell against the wall, the backs of my legs quivering, the .45 on the floor by my foot, the hammer on full cock.

Andropolis kicked the screen out of the window, placed one foot on the jamb, and leaped outside.

He stared back at me, the clouds etched with purple fire behind his head.

'When your mother died? I hope it didn't go like I think it probably did. I hope they hurt her,' he said.

He ran through the shallow water across the mudflat toward a distant clump of willow trees. The water splashing from under the impact of his feet had the same amber brilliance in the sunlight as whiskey splashed in a thick beer glass. I sighted the .45 on the middle of his back and felt my finger begin to tighten inside the trigger guard.

Clete Purcel exploded the dead bolt off the men's room door frame with one thrust of his massive shoulder.

'What are you doing, Dave?' he said incredulously.

I lay my forehead down on my arms and closed my eyes, my heart thundering in my ears, a vinegar-like odor rising from my armpits.

The next afternoon I drove out to the Labiche house on the bayou and was told by a black kid watering down the azaleas in front that Passion was at the cafe and nightclub she owned outside St Martinville. I drove to the club, a flat-roofed, green building with rusty screens and a fan-ventilated, hardwood dance floor. The sun's glare off the shale parking lot was blinding. I went in the side door and walked across the dance floor to the bar, where Passion was breaking rolls of quarters and dumping them into her cash drawer.

In the far corner stood the ancient piano that Letty used to play nightly. The keys were yellow, the walnut edges of the casement burned by cigarettes. Letty was one of the best rhythm-and-blues and boogie-woogie piano players I had ever seen perform. You could hear Albert Ammons, Moon Mulligan, and Jerry Lee Lewis in her music, and whenever she did 'Pine Top's Boogie,' the dance floor erupted into levels of erotic behavior that would have received applause at the baths of Caracalla.

Passion sometimes played in the house band as a bass guitarist, but she had never possessed her sister's talent. To my knowledge, no one had sat seriously at the piano since Letty had been arrested for the murder of Vachel Carmouche. At least not until today.

'You're walking with a list, chief,' Passion said.

'Really?' I said.

'You get hurt or something?'

'I'm doing fine. How about you, Passion?'

I sat at the bar and looked at an empty, oversized beer mug in front of me. The near side of the mug was coated with a thick, orange residue of some kind.

'The governor of Louisiana just drank out of that. I'm not sure if I should boil it for germs or not,' Passion said. She wore a white cotton dress printed with flowers. The light colors made her look even bigger than she was, and, in a peculiar way, more attractive and forceful.

'Belmont Pugh was here?' I said.

'He played Letty's piano. He's not bad.'

'What did he want from you?'

'What makes you think he wanted anything?' she asked.

'Because I know Belmont Pugh.'

Then she told me. It was vintage Belmont.

*

67

His black Chrysler had braked to a stop in the shell parking lot, drifting a dry, white cloud of dust across the building, and Belmont had come through the front door, stooping under the door frame, moisture leaking out of his hat, his silver shirt glued to his skin, a sweaty aura of libidinal crudeness and physical power emanating from his body.

'I'm in need of massive liquids, hon,' he said, and sat with his face in his hands while Letty drew a draft beer for him. 'Sweetheart, that little-bitty glass ain't gonna cut it. Give me that big 'un yonder, bust three raw eggs in it, and tell my family I died in your arms.'

She laughed, her arms folded across her chest.

'I always heard you were unusual,' she said.

'That's why my wife threw me out, God bless her. Now what am I gonna do – heartbroken, hungover, too old to have a beautiful, young Creole thing like you in his life? It's a misery, girl. Fill this up again, will you? Y'all got anything good to eat?'

He played the piano while she fixed him a sandwich in the café. She put the sandwich on a plate and set the plate on the end of the bar. He sat down on the stool again and removed his hat and mopped his face with a handkerchief. The skin across the top of his forehead was as pale as a cue ball.

'That record your sister cut in jail? She's a major talent, if you ask me. The minister at my church says she's a fine woman, too,' he said.

Passion looked at him silently, her rump resting against the tin wash bin behind her.

'You wondering why I'm here? I don't want to see a good woman die. It's that simple. But y'all gotta hep me and give me something I can use,' he said.

'How?' Passion asked.

'That story y'all told the jury didn't do nothing but leave skid marks on the bowl. There wasn't no evidence

68

Carmouche ever molested anybody else. It's hard to believe after all those years your sister would suddenly decide to take the man apart with a mattock. Like she was bored and it just come to mind as the thing to do.'

'Would you like me to describe what he did to me and Letty?'

'Lord, it's hot in here. Why don't you fix your air conditioner? No, I don't want you to describe it. I suspect the man was everything you say he was. That's why I want you to find somebody who can support your story. Round up a mess of black people, talk to 'em, you hear what I'm saying, sometimes folks shut out bad memories, you gotta remind them of what happened. They call it "recovered memory." People get rich suing over it.'

'You want me to get some black people to lie for us?'

'Girl, please don't use that word. And I don't care if they're white or black. I'll get state investigators down here to take their deposition. But y'all gotta understand my situation. I cain't give clemency to a woman 'cause I like the way she plays the piano. People in the last election was already calling me the Silver Zipper.'

'Letty won't go along with it.'

'You better hear what I'm saying, Miss Passion, or it's gonna be on y'all's own self. Them sonsofbitches in Baton Rouge is serious.'

'You want a refill, Governor?'

His face was tired and poached-looking in the warm gloom of the bar. He pulled his shirt out from his chest with his fingers and shook the cloth, his mouth down-turned at the corners. 'Damn if I can ever find the right words to use to people anymore,' he said, and pushed his Stetson on his head and walked back out of the club, the electric fan by the door flapping back his coat just before he stepped into the heated whiteness of the day outside.

Passion walked to the door.

'I'll tell her,' she said as his car scoured dust out of the parking lot.

But Belmont did not hear her.

'Maybe Belmont's a little corrupt, but he's got his hand on it,' I said.

'Meaning?' she said, her face in a pout.

'Nobody bought y'all's story. Vachel Carmouche had been gone from here for years. The very night he returned, your sister killed him. Over deeds done to her as a child?'

'You came out here to put this in my face?'

'No. Little Face Dautrieve inasmuch told me she was there that night. But that's all she'll say. What happened that night? Is Little Face protecting somebody?'

'Ax her.'

'You want it this way?' I said.

'Pardon?'

'That I be your adversary? The guy you don't trust, the guy who makes a nuisance of himself?'

'I didn't mean to make you mad,' she said.

'Give me a Dr Pepper, will you?'

'There isn't no way out for us, Dave. My sister's gonna die. Somebody got to pay for that nasty old piece of white trash.'

She walked on the duckboards to the end of the bar, her back turned toward me so I couldn't see her face. Her large body was framed against the white glare of the parking lot, her smoke-colored hair wispy with light. She picked a rose out of a green bottle on the liquor counter and stared at it dumbly. The petals were dead, the color of a bruise, and they fell off the stem of their own weight and drifted downward onto the duckboards.

chapter eight

I got home late from work that evening. Alafair had gone to the City Library and Bootsie had left a note on the kitchen blackboard that said she was shopping in town. I fixed a cup of coffee and stirred sugar in it and sat on the back steps in the twilight and watched the ducks wimpling the water on the pond at the foot of our property.

But sometimes I did not do well in solitude, particularly inside the home where my original family had come apart.

In the gathering shadows I could almost see the specters of my parents wounding each other daily, arguing bitterly in Cajun French, each accusing the other of their mutual sins.

The day my mother had gone off to Morgan City with Mack, the bouree dealer, my father had been hammering a chicken coop together in the side yard. Mack's Ford coupé was parked on the dirt road, the engine idling, and my mother had tried to talk to him before she left me in his care.

My father was heedless of her words and his eyes kept lifting from his work to Mack's car and the sunlight that reflected like a yellow flame off the front windows.

'That li'l gun he carry? See what good it gonna do him he step his foot on my property,' he said.

The day was boiling hot, the air acrid with a smell like fresh tar and dust blowing off a gravel road. My father's skin was glazed with sweat, his veins swollen with blood, his size seeming to swell inside his overalls with the enormous range his anger was capable of when his pride had been injured.

I sat on the front steps and wanted to cover my ears and not hear the things my parents said to each other. I wanted to not see Mack out there on the road, in his fedora and two-tone shoes and zoot slacks, not think about the pearl-handled, two-shot derringer I had seen once in his glove box.

But my father looked from his work to me, then out at Mack and back at me again, and the moment went out of his face and he lay his ball peen hammer on a bench and picked up the side of the chicken coop and examined its squareness and felt its balance. I pushed my hands under my thighs to stop them from shaking.

When my mother drove away with Mack, I thought there might still be hope for our family. My father, Big Aldous, the grinning, irresponsible derrick man and saloon brawler, was still my father. Even at that age I knew he had chosen me over an act of violence. And my mother, Mae, was still my mother. Her lust and her inability to deal with my father's alcoholism made her the victim of bad men, but she was not bad herself. She loved me and she loved my father, or she would not have fought with him.

But now there were people who called my mother a whore.

I had never heard that word used in association with her. During my mother's lifetime whores didn't work in laundries for thirty cents an hour or wait tables in beer gardens and clapboard bars and hoe out victory gardens for a sack of string beans.

Had it not been for Clete Purcel, I would have squeezed off my .45 on the back of the jigger named Steve Andropolis because he called my mother a whore. In my mind's eye I still saw myself doing it. I saw a worthless, running, pitiful facsimile of a human being look back at me, his mouth round with a silent scream, his arms spread against a bloodred sky. I looked down at my hand, and it was tightened into a ball, the forefinger kneading against the thumb.

I threw my coffee into the flower bed and tried to rub the fatigue out of my face.

Bootsie's car turned into the drive and stopped in front, then I heard the crinkle of paper bags as she unloaded the groceries and carried them across the gallery. Normally she would have driven to the back of the house to unload, but our conversations had been few since the night of her revelation about her affair with Jim Gable.

Why had I demeaned him as Bootsie and I lay there in the dark? It had been the same as telling her she had somehow willingly shared her life and person with a degenerate. Her second husband, Ralph Giacano, had lied his way into her life, telling her he had a degree in accounting from Tulane, that he owned half of a vending machine company, that, in effect, he was an unexciting, ordinary but decent middle-class New Orleans business-man.

He was an accountant, all right, but as a bean counter for the Mob; the other half of the vending machine operation was owned by Didi Gee.

She had to fly to Miami to identify the body after the Colombians blew Ralph's face off. She also found out his dead mistress had been the bank officer who had set up the second mortgage on her house in the Garden District

73

and had helped Ralph drain her accounts and the equity portfolio the bank managed for her.

She had been betrayed, degraded, and bankrupted. Was it any wonder a man like Gable, a police officer of detective grade, supposedly a man of integrity, could insinuate his way into her life?

Bootsie opened the screen door behind me and stood on the top step. Out of the corner of my eye I could see her ankles and the tops of her feet inside the moccasins she wore.

'Did you eat yet?' she said.

'I had that potato salad in the icebox.'

'You might have to do an extra mile on your run,' she replied.

I leaned forward on my forearms and folded my hands between my knees. The ducks were turning in circles on the pond, their wings fluttering, sprinkling the water's surface.

'I think you're a great lady, Boots. I don't think any man deserves you. I know I don't,' I said.

The light had washed out of the sky; the wind blowing across my neighbor's cane field was touched with rain and smelled of damp earth and the wildflowers that grew along the coulee. Bootsie sat down on the step behind me, then I felt her fingertips on the back of my neck and in my hair.

'You want to go inside?' she asked.

Later that night the weather turned unseasonably cool and it started to rain, hard, sheets of it marching across marshlands, cane fields, tin roofs, bayous, and oak-lined communities up the Teche. In the little town of Loreauville, a man parked his pickup truck outside a clapboard bar and walked through the rain to the entrance. He wore jeans low on his hips, exposing his midriff, and pointed boots and black-rimmed glasses and a straw cowboy hat.

When he sat at the bar, which was deserted because of the bad weather, he removed his hat and set it crown-down on the stool next to him. He wiped his glasses with a paper napkin, then forgot they were dry and picked them up and wiped them again, his expression seemingly troubled by a concern or problem he couldn't resolve. Later the bartender described the man as 'handsome, with kind of a ducktail haircut . . . Likable, I guess, but I wouldn't make him for no dishware man.'

The man ordered a diet soda and opened a vinyl folder wrapped with rubber bands and filled with invoices of some kind.

'You know a family named Grayson back in the quarters?' he said.

'Cain't say I do,' the bartender replied.

The man looked down at his invoice folder, widening his eyes, as though bemused. 'They live next door to the Dautrieve family,' he said.

'Oh, yeah. Go back up the road till you see some shotgun cabins. The Dautrieves are on the second row,' the bartender said.

'They won a bunch of dishware.'

'Who?'

'The Graysons.' The man held up a brochure with pictures of dishes and cups on it to make his point.

The bartender nodded vaguely. The man with the invoice folder stared into space, as though he saw meaning in the air, in the lightning that trembled in the trees along the bayou. He paid for his diet drink and thanked the bartender and drove up the road, in the opposite direction from the quarters.

It was still raining the next night when Little Face Dautrieve's aunt left for her janitorial job at the hospital in New Iberia and Little Face changed her baby's diapers, put a pacifier in his mouth, and lay him down in his crib. The cabin had been built in the last century, but it stayed warm and dry and snug in bad weather. When it rained Little Face liked to open the bedroom window partway and let the breeze blow across the baby's crib and her bed.

In the middle of the night she thought she heard a truck engine outside and tires crunching on clamshells, then the sound disappeared in the thunder and she fell asleep again.

When she awoke he was standing over her, his form-fitting T-shirt molded wetly against his torso. His body had a fecund odor, like water in the bottom of a coulee; a nickel-plated revolver, the handles wrapped with electrician's tape, hung from his gloved right hand.

'I came in out of the rain,' he said.

'Yeah, you done that. There ain't no rain in the house,' she replied, raising herself up on her hands, a wishbone breaking in her throat.

'You mind if I stay here? I mean, stay out of the rain?' he asked.

'You here, ain't you?'

His palm opened and closed on the grips of the pistol, the edges of the tape sticking, popping on his skin. His face was pale, his mouth soft and red in the flashes of lightning outside. He wet his lips and cut his eyes at the window, where mist was drifting across the sill and dampening the baby's mattress.

The man pushed the window tight and gazed down at the baby, who slept with his rump in the air. A pillow was stuffed into an empty space where one of the wood runners was missing. For some reason, perhaps because of the noise the window made, the baby woke and started to cry. The man pried the pillow loose and kneaded it in his left hand and turned toward Little Face.

'Why'd you get mixed up with a bunch of geeks? Why'd you run your mouth?' the man said. His black hair was combed back neatly on both sides, his skin glistening with water, his navel rising and falling above his jeans.

'Write out a list of the people ain't geeks. I'll start hanging 'round wit' them,' she replied.

'Make that baby be quiet.'

'You done woke him up. Babies gonna cry when they get woke up.'

'Just shut him up. I can't think. Why don't you have a man to take care of you?'

'I can have all the men I want. Trouble is, I ain't met none I want, including present company.'

He looked at the baby again, then closed and opened his eyes. He took a breath of air through his mouth, holding it, as though he were about to speak. But no sound came out. He folded the pillow around the pistol and held both ends together with his left hand. The rims of his nostrils whitened, as though the temperature had dropped precipitously in the room.

'You make me mad. You're too dumb to understand what's happening. Get that look off your face,' he said.

'It's my house. I ain't axed you in it. Go back in the rain you don't like it,' she said quietly.

Then she saw into his eyes and her throat went dry and became constricted like a piece of crimped pipe and she remembered the word 'abyss' from a sermon at a church somewhere and she knew now what the word meant. She tried to hold her gaze evenly on his face and stop the sound that thundered in her ears, that made her own words distorted and unintelligible to her.

Her hands knotted the sheet on top of her stomach.

'My baby ain't part of this, is he?' she said.

The man drew an enormous breath of air through his nose, as though he were hyperventilating. 'No, what do you think I am?' He held up the pillow as though he had just discovered its presence. 'Don't put something like this in a crib. That's how babies suffocate,' he said, and flung the pillow across the room.

He shoved the revolver in his blue-jeans pocket, the butt protruding just above the edge of the cloth, his booted feet wide-spread, as though he were confronting an adversary that no one else saw.

'You gonna just stand there, Rain Man?' she asked, because she had to say something or the sound roaring in her ears would consume her and the shaking in her mouth would become such that her jawbones would rattle.

He waited a long time to answer her. 'I don't know what I'm gonna do. But you shouldn't be messing with my head, lady. You really shouldn't be doing that at all,' he said.

Then he went out the screen door into the storm and drove his truck in reverse down the clamshells to the two-lane state road, the rain blowing like shattered crystal in his backup lights.

I spent the next morning, along with my partner, Helen Soileau, interviewing Little Face and anyone else in Loreauville who might have seen the intruder into Little Face's home. Helen had started her career as a meter maid at NOPD, then had put in seven years as a patrolwoman in the Garden District and the neighborhood around the Desire Welfare Project, an area so dangerous and violent that black city councilmen tried to persuade President Bush to clean it out with federal troops. Finally she returned to New Iberia, where she had grown up, and was hired as a plainclothes investigator by the sheriff's department.

Helen wore slacks and khakis and jeans to work, was thick-bodied and muscular, and looked boldly into the world's face, her arms pumped, her waved, lacquered blond hair her only visible concession to femininity. As a rule, she had trouble with difficult people only once. She had shot and killed three perpetrators on the job.

We stood in the parking lot of the bar the intruder had visited the night before he had wedged a screwdriver blade into the lock on Little Face's cabin door. The sun was out, the air cool and rain-washed, the sky blue above the trees.

'You think he's the same guy who did Zipper Clum, huh?' Helen said.

'That's my read on it,' I said.

'He tells the bartender he's delivering dishware to a family named Grayson, who don't exist, then casually mentions the Graysons live next to the Dautrieves, and that's how he finds Little Face. We're dealing with a shitbag who has a brain?'

She didn't wait for me to answer her question. She looked back at the bar, tapping her palm on the top of the cruiser.

'How do you figure this guy? He must have known his contract was on a woman, but then he walks out on the job,' she said.

'She had the baby in the room with her. It sounds like he wasn't up to it.'

'All we need is another piece of shit from New Orleans floating up the bayou. What do you want to do now, boss man?'

'Good question.'

Just as we started to get in the cruiser, the bartender opened the screen door and leaned outside. He held up a brightly colored brochure of some kind in his hand.

'Is this any hep to y'all?' he asked.

'What you got there?' I said.

'The man you was axing about? He left it on the

counter. I saved it in case he come back,' the bartender said.

Helen's usual martial expression stretched into a big smile. 'Sir, don't handle that any more than you need to. There you go. Just let me get a Ziploc bag and you can slip it right inside . . . That's it, plop it right in. Lovely day, isn't it? Drop by the department for free doughnuts any time. Thank you very much,' she said.

It's called the Automated Fingerprint Identification System, or AFIS. It's a miracle of technology. A latent fingerprint can be faxed to a computer at a regional pod and within two hours be matched with a print that is already on file.

If the fingerprint has a priority.

Priorities are usually given to homicide cases or instances when people are in custody and there is a dramatic need to know who they are.

The man who had prized open Little Face Dautrieve's cabin door was de facto guilty of little more than breaking and entering. The possibility that he was the same man who killed Zipper Clum was based only on my speculation. Also, the Clum homicide was not in our jurisdiction.

No priority for the latent print we took off the dishware brochure the bartender had saved. Get a number and wait. The line in Louisiana is a long one.

I called the office of Connie Deshotel, the attorney general, in Baton Rouge.

'She's out right now. Can she call you back?' the secretary said.

'Sure,' I replied, and gave her my office number.

I waited until quitting time. No call. The next day was Saturday.

I tried again Monday morning.

'She's out,' the secretary said.

'Did she get the message I left Friday?' I asked.

'I think she did.'

'When will she be back?'

'Anytime now.'

'Can you have her call me, please?'

'She's just been very busy, sir.'

'So are we. We're trying to catch a murderer.'

Then I felt stupid and vituperative for taking out my anger on a secretary who was not to blame for the problem.

Regardless, I received no return call. Tuesday morning I went into Helen's office. Her desk was covered with paperwork.

'You want to take a ride to Baton Rouge?' I asked.

Connie Deshotel's office was on the twenty-second floor of the state capitol building, high above the green parks of the downtown area and the wide sweep of the Mississippi River and the aluminum factories and petroleum refineries along its shores. But Connie Deshotel was not in her office. We were told by the secretary she was in the cafeteria downstairs.

'Is there a line to kiss her ring?' Helen asked.

'Excuse me?' the secretary said.

'Take it easy, Helen,' I said in the elevator.

'Connie Deshotel was born with a hairbrush up her ass. Somebody should have straightened her out a long time ago,' she replied.

'You mind if I do the talking?' I asked.

We stood at the entrance to the cafeteria, looking out over the tables, most of which were occupied. Connie Deshotel was at a table against the back wall. She wore a white suit and was sitting across from a man in a blue sports coat and tan slacks whose thinning hair looked almost braided with grease.

'You make the gel head?' Helen said.

'No.'

'Don Ritter, NOPD Vice. He's from some rat hole up in Jersey. I think he's still in the First District.'

'That's the guy who busted Little Face Dautrieve and planted rock on her. He tried to make her come across for him and Jim Gable.'

'Sounds right. He used to shake down fudge packers in the Quarter. What's he doing with the attorney general of Louisiana?'

'Go easy, Helen. Don't make him cut and run,' I said.

'It's your show,' she said, walking ahead of me between the tables before I could reply.

As we approached Connie Deshotel, her eyes moved from her conversation onto my face. But they showed no sense of surprise. Instead, she smiled good-naturedly.

'You want some help with access to AFIS?' she said.

'How'd you know?' I asked.

'I called your office this morning. But you'd already left. The sheriff told me about your problem. I had him fax the latents to the pod. The ID should be on your desk when you get back to New Iberia,' she said.

The confrontation I had been expecting was suddenly gone. I looked at her in dismay.

'You did it,' I said.

'I'm glad my office could help. I'm only sorry I couldn't get back to you earlier. Would you like to join us? This is Don Ritter. He's at the First District in New Orleans,' she said.

Ritter put out his hand and I took it, in the way you do when you suppress your feelings and know that later you'll wish you hadn't.

'I already know Helen. You used to be a meter maid at NOPD,' he said.

'Yeah, you were tight with Jim Gable,' she said, smiling.

I turned and looked directly into Helen's face. But she didn't allow herself to see my expression.

'Jim's working liaison with the mayor's office,' Ritter said.

'How about that Zipper Clum getting wasted? Remember him? You and Jim used to leave him hooked up in the cage,' Helen said.

'A tragic event. Everybody laughed for five minutes at roll call the other day,' Ritter said.

'We have to go. Thanks for your help, Ms Deshotel,' I said.

'Anytime, Mr Robicheaux,' she replied. She looked lovely in her white suit, her olive skin dark with tan, the tips of her hair burned by the sun. The silver angel pinned on her lapel swam with light. 'Come see us again.'

I waited until we were in the parking lot before I turned my anger on Helen.

'That was inexcusable,' I said.

'You've got to make them wince sometimes,' she said.

'That's not your call, Helen.'

'I'm your partner, not your driver. We're working the same case, Dave.'

The air rising from the cement was hot and dense with humidity and hard to breathe. Helen squeezed my upper arm.

'In your mind you're working your mother's case and you think nobody's going to help you. It's not true, bwana. We're a team. You and I are going to make them religious on this one,' she said.

If indeed the man who had broken into Little Face's cabin was the same man who murdered Zipper Clum, the jigger named Steve Andropolis had been halfway right about his identity. The National Crime Information Center said the print we had sent through AFIS belonged to one Johnny O'Roarke, who had graduated from a

Detroit high school but had grown up in Letcher County, Kentucky. His mother's maiden name was Remeta. At age twenty he had been sentenced to two years in the Florida State Penitentiary at Raiford for robbery and possession of burglar tools and stolen property.

While in prison he was the suspect in the murder of a six-and-one-half-foot, 280-pound recidivist named Jeremiah Boone, who systematically raped every fish, or new inmate, in his unit.

Helen sat with one haunch on the corner of my desk, reading from the sheets that had been faxed to us by the Florida Department of Corrections in Tallahassee.

'The rapist, this guy Boone? He was Molotoved in his cell. The prison psychologist says O'Roarke, or Remeta, was the regular punch for eight or nine guys till somebody turned Boone into a candle. Remeta must have made his bones by torching Boone,' she said, then waited. 'You listening?'

'Yeah, sure,' I replied. But I wasn't. 'Connie Deshotel seemed to be on the square. Why's she hanging around with a wrong cop, the gel head, what's his name, Ritter?'

'Maybe they just ran into each other. She started her career at NOPD.'

'She stonewalled us, then fell over backwards to look right,' I said.

'She got us the ID. Forget it. What do you want to do about Remeta, or O'Roarke, or whatever he calls himself?' Helen said.

'He probably got front money on the Little Face hit. Somebody besides us isn't happy with him right now. Maybe it's a good time to start jacking up the other side.'

'How?' she said.

I glanced out the window just as Clete Purcel's maroon Cadillac pulled to the curb, with Passion Labiche in the passenger's seat.

chapter nine

I walked down the hallway toward the building's entrance, but the sheriff cut me off.

'Purcel's out there,' he said.

'I know. I'm going to meet him,' I said.

'Keep him out of here,' he replied.

'You're too hard on him.'

'You want my job, run for office. I don't want him in the building.'

I looked at his back as he walked away, his words stinging in my face. I caught up with him.

'It's not Purcel. It's who he's with. I think she bothers a few people's conscience around here,' I said.

'You're out of line.'

'With respect, so are you, sir,' I replied, and went outside.

Clete was walking toward me from the curb. He wore a light suit and a tan silk shirt and a dark tie with tiny flowers on it, and his porkpie hat had been replaced by a Panama with a green-tinted visor built into the brim.

'What are you doing with Passion?' I asked.

'I took her to the clinic over in Lafayette.'

'What for?'

'She sees a dermatologist there or something. She didn't want to talk about it.'

'You didn't answer my question. What are you doing with her?'

'None of your damn business, Streak.'

We stood there like that, in the heat of the afternoon, the shadows of the huge white courthouse falling on the lawn behind us. Then Clete's face relented and his eyes went away from me and came back again.

'I took her for a drive because I like her. We're going to dinner and a movie. You want to tag along?' he said.

'I want to talk to you in private.'

'Yeah, anytime I can be useful. Thanks for the hospitality,' he said, and got back into the Cadillac and drove away. Passion smiled at me, brushing her hair out of one eye with the ends of her fingers.

Clete came into the bait shop when I was closing up that night. He opened a bottle of Dixie beer and drank it at the counter. I sat down next to him with a Dr Pepper.

'I'm sorry about today. I just worry about you sometimes, Cletus,' I said.

'You think I'm over-the-hill for Passion?'

'You carried me down a fire escape with two bullets in your back. I don't like to see you get hurt.'

'She makes me feel young. What's wrong in that?'

I cupped my hand on the back of his neck. The baked scales on his skin were as stiff as blistered paint.

'Nothing's wrong with it,' I said.

'So why did you want to talk in private?'

'We think the Zipper Clum shooter is a Kentucky product by way of Michigan. His real name is Johnny O'Roarke but he goes by Remeta. He did a two-bit in Raiford. He also got to be an expert in jailhouse romance.'

'Same guy who was going to do Little Face?'

'That's the way I see it.'

'The jigger said Remeta didn't have a sheet.'

'You ever know a gumball yet who had the whole story right?'

'So Remeta blew off the hit and now he's in the shithouse with whoever gave him the contract. Is that what you were going to tell me?'

'That's about it.'

He grinned and drank out of his beer. 'And you think we should make life as messed up as possible for all bad guys involved?'

'Who's the best source for cold pieces around New Orleans?' I asked.

'It used to be Tommy Carrol, till somebody flushed his grits for him. Right now?' He scratched his hairline and thought. 'You ever hear of the Eighteenth Street gang in Los Angeles? They're here, kind of like sewer growth metastasizing across the country. I never thought I'd miss the greaseballs.'

I drove down East Main at sunrise the next day, under the arched canopy of live oaks that lined the street, and picked Clete up at the apartment he had rented downtown. The moon was still up, the air heavy with the smell of night-blooming flowers and wet trees and bamboo and water that has seeped deep into the soil and settled permanently around stone and brickwork.

But three hours later Clete and I were in a rural area north of New Orleans that in terms of toxicity probably has no environmental equivalent in the country. The petrochemical plants on the edge of the wetlands bleed their wastes into the drainages and woods, systemically killing all life in them, layering the soil with a viscous, congealed substance that resembles putty veined with every color in the rainbow.

The man we were looking for, Garfield Jefferson, lived at the end of a row of tin-roofed shotgun shacks left over from the days of corporate plantations. The rain ditch in front was blown with Styrofoam litter, the yard heaped with upholstered furniture.

'This guy's a gun dealer?' I said.

'He creates free-fire zones for other people to live in and keeps a low profile in Shitsville. Don't be deceived by his smile, either. He's a mainline grad of Pelican Bay,' Clete said.

Garfield Jefferson's skin was so black it gave off a purple sheen, at least inside the colorless gloom of his tiny living room, where he sat on a stuffed couch, legs spread, and grinned at us. The grin never left his face, as though his mouth were hitched on the corners by fishhooks.

'I'm not following y'all. You say you a cop from New Iberia and some dude give you my name?' he said.

'Johnny Remeta says you sold him the piece he did Zipper Clum with. That puts you deep down in the bowl, Garfield,' I said.

'This is all new to me, man. How come the guy is telling you this, anyway? He just running around loose, popping people, calling in information from the phone booth?' Jefferson said.

'Because he fucked up a hit for the wrong people and he knows his ass is hanging over the fire. So he wants to cut a deal, and that means he gives up a few nickel-and-dime pus heads like yourself as an act of good faith,' Clete said.

Jefferson looked out the window, grinning at nothing, or perhaps at the outline of a chemical plant that loomed over a woods filled with leafless trees. His hair was shaved close to the scalp, his wide shoulders knobby with muscle under his T-shirt. He fitted a baseball cap backwards on his head and adjusted it, his eyes glowing with self-satisfaction.

'A turned-around cap in Louisiana mean a guy don't do drugs. You white folks ain't caught on to that. You see a nigger with his hat on backwards, you think "Mean-ass motherfucker, gonna 'jack my car, get in my daughter's bread." I ain't dealt no guns, man. Tell this cracker he be dropping my name, I be finding his crib. I got too much in my jacket to sit still for this shit,' he said. He grinned innocuously at us.

Clete stood up from his chair and remained standing on the corner of Jefferson's vision. He picked up a ceramic lamp, the only bright object in the room, and examined the motel logo on the bottom of it.

'You got a heavy jacket, huh?' I said.

'Eighteen Streeters always get Pelican Bay. Twenty-three hour lockdown. But I'm through with all that. I come back here to be with the home folks,' Jefferson said.

Clete smashed the lamp across the side of Jefferson's head. Pieces of ceramic showered on the couch and in Jefferson's lap. For a moment his face was dazed, his eyes out of focus, then the corners of his mouth stretched upward on wires again.

'See, when people got a weight problem, they go around pissed off all the time, big hard-on 'cause they fat and ugly and don't want no full-length mirrors in their bathrooms,' Jefferson said.

'You think you're funny?' Clete said, and hit him with the flat of his hand on the ear. 'Tell me you're funny. I want to hear it.'

'Clete,' I said softly.

'Butt out of this, Streak.' Then he said to Jefferson, 'You remember those three elementary kids got shot at the playground off Esplanade? The word is you sold the Uzi to the shooter. You got something to say about that, smart-ass?'

'Free enterprise, motherfucker,' Jefferson said, evenly, grinning, his tongue thick and red on his teeth.

Clete knotted Jefferson's T-shirt with his left hand and drove his right fist into Jefferson's face, then pulled him from the couch and threw him to the floor. When Jefferson started to raise himself on his arms, Clete crashed the sole of his shoe into his jaw.

'It looks like you just spit some teeth there, Garfield,' Clete said.

'Get away from him, Clete,' I said.

'No problem. Sorry I lost it with this outstanding Afro-American. Do you hear that, Garfield? I'll come back later sometime and apologize again when we're alone.'

'I mean it, Clete. Wait for me in the truck.'

Clete went out into the yard and let the screen slam behind him. He looked back at me, his face still dark, an unlit Lucky Strike in his mouth. I helped Jefferson back onto the couch and found a towel in the bathroom and put it in his hand.

'I'm sorry that happened,' I said.

'You the good guy in the act, huh?' he replied.

'It's no act, partner. Clete will tear you up.'

Jefferson pushed the towel tight against his mouth and coughed on his own blood, then looked up at me, this time without the grin, his eyes lackluster with the banal nature of the world in which he lived.

'I didn't sell the piece to the cracker. He wanted one, but he ain't got it from me. He got some wicked shit in his blood. I don't need his grief,' he said.

'What are you talking about?'

'He do it for hire. But if there wasn't no money in it, he'd do it anyway. You say he fucked up a hit? I don't believe it. He gets off on it, man. Somebody done reamed that dude good.'

Clete and I drove into the French Quarter, then across the river into Algiers. We talked to hookers, pimps, house creeps, stalls, dips, strong-arm robbers, fences, money washers, carjackers, petty boosters and addicts and crack dealers, all the population that clings to the underside of the city like nematodes eating their way through the subsoil of a manicured lawn. None of them seemed to know anything about Johnny Remeta.

But an ex-prizefighter who ran a saloon on Magazine said he'd heard a new button man in town had bought a half dozen clean guns off some black kids who'd burglarized a sporting goods store.

'Who's he working for, Goldie?' I asked.

'If he waxed Zipper Clum, the human race,' he answered.

At dusk, when the sun was only an orange smudge over the rooftops and the wind was peppered with grit and raindrops, we found one of the kids who had broken into the sporting goods store. Clete pulled him out of a fig tree down the street from the St Thomas Welfare Project.

He was fourteen years old and wore khaki short pants and tennis shoes without socks. Sweat dripped out of his hair and cut lines in the dust on his face.

'This is the mastermind of the group. The ones who got away are younger than he is,' Clete said. 'What's your name, mastermind?'

'Louis.'

'Where's the guy live you sold the guns to?' Clete asked.

'Probably downtown somewhere.'

'How do you know that?' I asked.

' 'Cause he drove toward downtown. The same direction the streetcar go to.'

'Pretty smart deduction, Louis. How much did he give you for the guns?' Clete said.

'A hunnerd dollars.'

'For six guns?' Clete said.

'He said he didn't have no more money. He showed us his wallet. It didn't have no more money in it.'

'One of those guns was used to kill somebody, Louis,' I said.

He looked into space, as though my words and the reality they suggested had nothing to do with his life. He must have weighed eighty pounds. He looked like an upended ant, with small ears, hooked teeth, and eyes that were too large for his face. His knees and elbows were scabbed, his T-shirt glued to his chest with dried food.

'What'd you do with the money, partner?' I asked.

'Didn't get no chance to do nothing. Big kids took it. We was going to the show. Y'all got any spare change?'

His eyes blinked in the silence while he waited for an answer.

What had we accomplished? There was no way to tell. We had put the word on the street that Johnny Remeta was willing to give up people in the New Orleans underworld. Maybe either he or the people who had given him the contract on Zipper Clum and Little Face Dautrieve would be forced into the sunlight. But that night I was too tired to care.

When I was nineteen I worked on an offshore seismograph rig, called a doodlebug outfit in the oil field. It was the summer of 1957, the year that Hurricane Audrey pushed a tidal wave out of the Gulf of Mexico on top of Cameron, Louisiana, crushing the town flat, killing hundreds of people.

For weeks afterward bodies were found in the forks of gum trees out in the swamp or inside islands of uprooted cypress that floated out of the wetlands into the Gulf. Sometimes the long, rubber-coated recording cables we strung from the bow and stern of a portable drill barge got hung on a sunken tree in the middle of a bay or river and a crew member on the jugboat would have to go down after them.

The water was warm with the sun's heat, dark brown

with mud and dead hyacinths. The kid who went over the gunnel and pulled himself hand over hand down to the fouled place on the cable did so without light. The sun, even though it was absolutely white in the sky, could not penetrate the layers of silt in the water, and the diver found himself swimming blindly among the water-sculpted and pointed ends of tree branches that gouged at his face like fingers. If he was lucky, the cable came loose with one hard tug in the right direction.

On a late July afternoon I swam down fifteen feet until I touched the smooth, mud-encased trunk of an enormous cypress. I felt my way along the bark until I bumped into the root system, then unwrapped the cable and slid it toward me off the sides of a taproot.

A gray cloud of mud mushroomed around me, as though I had disturbed an envelope of cold air trapped inside the maw of the tree's root system. Suddenly the body of a woman rose out of the silt against mine, her hair sliding across my face, her dress floating above her underwear, the tips of her ringed fingers glancing off my mouth.

No one on the jugboat saw her and some of the crew did not believe the story I told them. But the woman who had been gripped and held fast by the cypress tree, set free only to be lost again, lived with me in my dreams for many years. Her memory had the power to close my windpipe and steal the air from my lungs.

Tonight she was back, although in a different form.

It was nighttime in the dream, the air thick and acrid and sweet at the same time with smoke from a distant stubble fire. I saw my mother, Mae Robicheaux, on a dirt road that led past a neon-lit dance hall. The road was bordered on each side by fields that were bursting with fat stalks of purple cane, their leaves rustling with wind. She was running down the dirt road in the pink uniform she wore to work at the beer garden, her hands outstretched, her mouth wide with a desperate plea. Two cops ran behind her, their hands holding their revolvers in their holsters to prevent them from falling out on the ground.

I was unable to move, watching impotently as a torrent of water surged out of the bay at the end of the dirt road and roared toward her between the walls of sugarcane. She tripped and fell and the root systems from the fields wrapped her body like white worms and held her fast while the water coursed around her thighs, her hips and breasts and neck.

I could see her eyes and mouth clearly now and read my name on her lips, then the current closed over her head and I sat up in bed, my face popping with sweat, my lungs burning as though acid had been poured in them.

I sat in the kitchen, in the dark, my heart twisting in my chest. I went into the bedroom and came back again, with my .45 in my hand, my palm damp on the grips. In my mind I saw the two cops who had chased my mother down the road, saw the sky blue of their uniforms, the glint of the moon on their shields and revolver butts and waxed gun belts, saw everything about them except their faces. I wanted to fire my weapon until the barrel was translucent with heat.

When Bootsie lay her hand on my back, I twitched as though touched with a hot iron, then placed the .45 on the table and buried my face in her stomach.

chapter ten

On Saturday I woke early, before sunrise, to help Batist, the elderly black man who worked for me, open the bait shop and fire the barbecue pit on which we prepared chickens and links for our midday customers. I unhooked Tripod, Alafair's pet three-legged coon, from his chain and set him on top of the rabbit hutch with a bowl of water and a bowl of fish scraps. But he hopped down on the ground and walked ahead of me through the pecan and oak trees and across the dirt road to the dock, his tail and rear end swaying.

He and Batist had been at war for years, Tripod flinging boudin all over the counter, destroying boxes of fried pies and candy bars, Batist chasing him down the dock with a broom, threatening to cook him in a pot. But finally they had declared a truce, either out of their growing age or their recognition of their mutual intractability. Now, whenever Alafair or I turned Tripod loose, he usually headed for the dock and worked the screen open and slept on top of the icebox behind the counter. Last week I saw Batist roaring down the bayou in an outboard, with Tripod sitting on the bow, his face pointed into the breeze like a hood ornament.

When I went inside the shop Batist was drinking a cup of coffee, looking out the screen window at the swamp.

'You ever seen a red moon like that this time of year?' he said.

'The wind's up. There's a lot of dust in the air,' I said.

He was a big man, the muscles in his upper arms like croquet balls; his bell-bottomed dungarees and white T-shirt looked sewn to his skin.

'Old people say back in slave days they poured hog blood in the ground under a moon like this,' he said.

'Why?' I asked.

'Make the corn and cane bigger. Same reason people kill a gator and plant it in the field,' he replied. 'I seen Clete Purcel with Passion Labiche.'

'Really?'

'Them girls are trouble, Dave. Their folks was pimps.'

'A good apple can come off a bad tree,' I said.

'Tell that to the man got his parts chopped up all over the flo'.'

'I think he had it coming,' I replied.

Tripod had crawled up on the counter and was sniffing a jar of pickles. Batist hefted him up in the crook of his arm. Tripod's tail was ringed with silver bands and it flipped back and forth between his upended legs.

'We was ten of us when I was growing up. My mama made a big pan of biscuits for breakfast every morning but we didn't have nothing to put on them. So she kept a jar of fig preserves on the table. We rubbed the biscuit on the side of the jar, then ate it. We all laughed when we done that. Everybody's road got glass on it, Dave. Don't mean you got the right to kill nobody,' he said.

'What does that have to do with Clete seeing Passion, Batist?'

'I knowed them girls since they was little. You seen one, you seen the other. They wasn't never more than a broom handle apart.'

'It's too early in the morning to argue with you, partner,' I said.

'I ain't arguing. The troot's the troot. I ain't got to prove nothing, me.'

He walked outside into the soft blue light and set Tripod on the handrail and began hosing down the spool tables on the dock, the moon dull red behind his head.

Later that morning I filled an envelope full of black-and-white photos taken at the Vachel Carmouche murder scene and drove out to Carmouche's boarded-up house on the bayou. The property itself seemed physically stricken by the deed that had been committed there. The yard was waist-high in weeds, the gallery stacked with old tires and hay bales that had gone gray with rot. Nests of yellow jackets and dirtdobbers buzzed under the eaves and a broken windmill clanged uselessly in a dry, hot wind.

I walked around back, re-creating in my mind's eye the path that Letty must have taken from the back porch to the rear of her house, where she stripped off her shoes and robe and washed the blood from her hair and body with a garden hose. The lock was already broken on the back door of Carmouche's house, and I pushed the door open, scraping it back on the buckled linoleum.

The air was stifling, like the inside of a privy in summer, rife with the smell of bat guano and pools of settled water under the floor, superheated by the tin roof and the closed windows. A green plant, as dark as spinach, had blossomed from the drain in the sink.

But the signs of Carmouche's agony from his crawl were still visible on the linoleum, like smeared reddish black paint that had dried and taken on the crisp, razored design of broken leaves. But there were other stains in the kitchen, too – a tentacle of connected dots on the wall by the stove and two similar streakings on the ceiling. I touched my fingers on the dots by the stove and felt what

I was sure were the crusted, physical remains of Louisiana's most famous electrician.

I looked through the crime scene photos again. Blood had been slung all over the floor, the walls, the curtains on the cabinets, the icebox, and even the screen of the television set, which had been tuned to an old Laurel and Hardy comedy when the photo was taken. But how would blood from a mattock, a heavy, two-handed tool used to bust up stumps and root systems, create whipped patterns like those on the ceiling and the wall?

I walked across the yard to the back of the Labiche house. The faucet where Letty had washed herself dripped water into the dust; the oil drum she had tried to destroy her robe and shoes in now smoldered with burning leaves; the house she had grown up in was ringed with roses and gardenias, and red squirrels leaped from the branches of the live oaks and clattered across the roof.

The home was weathered, the woodwork termite-eaten and the white paint cracked by the sun and dulled by smoke from stubble fires, but it was still a fine place in which to live, a piece of history from antebellum times, if only Letty were here to enjoy it, if only she had not traded off her life in order to kill a worthless man like Vachel Carmouche.

'You prowling 'round my house for a reason?' someone said behind me.

'What's the haps, Passion?' I said.

She wore sandals and baggy jeans and stood with her big-boned hands on her hips.

'Clete says you think he's a cradle robber, that I'm too young a chick for a man his age.'

'He tells that to women all the time. It makes them feel sorry for him,' I replied.

'What were you doing over at Carmouche's place?' she asked.

98

'An elderly black friend of mine was mentioning how you and Letty were inseparable. How if somebody saw one of you, he automatically saw the other.'

'So?'

'What were you doing the night Carmouche got it?'

'Read the trial report. I'm not interested in covering that same old territory again. Tell me something. You got a problem with your friend seeing me 'cause I'm Creole?'

'You'll have to find another pin cushion, Passion. See you around,' I said, and walked across the yard under the shade trees toward my truck.

'Yeah, you, too, big stuff,' she said.

When I drove back up the road, she was carrying a loaded trash can in each hand to the roadside, her chest and heavy arms swollen with her physical power. I waved, but my truck seemed to slide past her gaze without her ever seeing it.

That afternoon Governor Belmont Pugh held a news conference, supposedly to talk about casinos, slot machines at the state's racetracks, and the percentage of the gambling revenue that should go into a pay raise for schoolteachers.

But Belmont did not look comfortable. His tie was askew, the point of one collar bent upward, his eyes scorched, his face the color and texture of a boiled ham. He kept gulping water, as though he were dehydrated or forcing down the regurgitated taste of last night's whiskey.

Then one reporter stood up and asked Belmont the question he feared: 'What are you going to do about Letty Labiche, Governor?'

Belmont rubbed his mouth with the flat of his hand, and the microphone picked up the sound of his calluses scraping across whiskers.

'Excuse me, I got a sore throat today and cain't talk

right. I'm granting an indefinite stay of execution. Long as she's got her appeals up there in the courts. That's what the law requires,' he said.

'What do you mean "indefinite," Governor?'

'I got corn fritters in my mouth? It means what I said.'

'Are you saying even after her Supreme Court appeal, you're going to continue the stay, or do you plan to see her executed? It's not a complicated question, sir,' another reporter, a man in a bow tie, said, smiling to make the insult acceptable.

Then, for just a moment, Belmont rose to a level of candor and integrity I hadn't thought him capable of.

'Y'all need to understand something. That's a human life we're talking about. Not just a story in your papers or on your TV show. Y'all can take my remarks any damn way you want, but by God I'm gonna do what my conscience tells me. If that don't sit right with somebody, they can chase a possum up a gum stump.'

An aide stepped close to Belmont and spoke into his ear. Belmont's face had the flatness of a guilty man staring into a strobe light. It didn't take long for the viewer to realize that a rare moment had come and gone.

Belmont blinked and his mouth flexed uncertainly before he spoke again.

'I'm an elected official. I'm gonna do my duty to the people of Lou'sana. That means when the appeals is over, I got to uphold the law. I don't got personal choices . . . That's it. There's complimentary food and drink on a table in the back of the room.' He swallowed and looked into space, his face empty and bloodless, as though the words he had just spoken had been said by someone else.

The next morning I read the coroner's report on the death of Vachel Carmouche. It was signed by a retired pathologist named Ezra Cole, a wizened, part-time deacon in a fundamentalist congregation made up mostly of Texas oil people and North Louisiana transplants. He had worked for the parish only a short time eight or nine years ago. But I still remembered the pharmacy he had owned in the Lafayette Medical Center back in the 1960s. He would not allow people of color to even stand in line with whites, requiring them instead to wait in the concourse until no other customers were inside.

I found him at his neat gray and red bungalow out by Spanish Lake, sanding a boat that was inverted on sawhorses. His wife was working in the garden behind the picket fence, a sunbonnet on her head. Their lawn was emerald green from soak hoses and liquid nitrogen, their bamboo and banana trees bending in their backyard against the blueness of the lake. But in the midst of this bucolic tranquillity, Ezra Cole waged war against all fashion and what he saw as the erosion of moral tradition.

'You're asking me how blood got on the ceiling and the wall by the stove? The woman slung it all over the place,' he said.

He wore suspenders over a white dress shirt and rubber boots with the pants tucked inside. His face was narrow and choleric, his eyes busy with angry thoughts that seemed to have less to do with my questions than concerns he carried with him as a daily burden.

'The pattern was too thin. Also, I don't know how she could throw blood on the ceiling from a heavy tool like a mattock,' I said.

'Ask me how she knocked the eyeball out of his head. The answer is she probably has the strength of three men. Maybe she was full of dope.'

'The drug screen says she wasn't.'

'Then I don't know.'

'Was there a second weapon, Doctor?'

'It's all in the report. If you want to help that woman,

pray for her soul, 'cause I don't buy death row conversions.'

'I think the blood on the ceiling was thrown there by a knife or barber's razor or weed sickle,' I said.

His face darkened; his eyes glanced sideways at his wife. His hand pinched hard into my arm.

'Step over here with me,' he said, pushing and walking with me toward my truck.

'Excuse me, but take your hand off my person, Dr Cole.'

'You hear my words, Mr Robicheaux. I know Vachel Carmouche's relatives. They don't need to suffer any more than they have. There's nothing that requires a pathologist to exacerbate the pain of the survivors. Are you understanding me, sir?'

'You mean you lied on an autopsy?'

'Watch your tongue.'

'There *was* a second weapon? Which means there might have been a second killer.'

'He was sexually mutilated. While he was still alive. What difference does it make what kind of weapon she used? The woman's depraved. You're trying to get her off? Where's your common sense, man?'

At sunset that same day Batist phoned up from the dock.

'Dave, there's a man down here don't want to come up to the house,' he said.

'Why not?'

'Hang on.' I heard Batist put the receiver down on the counter, walk away from it, then scrape it up in his hand again. 'He's outside where he cain't hear me. I t'ink he's a sad fellow 'cause of his face.'

'Is his name Mike or Micah or something like that?'

'I'll go ax.'

'Never mind. I'll be right down.'

I walked down the slope toward the dock. A purple

haze hung in the trees, and birds lifted on the wind that blew across the dead cypress in the swamp. The man who was the chauffeur for Cora Gable was leaning on the rail at the end of the dock, looking out at the bayou, his face turned into the shadows. His shirtsleeves were rolled and his biceps were tattooed with coiled green and red snakes whose fangs were arched into their own tails.

'You're Micah?' I said.

'That's right.'

'Can I help you?' I asked.

'Maybe you can Ms Perez.'

'Jim Gable's wife?'

'I call her by her screen name. The man who marries her ought to take her name, not the other way around.'

His right eye glimmered, barely visible behind the nodulous growth that deformed the side of his face and exposed the teeth at the corner of his mouth. His hair was straw-colored and neatly barbered and combed, as though his personal grooming could negate the joke nature had played upon him.

'It's all about a racetrack. Outside of Luna Mescalero, New Mexico,' he said.

'Pardon?'

'Mr Gable got her to buy a spread out there. He's building a racetrack. He's been trying to do it for years. That's where I'm from. I was a drunkard, a carnival man, what they call the geek act, before that woman come into my life.'

'She seems like a special person,' I said.

He turned his face into the glow of the electric lights and looked me directly in the eyes.

'I did nine months on a county road gang, Mr Robicheaux. One day I sassed a hack and he pulled me behind the van and caned knots all over my head. When I tried to get up he spit on me and jabbed me in the ribs and whipped me till I cried. Ms Perez seen it from her

103

front porch. She called the governor of New Mexico and threatened to walk in his office with a reporter and slap his face unless I was released from jail. She give me a job and an air-conditioned brick cottage to live in when other people would hide their children from me.'

'I don't know what I can do, Micah. Not unless Jim Gable has committed a crime of some kind.'

He chewed the skin on the ball of his thumb.

'A man who doesn't respect one woman, won't respect another,' he said.

'Excuse me?'

He looked out into the shadows again, his head twisting back and forth on his neck, as though searching for words that would not injure.

'He speaks disrespectfully of Ms Perez in front of other men. She's not the only one. Is your wife's first name Bootsie?'

'Yes,' I replied, the skin tightening around my temples.

'He said dirty things about her to a cop named Ritter. They laughed about her.'

'I think it's time for you to go.'

He splayed open his hand, like a fielder's glove, and stared at it and wiped dirt off the heel with the tips of his fingers.

'I've been told to get off better places. I come here on account of Ms Perez. If you won't stand up for your wife, it's your own damn business,' he said, and brushed past me, his arm grazing against mine.

'You hold on,' I said, and lifted my finger at him. 'If you've got a beef to square with Jim Gable, you do it on your own hook.'

He walked back toward me, the teeth at the corner of his mouth glinting in the purple dusk.

'People come to the geek act so they can look on the outside of a man like me and not look at the inside of themselves. You stick your finger in my face again and I'll break it, policeman be damned,' he said.

It stormed that night. The rain blew against the house and ran off the eaves and braided and whipped in the light that fell from the windows. Just as the ten o'clock news came on, the phone rang in the kitchen.

The accent was East Kentucky or Tennessee, the pronunciation soft, the 'r' sound almost gone from the words, the vowels round and deep-throated.

'There's no point in trying to trace this call. I'm not using a ground line,' he said.

'I'm going to take a guess. Johnny Remeta?' I said.

'I got a hit on me. Maybe you're responsible. I can't be sure.'

'Then get out of town.'

'I don't do that.'

'Why'd you call me?'

'Sir, you told folks I was a snitch. What gives you the right to lie like that? I don't even know you.'

'Come in. It's not too late to turn it around. Nobody's mourning Zipper Clum.'

'You've got to set straight what you've done, Mr Robicheaux.'

'You're in the wrong line of work to demand redress, partner.'

'Demand what?'

'Listen, you wouldn't go through with the job at Little Face Dautrieve's place. Maybe you have qualities you haven't thought about. Meet me someplace.'

'Are you kidding?'

I didn't reply. He waited in the silence, then cleared his throat as though he wanted to continue talking but didn't know what to say.

The line went dead.

A hit man who calls you 'sir'?

chapter eleven

At eight o'clock Monday morning the sheriff stopped me just as I walked in the front door of the department. A small square of blood-crusted tissue paper was stuck to his jawbone where he had cut himself shaving.

'Come down the hall and talk with me a minute,' he said.

I followed him inside his office. He took off his coat and hung it on a chair and gazed out the window. He pressed his knuckles into his lower spine as though relieving himself of a sharp pain in his back.

'Close the door. Pull the blind, too,' he said.

'Is this about the other day?'

'I told you I didn't want Clete Purcel in here. I believe that to be a reasonable request. You interpreted that to mean I have problems of conscience over Letty Labiche.'

'Maybe you just don't like Purcel. I apologize for implying anything else,' I said.

'You were on leave when Carmouche was killed. You didn't have to put your hand in it.'

'No, I didn't.'

'The prosecutor asked for the death penalty. The decision wasn't ours.'

'Carmouche was a pedophile and a sadist. One of his

victims is on death row. That one just won't go down, Sheriff.'

The color climbed out of his neck into his face. He cut his head to speak, but no words came out of his mouth. His profile was as scissored as an Indian's against the window.

'Don't lay this off on me, Dave. I won't abide it,' he said.

'I think we ought to reopen the case. I think a second killer is out there.'

He widened his eyes and said, 'You guys in A.A. have an expression, what is it, "dry drunks"? You've got a situation you can't work your way out of, so you create another problem and get emotionally drunk on it. I'm talking about your mother's death. That's the only reason I'm not putting you on suspension.'

'Is that it?' I said.

'No. A New Orleans homicide cop named Don Ritter is waiting in your office,' he replied.

'Ritter's Vice.'

'Good. Clear that up with him,' the sheriff said, and leaned against the windowsill on his palms, stretching out his frame to ease the pain in his lower back.

Don Ritter, the plainclothes detective Helen called the gel head, was sitting in a chair in front of my desk, cleaning his nails over the wastebasket with a gold penknife. His eyes lifted up at me. Then he went back to work on his nails.

'The sheriff says you're Homicide,' I said.

'Yeah, I just changed over. I caught the Zipper Clum case.'

'Really?'

'Who told you and Purcel to question people in New Orleans about Johnny Remeta?'

'He's a suspect in a house invasion.'

'A house invasion, huh? Lovely. What are we supposed to do if you scare him out of town?'

'He says that's not his way.'

'He says?'

'Yeah, he called me up last night.'

Ritter brushed the detritus from his nails into the basket and folded his penknife and put it in his pocket. He crossed his legs and rotated his ankle slightly, watching the light reflect on his shoe shine. His hair looked like gelled pieces of thick twine strung back on his scalp.

'The home invasion? That's the break-in at Little Face Dautrieve's place?' he said.

'Little Face says you planted rock on her. She's trying to turn her life around. Why don't you stay away from her?'

'I don't know what bothers me worse, the bullshit about talking to Remeta or the injured-black-whore routine. You want to nail this guy or not?'

'You see Jim Gable?'

'What about it?'

'Tell him I'm going to look him up on my next trip to New Orleans.'

He chewed with his front teeth on something, a tiny piece of food perhaps.

'So this is what happens when you start over again in a small town. Must make you feel like staying in bed some days. Thanks for your time, Robicheaux,' he said.

I signed out of the office at noon and went home for lunch. As I drove down the dirt road toward the house, I saw a blue Lexus approach me under the long line of oak trees that bordered the bayou. The Lexus slowed and the driver rolled down her window.

'How you doin', Dave?' she said.

'Hey, Ms Deshotel. You visiting in the neighborhood?'

'Your wife and I just had lunch. We're old school chums.'

She took off her sunglasses, and the shadows of leaves moved back and forth on her olive skin. It was hard to believe her career in law enforcement went back into the 1960s. Her heart-shaped face was radiant, her throat unlined, her dark hair a reminder of the health and latent energy and youthful good looks that her age didn't seem to diminish.

'I didn't realize y'all knew each other,' I said.

'She didn't remember me at first, but . . . Anyway, we'll be seeing you. Call me for anything you need.'

She drove away with a casual wave of the hand.

'You went to school with Connie Deshotel?' I asked Bootsie in the kitchen.

'A night class at LSU-NO. She just bought a weekend place at Fausse Pointe. You look puzzled.'

'She's strange.'

'She's a nice person. Stop being psychoanalytical,' Bootsie said.

'She was having lunch in Baton Rouge with an NOPD cop named Don Ritter. He's a genuine lowlife.'

She hung a dishrag over the faucet and turned toward me and let her eyes rove over my face.

'What did he do?' she asked.

'He twists dials on black hookers. Helen says he used to extort gays in the Quarter.'

'So he's a dirty cop. He's not the only one you've known.'

'He's buds with Jim Gable.'

'I see. That's the real subject of our conversation. Maybe you should warn me in advance.'

'Gable has personal knowledge about my mother's death. I'm absolutely convinced of that, Boots.'

She nodded, almost to herself, or to the room, rather than to me, then began slicing a roast on the counter for our sandwiches. She cut harder, faster, one hand slipping on the knob of bone she used for a grip, the blade of the butcher knife knocking against the chopping board. She slid the knife in a long cut through a flat piece of meat and halved and quartered a bloodred tomato next to it, her knuckles whitening. Then she turned around and faced me. 'What can I tell you? That I loathe myself for the fact I slept with him? What is it you want me to say, Dave?'

At the end of the week I received a call from Connie Deshotel at the office.

'Dave, maybe we've had some luck. Do you know of a recidivist named Steve Andropolis?' she said.

'He's a spotter, what used to be called a jigger.'

'He's in custody in Morgan City.'

'What for?'

'Possession of stolen weapons. He says he knows you. This is his fourth time down. He wants to cut a deal.'

'Andropolis is a pathological liar.'

'Maybe. He says he has information on the Zipper Clum murder. He also says he knows how your mother died.'

The sun was high and bright in the sky, the tinted windows of the cars in the parking lot hammered with white daggers. I felt my hand tighten on the telephone receiver.

'How did he come by his information?' I asked.

'I don't know. Two detectives from NOPD are going to interview him this afternoon. You want to meet them there?'

'Is one of them Ritter?'

'Probably. He caught the case.'

'What's Andropolis' bond?'

'None. He's a flight risk.'

'I'll make arrangements to go over there in the next

110

two or three days. Thanks for passing this on, Ms Deshotel,' I said.

'You seem pretty casual.'

'His crime isn't in our jurisdiction. I don't have the legal power to do anything for him. That means he wants to use me against somebody else. Let him sweat awhile.'

'You should have been a prosecutor,' she said.

'What's he have to offer on Remeta?' I said as an afterthought.

'Ritter thinks he might have sold Remeta the weapon used in the Clum killing. Maybe he knows who ordered the hit.'

'The piece came from a sporting goods break-in. The thieves were black kids from the St Thomas Project. Andropolis is taking Ritter over the hurdles.'

'I thought I might be of help. Good luck with it, Dave. Give my best to your wife,' she said, and quietly hung up.

That evening the sky was filled with yellow and red clouds when Clete Purcel and I put a boat in the water at Lake Fausse Pointe. I opened up the outboard down a long canal that was thickly wooded on each side. Green logs rolled against the bank in our wake and cranes and snow egrets and great blue herons lifted into the light and glided on extended wings out over the bay.

We passed acres of floating lilies and lotus flowers that had just gone into bloom, then crossed another bay that flowed into a willow swamp and anchored the outboard off a stand of flooded cypress and tupelo gums and watched our wake slide between the trunks that were as gray as elephant hide.

Clete sat on a swivel chair close to the bow, his porkpie hat low on his eyes, his blue denim shirt damp with sweat between the shoulder blades. He flipped his casting rod with his wrist and sent his treble-hooked balsa-wood lure arching through the air.

'How's it going with you and Passion?' I asked.

'Very solid, big mon,' he replied, turning the handle on his spinning reel, the lure zigzagging through the water toward the boat.

I took a cold can of beer from the ice chest and touched the back of his arm with it. He took it from my hand without turning around. I opened a Dr Pepper and drank it and watched the breeze blow through the cypress, ruffling the leaves like green lace.

'Why don't you say what's on your mind?' Clete said.

'I went through the transcript of Letty Labiche's trial. Both Letty and Passion testified that Passion was auditioning at a Lake Charles nightclub for a record company scout the night Vachel Carmouche got it.'

' 'Cause that's where she was,' Clete said.

'They always performed together. Why would she audition by herself?'

Clete retrieved his lure and idly shook the water off it, rattling the two treble hooks against the tip of the rod.

'What are you trying to do, Streak? Drag Passion into it? What's to be gained?'

'I think both sisters are lying about what happened that night. What's that suggest to you? Letty is already on death row. She has nothing to lose.'

'The state's executioner got chopped into sausage links and somebody's going to pay for it. You remember the Ricky Ray Rector case up in Arkansas? The guy had been lobotomized. He looked like black mush poured inside a prison jumpsuit. But he'd killed a cop. Clinton refused to commute the sentence. Rector told the warden he wanted to save out his pecan pie on his last meal so he could eat it after he was executed. Clinton's president, Rector's fertilizer. I bet nobody in Little Rock gave up their regular hump the night he got it, either.'

Clete lit a Lucky Strike and set his Zippo on the top of

his tackle box and blew smoke out across his cupped hand.

'I thought you quit those,' I said.

'I did. For some reason I just started again. Dave, it's grim shit. Passion says her sister's scared of the dark, scared of being alone, scared of her own dreams. I came out here to get away from listening about it. So how about lightening up?'

He lay his rod across his thighs and stuck his hand behind him into the crushed ice for another beer, his face painted with the sun's dying red light, his eyes avoiding mine.

According to his obituary, Robert Mitchum, when released from jail after serving time for marijuana possession, was asked what it was like inside the slams.

He replied, 'Not bad. Kind of like Palm Springs without the riffraff.'

It's gone downhill since.

Unless you're a black kid hustling rock and unlucky enough to get nailed under the Three Strikes and You're Out law, your chances of doing serious time are remote.

Who are all these people in the jails?

Meltdowns of every stripe, pipeheads and intravenous junkies who use public institutions to clean their systems out so they can re-addict, recidivists looking for the womb, armed robbers willing to risk ten years for a sixty-dollar score at a 7-Eleven.

Also the twenty-three-hour lockdown crowd: sadists, serial killers, necrophiliacs, sex predators, and people who defy classification, what we used to call the criminally insane, those whose deeds are so dark their specifics are only hinted at in news accounts.

I could have interviewed the jigger named Steve Andropolis on Friday, the same day that Don Ritter did. But what was the point? At best Ritter was a self-serving bumbler who would try to control the interview for his own purposes, probably buy into Andropolis' manipulations, and taint any possibility of obtaining legitimate information from him. Moreover, Ritter was investigating a homicide and had a legal reach that I did not.

So I waited over the weekend and drove to Morgan City on Monday.

Just in time to see Andropolis' body being wheeled out of the jail on a gurney by two paramedics.

'What happened?' I asked the jailer.

' "What happened?" he asks,' the jailer replied, as though a third party were in the room. He was a huge, head-shaved, granite-jawed man whose oversized pale blue suit looked like it was tailored from cardboard.

'I got people hanging out the windows. I got escapees going through air ducts. I got prisoners walking out the door with "time served," when they're not the guys supposed to be walking out the door,' he said.

He took a breath and picked up his cigar from his ashtray, then set it back down and cracked his knuckles like walnuts.

'I locked Andropolis in with eleven other prisoners. The cell's supposed to hold five. There's three bikers in that cell the devil wouldn't let scrub his toilet. There's a kid who puts broken glass in pet bowls. One guy shoots up speedballs with malt liquor. Those are the normal ones. You ask what happened? Somebody broke his thorax. The rest of them watched while he suffocated. Got any other questions?'

He scratched a kitchen match across the wood surface of his desk and relit his cigar, staring through the flame at my face.

The truth was I didn't care how Andropolis had died or even if he was dead. He was evil. He had been a jigger on hit teams, a supplier of guns to assassins, a man who, like a pimp or an eel attached to the side of a shark, thrived parasitically on both the suffering and darkness of others.

The following day Connie Deshotel called me at my office.

'I'm at my camp on the lake. Would you like to meet me here?' she said.

'What for?'

'I have a tape. A copy of Don Ritter's interview with Andropolis.'

'Ritter and Andropolis are a waste of time.'

'It's about your mother. Andropolis was there when she died. Listen to the details on the tape. If he's lying you'll know . . . Would you rather not do this, Dave? Tell me now.'

chapter twelve

That evening Clete and I drove to a boat landing outside Loreauville and put my outboard in the water and headed down the long, treelined canal into Lake Fausse Pointe. A sun shower peppered the lake, then the wind dropped and the air became still and birds rose out of the cypress and willows and gum trees against a bloodred sky.

The alligators sleeping on the banks were slick with mud and looked like they were sculpted out of black and green stone. The back of my neck felt hot, as though it had been burned by the sun, and my mouth was dry for no reason that I could explain, the way it used to be when I woke up with a whiskey hangover. Clete cut the engine and let the outboard float on its wake through a stand of cypress toward a levee and a tin-roofed stilt house that was shadowed by live oaks that must have been over a hundred years old.

'I'd shit-can this broad now. She's jerking your chain, Streak,' he said.

'What's she got to gain?'

'She was with NOPD in the old days. She's tight with that greasebag Ritter. You don't let Victor Charles get inside your wire.'

'What am I supposed to do, refuse to hear her tape?'

'Maybe I ought to shut up on this one,' he replied, and speared the paddle down through the hyacinths, pushing us in a cloud of mud onto the bank.

I walked up the slope of the levee, under the mossy overhang of the live oaks, and climbed the steps to the stilt house's elevated gallery. She met me at the door, dressed in a pair of platform sandals and designer jeans and a yellow pullover that hung on the points of her breasts. She held a spoon and a round, open container of yellow ice cream in her hands.

She looked past me down the slope to the water.

'Where's Bootsie?' she said.

'I figured this was business, Ms Deshotel.'

'Would you please call me "Connie"? . . . Is that Clete Purcel down there?'

'Yep.'

'Has he been house-trained?' she said, raising up on her tiptoes to see him better.

'Beg your pardon?' I said.

'He's unzippering himself in my philodendron.'

I followed her into her house. It was cheerful inside, filled with potted plants and bright surfaces to catch the sparse light through the trees. In the kitchen she spooned ice cream into the blender and added pitted cherries and bitters and orange slices and a cup of brandy. She flipped on the switch, smiling at me.

'I can't stay long, Connie,' I said.

'You have to try this.'

'I don't drink.'

'It's a dessert.'

'I'd like to hear the tape, please.'

'Boy, you *are* a pill,' she replied. Then her face seemed to grow with concern, almost as though it were manufactured for the moment. 'What's on that tape probably won't be pleasant for you to hear. I thought I'd make it a little easier somehow.'

She took a battery-powered tape player out of a drawer and placed it on the kitchen table and snapped down the play button with her thumb, her eyes watching my face as the recorded voices of Don Ritter and the dead jigger Steve Andropolis came through the speaker.

I stood by the screen window and gazed out at the lake while Andropolis described my mother's last hours and the hooker and pimp scam that brought about her death.

I wanted to shut out the words, live inside the wind in the trees and the light ruffling the lake's surface, listen to the hollow thunking of a pirogue rocking against a wood piling, or just watch Clete's broad back and thick arms and boyish expression as he flipped a lure with his spinning rod out into the dusk and retrieved it back toward the bank.

But even though he had been a parasite, an adverb and never a noun, Andropolis had proved in death his evil was sufficient to wound from beyond the grave.

'The guys who whacked her weren't cops. They were off-duty security guards or something. She had this dude named Mack with her. He told everybody he was a bouree dealer but he was her pimp. Him and Robicheaux's mother, if that's what she was, just worked the wrong two guys,' Andropolis' voice said.

As through a sepia-tinted lens I saw wind gusting on a dirt road that lay like a trench inside a sea of sugarcane. Black clouds roiled in the sky; a red and white neon Jax sign swung on a metal pole in front of a dance hall. Behind the dance hall was a row of cabins that resembled ancient slave quarters, and each tiny gallery was lit with a blue bulb. In slow motion I saw my mother, her body obese with beer fat, lead a drunk man from the back of the dance hall to a cabin door. He wore a polished brass badge on his shirt pocket, and she kissed him under the light, once, twice, working her hand down to his loins when he momentarily wavered.

Then they were inside the cabin, the security guard naked now, mounted between her legs, rearing on his stiffened arms, buckling her body into the stained mattress, bouncing the iron bed frame against the planked wall. A freight train loaded with refined sugar from the mill roared past the window.

Just as the security guard reached orgasm, his lips twisting back on his teeth like a monkey's, the door to the cabin drifted back on its hinges and Mack stepped inside and clicked on the light switch, his narrow, mustached face bright with purpose. He wore pointed boots and striped pants and a two-tone sports coat and cocked fedora like a horse trainer might. He slipped a small, nickel-plated revolver out of his belt and pointed it to the side, away from the startled couple in the center of the bed.

'You just waiting tables, you?' he said to my mother.

'Look, bud. This is cash and carry. Nothing personal,' the security guard said, rolling to one side now, pulling the sheet over his genitalia, removing himself from the line of fire.

'You ain't seen that band on her finger? You didn't know you was milking t'rew another man's fence?' Mack said.

'Hey, don't point that at me. Hey, there ain't no problem here. I just got paid. It's in my wallet. Take it.'

'I'll t'ink about it, me. Get down on your knees.'

'Don't do this, man.'

'I was in the bat'room. I splashed on my boots. Right there on the toe. I want that spot to shine . . . No, you use your tongue, you.'

Then Mack leaned over and pressed the barrel of the revolver into the sweat-soaked hair of the naked man while the man cleaned Mack's boot and his bladder broke in a shower on the floor.

*

119

Connie Deshotel pushed the off button on the tape player.

'It looks like a variation of the Murphy scam gone bad,' she said. 'The security guard came back with his friend and got even.'

'It's bullshit,' I said.

'Why?' She set two bowls of her ice cream and brandy dessert on the table.

'Andropolis originally told me the killers were cops, not security guards. Andropolis worked for the Giacanos. Anything he knew had to come from them. We're talking about dirty cops.'

'This is from another tape. The security guard *was* a Giacano, a distant cousin, but a Giacano. He was killed in a car accident about ten years ago. He worked for a security service in Algiers about the time your mother supposedly died.'

Far across the lake, the sun was just a red ember among the trees. 'I tell you what, Ms Deshotel,' I said, turning from the screen.

'*Connie*,' she said, smiling with her eyes.

Then her mouth parted and her face drained when she heard my words.

I walked down the incline through the shadows and stepped into the outboard and cranked the engine. Clete climbed in, rocking the boat from side to side as I turned us around without waiting for him to sit down.

'What happened in there?' he asked.

I reached into the ice chest and lifted out a can of Budweiser and tossed it to him, then opened up the throttle.

It was almost dark when we entered the canal that led to the boat landing. The air was heated, the sky crisscrossed with birds, dense with the distant smell that rain makes in a dry sugarcane field. I ran the boat up onto the ramp and cut the engine and tilted the propeller out of the water and flung our life vests up onto the bank and lifted the ice chest up by the handles and waded through the shallows.

'You gonna tell me?' Clete said.

'What?'

'How it went in there.' His face was round and softly focused, an alcoholic shine in his eyes.

'I told her if Don Ritter ever repeats those lies about my mother, I'm going to jam that tape up his ass with a chain saw.'

'Gee, I wonder if she got your meaning,' he said, then clasped his huge hand around the back of my neck, his breath welling into my face like a layer of malt. 'We're going to find out who hurt your mother, Streak. But you're no executioner. When those guys go down, it's not going to be on your conscience. My old podjo had better not try to go against me on this one,' he said, his fingers tightening into my neck.

The next morning I woke before dawn to the sounds of rain and a boat engine on the bayou. I fixed a cup of coffee and a bowl of Grape-Nuts and ate breakfast at the kitchen table, then put on my raincoat and hat and walked down to the bait shop in the grayness of the morning to help Batist open up.

'Dave, I seen a man wit' a boat trailer by the ramp when I drove up,' Batist said. 'I got out of my truck and he started to walk toward me, then he turned around and drove off. Later a boat gone on by the shop. I t'ink it was him.'

'Who was he?' I asked.

'I ain't seen him befo'. It was like he t'ought I was somebody else. Maybe he was looking for you, huh?'

'Why's this guy so important, Batist?'

'My eyes ain't that good no more. But there was

somet'ing shiny on his dashboard. Like chrome. Like a pistol, maybe.'

I turned on the string of lights over the dock and looked out the screen window at the rain denting the bayou and the mist blowing out of the cypress and willow trees in the swamp. Then I saw one of my rental boats that had broken loose from its chain floating sideways past the window.

'I'll go for it,' Batist said behind me.

'I'm already wet,' I said.

I unlocked an outboard by the concrete ramp and headed downstream. When I went around the bend, I saw the loose boat tangled in an island of hyacinths close-in to a stand of flooded cypress.

But I wasn't alone.

An outboard roared to life behind me, and the green-painted aluminum bow came out of a cut in the swamp and turned into my wake.

The man in the stern was tall, dark-haired, his skin pale, his jeans and T-shirt soaked. He wore a straw hat, with a black ribbon tied around the crown, and his face was beaded with water. He cut his engine and floated up onto the pad of hyacinths, his bow inches from the side of my boat.

He placed both of his palms on his thighs and looked at me and waited, his features flat, as though expecting a response to a question.

'That's an interesting shotgun you have on the seat,' I said.

'A Remington twelve. It's modified a little bit,' he replied.

'When you saw them off at the pump, they're illegal,' I said, and grinned at him. I caught the painter on the boat that had broken loose and began tying it to the stern of my outboard.

'You know who I am?' he asked. His eyes were a dark

blue, the color of ink. He took a bandanna from his back pocket and wiped his face with it, then glanced upward at the grayness in the sky and the water dripping out of the canopy.

'We don't hear a Kentucky accent around here very often,' I said.

'Somebody shot at me yesterday. Outside New Orleans.'

'Why tell me?'

'You made them think I was gonna turn them in. That's a rotten thing to do, sir.'

'I hear you killed people for the wise guys out on the coast. You had problems a long time before you came to Louisiana, Johnny.'

His eyes narrowed at my use of his name. His mouth was effeminate and did not seem to go with his wide shoulders and heavy upper arms. He picked at his fingernails and looked at nothing, his lips pursing before he spoke again.

'This is a pretty place. I'd like to live somewhere like this. This guy who got killed in Santa Barbara? He raped a fourteen-year-old girl at an amusement park in Tennessee. She almost bled to death. The judge gave him two years probation. What would you do if you were her father?'

'You were just helping out the family?'

'I've tried to treat you with respect, Mr Robicheaux. I heard you're not a bad guy for a roach.'

'You came here with a sawed-off shotgun.'

'It's not for you.'

'Who were the other people you did?'

The rain had slackened, then it stopped altogether and the water dripping out of trees was loud on the bayou's surface. He removed his straw hat and stared reflectively into the cypress and willows and air vines, his eyes full of light that seemed to have no origin.

'A greaseball's wife found out her husband was gonna have her popped. By a degenerate who specialized in women. So the wife brought in an out-of-state guy to blow up her husband's shit. The degenerate could have walked away, but some guys just got to try. Nobody in Pacific Palisades is losing sleep.'

'Who paid you to do Zipper Clum and Little Face Dautrieve?'

'The money was at a drop. All I know is they tried to pop me yesterday. So maybe that puts me and you on the same team.'

'Wrong.'

'Yeah?'

'Yeah.'

His eyes seemed to go out of focus, as though he were refusing to recognize the insult that hung in the air. He pulled at his T-shirt, lifting the wetness of the cloth off his skin.

'You gonna try to take me down?' he asked.

'You're the man with the gun,' I replied, grinning again.

'It's not loaded.'

'I'm not going to find out,' I said.

He lifted the cut-down shotgun off the seat and lay it across his thighs, then worked his boat alongside my engine. He ripped out the gas line and tossed it like a severed snake into the cat-tails.

'I wish you hadn't done that,' I said.

'I don't lie, sir. Not like some I've met.' He pumped open the shotgun and inserted his thumb in the empty chamber. Then he removed a Ziploc bag with three shells in it from his back pocket and began fitting them into the magazine. 'I dropped my gun in the water and got my other shells wet. That's why it was empty.'

'You said "not like some." You calling me a liar?' I said.

'You spread rumors I was a snitch. I was in the Flat Top at Raiford. I never gave anybody up.'

'Listen, Johnny, you backed out on the Little Face Dautrieve contract. You're still on this side of the line.'

'What are you talking about?'

'Don't pretend you don't understand. Look at me.'

'I don't like people talking to me like that, Mr Robicheaux. Let go of my boat.'

I looked hard into his face. His eyes were dark, his cheeks pooled with shadow, like a death mask, his mouth compressed into a small flower. I shoved his boat out into the current.

'You got it, kid,' I said.

He cranked the engine and roared down the bayou, glancing back at me once, the bow of his boat swerving wildly to avoid hitting a nutria that was swimming toward the bank.

chapter thirteen

Later that morning I called the prison psychologist at Raiford in Florida, a social worker in Letcher County, Kentucky, and a high school counselor in Detroit. By quitting time I had received at least three dozen fax sheets concerning Johnny Remeta.

That afternoon Clete Purcel sat next to me on a wood bench at the end of the dock and read through the file I had put together on Remeta.

'He's got a 160 I.Q. and he's a button man?' Clete said.

'No early indications of violence, either. Not until he got out of Raiford.'

'You're saying he got spread-eagled in the shower a few times and decided to get even?'

'I'm just saying he's probably not a sociopath.'

Clete closed the manila folder and handed it back to me. The wind ruffled and popped the canvas awning over our heads.

'Who cares what he is? He was on your turf. I'd put one through his kneecap if he comes back again,' Clete said.

I didn't reply. I felt Clete's eyes on the side of my face.

'The guy's of no value to you. He doesn't know who

hired him,' Clete said. 'Splash this psychological stuff in the bowl.'

'The social worker told me the kid's father was a drunk. She thinks the old man sold the kid a couple of times for booze.'

Clete was already shaking his head with exasperation before I finished the sentence.

'He looked Zipper Clum in the eyes while he drilled a round through his forehead. This is the kind of guy the air force trains to launch nuclear weapons,' he said.

He stood up and gripped his hands on the dock railing. The back of his neck was red, his big arms swollen with energy.

'I'm pissed off at myself. I shouldn't have helped you fire this guy up,' he said.

'How's Passion?' I asked, changing the subject.

'Waiting for me to pick her up.' He let out his breath. 'I've got baling wire wrapped around my head. I can't think straight.'

'What's wrong?' I said.

'I'm going to drive her to the women's prison tomorrow to visit her sister.'

'You feel like you're involving yourself with the other side?'

'Something like that. I always figured most people on death row had it coming. You watch Larry King last night? He had some shock-jock on there laughing about executing a woman in Texas. The same guy who made fun of Clinton at a banquet. These are America's heroes.'

He went inside the bait shop and came back out with a sixteen-ounce can of beer wrapped in a paper towel. He took two long drinks out of the can, tilting his head back, swallowing until the can was almost empty. He blew out his breath and the heat and tension went out of his face.

'Dave, I dreamed about the Death House at Angola. Except it wasn't Letty Labiche being taken there. It was

Passion. Why would I have a dream like that?' he said, squeezing his thumb and forefinger on his temples.

But I was to hear Letty Labiche's name more than once that day.

Cora Gable had volunteered her chauffeur, Micah, to deliver a thousand-name petition on behalf of Letty to the governor's mansion. After he had picked up several friends of Cora's in New Orleans, driven them to the capitol at Baton Rouge, and dropped them off again in New Orleans, he ate dinner by himself in a cafe by the river, on the other side of the Huey Long Bridge, then headed down a dusky two-lane road into Lafourche Parish.

He passed through a small settlement, then entered a long stretch of empty road surrounded by sugarcane fields. A white car closed behind him; a man in the passenger's seat glanced back over his shoulder and clapped a battery-powered flashing red light on the roof.

The cops looked like off-duty narcs or perhaps SWAT members. They were thick-bodied and vascular, young, unshaved, clad in jeans and sneakers and dark-colored T-shirts, their arms ridged with hair, handcuffs looped through the backs of their belts.

They walked up on each side of the limo. Micah's windows were down now, and he heard the Velcro strap peeling loose on the holster of the man approaching the passenger door.

'Could I see your driver's license, please?' the man at Micah's window said. He wore pilot's sunglasses and seemed bored, looking away at the sunset over the cane fields, his palm extended as he waited for Micah to pull his license from his wallet.

'What's the problem?'

The man in sunglasses looked at the photo on the license, then at Micah's face.

'You see what it says over your picture? "Don't drink

and drive . . . Don't litter Louisiana," ' he said. 'Every driver's license in Louisiana has that on it. We're trying to keep drunks off the road and the highways clean. You threw a beer can out the window back there.'

'No, I didn't.'

'Step out of the car, please.'

'You guys are from New Orleans. You don't have authority here,' Micah said.

'Walk around the far side of the car, please, and we'll discuss that with you.'

They braced him against the roof, kicked his ankles apart, ran their hands up and down his legs, and pulled his pockets inside out, spilling his change and wallet onto the shale.

A car passed with its lights on. The two cops watched it disappear between the cane fields. Then one of them swung a baton into the back of Micah's thigh, crumpling it as though the tendon had been cut in half. He fell to one knee, his fingers trying to find purchase against the side of the limo.

The second blow was ineffective, across his shoulders, but the third was whipped with two hands into his tailbone, driving a red shard of pain into his bowels. Micah rolled in the dirt, shuttering, trying to control his sphincter muscle.

The cop who had taken his license dropped it like a playing card into his face, then kicked him in the kidney.

'You got a sheet in New Mexico, Micah. Go back there. Don't make us find you again,' he said.

'I didn't do anything,' he said.

The cop with the baton leaned over and inserted the round, wooden end into Micah's mouth, pushing hard, until Micah gagged and choked on his own blood.

'What's that? Say again?' the cop said, bending down solicitously toward Micah's deformed face.

*

Clete called me the next afternoon and asked me to meet him in Armand's on Main Street. It was cool and dark inside, and Clete sat at the antique, mirrored bar, a julep glass in his hand, an electric fan blowing across his face.

But there was nothing cool or relaxed about his demeanor. His tropical shirt was damp against his skin, his face flushed as though he had a fever. One foot was propped on the runner of the barstool; his knee kept jiggling.

'What is it, Clete?'

'I don't know. I probably shouldn't have called you. Maybe I should just drive up the stock price on Jack Daniel's by three or four points.'

'I got a call from Cora Gable. A couple of NOPD goons beat up her driver. She says they scared him so bad he won't press charges.'

'Jim Gable wants him out of town?'

'The driver had just delivered a petition for Letty to Belmont Pugh. Maybe the message is for Cora.'

'What's Gable's interest in Letty Labiche?'

'I don't know. You going to tell me why you called me down here?'

The affair had started casually enough. Clete had gone to her house at evening time and had found her working in back, carrying buckets of water in both hands from the house faucet to her garden.

'Where's your hose?' he asked.

'The boy who cuts the grass ran the lawn mower over it,' she replied.

They carried the water together, sloshing it on their clothes, pouring it along the rows of watermelons and strawberries, the sky aflame behind them. Her face was hot with her work, her dress blowing loosely on her body as she stooped over in the row. He walked back to the house and filled a glass of water for her and carried it to her in the garden.

She watched his face over the top of the glass as she drank. Her skin was dusty, the tops of her breasts golden and filmed with perspiration in the dying light. She lifted her hair off her neck and pulled it on top of her head.

He touched the roundness of her upper arm with his fingertips.

'You're a strong woman,' he said.

'Overweight.'

'Not to me,' he replied.

She kept brushing her hair back from the corner of her mouth, not speaking, letting her eyes meet his as though she knew his thoughts.

'I drink too much. I lost my badge in a bad shooting. I did security for Sally Dio in Reno,' he said.

'I don't care.'

She tilted up her face and looked sideways with her eyes, the wind blowing her hair back from her face.

'My ex said she could have done better at the Humane Society,' he said.

'What somebody else say got nothing to do wit' me.'

'You smell like strawberries.'

'That's 'cause we standing in them, Clete.'

She pushed the soft curve of her sandal across the hardness of his shoe.

They went upstairs to the third story of the house and made love in an oversized brass bed that was surrounded by three electric fans. She came before he did, then mounted him and came a second time, her hands caressing his face simultaneously. Later she lay close to him and traced his body with her fingertips, touching his sex as though it were a source of power, in a way that almost embarrassed him and made him look at her quizzically.

She wanted to hear stories about the Marine Corps and

Vietnam, about his pouring a container of liquid soap down a hood's mouth in the men's room of the Greyhound bus depot, about growing up in the Irish Channel, how he smashed a woman's greenhouse with rocks after he found out her invitation for ice cream had been an act of charity she extended at her back door to raggedy street children.

'I'm a professional screwup, Passion. That's not humility, it's fact. Dave's guy with the history,' he said.

She pulled him against her and kissed his chest.

He stayed away for two days, then returned to her house at sunrise, his heart beating with anticipation before she opened the door. She made love with him as though her need were insatiable, her thighs fastened hard around him, the small cry she made in his ear like a moment of exorcism.

Two weeks later he sat in her kitchen, a blue and white coffeepot by his empty plate, while Passion rinsed a steak tray under the faucet.

He ran his nails through his hair.

'I think you're looking for an answer in a guy who doesn't have any,' he said.

When she didn't reply, he smiled wanly. 'I'm lucky to have a P.I. license, Passion. New Orleans cops cross the street rather than talk to me. I've had the kind of jobs people do when they're turned down by the foreign legion.'

She stood behind him, kneading his shoulders with her large hands, her breasts touching the back of his head.

'I have to go to the doctor in the morning. Then I want to visit my sister,' she said.

Clete drank out of his julep and stirred the ice in the bottom of the glass.

'She told me all the details about what Carmouche did to her and Letty. Somebody should dig that guy up and chain-drag the corpse through Baton Rouge,' he said. Then he seemed to look at a thought inside his head and his face went out of focus. 'Passion would let him exhaust himself on her so he'd go easier on her sister.'

'Get this stuff out of your mind, Clete.'

'You think she's playing me?'

'I don't know.'

'Give me another julep,' he said to the bartender.

Bootsie was waiting for me in the parking lot after work.

'How about I buy you dinner, big boy?' she said.

'What's going on?'

'I just like to see if I can pick up a cop once in a while.'

We drove to Lerosier, across from the Shadows, and ate in the back room. Behind us was a courtyard full of roses and bamboo, and in the shade mint grew between the bricks.

'Something happen today?' I said.

'Two messages on the machine from Connie Deshotel. I'm not sure I like other women calling you up.'

'She probably has my number mixed up with her Orkin man's.'

'She says she's sorry she offended you. What's she talking about?'

'This vice cop, Ritter, taped an interview with a perpetrator by the name of Steve Andropolis. The tape contained a bunch of lies about my mother.'

Bootsie put a small piece of food in her mouth and chewed it slowly, the light hardening in her eyes.

'Why would she do that?' she said.

'Ask her.'

'Count on it,' she said.

I started to reply, then looked at her face and thought better of it.

But Connie Deshotel was a willful and determined

133

woman and was not easily discouraged from revising a situation that was somehow detrimental to her interests.

The next evening Belmont Pugh's black Chrysler, followed by a caravan of political sycophants and revelers, parked by the boat ramp. They got out and stood in the road, blinking at the summer light in the sky, the dust from their cars drifting over them. All of them had been drinking, except apparently Belmont. While his friends wandered down toward the bait shop for food and beer, Belmont walked up the slope, among the oaks, where I was raking leaves, his face composed and somber, his pinstripe suit and gray Stetson checkered with broken sunlight.

'Why won't you accept that woman's apology?' he asked.

'You're talking about Connie Deshotel?'

'She didn't mean to cast an aspersion on your mother. She thought she was doing her job. Give her a little credit, son.'

'All right, I accept her apology. Make sure you tell her that for me, will you? She actually got the governor of the state to drive out here and deliver a message for her?'

He removed his hat and wiped the liner out with a handkerchief. His back was straight, his profile etched against the glare off the bayou. His hair had grown out on his neck, and it gave him a distinguished, rustic look. For some reason he reminded me of the idealistic young man I had known years ago, the one who daily did a good deed and learned a new word from his thesaurus.

'You're a hard man, Dave. I wish I had your toughness. I wouldn't be fretting my mind from morning to night about that woman on death row,' he said.

I rested the rake and popped my palms on the handle's end. It was cool in the shade and the wind was blowing the tree limbs above our heads.

'I remember when a guy offered you ten dollars to take

a math test for him, Belmont. You really needed the money. But you chased him out of your room,' I said.

'The cafeteria didn't serve on weekends. You and me could make a can of Vienna sausage and a jar of peanut butter and a box of crackers go from Friday noon to Sunday night,' he said.

'I've witnessed two executions. I wish I hadn't. You put your hand in one and you're never the same,' I said.

'A long time ago my daddy said I was gonna be either a preacher or a drunk and womanizer. I wake up in the morning and have no idea of who I am. Don't lecture at me, son.' His voice was husky, his tone subdued in a way that wasn't like Belmont.

I looked beyond him, out on the dock, where his friends were drinking can beer under the canvas awning. One of them was a small, sun-browned, mustached man with no chin and an oiled pate and the snubbed nose of a hawk.

'That's Sookie Motrie out there. I hear he's the money behind video poker at the tracks,' I said.

'It's all a trade-off. People want money for schools but don't like taxes. I say use the devil's money against him. So a guy like Sookie gets to be a player.'

When I didn't reply, he said, 'A lot of folks think Earl K. Long was just an ignorant redneck. But Earl did good things people don't know about. A whole bunch of Negro women graduated from a new nursing program and found out right quick they couldn't get jobs nowhere. So Earl hears about it and says he wants a tour of the state hospital. He pumps hands all over the building, sticks his head in operating rooms, flushes toilets, then gets all the hospital's administrators in one room and locks the door.

'He says, "I just seen a shameful spectacle here. Y'all got white nurses hand-waiting on nigra patients, carrying out their bedpans and I don't know what all, and I ain't gonna stand for it. You either hire nigra nurses in those wards or every damn one of you is gonna be out of a job."

'The next week the state hospital had two dozen black nurses on staff.'

'Makes a good story,' I said.

'Stories are all the human race has got, Dave. You just got to find the one you like and stay with it,' he replied.

'Are you going to execute Letty Labiche?'

He replaced his hat on his head and walked down the slope to rejoin his entourage, jiggling his hands in the air like a minstrel man.

chapter fourteen

Farther to the south of us, in the working-class community of Grand Bois, a young attorney, two years out of law school, filed suit on behalf of the local residents against a large oil corporation. The locals were by and large Cajuns and Houma Indians, uneducated, semi-skilled, poor, without political power, and bewildered by the legal apparatus, the perfect community to target as the open-pit depository of oil sludge trucked in from a petroleum treatment plant in Alabama.

Company officials didn't argue with the contention the pits contained benzene, hydrogen sulfide, and arsenic. They didn't have to. Years ago, during a time of gas shortages, the U.S. Congress had granted the oil industry blanket exemptions from the regulations that govern most toxic wastes. Secondly, the state of Louisiana does not define oil waste as hazardous material.

The state, the oil corporation, and the community of Grand Bois were now in court, and Connie Deshotel's office was taking depositions from the people in Grand Bois who claimed their children were afflicted with vertigo, red eyes, skin rashes, and diarrhea that was so severe they had to keep buckets in their automobiles.

Two of those Grand Bois families had moved to New Iberia and were now living up on the bayou road, not far from Passion Labiche's nightclub. On Monday Helen Soileau was assigned to drive Connie Deshotel and her assistant out to their homes.

Later she told me of Connie Deshotel's bizarre behavior, although she could offer no explanation as to its cause.

It had rained hard that morning, then the sun had become a white orb in the center of a windless sky, evaporating the water out of the fields, creating a superheated dome of humidity that made you feel like ants were crawling inside your clothes.

The air-conditioning unit in the cruiser began clanking, then gasped once and gave out. Connie Deshotel had removed her white suit coat and folded it on her lap, trying to keep her composure while her male assistant talked without stop in the backseat. Her armpits were ringed with sweat and a hostile light was growing in her eyes.

Her assistant paused a moment in his monologue, then cracked a mint between his molars and began again.

'Why don't the people of Grand Bois move to a place where there's no oil industry? Get jobs as whalers in Japan. Could it be they've done scut work all their lives in the oil industry and couldn't fix ice water without a diagram?' he said.

He took the silence in the cruiser as indication his point was not understood.

'The Houma Indians have a problem with oil waste. But they want to build casinos and addict their own people to gambling. I think the whole bunch is ripe for a hydrogen bomb,' he said.

'I don't want to add to your irritability, Malcolm, but would you please shut up?' Connie said.

'Y'all want something cool to drink?' Helen asked.

'Yes, please,' Connie said.

They pulled into Passion's nightclub just as a storm

cloud covered the sun and the landscape dropped into shadow. Inside, electric fans vibrated on the four corners of the dance floor, and an ancient air-conditioning unit inserted in a sawed-out hole in the back wall blew a stream of refrigerated coolness across the bar.

Connie sat on a barstool and closed her eyes in the wind stream.

Helen whistled through the door that gave onto the café side of the building.

'Hey, Passion, you've got some customers in here,' she called.

Connie's eyes opened and she turned her blank face on Helen.

'Letty Labiche's sister owns this place. You know her?' Helen said.

'No.'

'From the way you looked, I thought you recognized the name or something.'

'Yes, I did recognize the name. That doesn't mean I know her,' Connie said.

'Yes, ma'am,' Helen said.

'I'd like to leave now,' Connie said.

'I thought you wanted a cold drink.'

'I just wanted to get out of the heat a few minutes. I'm fine now. We should make at least one other stop today,' Connie said.

'Too late,' her assistant, Malcolm, said, grinning from behind the bar. He opened two ice-cold bottles of Coca-Cola and set them in front of Helen and Connie just as Passion walked in from the café and tilted her head at the presence of the man behind her bar.

'Could I hep y'all?' she asked.

'Sorry, miss. I'm so dry I'm a fire hazard. I left the money on the register,' Malcolm said. He opened a long-neck bottle of beer for himself and stepped back from the foam as it slid over the neck.

Passion rang up the purchase, her back to them. 'Sorry I couldn't get over here to wait on y'all,' she said.

Connie's face looked stricken. She stared helplessly at the back of Passion's head, as though an element from a nightmare had just forced its way inexorably into her waking day.

Passion turned and placed a quarter and two dimes in front of the male assistant. Then her eyes fell on Connie's.

'You all right, ma'am?' she asked.

'Yes. Why do you ask?' Connie said.

'On days like this the tar on the road melts. You look like you got dehydrated. I got some aspirin.'

'Thank you. I don't need any.'

Passion started to turn away, then a look of vague recognition swam into her face.

'I seen you somewhere before, ma'am?' she asked.

'Perhaps. I'm the attorney general.'

'No, I seen you in an old photograph. Or somebody sure do look like you. You got nice features. They don't change with time,' Passion said.

'I'm sure that's a compliment, but I don't know what you're talking about.'

'It's gonna come. Y'all visiting New Iberia?' Passion asked.

Connie rose from her chair and extended her hand across the bar.

'It was very nice meeting you,' she said, even though they had not exchanged names or been introduced by a third party.

She walked out to the cruiser, her chin tilted upward, her face bloodless. The wind raked the branches of a live-oak tree against the side of the club and another rain shower burst from the heavens, clattering like marbles on the tin roof.

'I'm going to finish my beer. Who plays that piano?' Malcolm said.

Button man or not, Johnny Remeta obviously didn't fall easily into a predictable category.

The off-duty New Orleans cop who worked security at the historical museum on Jackson Square watched a lithe young man in shades and knife-creased khakis and half-topped boots and a form-fitting ribbed T-shirt with the sleeves rolled over the shoulders cross from the Café du Monde and walk through the park, past a string band playing in front of Pirates Alley, wrap his chewing gum in a piece of foil and drop it in a waste can, comb his hair and enter the museum's doorway.

Where had the off-duty cop seen that face?

A mug shot passed around at roll call?

No, he was imagining things. The mug shot was of a guy who was wanted in a shooting off Magazine. Yeah, the hit on Zipper Clum. A white shooter, which meant it was probably a contract job, somebody the Giacanos hired to wipe out an obnoxious black pimp. Contract shooters didn't wander around in museums under a cop's nose. Besides, this kid looked like he just got out of high school.

'You visiting from out of town?' the cop asked.

The young man still wore his shades and was looking at a battle-rent Confederate flag that was pressed under glass.

'No, I live here. I'm an artist,' he replied. He did not turn his head when he spoke.

'You come here often?'

'About every three days.' He removed his shades and looked the cop full in the face, grinning now. 'Something wrong?'

'Yeah, my feet hurt,' the cop said.

But later the cop was still bothered. He followed the

141

young man across Jackson Square to Decatur, took down the license number of his pickup truck, and called it in.

One block away, a police cruiser fell in behind the pickup truck. Just as the uniformed cop behind the wheel was about to hit his flasher, the pickup truck turned back into the Quarter on Bienville and drove the short two-block distance to the police station at Royal and Conti.

The young man in shades parked his truck and went inside.

The cop in the cruiser kept going, shaking his head disgustedly at the cavalier misuse of his time.

Inside the police station, the young man gazed idly at Wanted posters on a corkboard, then asked the desk sergeant for directions to the battlefield at Chalmette.

The desk sergeant watched the young man walk out of the door of the station and get in his truck and drive down Conti toward the river. Then the sergeant was out the door himself, his arms waving in the air at two motorcycle cops who were coming up the walk.

'The guy in the black pickup! You can still get him!' he yelled.

Wrong.

Johnny Remeta cut across the Mississippi bridge onto the West Bank, caught Highway 90, wove five miles through residential neighborhoods and strip malls, and dumped the pickup in St Charles Parish and boosted an Oldsmobile out of a used-car lot.

He took back roads through Chacahoula and Amelia, crossed the wide sweep of the Atchafalaya at Morgan City, and hot-wired an ancient Volkswagen bus at the casino on the Chettimanchi Indian Reservation.

He created a one-man grand-auto crime wave across southwestern Louisiana, driving off idling automobiles from a Jiffy Lube and a daiquiri take-out window, blowing out tires and engines, lighting up emergency dispatcher screens in six parishes.

He almost eluded the army of state police and sheriff's deputies that was crisscrossing Highway 90, virtually colliding into one another. He swung onto a side road in St Mary Parish, floored the souped-up stock-car racer he had stolen out of a mechanic's shed, scoured a balloon of dust out of a dirt road for two miles through sugarcane fields that shielded the car from view, then swung back onto 90, a half mile beyond a police barricade, and looked down the long corridor of oaks and pines that led into New Iberia.

He shifted down, turned across a stone bridge over the bayou, arching a crick out of his neck, knotting his T-shirt in his hand, wiping the sweat off his face with it.

He'd outrun them all. He filled his lungs with air. The smoke from meat fires drifted through the oaks on people's lawns; the evening sky glowed like a purple rose. Now, to dump this car and find a rooming house where he could watch a lot of television for a few days. Man, it was good to be alive.

That's when the First Assembly of God church bus hit him broadside, springing his doors, and propelled him through the air like a stone, right through a canebrake into Bayou Teche.

He sat on a steel bunk in the holding cell, barefoot, his khakis and T-shirt splattered with mud, a bandage wrapped around his head. He pulled a thin strand of bamboo leaf from his hair and watched it tumble in a shaft of light to the cement floor.

The sheriff and I looked at him through the bars.

'Why didn't you get out of New Orleans when you had the chance?' I asked.

'It's a free country,' he replied.

'Not when you kill people,' I said.

'I'll ask you a better question. Why didn't you stay where you were?' the sheriff said.

143

Johnny Remeta's eyes lifted into the sheriff's face, then they emptied of any perception or thought. He looked at the wall, stifling a yawn.

'Get him processed. I want those detectives from New Orleans to have him out of here by noon tomorrow,' the sheriff said, and walked down the corridor and banged the heavy door behind him.

'What's his problem?' Remeta said.

'Our space is full up with local wise guys. We don't need imports. Why'd you come to New Iberia?'

'A guy looks for friends where he can.'

'I'm not your friend. You were hanging around New Orleans to pop the guys who took a shot at you, weren't you?'

'You blame me?'

'You know who they are?'

'No. That's why I hung around.'

I looked at him a long time. He dropped his eyes to the floor.

'You told the cop at the museum you were an artist,' I said.

'I paint ceramics. I've done a mess of them.'

'Good luck, kid. I think you're going to need it,' I said, and started to go.

He rose from the bunk and stood at the bars. His face was no more than three inches from mine.

'I've got money put away for a lawyer. I can beat the beef on Zipper Clum,' he said.

'So?'

'I have a feeling my kite's going down before I ever see that lawyer.'

His breath was like the stale odor of dead flowers.

His grief was his own, I told myself as I went home later that evening.

But I couldn't rest. Zipper Clum's dying statement,

taped on the boom box in the lawn-mower shop off Magazine, said Johnny Remeta was the trail back to my mother's death.

I ate a late supper with Bootsie on the picnic table in the backyard and told her about Johnny Remeta's fears. I expected her to take issue with my concerns, which I seemed to bring home as a matter of course from my job. After I stopped talking, she was pensive, one tooth biting into her bottom lip.

'I think Remeta's right. Zipper Clum was killed because of what he knew about your mother's death. Now Connie Deshotel has taken a special interest in you. She called again, by the way.'

'What about?'

'She said she wanted to tell you Clete Purcel's license problems have been straightened out. How nice of her to call us rather than him.'

'Forget her.'

'I'd like to. Dave, I didn't tell you everything about my relationship with Jim Gable. He's perverse. Oh, not with me. Just in things he said, in his manner, the way he'd stand in his undershorts in front of the mirror and comb his hair, the cruelty that was threaded through his remarks.'

The blood had risen in her face, and her eyes were shiny with embarrassment.

'You didn't know what he was like, Boots.'

'It doesn't help. I think about him and want to wash my body with peroxide.'

'I'm going to help Batist close up, then we'll go for some ice cream,' I said.

I walked down to the bait shop and called Dana Magelli, my NOPD friend, at his home and got the unlisted number for Jim Gable's condo in New Orleans.

'Why are you messing with Gable?' Magelli asked.

'Cleaning up some paperwork, interdepartmental cooperation, that sort of thing.'

'Gable leaves shit prints on everything he touches. Stay away from him. It's a matter of time till somebody scrambles his eggs.'

'It's not soon enough.'

I punched in Jim Gable's number. I could hear opera music playing in the background when he answered the phone.

'Y'all are picking up Johnny Remeta tomorrow,' I said.

'Who is this?' he asked.

'Dave Robicheaux. Remeta thinks somebody might want to blow up his shit.'

'Hey, we owe you a big thanks on this one. You made the ID through that home invasion in Loreauville, didn't you?'

'He'd better arrive in New Orleans without any scratches on the freight.'

'You're talking to the wrong man, my friend. Don Ritter's in charge of that case.'

'Let me raise another subject. I understand you've made some remarks about my wife.'

I could hear ice cubes rattle in a glass, as though he had just sipped from it and replaced it on a table.

'I don't know where you heard that, but it's not true. I have the greatest respect for your wife,' he said.

I stared out the bait shop window. The flood lamps were on and the bayou was yellow and netted with torn strands of hyacinths, the air luminescent with insects. My temples were pounding. I felt like a jealous high school boy who had just challenged a rival in a locker room, only to learn that his own words were his worst enemy.

'Maybe we can take up the subject another time. On a more physical level,' I said.

I thought I heard the voice of a young woman giggling

in the background, then the tinkle of ice in the glass again.

'I've got to run. Get a good night's sleep. I don't think you mean what you say. Anyway, I don't hold grudges,' Gable said.

The woman laughed again just before he hung up.

But the two New Orleans detectives who were assigned to take Johnny Remeta back to their jurisdiction, Don Ritter and a man named Burgoyne, didn't show up in the morning. In fact, they didn't arrive at the department until almost 5 p.m.

I stayed late until the last of the paperwork was done. Ritter bent over my desk and signed his name on a custody form attached to a clipboard, then bounced the ballpoint pen on my desk blotter.

'Thanks for your help, Robicheaux. We won't forget it,' he said.

'You taking the four-lane through Morgan City?' I said.

'No, I-10 through Baton Rouge,' Burgoyne, the other detective, said.

'The southern route is straight through now. You can be in New Orleans in two hours and fifteen minutes,' I said.

'The department uses prescribed routes for all transportation of prisoners. This one happens to go through Baton Rouge,' Burgoyne said. He grinned and chewed his gum.

He was young, unshaved, muscular, his arms padded with hair. He wore a faded black T-shirt and running shoes and Levi's with his handcuffs pulled through the back of his belt. He wore his shield on a cord around his neck, and a snub-nosed .38 in a clip-on holster on his belt.

'We've had Remeta in a holding cell since this morning. He didn't eat yet,' I said.

'We'll feed him at the jail. I'll ask him to drop you a card and tell you about it,' Burgoyne said, his eyes merry, his gum snapping in his jaw.

Ten minutes later I watched Ritter and Burgoyne lead Johnny Remeta, in waist and leg chains, to the back of a white Plymouth and lock him to a D-ring anchored on the floor. When they pulled out of the parking lot, Remeta stared out the side window into my face.

I went back inside the building, the residue of a burned-out, bad day like a visceral presence on my skin.

Why had they waited until quitting time to pick up Remeta? Why were they adamant about returning to New Orleans through Baton Rouge, which was the long way back? I was bothered also by the detective named Burgoyne. His clothes and looks and manner reminded me of the description that Micah, Cora Gable's chauffeur, had given of one of the cops who had beaten and terrorized him.

I signed out a cruiser, hit the flasher, and headed for the four-lane that led to Lafayette and Interstate 10 East.

It was almost sunset when I crossed Henderson Swamp on the causeway. There was no wind, and the miles of water on each side of the road were bloodred, absolutely still, the moss in the dead cypress gray and motionless against the trunks. I stayed in the passing lane, the blue, white, and red glow of the flasher rippling across the pavement and cement railings in the dying light.

Then I was on the bridge above the Atchafalaya River, rising above its wide breadth and swirling current and the deep green stands of gum trees along its banks. Only then did I realize the white Plymouth was behind me, off the highway, in the rest area on the west side of the river.

I'd blown it. I couldn't remember the distance to the next turnaround that would allow me to double back and recross the river. I pulled to the shoulder, put the cruiser in reverse, and backed over the bridge to the rest area exit while two tractor-trailers swerved around me into the passing lane.

The rest area was parklike, green and freshly mowed and watered, with picnic tables and clean rest rooms, and a fine view of the river from the levee.

But the Plymouth was not by the rest rooms. It was parked not far from the levee and a stand of trees, in a glade, its doors open, its parking lights on.

I entered the access road and clicked off the flasher and parked behind a truck and saw Ritter and Burgoyne walking from the Plymouth to the men's room. Burgoyne went inside while Ritter smoked a cigarette and watched the Plymouth. Then Burgoyne came back outside and both of them sat at a picnic table, smoking, a thermos of coffee set between them. They watched the Plymouth and the T-shirted, waist-chained form of Johnny Remeta in the backseat.

I thought they would finish their coffee, unlock Remeta from the D-ring, and walk him to the men's room. The sodium lamps came on overhead and still they made no move toward the Plymouth.

Instead, Ritter went to a candy machine. He peeled off the wrapper on a candy bar and dropped the wrapper on the ground and strolled out toward the parking lot and used a pay phone.

The wind started to blow off the river, then I heard a solitary *pop*, like a firecracker, in a clump of trees by the levee.

Johnny Remeta pitched forward in the seat, his shoulders curled down toward the floor, his chained wrists jerking at the D-ring. There were three more reports inside the trees; now I could see a muzzle flash or light reflecting off a telescopic lens, and I heard the rounds biting into metal, blowing glass out the back of the car.

I pulled my .45 and ran toward the picnic table where Burgoyne still sat, his cigarette burning on the edge of the wood, his hands motionless in front of him. Ritter was nowhere in sight. The few travelers in the rest area had either taken cover or flattened themselves on the lawn.

I screwed the .45 into Burgoyne's spine.

'You set him up, you shitbag,' I said, and hoisted him up by his T-shirt.

'What are you doing?'

'Walk in front of me. You're going to stop it. You touch your piece and I'll blow your liver out on the grass.'

I knotted my fist in the back of his belt, pushing him ahead of me, into the mauve-colored twilight and the smell of cut grass and the wind that was filled with newspaper and dust and raindrops that stung like hail. I tried to see over his shoulder into the clump of trees by the levee, but the limbs were churning, the leaves rising into the air, and the light had washed out of the sky into a thin band on the earth's rim.

'I'm not part of this, Robicheaux. You got it all wrong,' Burgoyne said.

'Shut up. Get your cuff key out. Throw it to Remeta.'

We were on the lee side of the Plymouth now and Burgoyne's face had gone white. He thumbed his key out of his watch pocket and threw it inside the backseat. He tried to turn his head so he could see my face.

'Let me go, man. I'll give you whatever you want,' he said.

The shooter in the trees let off two more rounds. One whanged off the door jamb and the second round seemed to go long. But I heard a hollow *throp*, just like someone casually plopping a watermelon with his fingers. Burgoyne's head slammed against mine and his knees collapsed under him. My hand was still hooked inside his belt, and his weight took me down with him.

I was kneeling in the grass now, behind the shelter of the car, the events of the last few seconds out of sequence in my head. Johnny Remeta was working furiously to unlock his hands and ankles from his chains. His eyes were riveted on me, a look of revulsion on his face.

'What's the matter with you?' I said.

'The guy's brains are in your hair, man.'

The shooter opened up again, firing indiscriminately, burning the whole magazine.

'Get out of here,' I said.

'What?'

'The keys are in the ignition. When I put down masking fire, you get out of here.'

I didn't wait for him to answer. I crawled to the front of the car, then extended one hand out beyond the fender and began firing the .45 into the clump of trees. The sparks flew into the darkness and the recoil snapped my wrist four inches up in the air with each shot. I fired eight rounds in a row, the brass casings flicking past my eyes, until the breech locked open. Then I released the empty magazine and shoved in a fresh one.

The Plymouth's engine roared to life and the back tires spun in reverse on the wet grass. Johnny Remeta whipped the car around in the opposite direction, shifted into low, and floored the accelerator across the glade toward the entrance to the highway.

A full minute must have passed; there was no sound except a boat engine starting up on the river and the whir of tires on the bridge. The people by the rest rooms rose to their feet and stood like figures in a trance under the smoky glow of the sodium lamps. I pulled off my shirt, my hands trembling, and wiped my hair and face with it. Then I vomited into the grass. The detective named Burgoyne lay on his side, his head on one arm, his jaws

151

locked open, his eyes looking vacuously into space, as though a terrible revelation about his life had just been whispered in his ear.

chapter fifteen

The sheriff paced back and forth in his office, reading from the folded-back front page of the *Baton Rouge Morning Advocate*. While he paced and read, he kept touching one eyebrow with a fingernail and widening his eyes, as though denying himself the luxury of an emotion that would turn his face crimson.

The story was a long one, of the kind written by a journalist who has learned the advantages of professional credulity over skepticism:

HENDERSON – In what authorities believe was an attempted gangland assassination gone awry, a New Orleans city police officer was killed and a murder suspect escaped custody by stealing an unmarked police vehicle and driving it through a hail of gunfire.

Dead upon arrival at Our Lady of Lourdes Hospital in Lafayette was Detective Sergeant James F. Burgoyne. Burgoyne and an Iberia Parish Sheriff's Department detective, David Robicheaux, tried to save the life of the intended victim, John Remeta, a suspect in a New Orleans homicide, investigators on the scene said.

The shooting took place in an I-10 rest area close by the Atchafalaya River. Remeta was being transported in chains from New Iberia to New Orleans.

Both officers advanced across an open field into sniper fire while Remeta huddled on the backseat of the unmarked police vehicle. When the officers freed Remeta of his handcuffs, Remeta escaped in the confusion and a bullet meant for him struck Burgoyne in the head, according to the crime scene investigator.

Authorities believe Remeta has ties to organized crime and that a contract was placed on his life. A second New Orleans police officer, Lieutenant Don Ritter, is credited with coming to the assistance of Robicheaux and Burgoyne, putting himself in the line of fire.

A St Martin Parish deputy sheriff on the scene said the behavior of all three officers was the bravest he had seen in his twenty years of police experience.

And on and on.

The sheriff tossed the newspaper on his desk and continued pacing, twisting the stem of his pipe in and out of the bowl.

Then he picked up a fax of the scene investigator's report and reread it and let it drift from his hand on top of the newspaper.

'The dead cop, what's his name, Burgoyne? He still had his piece in his holster. How do you explain that?' the sheriff said.

'Ask the scene investigator.'

'I'm asking you.'

'I'm not sure you want to know.' I looked at a spot on the wall.

'Ritter impressed me as a self-serving asswipe. He had a sudden conversion and ran into incoming fire to help you out?'

'I never saw Ritter. Not until the state police were coming down the ramp.'

'You'd better tell me what happened out there.'

'I made Burgoyne walk in front of me and give Remeta

his cuff key. If Remeta hadn't taken off in the unmarked vehicle, the shooter would have nailed us both.'

The sheriff ran one hand through his hair. 'I don't believe this,' he said.

'Ritter fabricated the story to cover himself. I didn't contradict him. If I had, I would have been in custody myself.'

'Did you hold a gun on Burgoyne?'

'Yes.'

'You got a cop killed, Dave.'

'They had that kid staked out like a goat under a tree stand.'

The sheriff was breathing hard through his nostrils. His face was dark, his candy-striped snap-button shirt tight across his chest.

'I can't quite describe how angry this makes me,' he said.

'You wanted the truth.'

'You're damn right I do. Stay right there.'

He went out the door and down the corridor, then came back five minutes later, his blood pressure glowing in his face, the lines around his eyes like white thread.

'I've got Don Ritter and an IAD man in New Orleans on the line,' he said, and hit the button on his conference phone.

'What are you doing, skipper?' I said.

He held up his hand for me to be quiet. 'Ritter?' he said, standing erect in the middle of the office.

'What can I do for you, Sheriff?' Ritter's voice said through the speaker.

'Listen and keep your mouth shut. You set up a prisoner from my jail to be murdered and you almost got one of my people killed. You set foot in my parish again and I'm going to find a way to bury your sorry ass on Angola Farm. In the meantime, you'd better pray I don't get my hands on you . . . Is that IAD man still there?'

There was a pause, then a second voice said through the speaker, 'Yes, sir, I'm right here.'

'If the media want to buy that pig flop you people put out about y'all cleaning up your act, that's their business. But you either get to the bottom of this or I'm going to put an open letter on the Internet and notify every law enforcement agency in the country of the kind of bullshit you pass off as police work. By the way, spell your full name for me,' the sheriff said.

After the sheriff hung up, his throat was blotched with color.

'Hypertension is going to put me in a box,' he said.

'I wish it had worked out different. I never got a clear shot.'

He drank a glass of water and took a deep breath, then his eyes settled on my face.

'Burgoyne's brains splattered on you?' he said.

'Yes.'

'It happened to me in Korea. The guy was a prisoner I was taking back to the rear. I used to get up in the middle of the night and take showers and wash my hair and swim in the ocean and all kinds of crazy stuff. What's the lesson? Better him than me.'

His hand rested on the end of my shoulder and he kept massaging it like a baseball coach working a stiff place out of his pitcher's arm.

That night a fisherman on Calcasieu Lake, over by the Texas border, saw a man park a white automobile by the water's edge and start to walk away. Then the man looked back at the car as though he had forgotten something, or as though he'd had an argument with someone and could not quite bear to leave the other party with the last word. The man gathered an armload of creek wood and dry weeds and yellowed newspaper and sifted it through the windows on the seats, his face

156

averted from the dust. He brushed his hands and shirt clean and took an emergency flare from the glove box and popped it alight. Then he methodically fired the inside of the car and stepped back from his work just before flames curled out over the roof. He tossed the flare hissing into the lake and walked down the road.

The next morning, which was Friday, the car was identified as the one stolen from NOPD by Johnny Remeta.

But he had dumped it over on the Texas border, I told myself. Which meant he was probably fleeing Louisiana and did not want to add a federal beef for interstate transportation of stolen property to the charges already pending against him.

Good. I was sick of Johnny Remeta.

I tried to forget that he had a 160 I.Q. That he was just the kind of perp who would burn a stolen car on the state line to let people think he was gone.

The call came at noon.

'Why'd you do that out there in that glade? I mean, walk into all that shooting and cut me loose?' he said.

'It's none of your business why I do anything,' I replied.

'I never saw anybody do anything like that.'

'You're an escaped felon. I'm a police officer. Don't get the wrong idea, Johnny.'

'I called to say thank you. You don't want my thanks, it's on you. But we got a mutual interest, Mr Robicheaux.'

'No, we don't. Get that out of your head. You come around here again and you're going to be back in custody.'

'You want the guys who killed your mother. That's the word on the street. You think they're the same guys who're trying to pop me.'

While he was talking I was waving my hand at Helen

Soileau out in the hall, pointing at the phone so she would start a trace on the call.

'I met Jimmy Figorelli when I first got to New Orleans. He said if I wanted some work, I should rent a post office box and leave the box number for somebody named M.G. at a café across from the open-air market on Decatur. I wrote the box number down on a piece of paper and put it in an envelope and wrote M.G. on the outside and gave it to a black lady behind the register at the café. When I was going out, she said, "Maggie only eats here on the weekend. I'll give it to her then, okay?"'

'I'm writing all this down. You've got to go slower,' I said.

'Good try.'

Change the subject, I thought.

'What was the front money?' I asked.

'I didn't say I got any front money. Sir, I didn't say anything that indicates I committed a crime.'

'Did you burn the car to make us think you'd blown the state?'

'I started thinking about those cops leaving me chained up while a sniper tried to cut all my motors. That's what they call it. They use a hollow point or a steel-claw bullet to core a plug out of your head. If the target is armed, his motors shut down and all his muscles die . . . Anyway, their car got burned. They can buy a new one . . . Say, forget about waving to that woman cop to trace this call. I'm on a cell phone.'

He broke the connection.

I dropped the receiver on the desk blotter and went to the window.

The parking lot was full of cars and noon-hour traffic was backed up on the streets from a passing freight train. Then the caboose of the train clicked down the track, the red-and-white-striped mechanical guard rose into the air, and the traffic flowed out of the side streets and the parking lot, the white sun reflecting blindingly off the windows like the swimming, mismatched eyes of the mythological Argus.

I went into Helen's office.

'He was outside?' she said.

'He had to be.'

'He knows the drill. He was guessing. Every one of these morons wants us to think he's a criminal genius.'

'He knew I waved to a "woman cop." '

'You put out an APB?'

'Yeah. No luck.'

She put a stick of gum in her mouth and chewed it while she read the notes on my legal pad. Her hair was bright yellow and waved and molded into place with chemical spray.

'The go-between on the hit is somebody with the initials M.G.?' she said.

'First name Maggie,' I said.

Our eyes locked on each other's.

'Maggie Glick? I thought Maggie Glick was doing fifteen in St Gabriel,' Helen said.

'Let's take a ride to New Orleans Monday morning.'

She stood a ballpoint pen upside down on its cap and studied it.

'I've got a lot of work in my basket, Dave. I think right now this guy is NOPD's headache.'

I nodded and went back out in the hall and closed her door softly behind me.

She followed me into my office.

'I know I said I'd help, but this stuff is starting to eat you up,' she said.

'What stuff?'

'About your mother. Sometimes you just have to let the bad guys drown in their own shit.'

'You're probably right,' I said.

Ten minutes before 5 p.m. she opened the door to my office and leaned inside.

'Did you see the B&E report on Passion Labiche's house?' she asked.

'No.'

'I didn't know about it, either, not till a few minutes ago. Somebody came through a screen and tore her house up but didn't take anything except a box of old photos.'

'Photos?'

'Remember I told you about Passion saying she'd seen Connie Deshotel's face in an old photo?'

'Yeah, but Passion and Connie Deshotel just don't connect for me,' I said.

'You still want to go to the Big Sleazy?'

'With you, always,' I said.

'Hey, bwana?'

'What?'

'Connie Deshotel's dirty.'

The next morning, Saturday, I drove out to Passion Labiche's house. She unlatched the front door and asked me to follow her into the kitchen, where she was canning tomatoes. She lifted a boiling cauldron off the stove with hot pads, pouring into the preserve jars on the drainboard while the steam rose into her face. She had placed a spoon into each of the jars to prevent the glass from cracking, but one of them suddenly popped and stewed tomatoes burst in a pattern like a broken artery on her arm and the front of her dress.

She dropped the cauldron into the sink, her face bright with pain.

'You okay?' I said.

'Sure,' she said, wiping at her arm and dress with a dishrag.

She continued to wash her arm and scrub at her dress,

rubbing the stain deeper into the fabric, spreading a huge damp area under her breasts.

'I have to change. Fix yourself something, or do whatever you feel like,' she said, her face sweating, her eyes dilated.

She ran up the stairs. When she came back down she had washed her face and tied her hair up on her head and put on a yellow dress. She cleaned off the drainboard with the heavy-breathing, self-enforced detachment of someone who might have just stepped back from a car wreck.

'I went over the breaking-and-entering report on your house. The intruder took nothing but a box of photos?' I said.

'That's all I'm missing so far. I wouldn't have known they were gone, except some shoes fell down from the shelf,' she said.

'You told Connie Deshotel you'd seen her in an old photo. Is there any reason she wouldn't want you to have a photograph of her?'

'It was probably kids. Who cares? Why you spending time on this, anyway? None of this got anything to do with my sister.'

'Was there a picture of Connie in the box that was stolen?'

'I don't know and I don't care. You stop bothering me with this.' She rubbed butter on the place where she had scalded herself with stewed tomatoes.

'Why'd that stain on your dress disturb you, Passion?'

She looked out the window at her garden and barn and the pecan trees down by the bayou, the skin twitching at the corner of her mouth.

'You better go about your business, Dave. I don't make good company some days. Funny how a policeman gives the grief to the person he can get his hands on, huh?' she said.

*

Monday morning Helen and I took an unmarked car to New Orleans and parked behind the old U.S. Mint on the river and cut through the open-air market on Decatur. The pavilion was crowded with people, and farther up the street a Dixieland band was playing in a courtyard and a man was selling snowballs from an umbrella-shaded cart on the sidewalk. We crossed Decatur to the café where Johnny Remeta had dropped off the number of his post office box.

It was not a place for the conventional tourist, particularly not someone with a history of coronary or vascular trouble. It had screen doors, electric fans instead of air-conditioning, an interior that looked painted with fingernail polish, and cuisine that featured sausage, bacon, cob corn glistening with butter, deep-fried pork chops, greens cooked in ham fat, potatoes floating in grease, and mounds of scrambled eggs that lay in bubbling heaps on a grill that probably hadn't been scraped clean since World War II.

'Does Maggie Glick come in here?' I asked the black woman who sat behind the counter, fanning herself with a magazine.

'Who want to know, darlin'?' she said.

I opened my shield.

'She eat breakfast here on the weekend,' the woman said.

'Do you remember somebody leaving a note for her a while back, one with the initials M.G. on the envelope?' I said.

'Could be. Don't remember.'

'I think it's a good time to focus on your memory skills,' Helen said.

The black woman kept flapping the magazine in her face. Her hair was threaded with gray and it rose and fell in the current of warm air generated by the magazine. She did not look at us when she spoke again.

'You see, Maggie comes over here to eat breakfast on the weekend 'cause she don't like the place where she lives or the work she do. When she was a li'l girl, she belonged to the same church as me over in Algiers. I still remember the li'l girl. Every time Maggie comes in here, I still remember that same li'l girl, I surely do. That enough for you, ma'am?'

We drove across the river into Algiers and parked on a narrow street lined with ancient buildings that looked like impacted teeth. The foundations had settled and the upper stories leaned into the sidewalks, the rooftops tipping downward against the light like the brim of a man's fedora. The hotels were walk-ups with stained sacks of garbage propped by the entrances, the taverns joyless, dark places where fortified wine was sold by the glass and where a person, if he truly wanted to slip loose his moorings, could create for himself the most violent denouement imaginable with a casual flick of the eyes at the bikers rubbing talcum into their pool cues.

But the real business on this street was to provide a sanctuary that precluded comparisons, in the same way that prisons provide a safe place for recidivists for whom setting time in abeyance is not a punishment but an end. The mulatto and black girls inside Maggie Glick's bar rejected no one. No behavior was too shameful, no level of physical or hygienic impairment unacceptable at the door. The Christmas tinsel and wreaths and paper bells wrapped with gold and silver foil stayed up year round. Inside Maggie Glick's, every day was New Year's morning, sunless, refrigerated, the red neon clock indicating either the a.m. or the p.m., as you wished, the future as meaningless and unthreatening as the past.

Maggie's father had been a Lithuanian peddler who sold shoestrings from door to door and her mother a washerwoman in an Algiers brothel. The tops of Maggie's gold breasts were tattooed with roses and her hair was the same shiny black as the satin blouse she wore with her flesh-tight jeans and purple heels. She was lean and hard-edged, and like most longtime prostitutes, withdrawn, solipsistic, bored with others and with what she did, and curiously asexual in her manner and behavior, particularly around johns.

Maggie sat at the far corner of the bar, a cup of tea on a napkin in front of her. She glanced at me, then at Helen, her eyes neutral, then picked up her cup and blew on her tea.

'You don't have to show me your badge. I know who you are,' she said.

'I thought you were in St Gabriel,' I said.

'Those cops who got fired or went to jail themselves? One of them was the narc who planted crystal in my apartment. He's in Seagoville, I'm outside. Everybody feeling good about the system now.'

'The word is you set up the drop for the contract on Zipper Clum. When'd you start fronting points for button men?' I said.

'Johnny Remeta told you that?'

'How do you know about Johnny Remeta?' Helen asked.

' 'Cause I read y'all had him in y'all's jail. 'Cause everybody on the street knows he did Zipper Clum. 'Cause he used to come in here. The boy has some serious sexual problems. But who want to go into details about that kind of thing?'

'That's so good of you,' Helen said, stepping close-in to the elbow of the bar, her forearm pressed flat on the wood. 'Is there something wrong about the words we use you don't understand? We're talking about conspiracy to commit murder for hire. There's a woman on death row right now. Would you like to join her there?'

Maggie picked up her cup again and drank from it. She watched her bartender break open a roll of quarters and spill the coins into the drawer of the cash register, then watched a man redeem a marker by counting out a stack of one-dollar bills one at a time on the bar. A young black woman sitting next to a white man in a suit quietly picked up her purse and went out the front door. Maggie Glick looked at the clock on the wall.

'The lady at the café across from the French Market said you used to go to her church when you were a little girl,' I said.

Maggie Glick's eyes cut sideways at me, her lips parting slightly.

'You're not a killer, Maggie. But somebody used you to set up a hit. I think the person who used you may have been involved in the murder of my mother,' I said.

Her eyes stayed fixed on mine, clouding, her brow wrinkling for the first time.

'Your mother?' she said.

'Two cops killed her. Zipper Clum was going to dime them. You're a smart lady. Put the rest of it together,' I said.

Her eyes shifted off mine and looked straight ahead into the gloom, the red glow of the neon tubing on the wall clock reflecting on the tops of her breasts. She tried to keep her face empty of expression, but I saw her throat swallow slightly, as though a piece of dry popcorn were caught in it. Her chest rose briefly against her blouse, then the moment passed and her face turned to stone and the slashes of color died in her cheeks. She raised her cup again, balancing it between the fingers of both hands, so that it partially concealed her mouth and made her next statement an unintelligible whisper.

'What?' I said.

'Get out of here. Don't you be talking about the church I went to, either. What you know about how other people grew up? You used to come in here drunk, but you don't remember it. Now you think you got the right to wipe your feet on my life?' she said.

She wheeled the top of her barstool around and walked toward the fire exit in back, her long legs wobbling slightly on her heels.

Perhaps it was my imagination, but I thought I saw a flash of wetness in the side of her eye.

That night Bootsie and I went to a movie in New Iberia, then bought ice cream on the way home and ate it on the redwood table under the mimosa tree in back. Clouds tumbled across the moon and my neighbor's cane field was green and channeled with wind.

'You look tired,' she said.

'I can't see through this stuff,' I said.

'About your mother?'

'All the roads lead back to prostitution of some kind: Zipper Clum, Little Face Dautrieve, this woman Maggie Glick, the story the jigger told about my mother working a scam with Mack—'

'It's the world they live in, Dave – prostitution, drugs, stealing, it's all part of the same web.' She looked at my expression and squeezed the top of my hand. 'I don't mean your mother.'

'No, it's not coincidence. Jim Gable –' I hesitated when I used his name, then looked her evenly in the eyes and went ahead. 'Gable and this vice cop Ritter are mixed up with hookers. Passion and Letty Labiche's parents were procurers. Connie Deshotel wet her pants when she thought Passion recognized her. Somehow it's all tied in together. I just don't know how.'

'Your mother wasn't a prostitute. Don't ever let anyone tell you that.'

'You're my buddy, Boots.'

She picked up the dishes to take them inside, then stopped and set them down again and stood behind me.

Her fingers touched my hair and neck, then she bent over me and slipped her hands down my chest and pressed her body against me, her stomach and thighs flattening into my back, her mouth on my ear.

Later, in bed, she lay against me. Her fingertips traced the shrapnel scars that were like a spray of raised arrowheads on my hip. She turned her head and looked at the limbs of the oaks and pecan trees moving against the sky and the shadows the moon made in the yard.

'We have a wonderful family,' she said.

'We do,' I replied.

That's when the phone rang. I went into the kitchen to answer it.

It was an intern at Iberia General. 'An ambulance brought in a man named Clete Purcel. A gun fell out of his clothes,' he said.

'He's a P.I. He has a license to carry it. What happened to him?'

'Maybe you'd better come down.'

Clete had many enemies. Outside of the Mob, which bore him a special grudge, the worst were his ex-colleagues inside the New Orleans Police Department.

He had gone down to Cocodrie for the weekend, on Terrebonne Bay, where he still kept a rented cabin and a small boat. On Saturday morning he went south into the Gulf until the coast was only a low, green line on the horizon, then he floated with the tide and fished in the swells for white trout, baking shirtless under the sun all day, consuming one can of beer after another, his whole body glistening like an oiled ham.

At sunset, when he headed for shore, the crushed ice in his cooler was layered with trout, his empty beer cans floated in the bilge, and the flying fish leaping out of the crests of waves and the raindrops that dented the swells were the perfect end to a fine day.

He winched his boat onto his trailer and put on his tropical shirt, but his skin was stiff with sunburn and dried salt, and he was sure the only remedy for his discomfort was a foot-long chili dog and a six-pack of Dixie to go.

The 911 Club was built out of cinder blocks and plywood on a sandy flat by the side of the road. It was owned by an ex-Jefferson Parish deputy sheriff who supposedly welcomed everyone at his bar, but most of his clientele, particularly on weekends, was made up of police officers, male and female, or those who wished to imitate them.

A gathering of sports trappers was taking place at the bar and in the parking lot when Clete came down the road. The trappers wore olive-green T-shirts, dog tags, camouflage pants they tucked inside combat boots, goatees that bristled on the chin. They automatically crushed their aluminum cans in their hands after draining them, lit their cigarettes with Bic lighters, sucking in on the flame with the satisfaction of dragons breathing smoke, touching their genitalia when they laughed.

But Clete didn't care about the trappers. He saw at least four men and two women, white and black, he knew from the Second and Third districts in New Orleans. They crossed the parking lot and went inside the double screen doors. They were carrying open cans of beer and laughing, the way people would at a private party.

Just go on up the road, Clete thought.

He did. For a hundred yards. But if he didn't buy beer and something to eat at the 911 Club, he would have to drive two miles farther up the road.

There was a difference between caution and driving two extra miles because you were afraid of the people you used to work with.

He made a U-turn and pulled his Cadillac and boat

trailer onto the oyster shells of the 911 parking lot and went in the side door.

Don Ritter was at the bar, peeling a hard-boiled egg while he told a story to the men around him.

'The Kit Carsons were V.C. who'd gone over to our side,' he said. 'This one little sawed-off dude, we called him "Bottles" because of his glasses, he kept saying, "Boss, you leave me behind, V.C. gonna make it real hard."

'So I told him, "I'd like to help you, little buddy, but you haven't showed us a lot. Let's face it. Your ville's V.C. Those are your relatives, right? A lot of people might question your loyalties."

'He goes, "Time running out, boss. Americans going home. Bottles gonna be in the shitter." I go, "Wish I could help. But you know how it is. You got to bring us something we can use." '

Both of Ritter's elbows were propped on the bar while he picked tiny pieces of eggshell off his egg, grinning at the backs of his fingers.

'So what'd he bring you?' another man said.

'Can you believe this? He and his brother-in-law stole a slick from the ARVN and loaded it with these fifty-gallon drums of gasoline. They taped frags to the tops of the drums and flew over their own ville and burned it to the ground. He comes to me and says, "Ville gone, boss. That good enough?" '

Ritter started laughing. He laughed so hard tears coursed down his cheeks and a violent cough hacked in his chest. He held a paper napkin to his mouth, then began laughing and coughing again.

The cops and trappers standing around Ritter waited.

'What happened to Bottles?' another man asked.

'You got me. I was on the Freedom Bird the next week . . . Oh, he probably did all right,' Ritter said, wiping his eyes, lifting his glass to his mouth.

Clete ordered a chili dog and a draft and went to the

men's room. Ritter's eyes followed him, then the eyes of the other men turned and followed him, too.

When Clete came back out, the jukebox was playing and someone was racking pool balls. At first he wasn't sure about the references he was now hearing in the story Ritter was telling his friends.

'His wife was a muff-diver. That's not exaggeration. My wife knew her. She dumped him for another dyke and went off to a Buddhist monastery in Colorado. Can you dig it? The guy comes home and thinks he's finally nailed her in the sack with the milkman and she's getting it on with another broad?' Ritter said.

They're shitheads. Walk away from it, Clete thought.

But the bartender had just set Clete's foot-long chili dog, smothered with melted cheese and chopped onions, in front of him and was now drawing a schooner of beer for him. So Clete hunched over his plate and ate with a spoon, his porkpie hat tilted over his forehead, and tried to ignore Ritter and his friends, whose conversation had already moved on to another subject.

When he had finished eating and had drained the last of his beer, he started to get up from the stool and leave. But he paused, like a man who can't make up his mind to get on the bus, then sat back down, his skin crawling with dried salt under his shirt. What was it he had to set straight? The lie that still hung in the air about his ex-wife? That was part of it. But the real problem was that Ritter could ridicule and sneer with impunity because he knew Clete was chained by denial to his past and would always be an object of contempt in the eyes of other cops.

'My ex left me because I was a drunk and I took juice and I popped a bucket of shit in Witness Protection,' Clete said. 'She wasn't a dyke, either. She just had the poor judgment to hang with your wife. The one who gave head to a couple of rookies at that party behind Mambo Joe's.'

They caught him in the parking lot, as he was opening his car door, Ritter and one of the trappers and an unshaved man who wore canvas pants and rubber boots and firehouse suspenders on his bare torso.

The man in suspenders hit Clete in the back of the head with brass knuckles, then hooked him above the eye. As Clete bounced off the side of the Cadillac and crashed onto the shells, he saw the man in suspenders step away and Ritter take a long cylindrical object from him and pull a leather loop around his wrist.

'You think you're still a cop because you throw pimps off a roof? In Camden guys who look like you drive Frito trucks. Here's payback for that crack about my wife. How you like it, skell?' Ritter said.

chapter sixteen

'He used a baton on you?' I said.

'Mostly on the shins,' Clete said. He lay propped up in the hospital bed. There was a neat row of black stitches above his right eye and another one inside a shaved place in the back of his head.

'How'd you get out of it?'

'Some other cops stopped it.' He took a sip from a glass of ice water. His green eyes roved around the room and avoided mine and showed no emotion. He pulled one knee up under the sheet and his face flinched.

'This happened on Saturday. Where have you been since then?' I said.

'Laid up. A lot of Valium, too much booze. I ran off the road tonight. The state trooper let me slide.'

'You weren't laid up. You were hunting those guys, weren't you?'

'The one in canvas pants and suspenders, the dude who gave Ritter the baton? He was buds with that plain-clothes, Burgoyne. I bet they were the two guys who beat the shit out of Cora Gable's chauffeur. By the way, I called the chauffeur and shared my thoughts.'

'Don't do this, Clete.'

'It's only rock 'n' roll.'

'They're going to put you in a box one day.'
'Ritter called me a skell.'

Tuesday morning the sheriff came into my office.

'I need you to help me with some P.R.,' he said.

'On what?'

'It's a favor to the mayor. We can't have an ongoing war with the city of New Orleans. She and I are having lunch with some people to try and establish a little goodwill. You want to meet us at Lerosier?'

'Bootsie's meeting me in the park.'

'Bring her along.'

'Who are these people we're having lunch with?'

'P.R. types, who else? Come on, Dave, give me a hand here.'

Bootsie picked me up at noon and we drove down East Main and parked up from the Shadows and crossed the street and walked under the canopy of oaks toward the restaurant, which had been created out of a rambling nineteenth-century home with a wide gallery and ventilated green shutters.

I saw the sheriff's cruiser parked in front of the restaurant, and, farther down, a white limousine with charcoal-tinted windows. I put my hand on Bootsie's arm.

'That's Cora Gable's limo,' I said.

She slowed her walk for just a moment, glancing at the flowers in the beds along the edge of the cement.

'I just wish I could get my hydrangeas to bloom like that,' she said.

We walked up the steps and into a foyer that served as a waiting area. I could see our newly elected woman mayor and the sheriff and three men in business suits and Cora Gable at a table in a banquet room. At the head of the table, his face obscured by the angle of the door, sat a

173

man in a blue blazer, with French cuffs and a heavy gold watch on his wrist.

'I have to go into the ladies' room a minute,' Bootsie said.

A moment later I looked through the glass in the front door and saw Micah, the chauffeur, come up the walk and sit in a wicker chair at the far end of the gallery and light a cigarette.

I went back outside and stood by the arm of his chair. He smoked with his face averted and showed no recognition of my presence. Even though his forehead was freckled with perspiration, he did not remove his black coat or loosen his tie or unbutton his starched collar.

'Miss Cora said you won't press charges against the two NOPD cops who worked you over,' I said.

'I'm not sure *who* they were. Waste of time, anyway,' he replied, and tipped his ashes into his cupped palm.

'Why?'

He moved his neck slightly, so that the skin brushed like sandpaper against the stiff edges of his collar.

'I got a sheet,' he said.

'People with records sue the system all the time. It's a way of life around here.'

'New Orleans cops have murdered their own snitches. They've committed robberies and murdered the witnesses to the robberies. Go work your joint somewhere else,' he said, and leaned over the railing and raked the ashes off his palm.

'You afraid of Gable?' I asked.

He brushed at the ashes that had blown back on his black clothes. Sweat leaked out of his hair; the right side of his face glistened like a broken strawberry cake.

I went back inside just as Bootsie was emerging from the ladies' room. We walked through the tables in the main dining area to the banquet room in back where Jim

Gable stood at the head of the table, pouring white wine into his wife's glass.

'Jim says y'all know each other,' the sheriff said to me.

'We sure do,' I said.

'Bootsie's an old acquaintance, too. From when she lived in New Orleans,' Gable said, the corners of his eyes threading with lines.

'You look overheated, Dave. Take off your coat. We're not formal here,' the mayor said. She was an attractive and gentle and intelligent woman, and her manners were sincere and not political. But the way she smiled pleasantly at Jim Gable while he poured wine into her glass made me wonder in awe at the willingness of good people to suspend all their self-protective instincts and accept the worst members of the human race into their midst.

There was something obscene about his manner that I couldn't translate into words. His mouth constricted to a slight pucker when he lifted the neck of the wine bottle from the mayor's glass. He removed a rose that was floating in a silver center bowl and shook the water from it and placed it by her plate, his feigned boyishness an insult to a mature woman's intelligence. During the luncheon conversation his tongue often lolled on his teeth, as though he were about to speak; then his eyes would smile with an unspoken, mischievous thought and he would remain silent while his listener tried to guess at what had been left unsaid.

With regularity his eyes came back to Bootsie, examining her profile, her clothes, a morsel of food she was about to place on her lips.

When he realized I was looking at him, his face became suffused with an avuncular warmth, like an old friend of the family sharing a mutual affection.

'Y'all are fine people, Dave,' he said.

Just before coffee was served, he tinked his glass with a spoon.

'Ms Mayor and Sheriff, let me state the business side of our visit real quickly,' he said. 'Our people are looking into that mess on the Atchafalaya. Obviously some procedures weren't followed. That's our fault and not y'all's. We just want y'all to know we're doing everything possible to get to the bottom of what happened . . . Dave, you want to say something?'

'No,' I said.

'Sure?' he said.

'I don't have anything to say, Gable.'

'Friends don't call each other by their last names,' he said.

'I apologize,' I said.

He smiled and turned his attention away from the rest of the table. 'You lift, don't you? I've always wanted to get into that,' he said to me.

'I haven't had much time. I'm still tied up with that Little Face Dautrieve investigation. Remember Little Face? A black hooker who worked for Zipper Clum?' I said.

'No bells are going off,' he said.

'We hope to have all of you to a lawn party as soon as the weather cools,' Cora Gable said. 'It's been frightfully hot this summer, hasn't it?'

But Gable wasn't listening to his wife. His arm rested on top of the tablecloth and his eyes were fixed indolently on mine. His nails were clipped and pink on his small fingers.

'I understand Clete Purcel had trouble with some off-duty cops. Is that what's bothering you, Dave?' he said.

I looked at my watch and didn't answer. Gable lit a thin black cigar with a gold lighter and put the lighter in his shirt pocket.

'What a character,' he said, without identifying his reference. 'You and Purcel must have made quite a pair.'

'Please don't smoke at the table,' Bootsie said.

Gable looked straight ahead in the silence, a smile

176

frozen on his mouth. He rotated the burning tip of his cigar in the ashtray until it was out, and picked up his wineglass and drank from it, his hand not quite hiding the flush of color in his neck.

From behind the caked makeup on her face, Cora Gable watched her husband's discomfort the way a hawk on a telephone wire might watch a rabbit snared in a fence.

After lunch, as our group moved through the dining room and out onto the gallery and front walk, the sheriff hung back and gripped my arm.

'What the hell was going on in there?' he whispered.

'I guess I never told you about my relationship with Jim Gable,' I said.

'You treated him like something cleaned out of a drainpipe,' he said.

'Go on?' I said.

But Jim Gable was not the kind of man who simply went away after being publicly corrected and humiliated. While Micah was helping Cora Gable into the back of the limo, Gable stopped me and Bootsie as we were about to walk back to our car.

'It was really good to see y'all,' he said.

'You'll see more of me, Jim. I guarantee it,' I said, and once again started toward our car.

'You look wonderful, Boots,' he said, and took her hand in his. When he released it, he let his fingers touch her wrist and trail like water down the inside of her palm. To make sure there was no mistaking the insult, he rubbed his thumb across her knuckles.

Suddenly I was standing inches from his face. The sheriff was out in the street and had just opened the driver's door of his cruiser and was now staring across the roof at us.

'Is there something wrong, Dave?' Gable asked.

'Would you like to have a chat over in the alley?' I said.

'You're a lot of fun,' he said, and touched my arm good-naturedly. 'Twenty-five years on the job and you spend your time chasing down pimps and whores and talking about it in front of your new mayor.' He shook the humor out of his face and lit another cigar and clicked his lighter shut. 'It's all right to smoke out here, isn't it?'

I went back to the office and spent most of the afternoon doing paperwork. But I kept thinking about Jim Gable. In A.A. we talk about putting principles before personalities. I kept repeating the admonition over and over to myself. Each time I did I saw Gable's fingers sliding across my wife's palm.

When the phone rang I hoped it was he.

'I thought I'd check in,' the voice of Johnny Remeta said.

'You have a thinking disorder. You don't check in with me. You have no connection with my life.'

'You know a New Orleans cop named Axel?'

'No.'

'When I was chained up in that car, that cop Burgoyne, the one who got smoked? He kept telling that other cop not to worry, that Axel was gonna be on time. He said, "No fuss, no muss. Axel's an artist." '

'What's that supposed to mean?'

'I found out Burgoyne partnered with a guy named Axel. He's a sharpshooter, the guy they use for, what do they call it, a barricaded suspect. He's got two or three kills.'

'Maggie Glick says you used to come to her bar.'

'I never heard of her. I don't even drink. Does everybody down here lie?'

'Don't call here again unless you want to surrender

yourself. Do you understand that? Repeat my words back to me.'

'You saved my life. I owe you. It's a matter of honor, Mr Robicheaux. You got a cell phone in case I can't reach you at home?'

After I'd hung up on him I punched in Clete's apartment number.

'You know anybody named Axel?' I asked.

'Yeah, Axel Jennings. He's Don Ritter's buddy, the one who hit me in the back of the head with a set of brass knuckles.'

'Johnny Remeta just called me again. Maybe Jennings is the shooter who did Burgoyne by mistake.'

'I've got some plans about this guy Jennings. Worry about Remeta. He's got you mixed up with his father or something.'

'What do you mean you've got plans for Jennings?' I asked.

'How about I take y'all to dinner tonight? Dave, Remeta's a head case. Ritter and Axel Jennings are wind-ups. Don't lose the distinction.'

chapter seventeen

A storm had moved into the Gulf and the morning broke gray and cool and shrouded with mist, then it began to rain. I glanced out my office window and saw Passion Labiche get out of a car and step over the flooded curb and run up the front walk of the courthouse. Her hair and skin were shiny with water when she knocked on my office glass. Under her right arm she carried a scrapbook or photo album wrapped in a cellophane bag.

'You want to dry off?' I asked.

'I'm sorry for the way I talked to you at my house. I have days I don't feel too good,' she said.

'It's all right. How about some coffee?'

She shook her head. 'I found that picture of Ms Deshotel. The one I told her about when she came to my club. It was in the attic. My parents kept all the pictures of the places they lived and visited.'

She sat down in front of my desk and took a handkerchief from her purse and touched at her face.

'Why'd you decide to bring it in?' I asked.

' 'Cause you axed about it. 'Cause you been good to us.'

Passion turned the stiff pages of the album to a large black-and-white photo taken in a nightclub. The bar mirror was hung with Santa sleighs and reindeer and

Styrofoam snowballs, and a group of five people, including Passion's parents, sat on stools looking back at the camera, their drinks balanced on their knees, their faces glowing with the occasion.

Someone had inked 'Christmas, 1967' in the corner of the photo, but there was no mistaking Connie Deshotel. She was one of those women whose facial features change little with time and are defined by their natural loveliness rather than by age or youth. She wore a black, sequined evening dress with straps and a corsage, and her champagne glass was empty and tilted at an angle in her hand. She was smiling, but, unlike the others, at someone outside the picture.

'Why should this picture be important to anybody?' Passion asked.

'Your folks were in the life. Connie Deshotel is attorney general.'

'They owned three or four dance halls. All kinds of people came in there. The governor, Earl K. Long, used to go in there.'

'Can I keep the photo?'

She popped the glued edges loose from the backing and handed it to me. Her consciousness of its content, or any importance it might have, seemed to be already lost by the time I had taken it from her hand.

'My sister's got only one lawyer working on her case now. He's twenty-five years old,' she said.

'I think you helped Letty kill Vachel Carmouche. I don't think you're going to get anywhere until that fact is flopping around on the table,' I said.

She stared back at me with the transfixed expression of an animal caught in a truck's headlights.

She literally ran from the building.

I hated my own words.

I grew up in the South Louisiana of the 1940s and '50s. I

remember the slot and racehorse machines, their chromium and electric glitter among the potted palms in the old Frederic Hotel on Main Street, and the cribs on each side of the train tracks that ran the length of Railroad Avenue. I collected for the newspaper on Saturday afternoons, and the prostitutes would be sitting on their galleries, smoking the new filter-tipped cigarettes and sometimes dipping draft beer out of a bucket a pimp would bring them from Broussard's Bar. They were unattractive and physically dissolute women, and they wore no makeup and their hair was uncombed and looked dirty. Sometimes they laughed like deranged people, a high, cackling sound that climbed emptily, without meaning, into the brassy sky.

None of them had Cajun accents, and I wondered where they came from. I wondered if they had ever gone to church, or if they had parents anywhere, or perhaps children. I saw a pimp strike one of them on the gallery once, the first time I had ever seen a man hit a woman. Her nose bled on her hand. Her pimp had oiled black hair and wore purple slacks that fitted him as tightly as a matador's pants.

'You got your money, kid?' he said to me.

'Yes, sir.'

'Better get on it, then,' he said.

I rode away on my bike. When I passed the crib again, she was sitting on a swing next to him, weeping into a red-spotted dish towel, while he consoled her with one arm around her shoulders.

I also remembered the gambling clubs in St Martin and St Landry parishes during the 1950s. Bartenders, bouncers, and blackjack dealers wore the badges of sheriff's deputies. No kid was ever turned away from the bar or a table. The women were brought in by the Giacanos in New Orleans and a Syrian family in Lafayette and worked out of air-conditioned trailers behind the clubs. The head of the state police who tried to enforce the law and shut down gambling and prostitution in Louisiana became the most hated man in the state.

Most of those same clubs stayed in business into the 1960s. Passion was right. People of every stripe visited them. Would Connie Deshotel need to hire someone to steal an old photograph showing her in the company of people whom she may have known in only a casual way?

I decided to find out.

'I'm sorry to bother you with a minor situation here,' I said when I got her on the phone.

'I'm happy you called, Dave,' she replied.

'There was a B&E at Passion Labiche's house. Somebody stole a box of photographs out of her closet.'

'Yes?'

'Passion says she'd told you about seeing you in an old photo she had. Is there any reason anybody would want to steal something like that? A political enemy, perhaps?'

'You got me.'

'I see. Anyway, I thought I'd ask. How you doin'?'

'Fine. Busy. All that sort of thing,' she said.

'By the way, the thief didn't get the photo. I have it here. It shows you with Passion's parents sometime around Christmas of 1967.'

'Could be. I don't know much about her family. Maybe I met them at one time. Dave, when my political enemies want to do me damage with pictures, they put them on dartboards. Say hello to Bootsie.'

The next afternoon Dana Magelli at NOPD returned a call I had placed earlier in the day.

'Can you pull the jacket of a cop named Axel Jennings?' I said.

'Why?'

'He and Don Ritter and another guy worked over Clete Purcel down by Cocodrie. I also think this Jennings character is a good guy to look at for the Burgoyne shooting.'

'Jennings shot his own partner on the Atchafalaya? You come up with some novel ideas, Dave.'

'Can you get his jacket?'

'I have it sitting in front of me. I was just going to call you about Purcel. Where is he?'

I had put my foot in it.

Axel Jennings lived uptown in the small yellow bungalow on Baronne in which he had grown up. It had a neat green yard, a stone porch, and an alleyway with palm trees that grew between the garages. The neighborhood was like neighborhoods had been during World War II, places where people cut the grass on Saturday evening and listened to the ball game on radios that sat in open windows. At least that's what his father had said.

Axel's father had flown with General Curtis LeMay on incendiary raids against Japanese targets between the dropping of atom bombs on Hiroshima and Nagasaki. LeMay's raids didn't do any good. It took a second atom bomb to vaporize another city to bring the war to an end. Most civilians, particularly these peace types, didn't know squat about what went on over there. That's what Axel's father had said.

Axel had three loves: firearms, model railroading, and the memory of his father, whose picture in uniform he kept on the mantel.

He was a member at a gun range in St Charles Parish, and almost every weekend he packed up his boxes of hand-loaded ammunition and his three favorite weapons – his .45 auto, a scoped '03 Springfield, and the civilian equivalent of the M-14 rifle – and fired them from under a wood shed at paper targets clipped to wires in front of a dirt embankment.

His father used to say marksmanship was simply the

coordination of angles with the beat of your heart and the rise and fall of your lungs. The bullet's behavior was mathematically predictable and was governed by no rules other than physical principles. You simply had to make the weapon an extension of blood and sinew and thought so that the squeeze of your finger created a geometric certainty for your target.

It was all about control and order.

The same way with life, his father had said. People didn't respect authority anymore. You had to find a leader, a man you could respect, and put your faith in him, just as he placed his faith in you. His father called it a reciprocity of personal honor.

Axel's sunporch and guest room were covered with electric trains. The tracks ran across floors and tables and sections of plywood screwed down on sawhorses. The tracks wound through papier-mâché mountains and tiny forests, past water towers and freight depots and miniature communities; there were toy brakemen and gandy walkers along the tracks and switches that diverted locomotives past each other at the last possible moment, and warning bells and flashing lights at the crossings.

When Axel cranked up all his trains at once, the smells of warm metal and oil and overheated electrical circuits reminded him of the clean acrid smell of gunpowder at the range.

Two kills with a department-issue M-16, a third kill shared with Burgoyne.

He thought he might feel bad about the first barricaded suspect he popped.

He didn't. The guy had every opportunity to come out of the building. Instead, he turned on the gas jets and was going to take his child out with him. Just as the guy was about to light the match, Axel, in a prone position on a rooftop, sucked in his breath, exhaled slowly, and drilled a round through a glass pane and nailed him through both temples.

You believed in what you did. You trusted the man you took orders from. And you didn't look back. That's what his father had said.

It must have been grand to be around during World War II. Working people made good money and for fun went bowling and played shuffleboard in a tavern and didn't snort lines off toilet tanks; you walked a girl home from a café without gangbangers yelling at her from a car; blacks lived in their own part of town. Kids collected old newspapers and coat hangers and automobile tires and hauled them on their wagons down to the firehouse for the war effort. The enemy was overseas. Not in the streets of your own city.

Axel's occasional girlfriend, a barmaid named Cherry Butera, said he'd been depressed since Jimmy Burgoyne was killed in that shooting on the Atchafalaya. He'd taken a couple of vacation days, and he and the girlfriend had driven down to Grand Isle. A storm was tearing up the Gulf and the sky had turned green and the surf was wild and yellow with churning sand.

'There's a Nazi sub out there. The Coast Guard sunk it with planes in '42,' he said. 'I wish I'd been alive back then.'

'What for?' she asked.

'I would have been there. I would have been part of all that,' he replied.

They drove back to New Orleans in the rain and drank beer in a small pizza joint two blocks from his house. Banana trees thrashed against the side of the building, and the shadows from the neon signs in the windows cascaded like water down Axel's face.

'Somebody's following me,' he said.

'You're blaming yourself because you weren't there when Jimmy was killed,' his girlfriend said.

He looked at her a moment, then his eyes disconnected from hers and looked at nothing. He peeled the gold and green label off his beer bottle and rolled it into tiny balls.

'I saw somebody outside my window. He was behind us on the road tonight,' he said.

'The road was empty, hon. The bad guys are afraid of you. Everybody knows that.'

'I wish Jimmy was here. I wish he wasn't dead,' he said.

At 11 p.m. they went out the back of the café and walked down the alley toward his car. Rain blew in a vortex from a streetlight out by the sidewalk, and the palm trees between the garages filled with wind and raked against the wood walls.

The man waiting in the shadows wore a wide hat and a black raincoat with the collar up. The piece of lumber he held in his hands was thick and square and probably three feet long. Leaves clung wetly to his shoulders and hat, so that he looked like an extension of the hedge when he stepped into the alley. He swung the piece of lumber with both hands, as he would a baseball bat, into Axel's face.

Axel crashed backwards into a row of garbage cans, his forehead veined with blood and water. Then the man in the wide hat leaned over and drove the piece of lumber into Axel's throat and the side of his head.

The man stood erect, water sluicing off his hat brim, his face a dark oval against the streetlight at the end of the alley.

'Haul freight, unless you want the same,' he said to the woman.

She turned and ran, twisting her face back toward the hatted man, her flats splashing through puddles that were iridescent with engine oil. The hatted man tossed the piece of lumber in the hedge, then picked up a whiskey bottle and broke it against the side of a garage.

He stooped over Axel's body, the streetlight glinting on the jagged shell of the bottle, his extended arm probing downward into the darkness, soundlessly, like a man doing a deed he had conceived in private and now performed without heat or surprise.

'It'd take a real sonofabitch to do something like that, Dave,' Magelli said.

'It wasn't Clete.'

'How do you know?'

'Check out Jim Gable's chauffeur. He's an ex-carnival man named Micah. His face is disfigured.'

'Why don't you let Purcel cover his own ass for a change?'

'Jennings is a rogue cop. He brought this down on himself. Lay off of Clete,' I said.

'Tell it to Jennings. The doctor had the mirrors taken out of his hospital room.'

chapter eighteen

A week passed, and I didn't hear anything more from Dana Magelli. The night Jennings had been attacked Clete was picking up a bail skip for Wee Willie Bimstine and Nig Rosewater in Baton Rouge, which didn't mean he couldn't have attacked Jennings after he dumped the skip in Willie and Nig's office. But Clete Purcel had boundaries, even though they were a little arbitrary, and they didn't include mutilating a half-conscious man who was already on the ground.

I wanted to empty my head and caseload and go to Key West with Bootsie and Alafair and fish for three weeks. I was tired of other people's problems, of breaking up domestic arguments, of hosing vomit out of a cruiser, of washing spittle off my face, of cutting slack to junkies because they had the virus, only later to have one try to bite me when I cuffed him.

I was tired of seeing the despair in the faces of black parents when I told them their children had overdosed on meth or heroin or had been gunned down in a robbery. Or vainly trying to reassure a store owner of his self-worth after he had been forced at gunpoint to kneel and beg for his life. Nor did I ever again want to look into the faces of women who had been raped, sodomized, burned with cigarettes, and beaten with fists, every ounce of dignity and self-respect they once possessed systematically ripped out of their bodies.

If you meet longtime street cops who don't drink or use, they're usually either in twelve-step programs or brain-dead or they have criminal propensities themselves.

But each time I cleared my head and tried to concentrate on all the potential that every day could bring – the sun showers that blew in from the Gulf, Bootsie's meeting me for lunch at Victor's or in the park, the long summer evenings and the way the light climbed high into the sky at sunset, picking up Alafair at night at the City Library and going for ice cream with her high school creative writing group – my mind returned again and again to thoughts about my mother's fate, the pleas for help she must have uttered, and the fact her killers were still out there.

But it was more than my mother's death that obsessed me. Long ago I had accepted the loss of my natal family and my childhood and the innocence of the Cajun world I had been born into. You treat loss just like death. It visits everyone and you don't let it prevail in your life.

What I felt now was not loss but theft and violation. My mother's memory, the sad respect I had always felt for her, had been stolen from me. Now the tape-recorded lie left behind by a dead jigger in the Morgan City jail, that my mother was a whore and a thief, had become part of a file at the New Orleans Police Department and I had no way to change it.

'Something on your mind?' Helen Soileau said in my office.

'No, not really,' I replied.

She stood at the window and rubbed the back of her neck and looked out at the street.

'Connie Deshotel just kind of disappeared? Being photographed with a couple of procurers didn't rattle her?' she said.

'Not that I could tell,' I said, tilting back in my chair.

'She was in her office. All her power was right there at her fingertips. Don't let her fool you, Dave. That broad's got you in her bombsights.'

But it was Friday afternoon and I didn't want to think any more about Connie Deshotel. I signed out of the office, bought a loaf of French bread at the market, and drove down the dirt road toward my house, the sun flashing like pieces of hammered brass in the oak limbs overhead.

Alafair and Bootsie and I ate dinner at the kitchen table. Outside the window, the evening sky was piled high with rain clouds, and columns of sunlight shone through the clouds on my neighbor's sugarcane. Alafair ate with her book bag by her foot. In it she kept her short stories and notebooks and felt pens and a handbook on script writing. By her elbow was a thick trade paperback with a black-and-white photo of a log cabin on the cover.

'What are you reading?' I asked.

'*Night Comes to the Cumberland*. It's by a lawyer named Harry Caudill. It's a history of the southern mountains,' she said.

'For your creative writing group?' I asked.

'No, a boy at the library said I should read it. It's the best book ever written about the people of Appalachia,' she replied.

'You're going to read your new story tonight?' I said.

'Yeah,' she said, smiling. 'By the way, I might get a ride home tonight.'

'With whom?' Bootsie said.

'This boy.'

'Which boy?' I asked.

'The one who told me about *Night Comes to the Cumberland*.'

'That nails it down,' I said.

'Dave, I *am* sixteen now . . . Why are you making that face?'

'No reason. Sorry,' I said.

'I mean, lighten up,' she said.

'You bet,' I said, looking straight ahead.

A few minutes later Alafair got into the car with Bootsie to ride into town. Under the trees the sunlight was red on the ground, and I could smell humus and the wet, dense warm odor of the swamp and schooled-up fish on the wind.

'No riding home with boys we don't know, Alafair. We got a deal?' I said.

'No,' she said.

'Alf?' I said.

'You have to stop talking to me like I'm a child. Until you do, I'm just not going to say anything.'

Behind Alafair's angle of vision Bootsie shook her head at me, then she said, 'I'll be back in a little while, Dave,' and I watched them drive down the road toward New Iberia.

I don't know how good a father I was, but I had learned that when your daughter is between the ages of thirteen and seventeen, you will never win an argument with her, and if you fall back on anger and recrimination and coercion to prevail over her, you will come to loathe your triumph and the weakness it disguises and you will not easily find forgiveness for it in either her or yourself.

I read the newspaper on the gallery, then the dusk gathered inside the trees and the leaves on the ground darkened and became indistinct and a car passed on the road with its headlights on. I saw Batist walk out of the bait shop and scoop the hot ashes out of the barbecue into a bucket and fling them in a spray of burning embers onto the bayou's surface.

I went inside and lay down on the couch with the newspaper over my face and fell asleep. In my dream I saw the sculpted, leafless branches of a tree on an alkali plain, and in the distance purple hills and piñon and cedar trees and cactus and rain bleeding like smoke out of the clouds. Then a flock of colored birds descended on the hardened and gnarled surfaces of the barren tree, and green tendrils began to grow from the tree's skin and wind about its branches, and young leaves and flowers unfolded with the sudden crispness of tissue paper from the ends of the twigs, so that the tree looked like a man raising a floral tribute toward the sky.

But a carrion bird descended into the tree, its talons and beak flecked with its work, its feathers shining, its eyes like perfectly round drops of black ink that had dried on brass. It extended its wings and cawed loudly, white insects crawling across its feathers, its breath filling the air with a scrofulous presence that enveloped the tree and the tropical birds in it like a moist net.

I sat up on the couch and the newspaper across my face cascaded to the floor. I closed and opened my eyes and tried to shake the dream out of my mind, although I had no idea what it meant. I heard Bootsie's car outside and a moment later she opened the front screen and came inside.

'I fell asleep,' I said, the room still not in focus.

'You okay?' she said.

'Yeah, sure.' I went into the bathroom and washed my face and combed my hair. When I came back out Bootsie was in the kitchen.

'I had a terrible dream,' I said.

'About what?'

'I don't know. Is Alf all right?'

'She's at the library. She promised me she'd call or get a ride from somebody we know.'

I took two glasses out of the cabinet over the drainboard and filled them from a pitcher of tea in the icebox.

'Why wouldn't she tell me who this boy is?' I asked. 'The one who recommended the book about the Appalachians?'

'Yes.'

'Because she's sixteen. Dave, don't see a plot in everything. The kid she's talking about is studying to be an artist.'

'Say again?'

'Alafair said he's a painter. He paints ceramics. Does that sound like Jack the Ripper to you?'

I stared stupidly at Bootsie, and in my mind's eye I saw the humped black shape of the carrion bird in the midst of the flowering tree.

I dialed 911 and got the city dispatcher, then I was out the back door and in the truck, roaring backwards in the driveway, the rear end fishtailing in a plume of dust out on the road. The dust drifted out onto the glare of the electric lights over the dock, glowing as brightly as powdered alkali under the moon.

I came down East Main, under the oaks that arched over the street, and pulled into the City Library. The outside flood lamps were on and the oak trees on the lawn were filled with white light and shadows that moved with the wind, and next to the parking lot I could see a wall of green bamboo and the stone grotto that contained a statue of Jesus' mother.

A city police cruiser was parked under a tree by the grotto, and an overweight, redheaded cop, his cap at an angle on his brow, leaned against the fender, smoking a cigarette. He was a retired marine NCO nicknamed Top, although he had been a cook in the corps and never a first sergeant.

'I've already been inside, Dave. Your daughter's with a bunch of kids upstairs. I don't see anything unusual going on here,' he said.

'You didn't see a tall kid, wide shoulders, dark hair, real white skin, maybe wearing glasses with black frames?'

'How old?'

'It's hard to tell his age. He doesn't always look the same.'

He took the cigarette out of his mouth, and, without extinguishing it, tossed it in a flower bed.

'That's what I need. To be hunting down Plastic Man,' he said.

We entered the building and walked through a large reading area, then went up the stairs. I saw Alafair sitting with five or six other high school kids around a table in a side room. I stood just outside the door until she noticed me. Her concentration kept going from me to the creative writing teacher, a black writer-in-residence at USL in Lafayette who volunteered his time at the library. Alafair got up from the table and came to the door, her eyes shining.

'*Dave* . . . ,' she said, the word almost twisting as it came out of her mouth.

'The kid who paints ceramics? Is he here tonight?' I said.

She squeezed her eyes shut, as though in pain, and opened them again. 'I knew that was it.'

'Alf, this guy isn't what you think he is. He's a killer for hire. He's the guy who escaped custody in the shoot-out on the Atchafalaya.'

'No, you're wrong. His name's Jack O'Roarke. He's not a criminal. He paints beautiful things. He showed me photographs of the things he's done.'

'That's the guy. O'Roarke was his father's name. Where is he?'

A fan oscillated behind her head; her eyes were moist and dark inside the skein of hair that blew around her face.

'It's a mistake of some kind. He's an artist. He's a gentle person. Jack wouldn't hurt anybody,' she said.

'Alf, come with me,' I said, and put my hand on her forearm, my fingers closing around the skin, harder than I meant to.

'No, I'm not going anywhere with you. You're humiliating me.'

I could see the veins in her forearm bunched like blue string under the skin, and I released her and realized my hand was shaking now.

'I'm sorry,' I said.

'Everybody's looking at us. Just go,' she said, her voice lowered, as though she could trap her words in the space between the two of us.

'He's here, isn't he?'

'I'll never forgive you for this.'

'Alafair, I'm a police officer. I was almost killed because of this man.'

She squeezed her eyes shut again and I saw the tears well out of her eyelids and shine on her lashes. Then inadvertently she glanced beyond me.

'The rest room?' I said.

But she wouldn't answer.

I waited until the area around the door of the men's room was clear, then I slipped my .45 from its clip-on holster under my coat, holding it close against my thigh, and went inside.

No one was at the urinals or lavatories. I pushed open each of the stall doors, standing back as they swung emptily against the partitions. I put the .45 back in my holster and went outside and motioned to the city cop to follow me. I saw Alafair looking at me, hollow-eyed, from across the room.

We went back down to the first floor and I described Johnny Remeta to the librarian at the circulation desk. She removed the glasses from her face and let them hang from a velvet ribbon around her neck and gazed thoughtfully into space.

'Did he have on a straw hat?' she asked.

'Maybe . . . I don't know,' I said.

'He walked past me a few minutes ago. I think he's in the historical collection. That room in the back,' she said, and pointed past the book stacks.

I walked between the stacks, the city cop behind me, to a gray metal door inset with a small rectangle of reinforced glass. I tried to look through the glass at the entirety of the room but I saw only bookshelves and an austere desk lighted by a reading lamp. I pulled my .45 and held it down against my thigh, then shoved open the door and stepped inside.

The side window was open and a straw hat, with a black ribbon around the crown, lay brim-down on the floor. A bound collection of Civil War-era photographs lay open on the narrow desk. The photographs on the two exposed pages showed the bodies of Confederate and Union dead at Dunker Church and the Bloody Angle.

'This place is like a meat locker,' the city cop said.

I looked out the window into the summer night, into the sounds of crickets and frogs on the bayou and the easy creak of wind in the oak trees. But the air inside the room was like the vapor from dry ice.

'You believe in the angel of death, Top?' I said.

'Yeah, I knew her well. My ex-wife. Or maybe she was the Antichrist. I've never been sure,' he replied.

I climbed through the window and dropped onto the lawn. I walked out on the street, then through the parking lot and down to the bayou. I heard the horns on a tugboat in the distance, then the drawbridge at Burke Street clanking heavily into the air. There was no sign of Johnny Remeta. The sky had cleared and was as black as velvet and bursting with stars, like thousands of eyes looking down at me from all points on the compass.

Later, when we drove home, Alafair sat on the far side of the truck's seat, staring out the window, her anger or regret or humiliation or whatever emotion she possessed neutralized by fatigue and set in abeyance for the next day.

'You want to talk with Bootsie?' I said.

'No. You're just the way you are, Dave. You're not going to change.'

'Which way is that?' I said, and tried to smile in the darkness.

'I don't want to talk about it.'

After I pulled into the drive and cut the engine, she got out and walked to the front yard and went into the house through the living room so she wouldn't have to see me again that night.

'What's going on, Dave?' Bootsie said in the kitchen.

'It was Remeta. I tried to take him down in the library. He got away.'

The phone rang. I heard Alafair walking toward the extension that was in the hallway by her room. I picked up the receiver off the wall hook in the kitchen, my heart beating.

'Hello?' I said.

'You came after me like I was a germ,' Remeta said.

'How'd you get this number?' I said.

'What do you care? I got it.'

'You stay the fuck away from my daughter,' I said.

'What's with you? Don't talk to me like that.'

My temples were hammering, the inside of my shirt cold with sweat, my breath sour as it bounced off the receiver.

'So far I've got nothing against you personally. Drag your crazy bullshit into my family life, you'll wish you were still somebody's hump back in Raiford.'

I could hear his breath on the phone, almost a palpable physical presence, like an emery cloth brushing across the receiver.

When he spoke again, his voice was not the same. It came out of a barrel, dipped in blackness, the youthful face dissolving in my mind's eye.

His words were slow and deliberate, as though he were picking them one by one out of a cardboard box. 'You're not a smart man, after all, Mr Robicheaux. But I got an obligation to you. That makes you . . . a lucky man. Word of caution, sir. Don't mess with my head,' he said.

There was a click in his throat, then an exhalation of breath like a damp match flaring to life.

chapter nineteen

A week and a half went by and I heard nothing else from Johnny Remeta or about Axel Jennings or Micah the chauffeur or Jim and Cora Gable, and I began to feel that perhaps they would simply disappear from my life.

But my conclusions were about as wise as those of a man floating down a wide, flat stream on a balmy day, when the mind does not want to listen to the growing sounds of water cascading over a falls just beyond a wooded bend.

'You ought to go easy on the flak juice, hon,' Cherry Butera said to him.

Axel Jennings sat at the kitchen table in an undershirt and camouflage pants and house slippers without socks, a bottle of tequila and a sliced lime on a saucer in front of him. He poured into a jigger and knocked it back and licked salt from between his thumb and index finger and sucked on the lime. His shoulders were as dark as mahogany, hard and knobbed along the ridges, the skin taut and warm and smooth and sprinkled with sun freckles. He wasn't a handsome man, not in the ordinary sense, but he had beautiful skin and she loved to touch it and to feel that she was pressing his power and hardness inside her when she spread her fingers across his shoulders and ran them down to the small of his back.

The barmaids she worked with said she could do a lot better. They said Axel had a violent history. They should talk. Their boyfriends hit them, hung paper and cadged drinks at the bar, and usually had somebody on the side. He killed those guys in the line of duty; that's what cops got paid to do. Besides, he didn't talk about that part of his life, and the people he hurt deserved it. Nobody came on to her or treated her disrespectfully when she was with Axel.

But it had sure gone south since Jimmy Burgoyne got killed out by the Atchafalaya. Axel brooded all the time, like he was responsible for Jimmy getting killed. Now there was even a worse problem, and she didn't have an answer for it, either.

'Drinking don't hurt anything,' he said. 'A man decides how much he takes out of the bottle. Then he puts the cork in it. He controls the situation. That's what my dad said.'

He had taken off his bandages and lain out in the backyard in his Jockey undershorts with a wet washcloth rolled across his eyes and talked for a half hour on his remote phone to another cop. When he came in he started up all his electric trains and poured himself a drink and didn't replace his bandages. The collective hum of the electric trains made the house reverberate like an enormous sewing machine.

'Maybe I'd better be getting home. I mean, so's you can rest,' she said.

'Come over here,' he said.

He extended his hand toward her, waiting for her to take it and sit on his lap. She placed her fingers in his, but remained standing, her vision fixed so his face did not come into focus.

'The doctor says you got to take care of yourself,' she said.

'You got a problem with this, Cherry?' he said, lifting one finger toward his face.

'No, baby,' she said.

He released her hand and watched two calico kittens out the window. The kittens raced after each other in a flower bed, their fur a patchwork of color among the elephant ears.

'Why'd you bag out on me?' he said, his eyes still concentrated out the window.

'Bag out on you?'

'In the alley. When the perp told you to boogie, you hoofed it big-time.'

'I called 911. I got help.'

'You didn't scream. That's what women always do when they're at risk. You didn't do that, Cherry.'

'You think I was in on it?'

'You knew you were safe as long as you didn't scream. It's funny how fast people can add up the score when they're scared.'

She stood motionless for a long moment, her mind back in the alley now, inside the vortex of rain. She saw herself running through the rain puddles that were rainbowed with engine oil, her windpipe constricted, her breasts bouncing shamelessly in her blouse, and she knew what he said was true, and that an even greater, uglier truth was about to surface in her mind, that she was glad it had happened to him and not her.

The house was hot, full of morning sun trapped between the glass and the freshly painted yellowed walls. The electric trains coursing down the tracks, emerging from tunnels, clicking across the switches, seemed to amplify in her head. She made herself look directly into Axel's face. The jaws and chin line and brow looked like they had been disassembled and then rejoined and sealed together like the sunken and uneven pieces of an earthen pot.

He touched the point of a canine tooth and looked at the spittle on the ball of his finger, just the way he once did right before he hurt a man in a bar. She saw the network of red lines on his face transferred to hers and she wanted to weep.

'I'll leave, Axel. I mean, if that's what you want,' she said, and folded her arms suddenly across her chest, gripping her elbows as though she were cold.

He closed and opened his hand and watched the veins pump with blood in his forearm. Then he picked an apple out of a bowl of fruit and began peeling off the skin with a paring knife, watching it curl like a red and white wood shaving over his thumbnail.

'I'm gonna have a lot of money. I think I'm going to South America and start up a business. You can come,' he said.

'Sure, baby,' she said, and she realized she was trembling inside.

'So you go home and think about it. Get in touch with your inner self. Then come back tomorrow and let me know . . . You want to use the bathroom before you go? You look like maybe you're gonna have an accident.'

Clete had sublet his apartment from a couple who wanted it back, evidently after the manager had called them in Florida and told them Clete sometimes parked the Cadillac in front with bail skips handcuffed to a D-ring in the backseat while he showered and changed clothes or fixed lunch in the apartment. One of the skips yelled out the window for fifteen minutes, announcing to the whole neighborhood that he had to use the bathroom.

On Saturday afternoon Bootsie went to visit her sister in Lafayette and Alafair and I helped Clete move to a tan stucco cottage in a 1930s motor court down Bayou

Teche. The motor court was hemmed in by live-oak and banana and palm trees, and toward evening working-class people cooked on barbecue grills outside the cottages. The sunlight off the bayou glowed through the tunnel of trees like the amber radiance of whiskey held up against firelight.

After we finished unloading Clete's things from my truck, Clete and I tore up the packing cartons and stuffed them in a trash barrel while Alafair put away his kitchen utensils inside.

'I'm gonna get us some po' boys,' he said.

'We'd better go,' I said.

'Y'all got to eat. Relax, big mon. Cletus is in charge,' he said, then got in his Cadillac and bounced out the drive onto East Main before I could argue.

Alafair walked out of the cottage and looked in both directions. She wore blue-jeans shorts that were rolled high up on her thighs, and a Clorox-stained lavender T-shirt that seemed to hang off the tips of her breasts. A man playing a guitar in front of the cottage next door let his gaze wander over the backs of her legs. I stared at him and he looked away.

'Where's Clete?' she asked.

'He went for some food.'

She made a pout with her mouth and blew her breath out her nose. 'I have a date, Dave.'

'With whom?'

'It's somebody I go to school with. He doesn't have two heads. He's very safe. In fact, he's gay. How's that?'

'I wouldn't have it any other way, Alf.'

'My name's Alafair. If you don't want to call me that, why didn't you give me another name?'

'Take the truck. I can get a ride with Clete,' I said.

She raised her chin and tapped her foot and put her hands on her hips and looked at the barbecue smoke drifting in the trees. 'It's not that big a deal,' she said.

I shook my head and walked out to the street and waited for Clete. He turned into the motor court, cut his engine, then walked back to the entrance and looked up East Main.

'What is it?' I asked.

'I'd swear somebody was watching me with binoculars from the Winn-Dixie parking lot,' he said.

'Who?'

'You got me. I circled around to get a look and he'd taken off.'

'Have you messed with Ritter or this guy Jennings again?' I said.

'I figure Jennings already got his. I'll catch up with Ritter down the road.'

We walked back to the cottage, but he kept glancing over his shoulder.

'Alafair, take the truck on home, would you?' I said.

'Just stop telling me what to do, please,' she said.

Clete raised his eyebrows and glanced upward at the mockingbirds in the trees as though he'd suddenly developed an interest in ornithology.

'Y'all want to eat on that table by the water?' he said, and lifted a sack of po' boys and a six-pack of Dr Pepper out of the Cadillac, an unlit Lucky Strike hanging from his mouth. He waited until Alafair was out of earshot, put the cigarette behind his ear, and said, 'Tell me, Streak, if I quit the juice and start going to meetings, can I enjoy the kind of serenity you do?'

While we ate at a table among a cluster of pine trees, a tall, sinewy man in a small red Japanese station wagon drove farther south of town, crossed a drawbridge, then followed the road back up the Teche to a grassy slope directly opposite the motor court.

He pulled his car down the slope and parked by a canebrake and walked down to the water's edge with a fishing rod and a bait bucket and a folding canvas chair that he flopped open and sat upon.

An elderly black man who had caught no fish was walking up the slope to the road. He glanced into the tall man's face, then looked away quickly, hiding the shock he hoped had not registered in his own face.

The tall man seemed disconcerted, vaguely irritated or angry that someone had looked at him. He gazed at his bobber floating among the lily pads, his back to the black man, and said, as though speaking to the bayou, 'You have any luck?'

'Not a bit. Water too high,' the black man said.

The tall man nodded and said nothing more, and the black man gained the road and walked toward the distant outline of the house where he lived.

It was dusk now. Across the bayou, Clete Purcel lighted a chemically treated candle that repelled mosquitoes. The fisherman sitting on the canvas stool watched through a pair of opera glasses from the edge of the canebrake as our faces glowed like pieces of yellow parchment in the candlelight.

He went back to his station wagon and opened the front and back doors on the driver's side, creating a kind of blind that shielded him from view. He removed a rifle wrapped in a blanket from the floor and carried it down to the bayou and lay it in the grass at his feet.

It was all about breathing and heartbeat, locking down on the target, remembering the weapon is your friend, an extension of angles and lines whose intersection your mind created. That's what his father had said.

He began to feel the old excitement pumping inside him and he had to refrain from beating his fists together. It was too good, a trio of faces bent around a candle flame, an alcove of shadow surrounding their heads. It wasn't just a hit now, but the perfect challenge, to drill a clean shot into the target, snip all his wires, and leave the people around him intact, with stunned, disbelieving looks on their faces and a sudden jellylike presence on the skin they were afraid to touch.

The beauty of it was they'd never hear the shot. While people ran in circles and screamed and crawled under tables and hid behind parked cars, he would recover his brass and get back in his station wagon and drive away. People talking on trash TV about using politics and sex for power and control? Forget it.

The Bobbsey Twins from Homicide. What a joke. A drunk and a pile of whale sperm with a P.I. license. He bit down softly on his lower lip in anticipation of the moments to come.

Then, for just a second, he saw Jimmy Burgoyne's brains exploding in that gig gone bad on the Atchafalaya and he had to squeeze his eyes shut until the image disappeared from his mind.

It was starting to sprinkle. The bayou was suddenly dotted with rain rings and the bream started popping the surface among the hyacinths. He opened his eyes as though awakening from sleep and took a deep breath and resolved to order more flowers for Jimmy's grave, to send another card to the family, to continue making those incremental gestures that temporarily lifted the guilt for Jimmy's death from his soul.

Then anger bloomed in his chest like an old friend, cleansing his mind of all his self-accusatory thoughts.

Show time, boys and girls.

He flipped back the blanket that was folded around the M-1A rifle, the semiauto civilian equivalent of the old M-14. It was a far better piece than any of the other modified military weapons, silenced and scoped, deadly accurate, rapid-firing, the twenty-round magazine packed tight with soft-nosed .308s. He worked the blanket out from under the rifle and draped it over his head like a tent. Then he gathered up the weight of the rifle, knelt on one knee, and fitted the stock against his shoulder and cheek.

A man's head swam into the lens of his telescopic sight, and Axel's mouth opened wetly against the stock, almost like his lips were pressing at a twisted angle into a woman's throat. He exhaled slowly and tightened his finger inside the trigger guard. This one's for Jimmy and me, both, he thought.

'I heard you were queer bait with Vice before NOPD let you start blowing heads,' a voice said behind him.

Axel jerked around, the blanket sliding off his head and shoulders, and stared into the face of a kid who looked like a 1950s greaser. Where had he seen that face before? On a composite? The kid smiled briefly, as though he were about to introduce himself, then shot Axel with a .22 Ruger automatic between the eyes. The kid watched Axel tumble into the cane, then nudged Axel's head to one side with his shoe and leaned over and fired a second round into his ear and a third into his temple.

The splatter hit the barrel of his pistol and he used the blanket to wipe it off.

When the shots went off, the elderly black man had been walking back down the bank to look for a pocketknife he had lost. He stood stark still, his heart racing, and watched the young dark-haired man with white skin, who only a moment ago had seemed like a fellow taking a stroll, straighten up from his work and mount the slope, a pistol hanging from his hand.

The black man thought he should run, but his feet would not move. He was going to say, 'White people fightin' ain't my bidness,' but he never got the chance.

'How's it goin', cappie?' the young man said, and passed him by, shaking a pair of black-framed glasses loose from their case and slipping them on his face.

The black man watched him wrap his pistol in a paper

bag and cross the road and toss the pistol on his car seat and drive away, his turn indicátor clicking to warn oncoming traffic of his presence.

chapter twenty

The night was absolutely black when Alafair and I got home two hours later. In the dash light her face was drawn, her eyes filled with questions that she didn't have adequate words for. And I was both depressed and angry with myself for having taken her to Clete's when I knew Axel Jennings might be coming after him.

I pulled into the drive and parked next to the gallery.

'I've got to help Batist close up. I'll see you in the house, okay?' I said.

But she didn't move. The light on the gallery shone through the trees and made shadows inside the truck. She stared at nothing, her eyes almost luminous in their solitary concern.

'You sure it was Johnny?' she said.

'That old black fellow picked out his photo from five others,' I replied.

'He shot point-blank in the man's ear? It wasn't self-defense or something?'

'It was an execution, Alafair.'

'But you said it saved Clete's life.'

'Remeta thought he owed me a debt and I guess this is how he paid it.'

'Then he's not all bad, Dave.'

'When people kill other people, they find a flag of some

kind to do it under. But their motivation is always the same. They enjoy it.'

'I don't believe that about Johnny.'

She got out of the truck and walked across the yard to the front door. But she paused before she went inside and looked back at me, as though seeking approval or just the knowledge that I did not condemn her for her humanity.

'Alf?' I said.

She opened the screen and went inside.

I walked down to the dock and helped Batist total up the receipts and hose the dried fish blood and cut-bait off the dock.

Clete Purcel's Cadillac came down the road, bouncing through the rain puddles. Then Clete pulled up at an angle across the cement boat ramp and cut the engine and got out and left the door open. He walked toward me with a can of beer in one hand and a pint bottle wrapped in a brown bag in the other. Under the string of electric lights his face was oily and distorted, his mouth unnaturally red.

'I can't believe I let that asswipe get behind us,' he said.

'I love you, Cletus, but you're not using my shop to get drunk in tonight,' I said.

'I've got local leper status now?'

'Your skin's crawling because a shithead had you in his crosshairs. Booze only tattoos the fear into your sleep. You know that.'

'You're pissed off because you think I put your daughter at risk.'

'You didn't have anything to do with it.'

I used the pressure nozzle on the hose to blow the dock and railing clean. When I released the handle I could hear the water draining between the boards into the darkness below. Clete stood silently and waited, his booze in each hand, the hurt barely concealed in his face.

'Let me hold that for you,' I said, and eased the pint bottle from his hand.

'What do you think you're doing?' he said.

'I've got a couple of steaks in the cooler. You're going to eat one and I'm going to eat the other,' I said.

'I don't get to vote about my own life?' he asked.

'I'll do it for you.'

I lit the gas stove inside the bait shop, seasoned the T-bone steaks, and lay them on the grill. Clete sat at the counter and drank from his beer and watched me. He kept touching at his forehead, as though an insect were on his skin.

'What's with this kid Remeta?' he asked, forcing his concentration on a subject other than his self-perceived failure.

'You were right the first time. He's nuts.'

'He was putting moves on Alafair?'

'Who knows?'

The phone on the counter rang. I picked it up impatiently, waiting once again to hear the voice of Johnny Remeta. But it was the sheriff.

'I thought this shouldn't wait till tomorrow,' he said. 'Levy and Badeaux tore apart Axel Jennings' station wagon. There was fourteen thousand dollars in new bills hidden in the trunk. He also had a passport and an Iberia Parish map with an inked line from I-10 to just about where your house is.'

'My house?' I said.

'Your picture and an article about the shoot-out on the Atchafalaya were in a newspaper on the floor. He'd drawn a circle around your head. Purcel wasn't the target.'

I could feel the heat and moisture trapped between my palm and the phone receiver. A drop of sweat ran from my armpit down my side.

Clete lowered his beer can from his mouth and looked curiously at my expression.

Later I lay in the dark next to Bootsie, the window fan blowing across us, and tried to put together the events of the day. A rogue cop doing a hit for hire on another police officer? It happened sometimes, but usually the victim was dirty and shared a corrupt enterprise with the shooter. Who would be behind it, anyway? Jim Gable was obnoxious and, in my view, a sexual degenerate, but why would he want me killed?

The contract could have been put out by a perpetrator with a grudge, but most perpetrators thought of cops, prosecutors, and judges as functionaries of the system who were not personally to blame for their grief; their real anger was usually directed at fall partners who sold them out and defense attorneys who pled them into double-digit sentences.

The only other person with whom I was currently having trouble was Connie Deshotel. The attorney general putting a whack on a cop?

But all the syllogisms I ran through my head were only a means of avoiding a nightmarish image that I couldn't shake from my mind. I saw Alafair seated next to me at the plank table, petting a cat in the glow of the candle Clete had just lighted. Then, in my imagination, I saw a muzzle flash across the bayou, a brief tongue of yellow flame against the bamboo, and an instant later I heard the sound a soft-nosed round makes when it strikes bone and I knew I had just entered a landscape of remorse and sorrow from which there is no exit.

I picked up my pillow and went into Alafair's room. She wore a cotton nightgown and was sleeping on her stomach, her face turned toward the wall, her black hair fanned out on the pillow. The moon had broken out of the clouds, and I could see the screen hanging ajar and

Tripod curled in a ball on Alafair's rump. He raised his nose and sniffed at the air, then yawned and went back to sleep.

I lay down on the floor, on top of Alafair's Navaho rug, and put my pillow under my head. Her shelves were lined with books, stuffed animals, and framed photographs and certificates of membership in Madrigals and Girls State and the school honor society. Inside a trunk I had made from restored cypress wood were all her possessions we had saved over the years: a Baby Orca T-shirt, red tennis shoes embossed with the words 'Left' and 'Right' on the appropriate shoe, a Donald Duck cap with a quacking bill, her Curious George and Baby Squanto Indian books, a brown, cloth Sodality scapular, the mystery stories she wrote in elementary school, with titles like 'The Case of the Hungry Caterpillar,' 'The Worm That Lost Its Wiggle,' and, most chilling of all, 'The Roller Rink Murders.'

Outside, the wind lifted the moss in the trees and I drifted off to sleep.

It was around 3 a.m. when I heard her stir in bed. I opened my eyes and looked up into her face, which hung over the side of the mattress.

'Why are you sleeping down there?' she whispered.

'I felt like it.'

'You thought something was going to happen to me?'

'Of course not.'

She made a solitary clicking sound with her tongue, then got out of bed and went out to the hall closet and came back and popped a sheet open and spread it across me.

'You are so crazy sometimes,' she said, and got back in bed, folding Tripod in the crook of her arm. She leaned over the side of the bed again and said, 'Dave?'

'Yes?'

'I love you.'

I placed my arm across my eyes so she wouldn't see the water welling up in them.

The next morning was Sunday and Bootsie, Alafair, and I went to Mass together. After we returned home I went down to the dock and helped Batist in the bait shop. It was unusually cool, a fine day for going after bream and goggle-eye perch with popping bugs, and we had rented most of our boats. It showered just after lunch, and a number of fishermen came in and drank beer and ate links and chicken at our spool tables under the awning. But regardless of the balmy weather and the cheerful mood out on the dock, I knew it wouldn't be long before Johnny Remeta came back into our lives.

The call came at mid-afternoon.

'I figure we're square,' he said.

'You got it,' I said.

He was silent a moment. I picked up an empty Coke can and looked at the label on it, trying to slow my thoughts and avoid the anger that was always my undoing.

'When you came after me in the library? How far were you willing to go?' he said.

'That would have been up to you, Johnny.'

'Gives me a bad feeling, Mr Robicheaux.'

'That's the way it is, I guess.'

Again he was silent. Then he said. 'Those things you said to me on the phone that night? My father talked to me like that.'

'I can't give you the help you need, partner. But no matter how you cut it, you have to stay away from us. I'm saying this with all respect.'

'It's over when I get the people who shot at me.'

'That's between you and others. We're not involved.'

'You thought maybe I had an improper attitude toward Alafair?'

Hearing him use her name made my breath come hard in my throat.

'I'm off the clock. I'm also off the phone. Have a good life, Johnny,' I said, and gently replaced the receiver in the cradle.

I stared at the phone like it was a live snake, waiting for him to call back. I rang up a sale, served a customer an order of boudin on a paper plate, and scrubbed down the counter with a wet rag, the tension in my ears crackling with a sound like crushed cellophane.

When the phone did ring, it was Bootsie, asking me to bring a quart of milk from the cooler up to the house.

Johnny Remeta may have been temporarily out of the way, but Connie Deshotel's possible involvement with Axel Jennings was not.

In Vietnam I knew a self-declared Buddhist and quasi-psychotic warrant officer who would fly a Huey into places the devil wouldn't go. He used to say, 'The way to keep your house safe from tigers is to return the tiger to its owner's house.'

I got Connie Deshotel's address from our local state representative, then drove to Baton Rouge late Sunday afternoon. She lived off Dalrymple, in the lake district north of the LSU campus, in a gabled two-story white house with azaleas and willows and blooming crepe myrtle in the yard. Her Sunday paper still lay on the front porch, wrapped tightly in a plastic rain bag.

I didn't try to call before I arrived. Even if she wasn't home, I felt my business card in her mailbox would indicate, if indeed she was the money behind Axel Jennings, that her intentions were known, and another visit from one of her emissaries would lead right back to her door.

I lifted the brass door knocker and heard chimes deep inside the house. But no one came to the door. I dropped my card through the mail slot and was headed back down the walk when I heard the spring of a diving board and a loud splash from the rear of the house.

I walked though a side yard under a long trellis that was wrapped with trumpet vine. I opened the gate into the backyard and saw Connie Deshotel in a purple two-piece bathing suit, mounting the tile steps at the shallow end of her swimming pool.

She picked a towel off a sun chair and shook out her hair, then dried her face and neck and blotted the towel on her thighs and the backs of her legs. She placed her feet inside her sandals and poured a Bloody Mary from a pitcher into a red-streaked glass with a stick of celery blossoming out of the ice.

I started to speak, then realized she had seen me out of the corner of her eye.

'Did you bring Bootsie with you this time?' she asked.

'No, it's still all business,' I replied.

'Well,' she said, touching the towel to her forehead, her chin raised, as though taking pause with an unacceptable intrusion rather than allowing herself to be undone by it. 'What is it that's of such great concern to us this Sunday afternoon?'

'Can I sit down?'

'Please do. Yes, indeed,' she said.

She sat across from me at a glass-topped table under an umbrella that was made from wide, multicolored strips of tin.

'Friday the sheriff and I were talking about an interesting attribute everyone of our generation seems to share,' I said.

'Oh?' she said, her interest wandering out into the yard.

'What were you doing when you heard John Kennedy had been shot?'

'I was coming out of gym class. Some girls were crying in the hallway.'

'See?' I said, smiling. 'Everybody remembers that exact moment in his or her life. They never hesitate when they're asked.'

'What's the point?'

'It's that photo taken of you with the parents of the Labiche girls. It troubles the heck out of me. Here, I brought it along,' I said, and removed a manila envelope from the pocket of my coat.

But before I could pull the photo out, she leaned forward and took both of my hands in hers, pressing down hard with her thumbs, her eyes fastened on mine.

'Dave, give this up. You're a good man. But you've developed a fixation about something that means absolutely nothing,' she said.

I took my hands from hers and slipped the photo out of the envelope and lay it flat on the table.

'You remember being with the Labiches?' I asked.

'No, I don't.'

'See, up here in the corner, someone wrote, "Christmas, 1967." So here you are in a nightclub, back in the civil rights era, in an evening dress, with a corsage on, at Christmastime, with a notorious mulatto couple who pimped for a living, and you have no memory of it. Does that seem strange to you?'

She picked up a big leather bag with drawstrings on it from the flagstones and dug a package of cigarettes and a gold lighter out of it and set them on the tabletop.

'I really don't have anything more to say on the matter. Would you like a Diet Coke or lemonade or decaffeinated coffee or ice water or whatever it is you drink?'

'In '67 you hadn't been out of the police academy too long. Does it make sense that a young cop could be around the Labiches, perhaps on Christmas Eve, and not remember it? Look me in the face and tell me that.'

'Do me a great favor, Dave. Go home to your wife. Sell worms to your friends. Play mind games with your sheriff. Just . . . go.'

'There's a bad dude by the name of Johnny Remeta running loose. In case you haven't heard, he's the same perp who cut Axel Jennings' kite string. He's got an iron bolt through his head and thinks he's my guardian angel. I wouldn't want Remeta on my case. You get my drift, Connie?'

She didn't answer. Instead, a strange transformation seemed to take place in her. She rose from her chair, an unlit cigarette dangling between her fingers, a gold lighter in her other hand, and studied the shadows that the banana trees and palm fronds created on her brick wall. Her face was bladed with the glare of the late afternoon sun reflecting off the pool; her eyes were narrow and hard, her lips crimped on the end of her unlit cigarette as she clicked her lighter several times without the flint igniting a flame. Her skin looked coarse and grained, like that of a countrywoman or someone who had stepped into a cold wind.

I replaced the photo in the envelope and put it in my pocket and walked across the flagstones toward the gate. I turned around and looked back at her once more before I entered the side yard.

The gold lighter. It was an archaic type, thin and lightweight, with strips of veined, dark leather inset in the casement and a horizonal lever the smoker snapped downward on top and a tiny cap that automatically retracted from the flame.

It was the same type of stylish gold lighter that Jim Gable used to light his cigars.

She got her cigarette lit and blew her smoke at an upward angle, her sandaled feet slightly spread, one hand on her hip, a private thought buried in her eyes.

chapter twenty-one

Monday morning Little Face Dautrieve came to see me at my office. She wore a dark dress with green flowers printed on it, and a hibiscus in her hair, and hose and lavender pumps.

'You going somewhere special today?' I said.

'Yeah, you driving me and you to New Orleans,' she replied.

'Is that right?'

'The reason I call you "Sad Man" ain't 'cause of the way you look. It's 'cause you let Zipper Clum play you for a fool,' she said.

'Say again?'

'Zipper liked to make other people hate themselves. That's how he got people like me to work for him. That and the rock he give me.'

'You're not making a whole lot of sense, Little Face.'

'You never axed me how I got in the life. It was t'rew my auntie in New Orleans. She knowed Zipper. I visited my auntie this weekend. She say Zipper tole you a bunch of lies about your mother.'

I signed out a cruiser, and Little Face and I took the four-lane through Morgan City to New Orleans. The sugar-cane was high and thickly clustered and pale green in the fields, and the cruiser was buffeting in the wind off the Gulf.

'Why are you doing this?' I asked.

'I seen the story in the paper. People trying to shoot at you and Fat Man. He doin' all right?'

'Sure.'

'Tell Fat Man I been going to meetings,' she said, her face pointed straight ahead to hide whatever emotion was in it.

'You still don't trust me enough to tell me how Vachel Carmouche died?'

'A lawman get killed in Lou'sana, somebody gonna pay. It don't matter who. Give them peckerwoods a chance, they'll strap another one down wit' her. Tell me I be wrong, Sad Man.'

The aunt lived on St Andrew, in a white shotgun house, between the streetcar line and the Mississippi River levee. She had been a prostitute thirty years ago, but her skin was smooth, unwrinkled, like yellow tallow, her gray-streaked hair combed out on her shoulders, her turquoise eyes and red mouth still seductive. At least until she opened her mouth to speak and you saw her bad teeth and the gums that were black and eaten with snuff.

She sat on the stuffed couch in her small living room, her hands clasped just below her knees to prevent the floor fan from puffing up her dress. From outside I could hear the streetcars grinding up and down the tracks on St Charles.

'You knew Mae Guillory?' I asked.

'I worked in a club in Lafourche Parish. Down on Purple Cane Road, almost to the salt water,' she said.

I repeated my question. The aunt, whose name was Caledonia Patout, looked at Little Face.

'Robicheaux been good to me, Callie,' Little Face said, her eyes avoiding mine, as though she had broken a self-imposed rule.

'The club was still for white people then. I worked out of the cribs in back. That's how I knew Mae Guillory,' Caledonia said.

'My mother worked out of the cribs?' I said, and coughed slightly in my palm, as though I had a mild cold or allergy.

'No, your mother wasn't no working girl. Zipper just putting some glass inside you. You seen that burn like a big ringworm on his cheek? Cops done that. Mae Guillory waited tables and hepped at the bar and cooked sometimes. She tole me she'd come there twenty years before with a man deal bouree. The bouree man got TB and died. So she just work there on and off. The rest of the time she work places around Morgan City and Thibodaux.'

'What happened to her, Caledonia?'

This is what she told me.

It was 1967, way down in the fall, hurricane weather. The sky turned green at evening and the air was palpable with the heavy, wet smell of seaweed laden with fish eggs and Portuguese men-of-war whose air sacs had popped and dried in a crusty web on the beach; it was weather that smelled of a storm-swollen tide surging over the barrier islands, bursting in geysers against jetties and sandspits.

The old owner of the nightclub had died and left his property to his half brother, a reckless, irreverent slaughter-house butcher by the name of Ladrine Theriot. Ladrine had always wanted to be a professional cook, and he remodeled the kitchen of the club and began to serve gumbos and chicken and dirty rice dinners. He loved to cook; he loved women, and, like my father, he loved to fight with anyone foolish enough to accept his challenge.

For Mae Guillory, Ladrine had walked right out of her past. But, unlike my father, Ladrine wasn't an alcoholic.

Mae was working at the bar the night the two police officers drove an unmarked vehicle to the back door and cut their lights and walked out of the darkness in rain slickers and hats. Through the door she could see Ladrine in an undershirt and apron, butchering a hog with a cleaver on top of an enormous wood block, chopping through ribs and vertebrae, his arms and shoulders curlicued with black hair that was flecked with tiny pieces of pink meat. She did not see the faces of the officers, only their shadows, which fell across the butcher block, but she clearly heard the conversation between one officer and Ladrine.

'Tell them dagos in New Orleans I ain't buying from them no more. One man tole me the rubber he got out of the machine got holes in it. Their beer's flat and the jukebox full of rock 'n' roll. Them people in New Orleans ain't got no Cajun music?' Ladrine said.

'You want to use another distributor, that's fine.'

Ladrine began paring the rinds off a stack of chops, his long, honed knife flicking the gray dissected pieces of fat sideways into a garbage barrel.

'There's another t'ing,' he said. 'I'm closing up them cribs, me. Don't be sending no more girls down here, no.'

His knife paused over the meat and he raised his eyes to make his point.

'That not a problem, Ladrine,' the officer said. 'But your brother owed the people in New Orleans forty-three hundred dollars and change. The debt comes with the club. What they call the vig, the points, the interest, is running, tick-tock, tick-tock, all day, all night. I'd pay it if I was you.'

'Oh, you need your money? Go to the graveyard. My brother's got a bunch of gold teet' in his mout'. You can have them. He don't mind,' Ladrine said.

He resumed his work, his knife going *chop, chop, snick, snick* against the wood.

*

223

Two nights later they were back. A storm had made landfall immediately to the south, the tidal surge warping and twisting boat docks, rippling the loose planks like piano keys, and the cane in the fields was white with lightning, slashing back and forth as though the wind were blowing from four directions at once.

The two police officers ran out of the rain into the dryness of the kitchen, and one of them loosened the bulb in the light socket that hung over the butcher block, dropping the kitchen into darkness.

The nightclub was almost deserted. Mae stood behind the bar on the duckboards and stared at the kitchen door, her pulse jumping in her neck. 'Callie and me need you to hep out here, Ladrine,' she said.

'He's all right. Go about your business,' one of the police officers said. 'You can fix us some coffee, if you want. Set it on the chair by the door. I'll get it.'

'Ladrine ain't caused no trouble,' Mae said.

'He's a good boy. He's going to stay a good boy,' the officer said. 'That's right, isn't it, Ladrine?'

'Stay out of it, Mae,' Callie whispered in her ear.

Mae could hear them talking now from inside the darkness, the lightning in the fields trembling like candle flame on their bodies. Ladrine was uncharacteristically subdued, perhaps even cowered by what he was being told, his shape like that of a haystack in the gloom.

'It's nothing personal. Debts have to be paid. We respect you. But you got to respect us,' the officer said.

The officer picked up the demitasse of coffee and the saucer and spoon and sugar cube that Mae had set on the chair for him. He stood in the doorway and sipped from it, his back to Mae, his small hands extended out of the black folds of his slicker. His nails were clean, and his face looked rosy and handsome when the light played on it.

'Them Giacanos pretty rough, huh?' Ladrine said.

'I wouldn't know. I stay on their good side,' the officer said.

'I'll t'ink about it, me,' Ladrine said.

'I knew you'd say that,' the officer said, and placed his hand on Ladrine's arm, then set down his empty cup and saucer and went out the door with his partner in a swirl of rain and wind.

'You okay, Ladrine? They ain't hurt you, huh?' Mae asked.

'Ain't nothing wrong with me,' he replied, his face bloodless.

The storm passed, but another was on its way. The next morning was dismal. The sky was the color of cardboard, the fields flooded, the dirt road like a long wet, yellow scar through the cane, and moccasins as thick as Mae's arms crawled from the ditches and bumped under her tires when she drove to work. She mopped floors and hauled trash to the rusted metal barrels in back until 10 a.m., when she saw Ladrine drive a pickup into the parking lot with a hydraulic lift in the rear. He got out, slammed the door of the cab, and thumped a hand truck up the wood steps into the bar.

Later, from in back, she heard him laboring with a heavy object, then she heard the hydraulic lift whining and his pickup truck driving away.

He returned at noontime and opened the cash register and counted out several bills and pieces of silver on the bar. As an afterthought he went back to the register drawer and removed an additional ten-dollar bill and added it to the stack on the bar.

'I got to let you go, Mae,' he said.

'What you fixing to do?' she said.

He broke a raw egg in an RC cola and drank it.

'I ain't done nothing,' he said.

'You a big fool don't have nobody to look after him. I ain't going nowhere,' she said.

He grinned at her, the corner of his mouth smeared with egg yoke, and she was reminded in that moment of a husband whose recklessness and courage and irresponsibility made him both the bane and natural victim of his enemies.

Ladrine opened the New Orleans telephone directory and thumbed through the white pages to the listings that began with the letter 'G'.

He reached under the bar and picked up the telephone and set it down heavily in front of him and dialed a number.

'How you doin', suh? This is Ladrine Theriot. I t'ought it over. I called my cousin in the legislature and tole him what you gangsters been doin' down here in Lafourche Parish. He said that ain't no surprise, 'cause ain't none of you ever worked in your life, and if you ain't pimping, you stealing from each other. By the way, if you want your jukebox back, it's floating down the bayou. If you hurry, you can catch it before it goes into the Gulf. T'anks. Good-bye.'

He hung up the phone and looked at it a moment, then closed his register drawer quietly and stared at the rain driving against the windows and the red and white Jax beer sign clanking on its chains, his eyes glazed over with thoughts he didn't share.

'Ladrine, Ladrine, what you gone and done?' Mae said.

Mae lived twenty miles up the state highway in a cabin she rented in the quarters of a corporation farm. The cabins were all exactly alike, tin-roofed, paintless, stained by the soot that blew from stubble fires in winter, narrow as matchboxes, with small galleries in front and privies in back. Once a week the 'rolling store,' an old school bus outfitted with shelves and packed with canned goods, brooms, overalls, work boots, pith helmets, straw hats, patent medicine, women's dresses, guitar strings, refrigerated milk and lunch meat, .22 caliber and twelve-gauge ammunition, quart jars of peanut butter and loaves of bread, rattled its way up and down the highway and braked with a screech and a clanking of gears in the quarters. People came out of their cabins and bought what they needed for the week, and sometimes with great excitement received a special order – perhaps a plastic guitar, a first communion suit, a cigarette rolling machine – from New Orleans or Memphis.

It was Saturday and Mae had bought a sequined comb to put in her hair from the rolling store, then had bathed in the iron tub and powdered her body and dressed in her best underthings, tying a string around her hips so her slip wouldn't show, the way Negro women did. She put on her purple suit and heels, drawing her stomach in as she stood sideways in front of her bedroom mirror while Callie sat watching her.

'You t'ink I'm too fat?' she asked, pressing her hand flatly against her stomach.

'What you got in your mind ain't gonna happen,' Callie said.

'Ladrine gonna take me to the movie in Morgan City. That's all we doin'.'

'He got in the dagos' face, Mae.'

'You hung around, ain't you?'

'Zipper Clum got a new sit'ation for me in New Orleans. White man want what I got, he gonna pay for it,' Callie said.

'Maybe me and Ladrine are gonna run off.'

'What are you telling yourself? He growed up here. Coon-asses don't go nowhere. You gonna die, woman.'

Mae turned from the mirror and looked at Callie, her

face empty, the words of self-assurance she wanted to speak dead on her lips.

Ladrine did not come for her that afternoon. She waited until almost dark, then drove to the club in her ancient Ford and was told by the bartender that Ladrine had left a note for her. It was written on lined paper torn from a notebook and folded in a small square, and the bartender held it between two fingers and handed it to her and went back to washing silverware. She spread the sheet of paper on the bar and looked down at it emptily, as though by concentrating on the swirls and slashes of Ladrine's calligraphy she could extrapolate meaning from the words she had never learned to read.

'I don't got my glasses, me. Can you make out what it says?' she said.

The bartender dried his hands again and picked up the sheet of paper and held it under the light. '"Dear Mae, I'm taking my boat out. Don't come back to the club no more. Sorry I couldn't call but you don't have no phone. Love, Ladrine,"' the bartender read, and handed the sheet of paper back to her.

The bartender's wrists were deep in the sink now, and she could see only his shining pate when he spoke again.

'I'd listen to him, Mae,' he said.

'Somet'ing's happened?'

'Some men from New Orleans was here. Know the way us little people get by? What you see, what you hear, you do this wit',' he said, and made a twisting motion with his fingers in front of his lips, as though turning a key in a lock.

'You tole them where Ladrine was at?'

'I ain't in this,' he said, and walked down the duckboards to the opposite end of the bar.

She drove in the rain to Ladrine's boat shed on the bayou. A pale yellow cusp of western sun hung on the horizon, then died, and the fields were suddenly dark. But a light attached to a pole over the shed was burning brightly, illuminating four or five cars that were parked in a semi-circle around the shed, like arrows pointed at a target.

The state highway was no more than fifty yards away, and cars and trucks were passing on it with regularity. Inside the warmth and dryness of those trucks and cars were ordinary people, just like her. They weren't criminals. They knew their only friends were their own kind. The ones who were lucky had jobs in the mill and hence were paid the minimum wage of one dollar and twenty-five cents an hour. The others worked for virtually nothing in the cane fields. But the highway was a tunnel of rain and darkness, and whatever happened out there by the bayou had nothing to do with those inside the tunnel. Their ability to see was selective, the fate of a friend and neighbor never registering on the periphery of their vision. That was the detail she would not be able to forget.

The planks in the board road that led to the boat shed were splintered and broken and half underwater, and Mae's car started to stall out when her front wheels sank into a flooded depression and steam hissed off her engine block. She put her car in reverse and backed up toward the highway, then cut the engine and lights and got out and walked down the incline, still dressed in her purple suit, the rain sliding like glass across the cone of light that shone down from the pole above the shed.

She could see them through the slats in the shed and the back door that yawed open above a mud-streaked wood pallet: Ladrine and two men in suits and two police officers in black slickers, the same officers who had tried to extort money from Ladrine; and a local constable, a big, overweight man who wore blue jeans, a cowboy hat, and a khaki shirt with an American flag sewn on the sleeve.

Ladrine had on strap overalls without a shirt or shoes, and his bare shoulders glowed like ivory in the damp air. He was shaking his head and arguing, when he seemed to look beyond the circle of heads around him and see Mae out in the darkness.

Then he called out, 'I ain't gonna talk to y'all no more. I'm going home. I'm gonna fix dinner. I'm gonna call up my grandkids. I'm gonna work in my garden tomorrow. I'm gonna do all them t'ings.'

He began to retreat in the opposite direction, inching backwards along the catwalk, stepping quickly out of the shed's far side into the darkness, then running along the mud bank, his bare feet slapping like flapjacks along the water's edge.

Someone turned on a large flashlight, and one of the raincoated police officers squatted in a shooter's position under the shed, the arms extended in a two-handed grip, and fired twice with a nickel-plated revolver.

Ladrine's head jerked upward, then he toppled forward, his left hand twisted palm-outward in the center of his back, as though he had pulled a muscle while running.

The group of five under the shed walked out into the rain, the flashlight's beam growing in circumference as they neared Ladrine. He had gone into convulsions, his wrists shaking uncontrollably, as though electricity were coursing through his body.

The shooter fired a third time, and Ladrine's chest seemed to deflate, almost like a balloon, his chin tilting back, his mouth parting, as though he wanted to drink the sky.

The other raincoated officer leaned over with a handkerchief-wrapped pistol in his hand and placed it in Ladrine's palm and wrapped Ladrine's fingers around the grips and steel frame and inside the trigger guard. The officer motioned for the others to step back, then depressed the trigger and fired a solitary round into the bayou just as a bolt of lightning struck in a sugarcane field on the opposite side of the highway.

That's when they saw her running for her car.

She drove twenty miles up the highway, in the storm, her car shaking in the wind. They had not tried to follow her, but her heart continued to pound in her chest, her breath catching spasmodically in her throat as though she had been crying. The quarters where she lived loomed up out of the green-black thrashing of the cane in the fields, and she saw lights in two of the cabins. She wanted to pull off the road, pack her suitcase and few belongings and retrieve the seventy dollars she kept hidden in the binder of a scrapbook, then try to make it to New Orleans or Morgan City.

But there was no telephone in the quarters and no guarantee the people who had shot Ladrine would not show up before she could get back on the road again.

She drove on in the rain, even though she had only three dollars in her purse and less than a quarter tank of gasoline. She would stop in the next filling station on the highway and use all her money to buy gasoline. If necessary she could sleep in the car and go without food, but every ounce of fuel she put in the tank bought distance between her and the people who had killed Ladrine.

Then she rounded a curve and realized all her decisions and plans and attempts at control were the stuff of vanity. Either high winds or a tornado had knocked down telephone and power poles as far as she could see, and they lay solidly in her path, extending like footbridges across the asphalt and the rain-swollen ditches.

She drove back to the quarters and sat on the side of

her bed the rest of the night. Perhaps the next day the highway would be cleared and she could drive to Morgan City and tell someone what she had seen. If she could just stay awake and not be undone by her fear and the sounds of the wind that were like fists thumping against the walls and doors of her cabin.

The morning broke cold and gray, and in her half-sleep she heard trucks out on the highway. When she looked through the window she saw people in the trucks, with furniture, mattresses, house pets, and farm animals in back.

She stripped the clothes off the hangers in the closet and stuffed them in her suitcase, pushed her dress shoes in the corners of the suitcase, pulled the seventy dollars from the binder of the scrapbook and lay it on top of her clothes. She hefted up the suitcase and ran outside into the dirt yard, her car keys already in her hand.

She stopped and stared stupidly at her car. It was tilted sideways on the frame. The right front and back tires were crushed down on the steel rims, the air stems cut in half.

An hour later a black man drove her down a dirt road through a cane field toward a weathered shack with a dead pecan tree in the yard. He wore a flannel shirt and canvas coat, and had tied down the leather cap on his head with a long strip of muslin.

'That's where you want to go?' he asked.

'Yes. Can you wait so I can make sure she's home?' Mae said.

'You didn't tell me it was Callie Patout. Ma'am, she work up at the nightclub. In the cribs.'

'I'll give you an extra half dollar if you wait. Then fifty cents more if you got to take me back.'

'Ladrine Theriot got killed shooting it out wit' a constable. I ain't having no truck with that kind of stuff.

232

Look, smoke's coming out of the chimney. See? Ain't nothing to worry about.'

Then she was standing alone in front of the shack, watching the black man's pickup disappear down the dirt road between the cane fields, the enormous gray bowl of sky above her head.

Callie sat on a wooden footstool by the fireplace, a cup of coffee between her fingers, and would not look at her.

'What I'm suppose to do? I ain't got a car,' she said. 'You the only one, Callie.'

'There's trucks up on the state road. There's people going by all the time.'

'I stand out there, they gonna get me.'

Callie pushed her hands inside her sleeves and stared into the fire.

'This white folks' trouble, Mae. Ain't right to be dragging colored peoples in it.'

'Where I'm gonna go, huh?'

'Just ain't right. What I got that can hep? I ain't even got a job. Ain't none of it my doing,' Callie said.

Mae stood a long time in the silence, watching the firelight flicker on Callie's averted face, embarrassed at the shame and cowardice that seemed to be both her legacy and that of everyone she touched.

Mae left the shack and began walking down the dirt road. She heard the door of the cabin open behind her.

'Zipper Clum suppose to pick me up this afternoon or tomorrow morning and take me to New Orleans. Where's your suitcase at?'

'My place.'

'You should have taken it, Mae. They would have thought you was gone.'

They waited through the afternoon for Zipper Clum, but no vehicles came down the road. The day seemed to have

233

passed without either a sunrise or a sunset, marked only by wind and a grayness that blew like smoke out of the wetlands. But that evening the temperature dropped, sucking the moisture out of the air, fringing the mud puddles with ice that looked like badgers' teeth, and a green-gold light began to rim the horizon.

Mae and Callie ate soda crackers and Vienna sausage out of cans in front of the fireplace, then Callie wiped her hands on a rag and put on a man's suit coat over her sweater and went outside to the privy. When she came back her face and eyes looked burned by the wind.

'Their car's coming, Mae. Lord God, they coming,' she said.

Mae turned and looked through the window, then rose slowly from her chair, the glow of the firelight receding from her body like warmth being withdrawn from her life. She shut her eyes and pressed a wadded handkerchief to her mouth, swallowing, her brow lined with thought or prayer or perhaps self-pity and grief that was of such a level she no longer had to contend with or blame herself for it.

'Get under the bed, you. Don't come out, neither. No matter what you hear out there. This all started when I run off with Mack. The ending ain't gonna change,' she said.

A four-door car that was gray with mud came up the road and stopped in front, and two police officers got out and stood in the dirt yard, not stepping up on the small gallery and knocking or even calling out, but simply reaching back into the car and blowing the horn, as though they would be demeaned by indicating that the home of a mulatto required the same respect and protocol as that of a white person.

Mae straightened the purple suit she still wore and stepped outside, the skin of her face tightening in the

234

cold, her ears filling with the sounds of seagulls that turned in circles above the sugarcane.

'Where's Callie?' the taller of the two officers said.

'She gone to Morgan City with a colored man. She ain't coming back,' Mae answered.

'Would you step out here, please? Don't be afraid,' the officer said.

'People call me Mae Guillory. But my married name is Robicheaux,' she said.

'We know that, ma'am. You saw something we think you don't understand. We want to explain what happened there on the bayou,' he said.

She ran her tongue over her lips to speak, then said nothing, her desire to respect herself as great as her desire to live, her pulse so thunderous she thought a vein would burst in her throat.

'Ladrine Theriot tried to kill a constable. So the constable had to shoot him. It was the constable. You saw it, didn't you?' the officer said. Then he began to speak very slowly, his eyes lingering on hers with each word, waiting for the moment of assent that had not come. 'The constable shot Ladrine Theriot. That's what you saw. There was no mistake about what happened . . . Okay?'

She stepped off the tiny gallery into the yard, as though she were in a dream, not making conscious choices now, stepping into the green light that seemed to radiate out of the fields into the sky.

'Ladrine was a good man. He wasn't like his brother, no. He done right by people. Y'all killed him,' she said.

'Yeah. Because we had to . . . Isn't that right?' he said.

'My name's Mae Robicheaux. My boy fought in Vietnam. My husband was Big Aldous Robicheaux. Nobody in the oil field mess with Big Aldous.'

'We'll take you to where Ladrine died and explain how it happened. Get in the car, ma'am.'

'I know what y'all gonna do. I ain't afraid of y'all no more. My boy gonna find you. You gonna see, you. You gonna run and hide when you see my boy.'

'You are one ignorant bitch, aren't you?' the officer said, and knocked her to the ground.

He unbuttoned his raincoat and exposed his holstered gun. He placed his fists on his hips, his jaw flexing, his raincoat flapping in the wind. Then a decision worked its way into his eyes, and he exhaled air through his nose, like a man resigning himself to a world that he both disdained and served.

'Help me with this,' he said to the other officer.

Mae's face was white and round when the two officers leaned out of the greenness of the evening, out of the creaking and wheeling of land-blown gulls, and fitted their hands on her with the mercy of giant crabs.

chapter twenty-two

The next day the Lafourche Parish Sheriff's Department faxed me all their file material on the shooting death of Ladrine Theriot in 1967. The crime scene report was filled with misspellings and elliptical sentences but gave the shooter's name as one Bobby Cale, a part-time constable, barroom bouncer, and collector for a finance agency.

I called the sheriff in Lafourche.

'The shooter wasn't the constable,' I said.

'Says who?' he replied.

'A woman by the name of Mae Guillory saw it happen.'

'You wired up about something?'

When I didn't reply, he said, 'Look, I read that file. The constable tried to serve a bench warrant on Ladrine Theriot and Theriot pulled a gun. Why would the constable take responsibility for a shooting he didn't do?'

'Because he was told to. Two other cops were there. They put a throw-down on the body.'

'I couldn't tell you. I was ten years old when all this happened. You guys running short of open cases in New Iberia?'

'Where's Bobby Cale now?'

'If you're up to it, I'll give you directions to his place.

Or you can get them from the Department of Health and Hospitals.'

'What do you mean "if I'm up to it"?'

'Maybe his sins are what got a fence post kicked up his ass. Check it out. Ask yourself if you'd like to trade places with him,' the Lafourche Parish sheriff said.

I drove my pickup truck to Morgan City, then down deep into Terrebonne Parish, toward the Gulf, almost to Point au Fer. The sky was gray and roiling with clouds and I could smell salt spray on the wind. I went down a dirt road full of sinkholes, between thickly canopied woods that were hung with air vines, dotted with palmettos, and drifting with gray leaves. The road ended at a sunless, tin-roofed cypress cabin that was streaked black with rainwater. A man sat in a chair on the front porch, his stomach popping out of his shirt like a crushed white cake, a guitar laid flat on his lap.

When I got out of the truck, the man leaned forward and picked up a straw hat from the porch swing and fitted it low on his head. In the shade his skin had the bloodless discoloration that an albino's might if he bathed in blue ink. He wore steel picks on the fingers of his right hand and the sawed-off, machine-buffed neck of a glass bottle on the index finger of his left. He slid the bottle neck up and down the strings of the guitar and sang, 'I'm going where the water tastes like cherry wine, 'cause the Georgia water tastes like turpentine.'

A mulatto or Indian woman who was shaped like a duck, with Hottentot buttocks and elephantine legs, was hanging wash in back. She turned and looked at me with the flat stare of a frying pan, then spit in the weeds and walked heavily to the privy and went inside and closed the door behind her by fitting a hand through a hole in a board.

'She ain't rude. She's just blind. Preacher tole me once

everybody's got somebody,' the man on the porch said. He picked up a burning cigarette from the porch railing and raised it to his mouth. His hand was withered, the fingers crimped together like the dried paw of an animal.

'You Bobby Cale?' I asked.

He pushed his hat up on his forehead and lifted his face, turning it at a slight angle, as though to feel the breeze.

'I look like I might be somebody else?' he said.

'No, sir.'

'I was in Carville fifteen years. That was back in the days when people like me was walled off from the rest of y'all. I run off and lived in Nevada. Wandered in the desert and ate grasshoppers and didn't take my meds and convinced myself I was John the Baptizer come back in modern times. I scared the hell out of people who turned up the wrong dirt road.'

I started to open my badge.

'I know who you are. I know why you're here, too. It won't do you no good,' he said.

'You didn't shoot Ladrine Theriot,' I said.

'The paperwork says otherwise.'

'The two other cops there had on uniforms. They wore black slickers. They made you take their heat because they were from another parish and out of their jurisdiction.'

He threw his cigarette out into the yard and looked into space. His nose was eaten away, the skin of his face drawn back on the bone, the cheeks creased with lines like whiskers on a cat.

'You know a whole lot for a man wasn't there,' he said.

'There was a witness. She used the name Mae Guillory,' I said.

'Everybody's got at least one night in his life that he wants to carry on a shovel to a deep hole in a woods and bury under a ton of dirt. Then for good measure burn the woods down on top of it. I wish I was a drunkard and could just get up and say I probably dreamed it all. I don't remember no witness.'

'The two other cops killed her. Except a hooker saw them do it.'

His eyes held on me for a long time. They were green, uncomplicated, and still seemed to belong inside the round, redneck face of an overweight constable from thirty years ago.

'You got an honest-to-God witness can hold them over the fire?' he said, his eyes lingering on mine.

'She never knew their names. She didn't see their faces well, either.'

The moment went out of his eyes. 'This world's briers and brambles, ain't it?' he said.

'You a churchgoin' man, Mr Cale?'

'Not no more.'

'Why not get square and start over? People won't be hard on you.'

'They killed Mae Guillory? I always thought she just run off,' he said, an unexpected note of sadness in his voice.

I didn't reply. His eyes were hooded, his down-turned nose like the ragged beak of a bird. He pressed the bottle neck down on the frets of the guitar and drew his steel picks across the strings. But his concentration was elsewhere, and his picks made a discordant sound like a fist striking piano keys.

'I had a wife and a little boy once. Owned a house and a truck and had money left over at the end of the month. That's all gone now,' he said.

'Mae Guillory was my mother, Mr Cale. Neither she nor I will rest until the bill's paid.'

He set his guitar in the swing and placed his hat

crown-down next to it and pulled the bottle neck and steel picks off his fingers and dropped them tinkling inside the hat.

'The old woman and me is going to eat some lima bean soup. You can stay if you want. But we're done talking on this particular subject,' he said.

'Those cops are still out there, aren't they?' I said.

'Good-bye, sir. Before you judge me, you might be thankful you got what you got,' he said, and went inside the darkness of the cabin and let the screen slam behind him.

Members in the fellowship of Alcoholics Anonymous maintain that alcohol is but the symptom of the disease. It sounds self-serving. It's not.

That night I sat at the counter in the bait shop and watched Clete Purcel use only one thumb to unscrew the cap from a pint bottle of whiskey, then pour two inches into a glass mug and crack open a Dixie for a chaser. He was talking about fishing, or a vacation in Hawaii, or his time in the corps, I don't remember. The beer bottle was dark green, running with moisture, the whiskey in the mug brownish gold, like autumn light trapped inside a hardwood forest.

The air outside was humid and thick with winged insects, and strings of smoke rose from the flood lamps. I opened a can of Dr Pepper but didn't drink it. My hand was crimped tightly around the can, my head buzzing with a sound like a downed wire in a rain puddle.

Clete tilted the glass mug to his mouth and drank the whiskey out of the bottom, then chased it with the beer and wiped his mouth on his palm. His eyes settled on mine, then went away from me and came back.

'Your head's back in that story the black hooker told you,' he said.

'My mother said her name was Mae Robicheaux,' I said.

'What?'

'Before she died, she said her name was Robicheaux. She took back her married name.'

'I'm going to use your own argument against you, Dave. The sonsofbitches who killed your mother are pure evil. Don't let them keep hurting you.'

'I'm going to find out who they are and hunt them down and kill them.'

He screwed the cap back on his whiskey bottle and wrapped the bottle in a paper bag, then drank from his beer and rose from the counter stool and worked the whiskey bottle into his side pocket.

'What are you doing?' I asked.

'Going back to the motel. Leaving you with your family. Taking my booze out of here.'

'That's not the problem.'

'It's not the main one, but you'd like it to be. See you tomorrow, Streak,' he said.

He put on his porkpie hat and went out the door, then I heard his Cadillac start up and roll heavily down the dirt road.

I chained up the rental boats for the night and was turning off the lights when Clete's Cadillac came back down the road and parked at the cement boat ramp. He met me at the end of the dock with a tinfoil container of microwave popcorn in his hand.

'I hate watching TV in a motel room by myself,' he said, and laid his big arm across my shoulders and walked with me up the slope to the house.

Early the next morning I put all the crime scene photos from the Vachel Carmouche homicide in an envelope and drove out to his deserted house on Bayou Teche. I pushed open the back door and once more entered the heated smell of the house. Purple martins, probably from the chimney, were flying blindly against the walls and windows, splattering their droppings on the floors and counters. I swatted them away from my face with a newspaper and closed off the kitchen to isolate the birds in the rest of the house.

Why was I even there? I asked myself. I had no idea what I was looking for.

I squatted down and touched a brownish flake of blood on the linoleum with my ballpoint pen. It crumbled into tiny particles, and I wiped my pen with a piece of Kleenex, then put my pen away and blotted the perspiration off my forehead with my sleeve.

All I wanted to do was get back outside in the wind, under the shade of a tree, out of the smell that Vachel Carmouche seemed to have bled into the woodwork when he died. Maybe I had to stop thinking of Passion and Letty Labiche as victims. I tried to tell myself that sometimes it took more courage to step away from the grief of another than to participate in it.

I felt a puff of cool air rise from the floor and I looked down through a crack in the linoleum, through a rotted plank, at a pool of water under the house with purple martins fluttering their wings in it. Then I realized the birds inside the house had not come from the chimney. But it wasn't the birds that caught my attention. One of the cinder-block pilings was orange with rust that had leaked from a crossbeam onto the stone.

I went back outside and lay flat on my stomach and crawled under the house. Three feet beyond the rear wall, wedged between the crossbeam and the cinder-block piling, was a one-handed weed sickle. I pried it loose and crawled back into the sunlight. The short wood handle was intact, but the half-moon blade had rusted into lace.

I slipped the sickle handle-first into a Ziploc bag and knocked on Passion's door.

'This is the instrument that slung blood on the ceiling

and walls. Letty hit him with the mattock and you used this,' I said when Passion came to the door.

'It look like a piece of junk to me,' she said.

'I came out here because I feel an obligation to your sister. But I don't have time for any more of y'all's bullshit. I'm going to bust Little Face Dautrieve as a material witness and make her life miserable. She'll stay in jail until she tells me what happened and in the meantime Social Services will take her baby. Is that how you want it to play out?'

'You seen the paper today?' she asked.

'No.'

'The Supreme Court won't hear any more of Letty's appeals. Unless Belmont Pugh commute her sentence, she's gonna die. You want to know what happened? I'm gonna tell you. Then you can carry it down to your office and do whatever you want to wit' it.'

Her face was wan, her eyes unfocused inside the gloom of the house, as though she didn't recognize the words she had just spoken. But suddenly I felt my victory was about to become ashes in my mouth. She studied my face through the screen, then pushed open the door and waited for me to come inside.

Eight years ago Passion and Letty looked out their side window in dismay at the return of their neighbor, Vachel Carmouche. In their minds he had been assigned to their past, to a world of dreams and aberrant memories that dissipated with time and had no application in their adult lives. Now they watched him blow his gallery clean of birds' nests with a pressure hose while crushing the tiny eggs under his rubber boots; they watched him pry the plywood covering from his windows, hoe out a vegetable patch, and drink lemonade in the shade, a small sip at a time, like a man who was stintful even with his own pleasure, his starched and pressed gray work clothes and gray cloth cap unstained by sweat, as though the rigidity that characterized his life allowed him to control the secretion in his glands.

They left the house and went grocery shopping, hoping somehow he would be gone when they returned and a rental sign would be standing in the yard. Instead, they saw him moving his belongings into the house, ignoring Passion and Letty as though they were not there. They saw him split open a ripe watermelon and ease chunks of it off a knife blade into his mouth, his face suffused with a self-contained sensual glow. In the evening shadows they saw him scythe weeds out of his front yard and fire a barbecue pit and impale a pork roast on its rotisserie; they saw him pack rock salt and ice into a hand-crank ice cream maker, then give a quarter to a twelve-year-old black girl to turn the crank for him. They saw him press the coin into her palm and fold his fingers over her fist and smile down at her, her upraised eyes only inches from his gleaming cowboy belt buckle and the flatness of his stomach and the dry heat that emanated from his clothes.

Letty went into the yard with a paper sack and walked among the trees in front, picking up scraps of paper that had blown off the road. She waited until Carmouche went into his house, then called the little girl over.

'What are you doing around here?' she asked.

'Visiting my auntie up the road,' Little Face replied.

'Go back home. Stay away from that white man.'

'My auntie left me here. She rent from Mr Vachel.'

Letty squatted down and looked directly into Little Face's eyes.

'Has he touched you? Put his hand somewhere he shouldn't?' she said.

'No, ma'am. He ain't like that.'

'You listen to me –' Letty began, squeezing the girl's arm. Then she looked past Little Face's head at the silhouette of Vachel Carmouche, who stood in the drive now, leaves swirling around his shoes, the early moon like a pink wafer in the sky behind him.

He pinched the brim of his cloth cap with two fingers.

'Been a long time. You grown into a handsome woman, Miss Letty,' he said.

'Why'd you come back?' she said.

'A lot of building going on. A man with electrical knowledge can make a good deal of money right now.'

'You get your goddamn feet off my property,' she said.

'You might be righteous now. But you and your sister were always switching your rear ends around when you wanted something.'

'I can't tell you how much I hate you,' Letty said, rising to her feet.

'What you hate are your own sins. Think back, Letty. Remember how you'd turn somersaults on the lawn, grinning and giggling at me? You were thirteen years old when you did that. Now you reprimand me and blaspheme God's name in front of a child.'

Carmouche put his hand in Little Face's and led her back onto his property. The white streaks of cornstarch that had been ironed into his gray clothes recalled an image out of Letty's memory that made her shut her eyes.

Letty worked in the back yard, raking the winter thatch out of her garden, thrusting a spade deep into the black soil, taking a strange pleasure when the blade crushed a slug or cut through the body of a night crawler. Her flannel shirt became heavy with sweat and she flung the spade on the ground and went inside the house and showered with hot water until her skin was as red and grained as old brick.

'We'll try to do something about him tomorrow,' Passion said.

'Do what?' Letty said, tying the belt around her terry-cloth robe.

'Call Social Services. Tell them about the little girl.'

'Maybe they'll hep her like they hepped us, huh?'

'What else you want to do, kill him?' Passion said.

'I wish. I really wish.'

Passion walked over to her sister and put her arms around her. She could smell a fragrance of strawberries in her hair.

'It's gonna be all right. We can make him move away. We're grown now. He cain't hurt us anymore,' she said.

'I want him to pay.'

Passion held her sister against her, stroking her back, feeling her sister's breath on her neck. Through the second-story window she could see down into Vachel Carmouche's backyard. Her face tingled and a bilious taste rose into her mouth.

'What is it?' Letty said, stepping back and looking at her sister's expression. Then she turned around and looked down into Vachel Carmouche's yard.

He had set Little Face on his knee and was feeding ice cream to her with a spoon. Each time he placed the spoon between her lips he smoothed back her hair, then wiped the drippings from the corners of her mouth with the backs of his fingers. He kissed her forehead and filled another spoonful of ice cream and placed a fresh strawberry on it. She opened her mouth like a bird, but he withdrew the spoon quickly, offering and withdrawing it again and again, and finally putting it into her mouth and lifting the spoon handle up so as not to drop any of the melted ice cream on her chin.

Letty charged barefoot down the stairs, tearing the sole of one foot on an exposed nailhead. She found a pair of work shoes in the downstairs closet and leaned against the wall with one arm and pulled them on.

'He used to keep a shotgun,' Passion said.

'He put his hand on it, I'll shove it up his ass. You coming or not?' Letty said.

They went out the back door, into the twilight, into the smell of spring and cut grass and newly turned dirt and night-blooming flowers opening in the cool of the evening. They crossed into Vachel Carmouche's property, expecting to see him on his back porch with the little girl, expecting to confront and verbally lacerate him for a deed he had committed out in the open, upon the person of a third victim, a deed he could not possibly deny, as though Passion's and Letty's knowledge of their own molestation had long ago lost its viability and had to be corroborated by the suffering of another in order to make it believable.

But Carmouche was nowhere in sight. The little girl sat on the back step, coloring in a crayon book.

'What did he do to you, honey?' Letty said.

'Ain't done nothing. He gone inside to eat his dinner,' the girl replied.

'Did he touch you?' Passion said.

The little girl did not look back at them. A bright silver dime was on the step by her shoe.

'Mr Vachel gonna take me up to the video store to get some cartoons,' she said.

'You come home wit' us. We'll call your auntie,' Letty said.

'She at work. I ain't suppose to go nowhere except Mr Vachel's.'

Letty mounted the steps and shoved open the back door. Carmouche was sitting at the kitchen table, his back erect, his whole posture as rectangular as his chair, a fork poised in front of his mouth. He laid the fork down and picked up a glass of yellow wine.

'I'd appreciate it if you'd show some respect toward my home,' he said.

'You sonofabitch,' she said, and stepped inside the

room. When she did, the belt around her waist came loose and her terry-cloth robe fell open on her body.

Carmouche's eyes moved over her breasts and stomach and thighs. He sipped from his wine and pushed back his chair and crossed his legs.

'Some say love's the other side of hate. You're a beautiful woman, Letty. An older man can bring a woman pleasure a younger man cain't,' he said, his voice growing more hoarse with each word.

He rose from his chair and approached her, his eyes liquid and warm under the bare electric light. She clutched her robe with one hand and stepped backwards, then felt her work shoe come down on the iron head of the mattock that was propped against the wall, knocking the handle into her back.

She reached behind her and picked the mattock up with both hands, her robe falling open again, and swung it into his face.

His nose broke and slung a string of blood across his shoulder. He stared at her in disbelief and she hit him again, this time directly in his overbite, breaking his upper teeth at the gums. His face quivered as though he had been electrically shocked, then the thousands of tiny wrinkles in his face flattened with rage and he attacked her with his fists.

He swung wildly, like a girl, but he was strong and driven by his pain and the disfigurement she had already done his face and she knew it was only a matter of time until he wrested the mattock from her.

His hands locked on the handle, his nose draining blood across his mouth, his broken teeth like ragged pieces of ceramic in his gums. She closed her eyes against the stench of his breath.

Passion picked up the weed sickle from the porch step and came through the door and drove the curved point into Carmouche's back, pushing with the heel of her hand against the dull side of the blade. His mouth fell open and his chin jutted upward like a man who had been garroted. He fell backwards, stumbling, reaching behind him with one hand as though he could insert a thumb in the hole that was stealing the air from his lung.

He collapsed on one knee, his eyes suddenly luminous, like a man kneeling inside a cave filled with specters whose existence he had long ago forgotten.

Letty hit him again and again with the mattock while Passion shut the back door so the little girl could not see inside the house. Letty's robe and work shoes and arms and thighs were splattered with Carmouche's blood, but her violence and anger found no satiation, and a muted, impotent cry came from between her teeth each time she swung the mattock.

Passion put her hand on her sister's shoulder and moved her away from Carmouche's body.

'What? What is it?' Letty said, as though awakening from a trance.

Passion didn't reply. Instead, she lifted the sickle above her head and looked into Carmouche's eyes.

'Don't . . . please,' he said, his hand fluttering toward his cowboy belt buckle.

Then Passion's arm came down and Letty pressed both her forearms against her ears so she would not hear the sound that came from his throat.

chapter twenty-three

I went home instead of returning to the office. I sat at one of the spool tables on the dock, the Cinzano umbrella popping in the breeze above my head, and looked at the blue jays flying in and out of the cypress and willow trees. I watched the clouds marble the swamp with shadow and light, and the wind from the Gulf straightening the moss on the dead snags. I stayed there a long time, although I didn't look at my watch, like a person who has strayed unknowingly into the showing of a pornographic film and would like to rinse himself of a new and unwanted awareness about human behavior.

The story of Carmouche's death was repellent. I wished I had not heard it, and I wished I did not have to make decisions about it.

I walked up to the house and told Bootsie of my morning with Passion Labiche.

She didn't say anything for perhaps a full minute. She got up from the kitchen table and stood at the sink and looked into the yard.

'What are you going to do?' she asked, her back to me.

'Nothing she told me can help her sister.'

'You have the sickle in the truck?'

'I put it back under the house.'

I went to the stove and poured a cup of coffee. She turned around and followed me with her eyes.

'You're going across a line, Dave,' she said.

'I virtually coerced a confession out of her. I don't know if Carmouche deserved to die the way he did, but I know the girls didn't deserve what happened to them.'

She walked to the stove and slipped her hand down my forearm and hooked her fingers under my palm.

'You know what I would do?' she said.

'What?' I said, turning to look at her.

'Start the day over. You set out to help Passion and Letty. Why bring them more harm? If Letty were tried today, she might go free. You want to enable a process that's already ignored the injury done to two innocent children?'

Bootsie was forever the loyal friend and knew what to say in order to make me feel better. But the real problem was one that went beyond suppression of non-exculpatory evidence in a crime of eight years ago. I was tired of daily convincing myself that what I did for a living made a difference.

I fixed a ham and onion sandwich for myself and ate it on the picnic table in the backyard. A few minutes later Bootsie came outside and sat down across from me, a small cardboard box in her hand.

'I hate to hit you with this right now, but this came in the morning mail. Alafair left it on her bed. I shouldn't have read the letter, but I did when I saw the name at the bottom,' she said.

The box was packed with tissue paper and contained a six-inch-high ceramic vase that was painted with miniature climbing roses and a Confederate soldier and a woman in a hoop dress holding each other's hands in an arbor of live oaks. The detail and the contrast of gray and red and green were beautiful inside the glazed finish.

The letter, handwritten on expensive stationery and folded in a neat square, read:

Dear Alafair,

I hope you don't think too badly of me by this time. Your father cares for you and wants to protect you, so I don't hold his feelings toward me against him. This is the vase I was working on. I tried to make the girl look like you. What do you think? You can't see the face of the Confederate soldier. I'll let you imagine who he is.

I wish I could have lived in a time like the soldier and the girl on the vase did. People back then were decent and had honor and looked after each other.

You're one of the best people I ever met. If you ever need me, I promise I will be there for you. Nobody will ever make me break that promise.

Your devoted friend from the library,
Johnny

'Where is she?' I asked.

'At the swimming pool.' Bootsie watched my face. 'What are you thinking?'

'That boy is definitely not a listener.'

I went back to the office and placed another call to the psychologist at the Florida State Penitentiary in Raiford. It wasn't long before I knew I was talking to one of those condescending, incompetent bureaucrats whose sole purpose is to hold on to their jobs and hide their paucity of credentials.

'You're asking me if he has obsessions?' the psychologist said.

'In a word, yeah.'

'We don't have an adequate vocabulary to describe what some of these people have.'

'You don't have to convince me of that,' I said.

'He was a suspect in a killing here. A gasoline bomb

253

thrown inside another inmate's cell. Your man was probably raped. You were faxed everything we have. I don't know what else to tell you about him.'

'Wait a minute. You didn't know him?'

'No. I thought you all understood that. Dr Louvas worked with O'Roarke, or Remeta, as you call him. Dr Louvas is at Marion now.'

'Excuse me for seeming impatient, but why didn't you tell me that?'

'You didn't ask. Is there anything else?'

I called the federal lockup at Marion, Illinois, and got Dr Louvas on the phone. His was a different cut from his colleague in Florida.

'Yeah, I remember Johnny well. Actually I liked him. I wouldn't suggest having him over for dinner, though,' he said.

'How's that?'

'He has two or three personalities. Oh, I don't mean he suffers dissociation, or any of that *Three Faces of Eve* stuff. He has an abiding sense of anger that he refuses to deal with. If he'd gotten help earlier, he might have turned out to be a writer or artist instead of a candidate for a lobotomy.'

'Because he was raped in prison?'

'His father would take him to a blind pig on skid row. That's what they call after-hours places in Detroit. According to Johnny, a couple of pedophiles would use him while the old man got drunk on their tab. Family values hadn't made a big splash in the Detroit area yet.'

'So he's hung up over his father?'

'You got it all wrong, Mr Robicheaux. He doesn't blame the father for what happened to him. He thinks the mother betrayed him. He's never gotten over what he perceives as her failure.'

'He's making overtures to my daughter.'

There was no response.

254

'Are you there?' I asked.

'You're asking me to tell you his future? My bet is Johnny will do himself in one day. But he'll probably take others with him,' the psychologist said.

The next morning I drove to Baton Rouge and went to Connie Deshotel's office. The secretary told me Connie used her lunch hour on Thursdays to play racquetball at a nearby club.

The club was dazzling white, surrounded with palm trees that were planted in white gravel; the swimming pool in back was an electric blue under the noon sun. Inside the building, I looked down through a viewing glass onto the hardwood floor of a racquetball court and watched Connie take apart her male opponent. She wore tennis shoes with green tubes of compressed air molded into the rubber soles, a pleated tennis skirt, and a sleeveless yellow jersey that was ringed under the neck and arms with sweat. Her tanned calves hardened with muscle when she bent to make a kill shot.

Her opponent, a tall, graying, athletic man, gave it up, shook hands good-naturedly, and left. She bounced the rubber ball once, served the ball to herself off the wall, then fired it into a low ricochet that sent it arching over her head, as though she were involved in a private celebration of her victory. Her eyes followed the ball's trajectory until they met mine. Then her face tightened, and she pushed her hair out of her eyes and left the court through a door in the back wall, slamming it behind her.

I went down the stairs and intercepted her in the lounge area.

'I have some information about my mother's death,' I said.

'Not here.'

'You're not going to put me off, Connie.'

'What is it?'

I gestured at a table.

'I'm leaving here in two minutes. But I'll make you a promise. You follow me anywhere again and I'll have you arrested,' she said.

'I have a witness.'

'To what?'

'My mother's murder. Two cops in uniform did it. In front of a cabin a few miles off Purple Cane Road in Lafourche Parish. One of them called her an ignorant bitch before he knocked her down.'

Her eyes stared into mine, unblinking, her lashes like black wire. Then they broke and she looked at nothing and pulled the dampness of her jersey off the tops of her breasts.

'Bring your witness forward,' she said.

'Nope.'

'Why not?'

'I think the individual would end up dead,' I said.

'You don't want to indicate the person's gender to me? I'm the attorney general of the state. What's the matter with you?'

'You trust Don Ritter. I don't. I think he tried to have both me and Johnny Remeta killed.'

She motioned at a black waiter in a white jacket. He nodded and began pouring a club soda into a glass of ice for her. She touched the sweat off her eyes with a towel and hung the towel around her neck.

'I'll say it again. My office is at your disposal. But a lot of this sounds like paranoia and conspiratorial obsession,' she said.

'The cops were NOPD.'

'How do you know this?'

'They killed a Lafourche Parish nightclub owner named Ladrine Theriot and made a local constable take the weight. They weren't backwoods coon-asses, either. They were enforcers and bagmen for the Giacanos. So if they weren't New Orleans cops, where did they come from?'

She took the club soda from the waiter's hand and drank it half-empty. The heat seemed to go out of her face but not her eyes.

'You have a larger agenda, Dave. I think it has something to do with me,' she said.

'Not me. By the way, you play a mean game of racquetball for a woman who smokes.'

'How kind.'

'The other day I noticed your gold and leather cigarette lighter. Did Jim Gable give you that? Y'all must be pretty tight.'

She got up from the table with her club soda in her hand.

'My apologies to Bootsie for saying this, but you're the most annoying person I've ever met,' she said, and walked toward the dressing room, her pleated skirt swishing across the tops of her thighs.

'You *read* my mail?' Alafair said. It was evening, the sun deep down in the trees now, and she was grooming Tex, her Appaloosa, in the railed lot by his shed. She stared at me across his back.

'The letter was lying on your bed. Bootsie saw Johnny's name on it. It was inadvertent,' I replied.

'You didn't have the right to read it.'

'Maybe not. Maybe you know what you're doing. But I believe he's a dangerous man.'

'Not the Johnny O'Roarke I know.'

'You always stood up for your friends, Alafair. But this guy is not a friend. The prison psychologist said he's a sick man who will probably die by his own hand and take other people with him.'

'Bullshit, bullshit, bullshit.'

'How about it on the language?'

'You admit he saved our lives, but you run him down and take his head apart, a person you don't know anything about, then you tell me to watch my language. I just don't expect crap like that from my father.'

'Has he tried to see you?'

'I'm not going to tell you. It's none of your business.'

'Remeta's a meltdown, Alf.'

'Don't call me that stupid name! God!' she said, and threw down the brush she had been using on Tex and stormed inside the house.

That night I dreamed about a sugar harvest in the late fall and mule-drawn wagons loaded with cane moving through the fog toward the mill. The dirt road was frozen hard and littered with stalks of sugarcane, and the fog rolled out of the unharvested cane on each side of the road like colorless cotton candy and coated the mules' and drivers' backs with moisture. Up ahead the tin outline of the mill loomed against the grayness of the sky, and inside I could hear the sounds of boilers overheating and iron machines that pulverized the cane into pulp. Immediately behind the mill a stubble fire burned in a field, creeping in serpentine red lines through the mist.

The dream filled me with a fear I could not explain. But I knew, with a terrible sense of urgency, I could not allow myself to go farther down the road, into the mill and the grinding sounds of its machinery and the fire and curds of yellow smoke that rose from the field beyond.

The scene changed, and I was on board my cabin cruiser at dawn, on West Cote Blanche Bay, and the fogbank was heavy and cold on the skin, sliding with the tide into the coastline. To the north I could see Avery Island, like two green humps in the mist, as smooth and firm-looking as a woman's breasts. The waves burst in strings of foam against the white sleekness of the bow, and I could smell the salt spray inside my head and bait fish in a bucket and the speckled trout that arched out of the waves and left circles like rain rings in the stillness of the swells.

When I woke I went into the kitchen and sat in the dark, my loins aching and my palms tingling on my thighs. I held a damp hand towel to my eyes and tried to think but couldn't. Even though I was awake now, I did not want to look at the meaning behind the dreams. I went back to bed and felt Bootsie stir, then touch my chest and turn on her hip and mold her body against me.

She was already wet when I entered her, and she widened her thighs and hooked her feet loosely inside my legs, slipping one hand down to the small of my back while she moved in a slow, circular fashion under me, as she always did when she wanted to preserve the moment for both of us as long as she could.

But I felt the heat rise in me, like fire climbing upward along a hard, bare surface, then my mouth opened involuntarily and I closed my eyes and pressed my face between her breasts.

I sat on the edge of the bed, depleted, my face in shadow, one hand still covering the tops of Bootsie's fingers, ashamed that I had used my wife to hide from the violent act I knew my alcoholic mind was planning.

chapter twenty-four

Early Sunday morning I heard a car with a blown muffler pull into the drive and continue to the back of the house before the driver cut the engine. I slipped on my khakis and went into the kitchen and looked into the backyard and saw Clete Purcel sitting alone at the redwood picnic table, his Marine Corps utility cap on his head. He had a take-out cup of coffee between his hands, and he kept looking over his shoulder at the dirt road.

I went outside and eased the screen shut so as not to wake Bootsie and Alafair.

'What are you doing?' I asked.

He looked sideways, then pulled on his nose and let his breath out.

'I went after Ritter. Nobody's been by?'

'No.'

'The shit went through the fan.'

'I don't want to know about it.'

'I was trying to help. You got somebody else willing to cover your back on a daily basis?'

He looked miserable. He rubbed his face, then knocked over his paper cup and spilled coffee on his hands.

'Tell me,' I said.

'Ritter had dials on this stripper, Janet Gish. She'd been washing stolen money at the Indian casinos for some Jersey wise guys. Ritter nailed the wise guys but he left her out of the bust. The deal was she had to come across for him at least once a month. Guess what? Janet developed the hots for Ritter, can you believe it? So he knew he had a good thing and he played along with her and said he was going to marry her as soon as he could dump his wife. In the meantime he was bopping Janet every Friday afternoon at a motel on Airline.

'Last week she's in the supermarket and who does she see? Ritter and his old lady. Ritter looks right through Janet and studies these cans of beans on the shelf like he's never seen one before. But what's Ritter supposed to do? she asks herself. Introduce her? Except she's in the next aisle now and she hears Ritter's old lady say, "Did you see that? She's got jugs like gallon milk bottles. With tattoos yet. You didn't notice?"

'Ritter says, "I was never attracted to Elsie the Cow types." They both thought that was a real laugh.

'Janet decides it's payback time. She's got a bond on a soliciting charge with Nig and Wee Willie and she calls me up and asks if I can get the DA to cut her loose on the soliciting beef if she gives up Ritter. I told her that was a possibility but the DA would probably make her take the weight on the money laundering deal and maybe there was a better way to spike Ritter's cannon.

'I got her to call up Ritter's old lady at midnight and tell her she was sorry Don didn't introduce the two of them at the supermarket because they probably have a lot in common. Then Janet goes into detail about Ritter's sex habits and says it's too bad Ritter uses the same old tired line with all his broads, namely that his wife is a drag at home and an embarrassment at departmental social functions and he's shit-canning her as soon as he can make sure all the bills and charge accounts are under her name.

'It took about ten minutes for Ritter to come tearing

across the bridge to Janet's place on the West Bank. She dead-bolted the back door on him and he got a ball peen hammer out of his convertible and started smashing the glass out of the door and trying to get his hand on the lock. That's when I clocked him with the bird bath.'

'You hit him with a cement bird bath?' I said.

'Hear me out, okay? Janet's brother owns this car wash behind the apartment. Ritter's half out of it, so I put him in the passenger seat of his convertible and hooked him up to the door handle with his cuffs and drove him up to the car wash entrance.

'I go, "Don, you're a dirty cop. Now's the time to rinse your sins, start over again, try keeping your flopper in your pants for a change. You set up that gig on the Atchafalaya and almost got my podjo, Dave, killed, didn't you?"

'He goes, "No matter how this comes out, you're still a skell, Purcel."

'So I drove his convertible onto the conveyor and pushed all the buttons for the super clean and hot wax job. The pressure hoses came on and those big brushes dipped down inside the car and were scouring Ritter into the seats. I shut it down and gave him another chance, but he started yelling and blowing the horn, so I turned everything back on and stalled the conveyor and left him there with the steam blowing out both ends of the building.'

'You're telling me Ritter's still in there?' I said.

'Yes and no.' His mouth was cone-shaped when he breathed through it. 'I had my hands full. Janet was getting hysterical and breaking things and throwing her clothes in a suitcase. Then I heard two popping sounds, like firecrackers in the rain. I went back to the car wash but there wasn't anybody around. Except Ritter floating face-down in all that soap and wax. He'd taken one in the ear and one through the mouth.'

I got up from the table and looked out at my neighbor's field and at the fog rising out of the coulee, my back turned to Clete so he couldn't see my face.

When I turned around again Clete's eyes were jittering with light, his lips moving uncertainly, like a drunk coming off a bender when he doesn't know whether he should laugh or not at what he has done.

Then his eyes fixed on mine and his expression went flat and he said, as though by explanation, 'This one went south on me.'

'Yeah, I guess it did, Clete.'

'That's all you're going to say?'

'Come inside. I'll fix you something to eat,' I said as I walked past him toward the house.

'Streak? . . . Damn it, don't give me that look.'

But I went through the kitchen into the bath and brushed my teeth and put cold water on my face and tried not to think the thoughts I was thinking or take my anger out on a friend who had put himself in harm's way on my account. But I believed Ritter'd had knowledge about my mother's death and now it was gone.

I dried my face and went back into the kitchen.

'You want me to boogie?' Clete said.

'Get the skillet out of the cabinet, then call Nig and Wee Willie and tell them you'll need a bond,' I said as I took a carton of eggs and a slab of bacon from the icebox.

After we ate breakfast, Bootsie, Alafair, and I went to Mass. When we got back, Clete was down at the dock, sitting at a spool table under an umbrella, reading the newspaper. From a distance he looked like a relaxed and content man enjoying the fine day, but I knew better. Clete had no doubt about the gravity of his actions. Once again his recklessness had empowered his enemies and he

263

now hung by a spider's thread over the maw of the system.

Television programs treat the legal process as an intelligent and orderly series of events that eventually punishes the guilty and exonerates the innocent. The reality is otherwise. The day you get involved with the law is the day you lose all control over your life. What is dismissed by the uninitiated as 'a night in jail' means sitting for an indeterminable amount of time in a holding cell, with a drain hole in the floor, looking at hand-soiled walls scrawled with pictures of genitalia, listening to other inmates yell incoherently down the corridors while cops yell back and clang their batons on the bars.

You ask permission to use a toilet. When you run out of cigarettes or matches, you beg them off a screw through the bars. Your *persona*, your identity, and all the social courtesy you take for granted are removed from your existence like the skin being pulled off a banana. When you look through a window onto the street, you realize you do not register on the periphery of what are called free people. Your best hope of getting back outside lies with a bondsman who secretes Vitalis through his pores or a twenty-four-hour Yellow Pages lawyer who wears zircon rings on his fingers and keeps a breath mint on his tongue. We're only talking about day one.

That afternoon I finally got Dana Magelli on the phone.

'Clete says the entry wounds look like they came from a .22 or .25,' I said.

'Thank him for his feedback on that.'

'He didn't do it, Dana. It was a professional hit. I think we're talking about Johnny Remeta.'

'Except Purcel has a way of stringing elephant shit behind him everywhere he goes.'

'You want me to bring him in?'

'Take a guess.'

'We'll be there in three hours.'

There was a long silence and I knew Magelli's basic decency was having its way with him.

'IAD has been looking at Ritter for a month. Tell Purcel to come in and give a statement. Then get him out of town,' he said.

'Pardon?'

'Janet Gish confirms his story. We don't need zoo creatures muddying up the water right now. You hearing me?'

'You're looking at some other cops?'

He ignored my question. 'I mean it about Purcel. He's not just a pain in the ass. In my view he's one cut above the clientele in Angola. He mixes in our business again, I'll turn the key on him myself,' Magelli said.

I replaced the receiver in the phone cradle on top of the counter in the bait shop. Through the screen window I could see Clete at a spool table, watching an outboard pass on the bayou, his face divided by sunlight and shadow. I walked outside the bait shop and looked down at him.

'That was Dana Magelli. You're going to skate,' I said.

He beamed at me, and I realized all the lessons he should have learned had just blown away in the breeze.

The next day NOPD matched the .25 caliber rounds taken from Don Ritter's body to the .25 caliber round that was fired into Zipper Clum's forehead.

That night Alafair went with friends to the McDonald's on East Main. She came home later than we expected her and gave no explanation. I followed her into her bedroom. Tripod was outside the screen on the windowsill, but she had made no effort to let him in. The light was off in the room and Alafair's face was covered with shadow.

'What happened tonight?' I asked.

'Whenever I tell you the truth about something, it makes you mad.'

'I've shown bad judgment, Alafair. I'm just not a good learner sometimes.'

'I saw Johnny. I took a ride with him.'

I ran my hand along the side of my head. I could feel a tightening in my veins, as though I had a hat on. I took a breath before I spoke.

'With Remeta?' I said.

'Yes.'

'He's wanted in another shooting. An execution at point-blank range in a car wash.'

'I told him I couldn't see him again. I'm going to sleep now, Dave. I don't want to talk about Johnny anymore,' she said.

She sat on the edge of her bed and waited for me to go out of the room. On the shelf above her bedstead I could see the painted ceramic vase Remeta had given to her, the Confederate soldier and his antebellum girlfriend glowing in the moonlight.

The call came at four in the morning.

'You told your daughter not to see me again?' the voice asked.

'Not in so many words,' I replied.

'That was a chickenshit thing to do.'

'You're too old for her, Johnny.'

'People can't be friends because they're apart in years? Run your lies on somebody else.'

'Your problems began long before we met. Don't take them out on us.'

'What do you know about my problems?'

'I talked with the prison psychologist.'

'I'm starting to construct a new image of you, Mr Robicheaux. It's not a good one.'

I didn't reply. The skin of my face felt flaccid and full of needles. Then, to change the subject, I said, 'You should have lost the .25 you used on Zipper Clum. NOPD has made you for the Ritter hit.'

'Ritter gave up your mother's killers, Mr Robicheaux. I was gonna give you their names. Maybe even cap them for you. But you act like I'm the stink on shit. Now I say fuck you,' he said, and hung up.

At 9 AM I sat in the sheriff's office and watched the sheriff core out the inside of his pipe with a pen knife.

'So you got to see the other side of Johnny Remeta?' he said, and dropped the black build-up of ash off his knife blade into the waste basket.

'He pumped Ritter for information, then blew out his light,' I said.

'This guy is making us look like a collection of web-toed hicks, Dave. He comes and goes when he feels like it. He takes your daughter for rides. He murders a police officer and calls you up in the middle of the night and tells you about it. Forgive me for what I'm about to say next.'

'Sir?'

'Do you want this guy out on the ground? It seems you and he and Purcel have the same enemies.'

'I don't think that's a cool speculation to make, Sheriff.'

'Let me put it this way. The next time I hear this guy's name, it had better be in conjunction with either his arrest or death. I don't want one of my detectives telling me about his phone conversations with a psychopath or his family's involvement with same. Are we clear?'

'There're pipe ashes on your boot,' I said, and left the room.

Ten minutes later I received a phone call from a woman

who did not identify herself but just started talking as though I already knew who she was. She had a heavy Cajun accent and her voice was knotted with anger and dismay and a need to injure.

'I t'ought you'd like to know what you done. Not that it makes no difference to somebody who t'inks he got the right to twist a sick man up wit' his words,' she said.

'Who is this?' I asked.

But she kept wading in. 'You was a lot smarter than him, you. You know how to put t'oughts in somebody's head, make him full of guilt, fix it so he cain't go nowhere in his head except t'rew one door. So it ain't enough leprosy eat him up and turn his hands to nutria feet. Man like you got to come along and push him and push him and push him till he so full of misery he gonna do what you want.'

Then I remembered the duck-shaped blind woman who had been hanging wash behind the cabin of Bobby Cale, the ex-constable, down by Point au Fer.

'Did something happen to Bobby?' I said.

She couldn't answer. She started weeping into the phone.

'Ma'am, tell me what it is,' I said.

'I smelled it on the wind. Out in the persimmon trees. He was gone t'ree days, then I found him and touched him and he swung in my hands, light as bird shell. You done this, suh. Don't be telling yourself you innocent, no. 'Cause you ain't.'

The side of my head felt numb after I hung up, as though a dirty revelation about myself had just been whispered in my ear. But I wasn't sure if my sense of regret was over the possibility that I was a contributing factor in the suicide of Bobby Cale or the fact I had just lost my only tangible lead back to my mother's killers.

chapter twenty-five

The Shrimp Festival was held each year at the end of summer down by the bay. On Friday, when the day cooled and the summer light filled the evening sky, shrimp boats festooned with pennants and flags blew their horns in the canal and a cleric blessed the fleet while thousands wandered up and down a carnival midway, drinking from beer cups and eating shrimp off paper plates. College students, the working classes, and politicians from all over the state took part. Inside the cacophony of calliopes and the popping of .22 rifles in the shooting galleries and the happy shrieks that cascaded down from a Ferris wheel, the celebrants took on the characteristics of figures in a Brueghel painting, any intimations about mortality they may have possessed now lost in the balm of the season.

Belmont Pugh was there, and Jim Gable and his wife, and by the Tilt-a-Whirl I saw Connie Deshotel in an evening dress, carrying a pair of silver shoes in one hand, her other on her escort's arm for balance, her cleavage deep with shadow.

But the figure who caught my eye was outside the circle of noise and light that rose into the sky from the midway. Micah, Cora Gable's chauffeur, sat beside the Gables' limo on a folding canvas stool, tossing pieces of dirt at a beer can, his jaws slack, like a man who doesn't care what others think of his appearance or state of mind. A rolled comic book protruded from the side pocket of his black coat.

I left Bootsie at the drink pavilion and walked into the parking area and stood no more than three feet in front of him. He raised his eyes, then tinked a dirt clod against the beer can, his face indifferent.

'Looks like you're in the dumps, partner,' I said.

He flexed his mouth, as though working a bit of food out of his gums. 'I'm finishing out my last week,' he replied.

'You're not working for Ms Gable anymore?'

'She thinks I sassed her. It was a misunderstanding. But I guess it helped her husband.'

'Sassed her?'

'We were passing all these shacks where the sugarcane workers used to live. Ms Perez says to herself, "The glory that was Rome."'

'So I say, "It sure wasn't any glory, was it?"'

'She says, "Beg your pardon?"'

'I say, "Rich man got the poor whites to fight with the coloreds so the whole bunch would work for near nothing while the rich man got richer." It got real quiet in the car.'

'Sounds like you got your hand on it, Micah,' I said.

'Tell me about it,' he said resentfully. 'I looked in the rearview mirror and her face was tight as paper, like it had got slapped. She says, "This land belonged to my family. So I suggest you keep your own counsel."'

He removed the comic book from his pocket and tapped it in his palm, his anger seeming to rise and fall, as though it could not find an acceptable target.

'Doesn't seem like that's enough to get a person fired,' I said.

'Gable's been acting good to her lately. I think she's

gonna let him have the money to build that racetrack out in New Mexico. I had to be a smart ass at the wrong time and give him what he needed to get me canned.'

'You cut up Axel Jennings, Micah?'

He opened his comic book and flopped the pages back on his knee, thinking, his deformed face like a melted candied apple in the glow from the midway.

'You're always trying to get another inch, aren't you? I'll give you something better to chew on,' he said. 'You know a woman named Maggie Glick, runs a bar full of colored whores in Algiers? It was Jim Gable got her out of prison. Gable's got a whole network of whores and dope peddlers working for him. That's the man gonna be head of your state police, Mr Robicheaux. Play your cards right and there might be a little pissant job in it for you somewhere.'

He smiled at the corner of his mouth, a glint in his good eye.

'Some people enjoy the role of victim. Maybe you've found what you were looking for, after all,' I said, and walked away, wondering if I, too, possessed a potential for cruelty I had chosen not to recognize.

When I returned to the pavilion I realized I had made a mistake. Belmont Pugh had cornered Connie Deshotel and Bootsie and there was no easy way of getting away from the situation. Belmont had launched into one of his oratorical performances, guffawing, gesturing at the air like Huey Long, slinging shrimp tails out into the darkness, the damp rawness of his body reaching out like a fist. He squeezed Connie with one arm while his wife, a black-haired woman with recessed dark eyes and a neck like a hog, looked on sternly, as though her disapproval of Belmont's behavior somehow removed her from all the machinations and carnival vulgarity that had placed her and her husband in the governor's mansion.

Sookie Motrie stood at Belmont's elbow, dressed in the two-tone boots and clothes of a horse tout at a western track, his salt-and-pepper mustache clipped and trim, his snubbed, hawk nose moving about like a weather vane. For years he had been an ambulance chaser in Baton Rouge and had self-published a detective novel that he tried to unload on every movie representative who visited the area. But he had found his true level as well as success when he became a lobbyist for Vegas and Chicago gambling interests. Even though he had been indicted twice on RICO charges, no door in the state legislature or at any of the regulatory agencies was closed to him.

He laughed when Belmont did and listened attentively to Belmont's coarse jokes, but still managed to watch everyone passing by and to shake the hand, even if quickly, of anyone he deemed important.

Jim and Cora Gable stood at the makeshift plank bar that sold mint juleps in plastic cups for three dollars. He wore a pale pink shirt and dark tie with roses on it and a white sports coat, his face glowing with the perfection of the evening. No, that's too simple. I had to hand it to Gable. He exuded the confidence and self-satisfaction of those who know that real power lies in not having to demonstrate its possession. Every gesture, every mannerism, was like an extension of his will and his ability to charm, a statement about a meticulous personality that allowed no exception to its own rules. He walked toward Belmont's circle and lifted a sprig of mint from his drink and shook the drops from the leaves, bending slightly so as not to spot his shoes.

Cora Gable started to raise her hand, her lipsticked mouth twisting with alarm, like someone left behind unexpectedly at a bus stop. But almost on cue, as though Gable were privy to all the unconscious anxieties that drove her life, he turned and said, 'I'll be just a minute, sweetheart. Order another julep.'

Belmont asked Connie if she knew Jim Gable.

'I'm not sure. Maybe we met years ago,' she replied.

'How do you do, Miss Connie? It's good to see you,' Gable said.

They did not look directly at each other again; they even stepped backwards at the same time, like people who have nothing in common.

I stared at the two of them, as though the moment had been caught inside a cropped photograph whose meaning lay outside the borders of the camera's lens. Both Gable and Connie had come up through the ranks at NOPD back in the late 1960s. How could they have no specific memory of each other?

Then Connie Deshotel lit a cigarette, as though she were distracted by thoughts that would not come together in her mind. But she did not have the lighter I had seen her use by her swimming pool, the one that was identical to the thin leather and gold lighter owned by Jim Gable.

His face split with his gap-toothed smile.

'It's the Davester,' he said.

'I was just talking with your chauffeur about your friendship with Maggie Glick,' I said.

'*Maggie*, my favorite madam,' he said.

'You got her out of prison?' I said.

'Right again, Davester. A wrong narc planted crystal on her. It's a new day in the department. Too bad you're not with us anymore,' he replied.

It started to rain, thudding on top of the tents, misting on the neon and the strings of electric lights over the rides. A barman dropped a tarp on one side of the drink pavilion, and the air was sweet and cool in the dryness of the enclosure and I could smell the draft beer and whiskey and mint and sweet syrup and melted ice in the plastic cups along the bar.

'Remember me, Dave?' Sookie Motrie said, and put

out his hand. After my hand was firmly inside his, he locked down on my fingers and winked and said, 'When I used to write bonds for Wee Willie Bimstine, I went to see you in the lockup once. I think you were doing extra-curricular research. Back in your days of wine and roses.'

I took my hand from his and looked out into the rain, then said to Bootsie, 'I promised Alf we'd be back early. I'll get the car and swing around behind the pavilion.'

I didn't wait for her to answer. I walked into the rain, out beyond the noise of the revelers in the tents and the rides whose buckets and gondolas spun and dipped emptily under the electric lights.

You just walk away. It's easy, I thought. You don't provoke, you don't engage. You keep it simple and your adversaries never have power over you.

I started Bootsie's car and drove through the mud toward the drink pavilion. Cora Gable had disappeared, but Jim Gable was at the plank bar, standing just behind Bootsie.

I kept working my 12-Step Program inside my head, the way a long-distance ocean swimmer breathes with a concentrated effort to ensure he does not swallow water out of a wave and drown. I told myself I did not have to live as I once did. I did not have to re-create the violent moments that used to come aborning like a sulfurous match flaring off a thumbnail.

Through the rain and the beating of the windshield wipers I saw Jim Gable standing so close behind Bootsie that his shadow seemed to envelop her body. She was dabbing with a napkin at a spot on the plank bar where she had spilled a drink and was evidently not aware of his closeness, or the way his loins hovered just behind her buttocks, the glaze that was on his face.

I stopped the car and stepped out into the rain, the car door yawing behind me.

Gable's nostrils were dilated as he breathed in the

smell of Bootsie's shampoo, the perfume behind her ears, the soap from her bath, the heat off her skin, the hint of her sex in her underthings. I could see the cloth of his slacks tightening across his loins.

Then I was running out of the rain toward him. I hit him so hard spittle and blood flew from his mouth onto a woman's blouse four feet away. I drove my fist into his kidney, a blow that made his back arch as though his spine had been broken, then I hooked him with a left below the eye and drove a right cross into his jaw that knocked him across a folding table.

A man I didn't know grabbed my arm, and a big uniformed policeman crashed into me from the other side, wrestling with both of his big meaty hands to get his arms around me and smother me against his girth. But even while the two men tried to pull me off of Gable, I kicked him in the side of the head and kicked at him once more and missed his face and shattered his watch on the cement.

I fell over a chair and stared stupidly at the faces looking down at me, like a derelict who has collapsed on a sidewalk and must witness from the cement the pity and revulsion he inspires in his fellowman. Bootsie was between me and Gable now, her face incredulous. A wet cigarette butt clung to my cheek like a mashed cockroach. I could smell whiskey and beer in my clothes and Gable's blood on my knuckles and I swore I could taste whiskey surging out of my stomach into my throat, like an old friend who has come back in a time of need.

Through the sweat and water that dripped out of my hair I saw the governor and people from the crowd lifting Jim Gable to his feet. He was smiling at me, his teeth like pink tombstones in his mouth.

chapter twenty-six

My hands still hurt the next morning. I ran cold water over them in the kitchen sink, then drank coffee out on the picnic table in the blueness of the dawn and tried not to think about last night. I walked along the coulee that traversed the back of our property and looked at the periwinkles along the bank, the caladiums and elephant ears beaded with moisture, the willows swelling in the breeze. I wanted to stay in that spot forever and not go into the department on Monday morning, not look at the early edition of the *Daily Iberian*, not deal with the people who would speak politely to me on a sidewalk or in a courthouse corridor, then whisper to one another after they thought I was out of earshot.

I walked back up toward the house just as the sun rose behind the cypress trees and seemed to flatten like fire inside the swamp. The back of the house was still deep in shadow, but I could see a white envelope taped to Alafair's screen. I pulled it loose and looked at her name written across the front in a flowing calligraphy. The flap was glued, with tiny felt-pen marks that transected both the flap and the body of the envelope so the dried glue could not be broken without the addressee knowing it.

I opened my pocket knife and slit the envelope all the

way across the top and removed the folded sheet of stationery inside.

I went down to the bait shop and called Wally, our 275-pound dispatcher at the department, and told him I was taking a vacation day on Monday and not coming in.

'You axed the old man?' he said.

'I have a feeling he'll get in touch,' I said.

'Hey, Dave, if I pass the detectives exam, can I hang around wit' y'all, solve big cases, mop the shrimp tails off the floor with New Orleans cops?'

But as I went back on the dock, I wasn't thinking about Wally's sardonic humor or my eventual encounter with the sheriff. I sat at a spool table and read again the letter that was written with the symmetry and baroque curlicues of a self-absorbed artist or what a psychologist would simply call a megalomaniac.

It read:

Dear Alafair,

I had a harsh conversation with your father. But he has tried to destroy our friendship and has also been asking people about my private life, about things that are none of his business.

At first I could not believe your words when you said you couldn't see me again. Did you really mean that? I would never betray you. Would you do that to me? I already know what the answer is.

Remember all our secret meeting places? Just be at any one of them and I'll find you. You're the best person I've ever known, Alafair. We're like the soldier and the girl on the vase. Even though they lived long ago and have probably moldered in the grave, they're still alive inside the arbor on the vase. Death can be beautiful, just like art, and once

277

you're inside either of them, you stay young forever and your love never dies.

See you soon.

As ever, Your loyal friend,
Johnny

I walked up the slope to the house and went into the bedroom with the letter and showed it to Bootsie.

'My God,' she said.

'I'm at a loss on this one.'

'Where is she?'

'Still asleep. I'd like to—'

'What?' Bootsie said. She was still in her nightgown, propped on one elbow.

'Nothing,' I said.

She sat up and took both my hands in hers. 'We can't solve all our problems with violence. Remeta's a sick person,' she said.

'It sounds like we're talking about last night instead of Remeta.'

She lay back down on the pillow, then turned her head and looked out the window at the pecan and oak trees in the yard, as though fearing that whatever she said next would be wrong.

'You know why I don't believe in capital punishment?' she said. 'It empowers the people we execute. We allow them to remake us in their image.'

'Gable's a degenerate. You didn't see him. I hope I ruptured his spleen.'

'I can't take this shit. I can't, I can't, I can't,' she said, and sat on the side of the bed, her back stiff with anger.

I found Clete that afternoon, drinking beer, half in the bag, in a St Martinville bar. The bar had lath walls and a high, stamped ceiling, and because it was raining outside, someone had opened the back door to let in the cool air, and I could see the rain dripping on a banana tree that grew by a brick wall. A group of bikers and their girlfriends were shooting pool in back, yelling each time one of them made a difficult shot, slamming the butts of their cues on the floor.

'Passion tell you I was here?' Clete said. His lap and the area around his stool were littered with popcorn.

'Yeah. Y'all on the outs?'

'She's wrapped up in her own head all the time. I'm tired of guessing at what's going on. I mean who needs it, right?'

'If I wanted to have somebody capped, who would I call?'

'A couple of the asswipes at that pool table would do it for a hand job.'

'I'm serious.'

'The major talent is still out of Miami. You're actually talking about having somebody smoked? You must have had a bad day, Streak.'

'It's getting worse, too.'

'What's that mean?'

'Nothing. I want to throw a steel net over Johnny Remeta. Most button men know each other.'

'I already tried. A stone killer in Little Havana, a guy who goes back to the days of Johnny Roselli? He hung up on me as soon as I mentioned Remeta's name. What's Remeta done now?'

'He's got a death wish. I think he wants to take Alafair with him.'

Clete's face was flushed and he wiped the heat and oil out of his eyes with a paper napkin. The pool players yelled at another extraordinary shot.

'How about putting it under a glass bell, Jack?' Clete said to them, then looked back at me, a half smile on his face, his eyes slightly out of focus. 'Say all that again?'

'I'll catch you another time, Cletus.'

He removed a slip of paper from his shirt pocket and stared at it.

'What's scareoderm mean? I couldn't find it in the dictionary,' he said.

'I don't know. Why?'

'I took Passion to the doctor yesterday. I heard the nurses talking about her. I wrote that word down.'

'You mean scleroderma?' I asked.

'That's it. That's what she has. What is it?'

His mouth was parted expectantly, his green eyes bleary with alcohol, while he waited for me to reply.

It continued to rain through the afternoon into the night. Little Face Dautrieve put her baby to bed in his crib and watched television until midnight in the front room of her cabin in the Loreauville Quarters. Then she undressed and put on a pajama top and lay down on top of her bed under the fan and listened to the rain on the tin roof. The wind was blowing hard against the slat walls and she knew the storm would be a long one. The occasional headlights on the state road looked like spiderwebs flaring on the windowpane.

From the edges of sleep she heard a raw scraping sound, like a rat clawing inside the walls. When she raised her head from the pillow, she saw the dead bolt on the back door rotating in its socket, then sliding free of the door frame.

The man other people called Johnny Remeta stepped into the room, water sliding off his hat and black raincoat, a metal nail file glinting in his right hand.

'I t'ought you was my auntie. She fixing to be here any minute,' Little Face said.

'Long drive from Lake Charles. Because that's where she moved to.'

Remeta sat down in a chair next to the bed and leaned forward on his hands, his hatted profile in silhouette against the lightning that leaped above the trees on the bayou.

'Can I take off my things? They're wet,' he said.

'We ain't got nothing you want, Rain Man. My baby's got the kroop. I melted Vicks in hot water. That's how come the room smell like it do. You stay here, you get sick.'

He removed his hat and set it crown-down on the floor, then pulled his raincoat off his shoulders and let it hang wet-side out on the back of the chair. His eyes settled on her face and mouth and she saw his throat swallow. She pulled the sheet up to her stomach.

'I ain't in that life no more,' she said.

He opened and closed his hands on top of his thighs, his veins cording under the skin.

'You've been with white men?' he asked.

'Down South the color line never got drawn when it come to the bedroom.'

Then he said something that was lost in the thunder or the thickness that caused his words to bind in his throat.

'I cain't hear you,' she said.

'What difference does one more make?'

'I ain't want your money. I ain't want you, Rain Man. You got to go back where you come from.'

'Don't talk to me like that,' he said.

The rain clattered on the roof and sluiced down over the windows. Little Face could feel her heart beating inside the thinness of her pajama top. The elastic of her nylon panties cut into her skin, but she knew she should not move in order to make herself more comfortable, although she could not explain why she knew this.

Remeta's breath came out in a ragged exhalation before he spoke.

'I've used a trick to scare people so I wouldn't have to hurt them. I'll show you,' he said.

He slipped a blue-black snub-nosed revolver from a holster that was attached to his ankle with a Velcro strap. He flipped the cylinder out of the frame and ejected all six rounds into his palm. They were thick and brass-cased and seemed too large for the size of the revolver. He inserted one back into a chamber and spun the cylinder, then flipped the cylinder back into the frame without looking at where the loaded chamber had landed.

'Ever read about Doc Holliday? His edge was everybody knew he didn't care if he lived or died. So I do this sometimes and it makes people dump in their drawers,' Remeta said.

He cocked the revolver, pressed the barrel against the side of his head, and pulled the trigger.

'See, your face jumped. Just like it was you instead of me about to take the bullet. But I can tell by the weight where the round is,' he said.

She pushed herself up on her hands so her back was against the headboard. She thought she was going to lose control of her bladder. She looked at her baby in the crib and at the glow of a television set inside the cabin of a neighbor who worked nights and at her plastic welfare charge card on the table and next to it the thirteen dollars she had to make last until the end of the week and at the cheap clothes that hung on hangers in her closet. She breathed the funk that rose from her armpits and a soapy odor that either came from her bedclothes or her pajama top, and her breasts seemed to hang like an old woman's dugs from her skeleton. Her stomach had stretch marks on it and felt flaccid and like a water-filled balloon at the same time, and she realized she owned absolutely nothing of value in this world, not even in her own person, nor could she call upon one friend or resource, to bargain for her and her baby's life, that if she was lucky the world would simply take what it needed from her and leave a piece of something behind.

'I ain't gonna fight you no more, Rain Man. I'm just a nigger.'

She pulled the sheet off her and sat on the side of the

bed, her feet not quite touching the floor, her eyes downcast.

'You shouldn't use racial words like that. It's what whites have taught you people to do. To feel bad about yourself,' he said, and sat beside her. He moved his arm around her waist but did not look at her. Instead, his lips moved silently, as though he were talking to other people in the room.

'You coming apart, Rain Man?' she said.

'You couldn't guess at what's in my head, girl.'

She unfastened his belt and unbuttoned the top of his trousers and pulled his zipper partway down. She placed one hand inside his underwear and looked into his eyes. They were black, then suddenly apprehensive in the flashes of light through the window, as though he were watching his own behavior from outside himself and was not sure which person he was.

Her hand moved mechanically, as though it were disconnected from her. She watched the side of his face.

She took her hand away and let it rest by his thigh.

'It ain't me you want,' she said.

'Yes, it is.'

'The one you want is the one you cain't have.'

He got up from the bed and stood in front of her, his legs slightly spread, his unbuttoned trousers exposing the top of his Jockey underwear. His stomach was as flat as a swimmer's, smooth as tallow in the flashes of lightning through the window.

'Take off your clothes,' he said.

'Won't do no good, Rain Man. Can kill me and my baby, both. But it ain't gonna get you no satisfaction.'

He made a sound that she could not interpret, like someone who knew his anger must always be called upon in increments and never allowed to have complete expression.

He tucked in his shirt and worked the zipper up on his

trousers and fastened the button at the top and began buckling his belt. But his fingers started shaking and he could not line up the hole in the leather with the metal tongue in the buckle.

She reached out to help him. That's when his fist exploded on the side of her face.

She found Bootsie and me that Sunday evening at Jefferson Island while we were eating supper in the restaurant by the lake, the sun glowing through the oak trees and Spanish moss. I watched her come up the winding walkway through the flower gardens and groups of tourists, her diapered baby mounted on her arm, her blue-jeans shorts rolled up high on her thighs, her face bruised like an overripe eggplant.

She marched into the restaurant and stopped in front of our table.

'Somebody shit in that white boy's brain. It ain't me done it, either. You better get him out of our lives, Sad Man. I mean now. 'Cause he come back around, I got me a gun now and I'm gonna blow his fucking head off,' she said.

I walked outside with her into the gardens and we sat down on a scrolled-iron bench. Through the restaurant windows I could see Bootsie by herself at our table, staring out at the lake, her coffee cold and her dessert uneaten.

'Did you file a report at the department?' I asked.

'They was real hepful. Man kept looking down my top to make sure Johnny Remeta wasn't hiding there.'

'I doubt Remeta will bother you again.'

'Where Fat Man at?'

'Why?' I asked.

''Cause he ain't like you. 'Cause he don't fool hisself. 'Cause people mess wit' him only once.'

'Remeta might try to kill my daughter, Little Face. I'm

sorry about what happened to you. But I'm tired of your anger,' I said.

I left her on the bench with her baby. When I went back inside the restaurant, Bootsie was gone.

The sheriff was at the bait shop before dawn Monday morning, but he did not come inside the building right away. He propped his hands on the dock railing and stared across the bayou at the cypress trees inside the fog. In his cowboy boots and pinstripe suit and Stetson hat, he looked like a cattleman who had just watched his whole herd run off by dry lightning. He took off his hat and walked through the cone of light over the screen door and entered the shop.

'You gave Jim Gable a concussion Friday night. Now you take a vacation day and don't even have the courtesy to call me?' he said.

'Johnny Remeta is stalking my daughter and leaving notes at my house. I don't care what happens with Gable,' I replied.

'Everything's personal with you, Dave. You use the department the way a prizefighter uses a rosin box. You're an employee of the parish. Which means I'm your supervisor, not a guy who follows you around with a dustpan and whisk broom. I don't like coming out here to explain that.'

'Did Gable press charges?'

'No.'

'Then it's a private matter.'

'As of this moment you're on suspension.'

'That's the breaks.'

'That casual, huh?'

'How'd you like Remeta creeping your place?'

'Do what you're thinking and I've got your cell already waiting for you.'

'I didn't call you because I can't prove what Gable was

doing behind my wife's person in that pavilion. It would only bring her embarrassment.'

'Behind her person? What the hell does that mean?'

'End of conversation.'

'You're right. It does no good to talk to you. I wish I hadn't come here,' he said. He tapped his Stetson against his leg and walked out into the mist, his mouth a tight seam.

I worked with Batist at the dock all day, then drove to the Winn-Dixie in town, filled the back of the pickup with soda pop and loaded the ice chest with lunch meat for the bait shop cooler. Right down the street was the ancient motel where Clete was living. I had not seen him since Saturday afternoon, when I had left him bleary-eyed and alone with a scrap of paper in his hand that could have been torn from the Doomsday Book.

I pulled into the motel entrance and drove under the canopy of oaks to the stucco cottage he rented at the end of the row. Leaves were drifting out of the oak branches overhead and he was dusting the exterior of his Cadillac with a rag, flicking the leaves off the finish as though no others would drop out of the tree, the hair on his bare shoulders glowing like a blond ape's in a column of sunlight.

'What's the haps, Streak?' he said without looking up from his work.

'You doing all right?' I said.

'I used the medical dictionary at the city library. From what it says, that stuff's like going to hell without dying.'

'There're treatments.'

'The victims look like they're wrapped in sheets of plastic?'

'How's Passion?'

'She doesn't talk about it. At least not to me.' His voice

286

was without tone or inflection. 'It's true, you tore up Jim Gable at the Shrimp Festival?'

'I guess I have to lose it about every six months to remind myself I'm still a drunk.'

'Save the dish rinse. You didn't lose it. He took it from you.'

'What?'

'Gable never does anything without a reason. You're trying to bring him down. Now nobody will believe anything you say about him.'

I stared at him. I felt like the confidence game mark who realizes his gullibility has no bottom. Clete threw his dust rag through the open front window of the Cadillac onto the front seat and walked over to my truck.

'You're just like me, Streak. You never left the free-fire zone. You think aspirin and meetings and cold showers are going to clean out your head. What you want is God's permission to paint the trees with the bad guys. That won't happen, big mon,' he said.

'I'm sorry about Passion.'

'Life's a bitch and then you die,' he replied.

chapter twenty-seven

Bed Check Charley still visited me in my dreams, crawling on his stomach through the rice fields, his black pajamas twisted like liquid silk on his dehydrated body. He used a French bolt-action rifle with iron sights, and Japanese potato mashers that he whacked on a banyan root, igniting the impact fuze prematurely, before he flung one into our midst. But even though his ordnance was antiquated, Bed Check was punctual and did his job well. We used him in our day as we would a clock.

We were almost disappointed when a stray gunship caught him under a full moon, running across a rice paddy, and arbitrarily took him out.

A predictable enemy is a valuable one.

I knew Remeta would be back. And I knew where he would come from.

He returned three nights after the sheriff put me on departmental suspension.

I heard the outboard deep in the swamp, then the engine went dead. I slipped on my khakis and shoes and lifted the AR-15 from under the bed and went outside and crossed the lawn. The trees were dripping with night damp, and I could barely see the bait shop in the fog.

But I could hear a boat paddle dipping into the water,

knocking against a cypress root, scudding softly against the worn gunnel of a pirogue.

I walked down the concrete boat ramp into the water and stepped under the dock and waited. The bayou was moving northward, rising with the tide, and I saw a dead nutria in the current with a bluepoint crab hooked onto its side.

It was airless under the dock, the water warm inside my clothes, and I could smell dead fish among the pilings. Then the breeze came up and I saw the fog roll like puffs of cotton on the bayou's surface and the bow of a pirogue emerge out of the swamp twenty yards down from the bait shop.

I had inserted a thirty-round magazine in the rifle. The bow of the pirogue moved into the bayou and now I could see the outline of a kneeling man, drawing the paddle through the water in silent J-strokes. Farther down the bayou, at the four corners, the owner of the general store had left on a porch light, and the man in the pirogue was now lighted from behind, his features distorting like a figure moving about under the phosphorescent glow of a pistol flare.

I steadied the rifle against a piling and sighted along the barrel, no longer seeing a silhouette but in my mind's eye a human face, one with teeth, a hinged jawbone, an eye glinting in profile, a skull with skin stretched over its bladed surfaces.

A line of sweat ran through my eyebrow. You just squeeze off and not think about it, I told myself. How many times did you do it before, to people you didn't even know? You just step across the line into E-major rock 'n' roll and the concerns of conscience quickly disappear in the adrenaline rush of letting off one round after another. The only reality becomes the muzzle flashes in the darkness, the clean smell of smokeless powder, the deadness in the ears that allows you to disconnect from the crumpling figure in the distance.

But I hadn't yet actually seen the face of Johnny Remeta.

I clicked on the electric switch mounted on the dock piling. Suddenly the bayou was flooded with light.

'You must get mighty tired if you stay out here in the mosquitoes every night,' he said. He was grinning, his face bathed with white light, his mouth strangely discolored in the brilliance of the flood lamps, as though it were painted with purple lipstick.

I could feel my finger tightening inside the trigger guard.

'You're a pisspot, Johnny,' I said.

'I've heard it all before, Mr Robicheaux. My father said my mother would have gotten rid of me when I was in the womb but she didn't want to waste a coat hanger,' he replied.

Then he opened his palms, as though accepting grace from above, his head tilted, taking my measure.

'Use your left hand and drop your weapon overboard,' I said.

'I don't have one.'

I waded out from under the dock so he could see me.

'You're under arrest. Pull the pirogue into shore,' I said.

'You couldn't pop me, could you?'

I could hear myself breathing and feel the oil and moisture on my finger inside the trigger guard. He stood up in the pirogue, balancing himself, his hands extended outward. He stared at the muzzle of the rifle, his lips pursed, waiting.

'So long, Mr Robicheaux. Tell Alafair I said hello.'

He hit the water in a long, flat dive, his weight flipping the pirogue over. With two strokes he was inside the cypress trees, running across sandspits and through the sloughs, cobwebs and air vines swinging behind him.

I was trembling all over, as though I had malaria. My head thundered and my palms were wet on the plastic stock of the rifle. I leaned over and vomited into the water.

I walked up the boat ramp, then onto the dock, and pulled off my T-shirt and sat down on the planks and pulled my knees up in front of me and rested my face on top of them.

I stayed there until the sun rose, then got up and slung the AR-15 muzzle-down on my shoulder and walked up the slope through the trees with the knowledge I had deliberately set out to murder another human being and had simultaneously failed as both assassin and police officer.

chapter twenty-eight

That afternoon I got a call from Wally, our departmental comedian.

'Enjoying your days off?' he asked.

'I'm cleaning the grease trap right now. Come on over.'

'I got a little problem. I'd like to finish my shift without being taken out of here in a box. My systolic is 190. I don't need race riots. I don't need black people shouting into the phone at me. I don't need no white lesbian crazy woman firing up a mob over on Hopkins.'

'You're talking about Helen Soileau?'

'I knew you could think it out. Way to go, Dave.'

I drove into town, then over to the west side to Hopkins Street, which, along with Railroad, used to comprise New Iberia's red-light district. Helen Soileau had just handcuffed two black kids, about age fifteen, through the cap chain on a fire hydrant.

I parked the pickup in front of a liquor store and walked through the crowd that had formed on the sidewalk and the lawn of two houses. Helen was bent over at the waist, her hands on her hips, venting her spleen at the two kids sitting on the cement. A city cop in a uniform was looking nervously up and down the street.

Helen raised up and stared at me, her face still heated.

Her slacks were torn at the thigh and mud was smeared on her white shirt. 'What are you doing here?' she said.

'I just happened by. What'd these guys do?'

'Not much. One shot a BB into a passing car and hit a six-week-old baby. This other little fuck put an M-80 under an old woman's bedroom floor.'

'I think we need to turn the butane down.'

'They're going to tell me where that BB gun is or stay here till they have to eat the paint on that hydrant. You hear that, you little pukes?'

'Walk over here with me, Helen,' I said.

'You got no business telling me what to do,' she replied.

'I can't argue with that. But we're on city turf. Let them handle it.'

She lifted her face into mine. Her eyes were blazing, her thick arms pumped.

'I'd like to punch you out, Dave. All the skipper needs is an apology and you're back on the clock,' she said.

'So let the city guy do his job and take the kids down.'

'Yeah, I give a shit,' she said, and bent over and unlocked the handcuffs on the boys' wrists, then cuffed them again and walked them to the city cruiser and shoved them inside and slammed the door behind them. Then she walked back to me and said, 'Buy me coffee, Pops.'

I expected one of Helen's harangues, but I was wrong. We went to the McDonald's on East Main and sat by the window. The sky had turned green and the wind was blowing the oaks on the street, and leaves were rising out of the crown of the trees high in the air.

'I was in Lafayette this morning. You know that tattoo and fortune-telling place right off the four-lane?' she said.

'An old cypress cabin with beads and colored lights hanging all over the gallery?'

'I saw Passion Labiche go in there. That girl bothers me.'

'How?'

'Vachel Carmouche was a shithead and everybody knew it. That whole trial sucked. I get pissed off every time somebody tells me Carmouche was a lawman . . . Why the face?'

'I found evidence she didn't do it by herself.'

'You're telling me Passion helped her?'

'Yeah, I am.'

'Big revelation,' Helen said. 'What else is bothering you today?'

'I set up an ambush on Johnny Remeta last night.'

'You did what?'

'I was going to flush his grits. I couldn't pull the trigger.'

She cleaned up our mess from the table and walked to the trash basket and stuffed it inside and came back to the table.

'This is a noisy place full of teenagers and echoes and cooks yelling and I couldn't quite make out what you were saying. See you around, bwana,' she said.

She walked out to her cruiser and drove away.

I slept that night with the remote phone under the bed. It rang just after 11 p.m. I picked it up and went into the kitchen before I clicked it on.

'You're in it for the long haul,' I said without waiting for him to speak.

'I figured you wrong last night. I thought honor required I tell you that, Mr Robicheaux.'

'Honor?'

'I said you didn't have in it you to drop the hammer on me. I know who popped your mother. That's why you let me live.'

'You're not even close, partner.'

I could hear him breathing on the mouth of the receiver. 'We're alike. I've seen it in your eyes,' he said.

'I always thought my mother betrayed me, Johnny. But I learned to forgive her. I did that so I don't have to be a drunk anymore.'

'You saying something about my mother now?'

'You're smart. Read Chaucer's story about the three guys who set out to find Death and slay him once and for all. They found him, all right. But things didn't work out as they expected.'

'Let me tell you what real revenge is. I'm gonna shake down the people who did your mother, then I'm gonna leave the country and have them killed by somebody else. But you'll never know for sure who they were.'

'Pull on your own pud, Johnny. This stuff is a real drag,' I said, and clicked off the phone. Then I walked through the house and pulled the phone connections from all the wall jacks.

The sheriff lived up Bayou Teche in a yellow and gray frame house with a wide gallery, set back under huge cedar and oak trees. When I drove out there Saturday afternoon, he was trimming back the climbing roses in his flower bed while his grandchildren played in the side yard. He wore a tattered straw hat to protect his head from the thorns, and his stomach hung heavily over his belt. In his home setting, clipping flowers and placing them gingerly in a bowl of water, his clothes stained with fungicide and house paint, the sheriff looked much older than he did at the department and nothing like a law officer.

I sat down on the front steps and picked up some pieces of bark from a bag of mulch and flicked them out into the grass.

'I made an ass out of myself when I attacked Jim

Gable. I also brought shame on the department. I want to apologize,' I said.

'You got to rein it in, Dave.'

'I believe you.'

'Five-day suspension without pay, effective last Monday. A letter of reprimand in your jacket. Is that fair?'

'There's something else I have to tell you,' I said. 'Passion Labiche told me she helped her sister kill Vachel Carmouche.' I waited for him to speak but he didn't. 'Number two, I had the chance to plant one in Johnny Remeta's cauliflower and didn't do it.'

He paused in his work but his face showed no expression.

'You froze?' he asked.

'I had him set up. I was going to cut all his motors.'

A mosquito buzzed at his face and he rubbed his cheek with the back of his wrist.

'I'm going to retire soon. I'm glad you told me what you did.'

'Sir?'

'I'd like you to be my successor,' he said.

'Come again?'

'What are you going to do with Passion's confession?' he asked, ignoring my incredulity.

'It'll be dismissed as an eleventh-hour attempt to stop Letty's execution,' I said.

'Maybe that's just what it is. You think of that? Where's Remeta now?'

'He inasmuch told me my mother's killers are the same people who tried to have him killed on the Atchafalaya. He says he's going to extort them, then hire a button man to take them out.'

'You actually had that guy locked down in your sights? Then didn't say anything about it till today?'

'That's it, more or less.'

He locked the clasp on his clippers and dropped them

in his pants pocket and looked at his grandchildren playing.

'Remeta is going to take you to your mother's killers, isn't he?' he said.

'That wasn't the reason, Sheriff.'

'Yeah, I know,' he said, scratching inside his shirt. 'Yeah—' But he didn't bother to continue, as though he were weary of contending with the self-serving machinations of others.

I ate an early dinner with Bootsie, then drove to New Orleans through Morgan City. The evening light still reached high into the dome of sky overhead when I parked my pickup truck down the block from Maggie Glick's bar across the river in Algiers. The street was busy with the type of people whose Saturday nights were spent in a facsimile of the places their fellow countrymen enjoyed: elderly pensioners who ate in decrepit diners that served a free glass of domestic wine with the special; young white couples without geographical origins or means of support who lived in walk-ups with no air-conditioning and strolled the sidewalks with no apparent destination; and the men whose thoughts made them wake each morning with a longing that seldom found satiation.

I walked down the alley and entered Maggie Glick's through the back door. It was crowded and dark and unbearably frigid inside. She was behind the bar, fixing a drink in a Collins glass, talking to a white man in a business suit. She had woven glass Mardi Gras beads into her hair and she wore a white knit blouse that exposed the roses tattooed on the tops of her breasts. The man did not sit but stood and grinned while she talked, his back stiff, his eyes drifting down the bar to a mulatto girl who could not have been older than eighteen.

His eyes met mine and he fiddled with a college or

fraternity ring of some kind on his finger and turned his face away, as though he had heard a sudden noise outside, and walked down to the far end of the bar, then glanced back at me again and went out the door.

'My competition send you 'round?' Maggie asked.

'Johnny Remeta says he was never in here. He says you were lying,' I said.

'You a sober, thinking man now. Let me ax you a question. Why would I lie and tell you a man like that was a customer? 'Cause it gonna be good for my bidness?'

'That's why I believe you.'

'Do say?'

'Where can I find him?' I asked.

'He *used* to come in here. He don't now. Man shop for the trade in here got to be functional, know what I mean?'

'No.'

'That boy get off with a gun. And it ain't in his pants. Here, drink a free soda. I'll bag it to go.'

'Jim Gable sprung you from St Gabriel, Maggie?'

'I got sprung 'cause I was innocent. Have a good night, darlin',' she said, and turned her back to me, lighting a cigarette. Her hair was jet black, her skin as golden as a coin in the flare of light.

I walked toward the front of the building and was about to push open the door onto the street when I saw a muscular blond man in a pale blue suit with white piping on the lapels at the corner of the bar. His hair was clipped and combed neatly on the side of his head, one eye like a small marble inside the nodulous skin growth on the right side of his face.

'I thought maybe you'd gone back to New Mexico, Micah,' I said.

He had a long-neck bottle of beer and a shot glass in front of him, and he sipped from the shot, then drank a small amount of beer afterwards, like a man who loves a vice so dearly he fears his appetite for it will one day force him to give it up.

'The heavyweight champion of the Shrimp Festival,' he said.

I sat down next to him and took a peanut out of a plastic bowl on the bar and cracked the shell and put the nut in my mouth.

'You ever see a guy by the name of Johnny Remeta in here?' I asked.

'What would you give to find out?'

'Not much.'

He lifted the shot glass again and tipped it into his mouth.

'I might buy half of a carnival. What do you think of that?' he said.

'Maybe you can give me a job. I got bumped from the department after I punched out Jim Gable.'

He watched an overweight, topless girl in heels and a sequined G-string walk out on a tiny stage behind the bar.

'Miss Cora give you a severance package?' I said.

'The smart man squeezes the man who milks the cow. That don't mean anything to you. But maybe one day it will,' he said.

'Really?' I said.

'You're an ignorant man.'

'You're probably right,' I said, and slapped him on the back and caused him to spill his drink on his wrist.

I went outside and walked down to the old docks and pilings on the waterfront. It was dark now, and rain was falling on the river and I could see the nightglow of New Orleans on the far bank and, to the south, green trees flattening in the wind and the brown swirl of the current as it flowed around a wide bend toward the Gulf of Mexico.

Somewhere down on that southern horizon my father's rig had blown out and he had hooked his safety belt onto the Geronimo wire and bailed off the top of the derrick into the darkness. His bones and hard hat and steel-toed boots were still out there, shifting in the tidal currents, and I truly believed that in one way or another his brave spirit was out there as well.

The cops who had murdered my mother had rolled her body into a bayou, as contemptuous of her in death as they were of her in life. But eventually her body must have drifted southward into the salt water, and now I wanted to believe she and Big Al were together under the long, green roll of the Gulf, all their inadequacies washed away, their souls just beginning the journey they could not take together on earth.

The rain was blowing hard in the streets when I walked back to my truck, and the neon above the bars looked like blue and red smoke in the mist. I heard men fighting in a pool room and I thought of Big Aldous Robicheaux and Mae Guillory and the innocence of a world in which inarticulate people could not tell one another adequately of either their pain or the yearnings of their hearts.

chapter twenty-nine

That night I dreamed of roses. I saw the sheriff trimming them in his garden and I saw them tattooed on Maggie Glick's breasts. I saw them painted in miniature on the vase Johnny Remeta had given Alafair. I also saw the rose with green leaves that was tattooed on the neck of Letty Labiche.

But just as I woke and was momentarily between all the bright corridors of sleep and the grayness of the dawn, the flowers disappeared from the dream and I saw a collection of Civil War photographs on a library table, the pages flipping in the wind that blew through the open window.

I wanted to dismiss the dream and its confused images, but it lingered with me through the day. And maybe because the change of the season was at hand, I could almost hear a clock ticking for a sexually abused woman waiting to die in St Gabriel Prison.

On Monday morning I was out at the firing range with Helen Soileau. I watched her empty her nine-millimeter at a paper target, her ear protectors clamped on her head. When the breech locked open, she pulled off her ear protectors and slipped a fresh magazine into the butt of her automatic and replaced it in her holster and began picking up her brass.

'You're dead-on this morning,' I said.

'I'm glad somebody is.'

'Excuse me?'

'You're off-planet. I have to say everything twice to you before you hear me,' she said, chewing gum.

'Where'd you see Passion Labiche?'

'I told you. Going into that fortune-telling and tattoo place in Lafayette.'

'What for?'

'Ask her.'

'You brought up the subject, Helen.'

'Yeah. And I dropped it. Two days ago,' she said.

I went back to the office and called Dana Magelli at NOPD.

'I've got a lead for you,' I said.

'I see. You're doing general oversight on our cases now?' he replied.

'Hear me out, Dana. Johnny Remeta told me he was going to squeeze the people who killed my mother.'

'Are you kidding me? You're in personal contact with an escaped felon who's murdered two police officers?'

'Saturday night I was in Maggie Glick's bar over in Algiers. I ran into Jim Gable's ex-chauffeur, a guy named Micah something or another. He said he was going to come into some money by squeezing the man who was milking the cow.'

'What?'

'Those were his words. I think he was saying Remeta is shaking down Jim Gable.'

'You're saying Jim Gable killed your mother?' he said.

'Remeta forced Don Ritter to give up the names of my mother's killers before he executed him. At least that's what he says.'

'What am I supposed to do with information like this? I can't believe I'm having this conversation,' Magelli said.

'Put Micah under surveillance.'

'Shake loose three or four detectives and follow a guy around who has no last name? This sounds like something Purcel thought up, maybe to get even with the department.'

'I'm serious, Dana.'

'No, you're obsessed. You're a good guy. I love you. But you're stone nuts. That's not a joke. Stay out of town.'

The next day I drove to the City Library and found the collection of Civil War-era photographs that Johnny Remeta had been looking at just before he jumped out of the reading room window. I used the index, then flipped to the grainy black-and-white pictures taken at the Bloody Angle and Dunker Church.

The images in the pictures told me nothing new about Remeta. He was simply a necromancer with broken glass in his head trying to find a historical context for the rage and pain his mother had bequeathed him. But if that was true, why had the image of the book, its pages turning in the wind, disturbed me in my dream?

Because I hadn't considered he was looking at something else in the collection, not just at the photos of Union and Confederate dead at Sharpsburg and Spotsylvania?

I flipped back two pages and was suddenly looking at a photograph of a two-story, narrow, columned house, surrounded by a piked iron fence. The picture had been taken in 1864, in uptown New Orleans, after the Union occupation of the city by General Butler.

According to the historical notes opposite the photograph, the house was owned by a young woman, believed to be a southern spy, who hid her lover, an escaped Confederate prisoner of war, from General Butler's soldiers. The soldier was badly wounded, and when she discovered her own arrest was imminent, the two of them drank poison and died upstairs in a tester bed.

I went back to the department and called Dana Magelli at NOPD again.

'We haven't found Remeta because he hides in plain sight,' I said.

'I knew it was going to be that kind of day.'

'Give it a rest, Dana. When he had a cop on his tail in the Quarter, he parked his truck and went inside the police station. How many perps have that kind of cool?'

'Give me a street address and we'll swing by.'

'He's imbued with this notion he's a Confederate hero of some kind and my daughter is his girlfriend. He was reading an account in our library about two lovers who committed suicide during the Civil War in a home on Camp Street.'

'That doesn't mean he's living in New Orleans.'

'You have something better to offer?'

'Every cop in the city has a mug shot of this guy. What else can we do?'

'Pull Jim Gable's personnel records for me.'

'Forget it.'

'Why?'

'We'll handle our own people. Am I communicating here? Gable is none of your business.'

That's what you think, I thought as I lowered the receiver into the phone cradle.

I worked late that evening, then drove home along the bayou road in the dusk. I could smell chrysanthemums and a smell like gas on the wind and see fireflies lighting in the gloom of the swamp. The house had already fallen into shadow when I turned into the drive and the television set was on in the living room, the sounds of canned laughter rising and falling in the air like an insult to the listener's credulity. I tried not to think about the evening that awaited Bootsie and me as soon as I entered the house, hours of unrelieved tension, formality that hid our mutual anger, physical aversion, and periods of silence that were louder than a scream.

I saw Batist chopping up hog meat on a butcher table he had set up by the coulee. He had taken off his shirt and put on a gray apron, and I could see the veins cord in his shoulder each time he raised the cleaver in the air. Behind him, the sky was still blue and the evening star was out and the moon rising, and his head was framed against the light like a glistening cannonball.

'Sold thirty-five lunches today. We run out of poke chops,' he said.

A cardboard box by his foot contained the hog's head and loops of blue entrails.

'You doin' all right?' I asked.

'Weather's funny. The wind's hard out of the west. I seen t'ings glowing in the swamp last night. My wife use to say that was the *loupgarou*.'

'It's swamp gas igniting or ball lightning, podna. You know that. Forget about werewolves.'

'I run my trot line this morning. Had a big yellow mudcat on it. When I slit it open there was a snake in its stomach.'

'I'll see you later,' I said.

'When the *loupgarou* come, somebody gonna die. Old folks use to burn blood to run it back in the trees.'

'Thanks for putting up the meat, Batist,' I said, and went inside the house.

Bootsie sat at the kitchen table reading from two sheets of lined paper. She wore blue jeans and loafers and a denim shirt with the sleeves cut away at the shoulders; wisps of her hair had fallen loose from her barrette and hung on the back of her neck. Her fingers were pressed to her temples while she read.

'Is that from Remeta?' I said.

'No. I went to an Al-Anon meeting today. Judy
Theriot, my sponsor, was there. She said I had a problem
with anger.'

'She did?' I said, my voice neutral.

'She made me do a Fourth Step and write out an
inventory. Now that I've read it again I'd like to wad it
up and throw it away.'

I went to the icebox and took out a pitcher of iced tea
and poured a glass at the sink. I raised the glass to my
mouth, then lowered it and set it back on the drainboard.

'Would you care for one?' I asked.

'You want to know what's in my inventory?' Bootsie
asked.

'I'm a little bit afraid of what's coming.'

'My first statement has to do with absolute rage.'

'That's understandable.'

'Hold your water, Streak, before I get charged up
again. Judy made me write out a list of all the things you
did that angered me. It's quite long.'

I looked out the window at Batist chopping meat on
the wood table by the coulee. He had started a trash fire
of leaves, and the smoke was blowing into my neighbor's
cane field. I could feel my scalp tightening as I waited for
Bootsie to recite her written complaint, and I wanted to
be outside, in the wind, in the autumnal smell of
smoldering leaves, away from the words that would force
me to look again at the on-going insanity of my behavior.

Then, rather than wait for her to speak again and
quietly accept criticism, I took the easier, softer way and
tried to pre-empt it. 'You don't have to tell me. It's the
violence. Nobody should have to live around it. I drag it
home with me like an animal on a chain,' I said.

'Judy made me look at something I didn't want to see. I
was often angry when you were protective of someone
else. You beat up Gable because you thought he was

306

treating me disrespectfully in public. Then I lectured you about your violent feelings toward Remeta.'

'You weren't wrong,' I said.

'What?'

'I set Remeta up the other night. I was going to dust him and take him out of Alafair's life.'

She was quiet a long time, staring into space, her cheeks spotted with color. Her mouth was parted slightly and I kept waiting for her to speak.

'Boots?' I said.

'You were actually going to kill him?'

'Yes.'

I could see the anger climbing into her face. 'In front of our home, just blow him away?' she said.

'I couldn't do it. So he'll be back. We can count on it.'

I could hear the wall clock in the silence. Her face was covered with shadow and I couldn't see her expression. I waited a moment longer, then rinsed out my glass and dried it and put it in the cupboard and went out on the front gallery. The screen opened behind me.

'He's coming back?' she said.

I didn't answer.

'I wish you had killed him. That's what I really feel. I wish Johnny Remeta was dead. If he comes around Alafair again, I'll do it myself. Get either in or out of the game, Streak,' she said.

'Your sponsor would call that rigorous honesty,' I said.

She tried to hold the anger in her face, then mashed her foot on top of mine.

The bedroom was filled with shadows and the curtains twisted and popped in the wind when Bootsie sat on my thighs and lowered her hand, then raised herself and placed me inside her. A few minutes later her mouth opened silently and her eyes became unfocused, her hair hanging in her face, and she began to say something that broke and dissolved in her throat; then I felt myself joining her, my hands slipping off her breasts onto her back, and in my mind's eye I saw a waterfall cascading over pink rocks and a marbled boulder tearing loose from its moorings, rolling heavily, faster and faster in the current, its weight pressing deeply into the soft pebbly bottom of the stream.

She kissed me and cupped her hand on my forehead as though she were checking to see if I had a fever, then pushed my hair up on my head.

'Alafair will be home soon. Let's take her to dinner at the Patio. We can afford an extra night out, can't we?' she said.

'Sure.'

I watched her as she put on her panties and bra; her back was firm with muscle, her skin as free of wrinkles as a young woman's. She was reaching for her shirt on the chair when an odor like scorched hair and burning garbage struck her face.

'Good Lord, what is that?' she said.

I put on my khakis and the two of us went into the kitchen and looked through the window into the backyard. The sun had dropped below the horizon, but the light had not gone out of the sky, and the full moon hung like a sliver of partially melted ice above my neighbor's cane. Batist flung a bucket filled with hog's blood onto the trash fire, and a cloud of black smoke with fire inside it billowed up into the wind and drifted back against the house.

'What's Batist doing? Has he lost his mind?' Bootsie said.

I rubbed the small of her back, my fingers touching the line of elastic across the top of her panties.

'It's a primitive form of sacrifice. He believes he saw the *loupgarou* in the swamp,' I said.

'Sacrifice?'

'It keeps the monster back in the trees.'
'You thinking about Letty Labiche?'
'About all of us, I guess,' I said.

chapter thirty

The next day was Wednesday. I don't know why, but I woke with a sense of loss and emptiness I hadn't experienced in many years. It was like the feelings I had as a child that I could never explain to priests or nuns or any other adults who tried to help me. But when that strange chemical presence would have its way with my heart, like weevil worms that had invaded my blood, I was convinced the world had become a gray, desolate place without purpose, with no source of heat other than a perpetual winter sun.

I walked down through the mist in the trees to the road and took the newspaper out of the metal cylinder and opened it on the kitchen table.

The lead story had a three-column headline that read: 'Governor Sets Execution for Labiche.'

Unless Belmont Pugh commuted her sentence, Letty had exactly three weeks to live.

I drove to the department in the rain and talked to the sheriff, then went to the prosecutor's office.

The district attorney was out of town and would be gone for a week, and the ADA I caught was Barbara Shanahan, sometimes known as Battering Ram Shanahan. She was over six-feet tall and had freckles and wore her light red hair cut short and wore a blue suit with white hose. She worked hard and was a good prosecutor, and I had always wanted to like her. But she seldom smiled and she went about her job with the abrasiveness of a carpenter building coffins with a nail gun.

'Passion Labiche has confessed she participated in the murder of Vachel Carmouche?' she said.

'Yes.'

'Where is it?' she asked.

'Where's what?'

'The statement, the tape, whatever.'

'I didn't take a formal statement from her.'

'So what is it you want from us?' she asked.

'I'm apprising you of the situation.'

'It sounds like you're getting your chain jerked.'

'The weed sickle she used is still under the house.'

'I think you should get out of law enforcement. Become a public defender. Then you can clean up after these people on a regular basis. Talk to the DA when he gets back. He's going to tell you the right person is going to be injected three weeks from now. I suggest you learn to live with it,' she said.

It was still raining outside, and through the window I could see the old crypts in St Peter's Cemetery and the rain dancing on top of the bricks and plaster.

'Passion was telling the truth,' I said.

'Good. Make the case and we'll indict for capital murder. Anything else you want?' she replied, and began sticking files in a cabinet, her back to me.

But Barbara Shanahan surprised me. And so did Connie Deshotel, who rang my phone just before 5 p.m.

'Your ADA called me. She says you have new evidence in the Carmouche case,' she said.

'Both sisters killed him,' I said.

'You know this for a fact?'

'Yes.'

'Put something together. I'll take it to the governor.'

'Why are you doing this?' I asked.

'Because I'm the attorney general of Louisiana. Because I don't want to overlook mitigating circumstances in a capital conviction.'

'I want to offer Passion Labiche immunity,' I said.

'That's between you and the prosecutor's office.'

'Belmont thinks he's going to be a vice-presidential candidate. He's not going to be easy to move.'

'Tell me about it,' she said.

After she hung up I put on my coat to leave the office. Through the window I could see rain and leaves blowing in the cemetery. Helen Soileau opened my office door and leaned inside.

'Give me a ride, boss man?'

'Sure. Why would Connie Deshotel want to help Letty Labiche?'

'Simple. She's humanitarian and is always willing to risk her ass for a cop killer,' Helen said.

'Right,' I said.

In the morning I drove out to Passion Labiche's house, but she wasn't home. I drove up the road, along the bayou, to her nightclub outside St Martinville and saw her pickup truck parked by the back door under a dripping tree. She was unloading groceries from the bed and carrying them, two sacks at a time, through a puddle of water into the small kitchen in back. She wore baggy strap overalls and a gray T-shirt and a red bandanna tied around her neck. Her feet were wet up to her ankles.

'Need a hand?' I asked.

'I got it. What you want, Dave?' she said.

I followed her through the screen door into the kitchen.

'I talked to the attorney general. She wants to take your statement about Carmouche's death to the governor,' I said.

'What statement?'

'Excuse me?'

'I said what statement you talking about?'

She put a huge gumbo pot on the gas range and split open a bag of okra on the drainboard and began rinsing the okra under hot water and rubbing it smooth with a dish towel. Her hair looked oily and unwashed and I could smell a sour odor in her clothes.

'If you want immunity, we have to wait till the DA comes back from Washington,' I said.

'I got scleroderma. He can give immunity from that?'

'I'm telling you what's available.'

'It don't matter what I do. They gonna kill my sister. Your friends, the attorney general and Belmont Pugh? I wish it was them gonna be strapped down on that table. I wish they could know what it feels like to sit in a cage and wait for people to tape a needle on your arm and steal the breath out of your chest. You don't die easy on that table, no. You strangle to death.' She raised one arm from her work, her back still to me, and wiped at the corner of her face. 'It's over, Dave. Don't be bothering me and Letty again.'

When I drove back to the office, the sugarcane in the fields waving against the grayness of the sky, I kept thinking of Passion's words. Was it just a matter of her peculiar use of the second person, or had she described the execution as though she were speaking of her own fate, not Letty's?

The following Monday I received a call from Dana Magelli in New Orleans.

'I'm patched in on Camp Street. We got a "911 shots-fired" a half hour ago. The neighbors say a blond guy drove up in a Honda, went inside, then suddenly *pow*, *pow*, and the Honda drives back off. We showed the neighbors Remeta's picture. They say he looks like the guy who's been living upstairs.'

'Somebody hit Remeta?'

'I'm not sure,' Magelli said.

'You haven't gone into the house?'

'It's burning. There's another problem, too. Gunfire's coming from the upstairs window. Whoever's in there is going down with the ship.'

Helen and I checked out a cruiser, hit the flasher, and took the four-lane through Morgan City into New Orleans. We made it in less than two hours. We came off I-10 onto St Charles Avenue, passed Lee Circle, and headed uptown toward the Garden District. When we turned onto Camp, the street was sealed off with emergency vehicles and plumes of black smoke were still rising from the scorched brick shell and cratered roof of the building I had seen in the historical photograph.

Magelli stood behind an NOPD cruiser, looking at the destroyed building, his face flinching slightly when a live round popped inside the heat.

'You nail him?' Helen said.

'We never saw him,' Magelli said.

'You couldn't get anybody into the first floor?' I asked.

'We kept within our perimeter. We've got nobody down. Is that all right with you?' he said.

'You bet,' I replied.

The defensiveness went out of his face.

'We've heard ammunition popping for two hours. How many were in a weapon is anybody's guess. At least two rounds hit a fire truck. Another one went through a neighbor's window,' he said.

The wind changed, and he turned his head and cleared his throat slightly and spit in the gutter.

'Well, you know what's inside. You want to take a look?' he said.

'I guess we won't have ribs for lunch today,' Helen said.

Magelli, two cops in uniform, and Helen and I went through the piked gate and started up the stairs to the second story, our weapons drawn. But the top of the stairs was partially blocked by a pile of burned laths and plaster. A raincoated fireman pushed his way past us and cleared a walkway, then kicked the door loose from the jamb.

The smell inside did not fit in time and place; instead, I thought of a village across the seas and I heard ducks quacking in terror and the grinding sounds of steel tracks on an armored vehicle.

The fire had probably started on or near the gas stove, and the entirety of the kitchen looked like a room carved out of soft coal. The canned goods in the pantry had superheated, and exploded glass from preserve or jelly jars had embedded like teeth in the walls. Portions of the roof had collapsed into the living room, half covering a desk by a front window. On the floor, among hundreds of brass shell casings and shards of broken window glass and a network of incinerated rug fibers, were the remains of two bolt-action rifles, their magazines filled with melted lead, and a .45 and a nine-millimeter pistol, the slides blown back and jammed open.

We neared the front windows, and a fireman gagged behind his face shield. I pressed my handkerchief to my mouth and nose and thought of water buffalo and grass huts and rice in wicker baskets and penned hogs and the kerosene-like smell of a flame arching into a ville from a vehicle we called zippo tracks and another smell that was like the sweet, sickening stench a rendering plant makes. The fireman used the point of his ax to drag a pile of drenched debris off a desk, and the stench rose from the desk well as palpably and thick as a cloud of insects.

'Sorry for the remark outside,' Helen said, her eyes

deliberately unfocused as she looked down at the shape curled inside the well.

'Is that Remeta?' Magelli asked.

There was little left of the dead man's features. The head was hairless, the skin burned black. His forearms were pressed against his ears, as though the flames had contained a sound he did not want to hear. The tissue around his right eye looked like a scorched and shriveled biscuit.

'He was a geek. I was wrong about him,' I said.

Magelli raised his eyes to mine, not understanding.

'It's Micah, Jim Gable's chauffeur. He used to be a carnival geek. He told me people paid to see the deformity on his face so they wouldn't have to look at the ugliness inside themselves.'

'So?' Magelli said.

'He was a carnie man. He knew better than to shake down a man like Remeta. He was sent here to kill him,' I said.

'You're saying Gable hired him?' Magelli said.

'A cop who had a whole family capped? Not a chance. I can't believe I was a meter maid here,' Helen said.

chapter thirty-one

The next morning I called Clete's motel but no one answered. I tried again later and a woman picked up the phone.

'Passion?' I said.

'What you want?'

'Where's Clete?'

'Asleep. Leave him alone.'

'How about a little show of manners?' I said.

'I'll tell him you called. Right now he needs his rest,' she said, and hung up.

That evening I drove to the motel. It had been hot all day, and the sky was purple and red in the west and it had just started to rain. When Clete opened the door his clothes looked like they had been slept in and I could smell alcohol deep down in his lungs.

'What's up, Streak?' he said.

'Did Passion tell you I called?'

'She must have forgot.'

He closed the door behind me. The room was dark and in disarray. A red bandanna, like the one I had seen Passion wear around her neck, was on the nightstand. He took an open can of beer out of the icebox and drank the can empty and dropped it in a trash basket.

'Jim Gable's chauffeur tried to hit Remeta. Remeta put

one in him and then set his own apartment on fire,' I said. I looked at the side of his face, his gaze that was focused on nothing. 'Clete?'

'Remeta wanted everybody to think the chauffeur was him?'

'Or to buy time till he could find Gable and cook his hash.'

'Gable set up the hit, huh?'

'That's my guess.'

He turned on the tap in the sink and washed his face with his hands. 'I'm out of hooch. I've got to get a drink,' he said.

'I thought you were breaking it off with Passion.'

'She's all alone. Her sister's going to be executed. She's got an incurable disease. What am I supposed to say? You were a good punch but hit the road?'

Then he started opening and closing cabinets, rooting in his suitcase, reopening the icebox, even though he already knew there was no more booze in the cottage.

'Passion wants me to go with her to Letty's execution. She got Letty to put my name on the list,' he said. 'You ever see the Stake in Saigon? I'm not up to this bullshit.'

He waved one meaty hand in the air, as though warning away an imaginary adversary. I sat down on the side of his bed and waited for his anger to pass. Then my gaze alighted on one of the pillows by the headboard.

'Who was bleeding?' I asked.

'Go home, Dave. Let me alone for a while. I'll be all right. I promise,' he said, and leaned heavily on the sink, his back swelling with breath like a beached whale's.

The next day I got another call from Connie Deshotel.

'I wasn't able to make any headway with Belmont,' she said.

'I see.'

'He's caught between his own inclinations and what his constituency wants. It's not easy for him,' she said.

'His inclinations? I'll float that by Letty Labiche if I get a chance.'

'I tried to help. I don't know what else you want.'

'Where's Belmont now?'

'I wouldn't know. Try his office. But I'm out of this. You understand? Frankly, I just don't want any more of your rudeness,' she said.

'What's your relationship with Jim Gable, Connie?' I said.

But the connection had already gone dead.

Connie Deshotel had said she didn't know Belmont Pugh's whereabouts. But today was Wednesday, and I knew where to find him. When Belmont had been a traveling preacher and broom salesman, he had made a regular midweek stop at a slat-board fundamentalist church outside the little settlement of Lottie, in the middle of the Atchafalaya Basin. The congregation had paid thirty-five dollars for every sermon Belmont gave, and today, either out of gratitude or the aura of humility his continued presence at the church brought him, Belmont was still a regular at Wednesday night meetings.

That evening I drove up through Opelousas and took Highway 190 toward Baton Rouge, then turned down a shale road and crossed a railroad track and went deeper into the Basin, past a community of small houses with rusted screens, to a church building with a blue neon cross on the roof.

The congregation had laid out dinner on plank tables by a grove of cedar trees. Among the cluster of pickup trucks and 1970s gas-guzzlers I saw Belmont's black Chrysler, a patina of gray mud on the fenders.

The windows were down in the Chrysler, and when I walked past it I could see a bored state trooper behind the wheel and a woman in back who was smoking a cigarette. She looked like she had been reconstructed in Dr Frankenstein's laboratory, with silicone implants, a face tuck, chemically dyed skin, and industrial-strength perfume. She blew her nose on a Kleenex and dropped it out the window on the grass.

Belmont's mouth was full of food, his Stetson pushed back on his head so that the ends of his hair were mashed against his forehead like a little boy's.

'You're not gonna punch nobody out, are you, son?' he said.

'I need to talk with you about Letty Labiche.'

'I knew it.'

'She's got two weeks.'

'You don't need to remind me of that. I got people marching with signs in front of the capitol. I got Italians calling me from the Vatican.'

'You don't want this on your conscience, Belmont.'

He tossed a chicken bone over his shoulder and got up from the table.

'Walk with me,' he said.

We went into the grove of cedars; the sky was purple now and filled with the drone of locusts. There was grease on his hands, and he kept opening and closing them and looking at the shine the grease made on his skin.

'I'll be right by the phone the night the death warrant is read. I get new evidence or hear from the federal court, I'll stop it. Otherwise, it goes forward,' he said.

'It's wrong. You know it.'

'I'm the governor. Not a judge. Not a jury. I didn't have a damn thing to do with that trial. It's on y'all's self, right down there in Iberia Parish. You quit carrying your guilt up to Baton Rouge and throwing it on my doorstep, you hear?'

He turned away from me and let out his breath. The

curls on the back of his neck moved like chicken feathers in the breeze. In the distance his black Chrysler was painted with a red light against the western sun. Someone inside the church turned on the neon cross.

'Who's the lady in the car?' I asked.

'She's a missionary, as in "missionary position." I'm a sinner. I don't hide it. You stop climbing my back, Dave.'

'Connie Deshotel warned me.'

'What?'

'She said she didn't get anywhere with you. I don't know why I thought I could.'

'It's Connie Deshotel been telling me Letty Labiche takes the needle or I go back to selling brooms and bathroom disinfectant. Where in God's name do you get your information, son?'

He walked back to the picnic and stopped by a water spigot. He turned it on and washed his hands, scrubbing them in the spray as though an obscene presence had worked its way into the grain of his skin. Then he pulled at least three feet of paper towel off a roll and wiped his hands and forearms and mouth and wadded up the paper and bounced it off the side of a trash barrel. His Stetson hat had turned a soft blue in the glow of the neon cross on the church.

Saturday afternoon Dana Magelli walked into my bait shop, carrying a tackle box and a spinning rod. His blue jeans and tennis shoes looked like they had just come out of the box.

'Got any boats for rent?' he asked.

'Take your pick,' I said.

He pulled a soda out of the cooler and wiped the melted ice off the can and put a dollar on the counter and sat down on a stool. A customer was dipping shiners with a net out of the aerated tank in back and dropping them in a shiner bucket. Dana waited until the customer had finished and gone outside, then he said, 'You and Purcel haven't been running a game on Jim Gable, have you?'

'What game?'

'He says he found glass in his soup at a restaurant. He says people are following him. He says he saw what he believes was a scoped rifle in a window.'

'Gee, that's too bad.'

'Evidently he's got a fuckpad with an unlisted number. One of his broads is getting calls that scare her shitless.'

'You think Clete and I are behind this?'

'Purcel's an animal. He's capable of anything. Last night somebody blew out Gable's car window with double-ought bucks and missed his head by about two inches.'

'It's Remeta.'

'You're not involved? I have your word?'

'I'm not involved, Dana.'

'You all right?' he said.

'Why?'

'Because you don't look it.'

'Must be the weather.'

He gazed at the sunlight and shadows on the bamboo and the willows bending in the breeze off the Gulf.

'You must have a funny metabolism,' he said.

I had given my word to Dana that I was not involved in the harassing of Jim Gable or the shotgun attack upon him. I had said nothing about future possibilities.

Early Sunday morning I drove to Lafourche Parish and headed south through the cane fields toward the Gulf. The wind was blowing hard and the sky had turned black and I could feel the barometer dropping. I drove down Purple Cane Road, past the general store and the dance hall where my mother used to work, while raindrops as big as marbles broke against my windshield. In the distance I could see the three-story, coffee-colored stucco house where Jim and Cora Gable lived, the palm trees blowing above the roof.

But no one came to the door. I waited in my truck until almost noon under a sky sealed with clouds that looked like black ink floating inside an inverted bowl. I don't know what I expected to do or to find, but I knew that my mother's murderers would never be apprehended by my simply letting the system move forward of its own accord. The temperature must have dropped fifteen degrees and through the window I could smell speckled trout schooling up in the bay and the cool, wet odor of dust blowing out of the cane, and when I shut my eyes I was a little boy again, driving down Purple Cane Road with my mother and the bouree man named Mack, wondering what had happened to my father, Big Aldous, and our home on the bayou south of New Iberia.

Then the front door opened and Cora Gable looked out at my truck, her face as white and threaded with lines as old plaster, her scalp showing when the wind blew her hair. I got out of the truck and walked toward her. Her mouth was bright red in the gloom, and she tried to smile, but the conflict in her face made me think of a guitar string wound so tightly on its peg that it seems to tremble with its own tension.

'Oh, Mr Robicheaux,' she said.

'Is Jim home?'

'Sir, this upsets me. You attacked my husband. Now you're here.'

'I think your husband is responsible for Micah's death, Miss Cora.'

'Micah went back to New Mexico. Jim gave him money to go. What are you telling me?'

'May I come in?'

'No, you may not. Jim said you'd do something like this. I think I have some things of your mother's. Wasn't

323

her name Guillory? They were in a shed. Maybe you should take them and go.'

'You have belongings of my mother?'

'Yes, I think I do.' Her face became disconcerted, wrapped in conflicting thoughts, as though she were simultaneously asking and answering questions inside her own head. 'I don't know where they are right now. I can't be responsible for other people's things.'

I stepped closer to the door. The rain was slanting out of the sky, running off the tiles on the roof, clicking on the banks of philodendron and caladium that lined the brick walkway.

'Go away before I call the police,' she said, and closed the heavy door with both hands and shot the bolt inside.

I drove back up the dirt road. Just as I reached the general store, I felt my left front tire go down on the rim. I pulled into the store's parking lot and got the jack, lug wrench, a pair of cloth gloves, and the spare out of the back and squatted down by the front fender and began spinning the nuts off the flat. I heard a car pull in next to me and someone walk toward the entrance of the store, then pause.

'Lo and behold, it's the Davester,' a man's voice said.

I looked up into the grinning face of Jim Gable. He wore a tweed sports coat and tan slacks and shined loafers and a pink shirt with a silver horse monogrammed on the pocket. There was only a yellow discoloration around one eye and the corner of his mouth from the blows he had taken at the Shrimp Festival.

He looked up at the gallery where an old man in overalls and a little boy sat on a wood bench, drinking soda pop and cracking peanuts.

'That's a mean-looking lug wrench in your hand. You're not in a volatile mood, are you?' he said.

'Not in the least, Jim.'

'Don't get up. I suspect you've already bothered my wife. I'll get the feedback from her later,' he said.

He walked past me, on up the steps and across the gallery, through the screen door and into the store. He shook hands with people, then opened the screen again in a gentlemanly fashion to let an elderly lady enter. I fitted the spare onto the axle and tightened down the wheel nuts and lowered the jack, then went inside the store.

Gable sat at a table with a checkerboard painted on top of it, drinking from a paper cup filled with coffee. The inside of the store smelled like cheese and lunch meat and microwave boudin and the green sawdust that was scattered on the floor. I turned a chair around and sat down facing Gable.

He grinned at me as he had outside, but his eyes wouldn't hold on mine.

'Remeta missed you with double-ought bucks? Maybe he's slipping. I'd hate to have him on my case,' I said.

He pulled at his collar and looked sideways out the window at the abandoned nightclub next door and the old Jax beer sign swinging on its chains.

'You don't have any idea of what's going on, do you?' he said.

'I don't have to. Time and Remeta are on my side.'

A family dressed in Sunday clothes came in, folding umbrellas, blowing and laughing at the rain.

'I've pulled your sheet. You have a violent, alcoholic history. You've spent a whole career discrediting yourself,' he said.

I stared directly into Gable's eyes.

'I know you murdered my mother. I know the words she spoke just before you and your partner killed her. "My name's Mae Robicheaux. My boy fought in Vietnam. My husband was Big Aldous Robicheaux." I'm going to smoke you myself or be there when you ride the needle, Jim,' I said.

He kept his eyes on mine now, so he would not have to look at the people who were staring at us from the grocery counter.

'I'm going to walk out of here now. These are my neighbors. You're not going to do anything. I'm carrying a weapon, but my hands are on the table. Everyone can see that,' he said.

'I promised Boots I wouldn't repeat my old behavior. I'm usually pretty good about keeping my word, Jim, but I'm just human. Also, I want you to understand the nature of our relationship and to form an idea of what will probably happen whenever we meet. So, in that spirit—' I said, and balled up my fist inside my cloth glove and leaned across the table and hooked him in the eye and knocked him into a stack of canned vegetables.

chapter thirty-two

Wednesday evening Alafair was eating at an outdoor table at the McDonald's on East Main when a red car pulled into the parking lot and a young man wearing a freshly pressed white shirt and starched khakis and sunglasses and a straw hat got out and walked toward her.

He stood in front of her, the fingers of one hand touching the tabletop, his face expressionless behind his sunglasses.

'Can I sit down?' he asked.

'You shouldn't be here, Johnny. People are looking for you,' she replied.

'That's nothing new.' He glanced over his shoulder at a Cherokee filled with high school kids in the parking lot. They were listening to white rap music that beat like a fist on the walls of the restaurant. He sat down at the table. 'Take a ride with me.'

'Dave says you beat up a black woman in the Loreauville Quarters. For no reason,' she said.

'I'm sorry about that. I got strange stuff that goes off in my head sometime. I told the woman that. That's the way it flushes sometime.'

The rap music from the Cherokee increased in intensity. He turned irritably and glared at the kids inside the vehicle. One of them threw a box of trash out on the pavement. Alafair looked at Remeta's hands. For some reason they weren't like those of an artist any longer. They were knobbed with bone and they curled spasmodically into fists, as though he wanted to crush something inside them. He turned back to her and stared at her expression.

'You got something on your mind?' he asked.

'Your arms are sunburned,' she said.

'I was out on Lake Fausse Pointe. It's full of herons and cranes and flooded cypress. It's beautiful.'

'I have to go now.'

'No,' he said, and placed his hand across her wrist. He leaned toward her, his mouth parting to speak, but the kids in the Cherokee had turned up their stereo even louder and he looked at them again over his shoulder. A pop can flew out of the Cherokee's window and clattered across the pavement.

'Wait here a minute,' Remeta said, and got up from the table.

He walked to the Cherokee and picked up all the Styrofoam cups and hamburger containers and dirty napkins that had been thrown on the pavement and stood with them at the driver's window.

'Turn off the radio,' he said.

The high school kid behind the wheel stopped talking to the others in the vehicle and looked dumbly at Remeta, then began turning down the dial on the stereo until the sound bled away into silence.

'You guys are seriously pissing me off,' Remeta said, pushing the trash through the window. 'The next time I see you throwing garbage on the ground, I'm going to kick the shit out of you. And if I hear that rap music again, I'm going to tear your stereo out of the dashboard and shove it up your ass. Now get out of here.'

The driver started the Cherokee, grinding the starter,

and bounced out onto the street, while his passengers looked back white-faced at Remeta.

He sat back down at the table, his eyes following the Cherokee down the street.

'That was mean,' she said.

'They deserve worse.'

'I'm going to the library now.'

'I'll drive you there. We can meet later.'

'No.'

'I had to shoot that guy. The one in the fire in New Orleans. He was sent to kill me.'

'Don't tell me about it. It's disgusting.'

There were shards of color in his cheeks and throat.

'I can't believe you're talking to me like that. Who did this to us, Alafair?' he said.

'You did. Go away, Johnny.'

She could not see his eyes through his dark glasses, but his head protruded on his neck toward her, and his breath seemed to reach out and touch her cheek like a dirty finger.

Then he drew his hand back off the table, his skin squeaking on the surface.

'The vase I gave you? I want you to break it. You're not one of the people in that painting anymore, Alafair,' he said.

He got up from his seat and stared down at her, his silhouette motionless against the late sun. She could see her reflection in his glasses. She looked small and diminished, her image distorted, as though it were she who was morally impaired and not he.

After a long moment, as though he had reviewed his judgment, he said, 'You're just a little traitor. That's all you ever were.'

She waited until he had driven out of the parking lot, then went to the pay phone and dialed 911.

*

Two days later Wally, the dispatcher, buzzed my office phone.

'There's a guy out here says he's Goldie Bierbaum from New Orleans,' he said.

'Send him back.'

'Didn't he fight Cleveland Williams?'

'Goldie fought everybody.'

A minute later I saw Goldie at my door. Even though he was almost seventy, his chest was still flat-plated, his muscular thighs wider than his waist. Before he had opened his saloon on Magazine back in the 1960s, he had fought in three weight divisions and had been a contender in two.

Goldie sat down and put a gumball in his mouth and offered the remaining one in his palm to me.

'Not right now,' I said.

'That button man you were looking for, the one who did Zipper Clum, you still after him?' he asked. His few strands of hair were coated with gel and looked like copper wire stretched across his scalp.

'Yeah, he's a real headache,' I said.

'I hear he's been living on Camp Street. He boosts cars all over the neighborhood, like the Garden District is the Hertz company.'

'Thanks, anyway, Goldie. That place burned down last week. Our man has moved on.'

'You're kidding?'

'Why didn't you report him to NOPD?'

'I don't have a good history with those guys.'

'Tell me, you remember a cop named Jim Gable, from back in the sixties?'

'Sure. He was a bum.'

'In what way?'

'He did scut work for the Giacanos.'

'You positive about that?'

'Hey, Dave, I got into Didoni Giacano for ten large.

The vig was four hundred a week. You know how it works. The principal don't ever go down. I was late a couple of times and Gable came by and picked it up. He'd leave the woman in the cruiser and drink a cup of coffee in back and talk about the weather like we were old friends. But he was a bum.'

'What woman?'

'She was a rookie. Maybe she didn't know what was going on. She's big shit in Baton Rouge. You know, what's-her-name, Deshotel, she's the attorney general now.'

That same evening Jim Gable told his wife he was going to cut his losses, take early retirement, and move the two of them to New Mexico. Dana Magelli had actually sicced IAD on him. Could you believe it? Two plain-clothes picked him up in the mayor's office and grilled him down at the district like a perp. A pair of polyester desk pilots who smelled like hair oil and made grade by jamming up other cops.

'What's your association with Maggie Glick?' one of them asked.

'I don't have one.'

'That's not what she says.'

'Let me give you guys a short history lesson,' Gable said. 'This used to be a good city. We knew who and where everybody was. People say they don't like vice. What they mean is they don't like it uncontrolled. We'd tell the dagos somebody was out of line and they'd throw him off a roof. Muggers got their noses broken with a blackjack. The whores didn't spread clap through the tourist trade. That's the way the old days were, boys. Go back to Dana Magelli and tell him to open a fruit stand.'

Jim Gable stood in his den, surrounded by his collection of ordnance, and drank from a glass of whiskey and ice. He opened a mahogany humidor and took a plump cigar from it and gingerly bit off the tip and lit it.

He could probably get around the IAD investigation. He was too high up in the department, too long term, and he knew too many secrets about the misdeeds of others to be a sacrificial offering now. When a police department got hosed, a few street cops and midlevel functionaries took the heat and did the time, if any indeed was ever forthcoming.

The real problem was this guy Johnny Remeta. How did he, Jim Gable, get mixed up with a psychopath, particularly one who could boost cars all over the state, smoke two police officers, and walk through walls as though he were invisible?

He didn't like to think about Remeta. Perps and lowlifes were predictable as a class. Most of them were dumb and did everything in their power to get caught. They sought authority in their lives and attention from father figures and were too stupid to know it. Remeta was different. He brought both intelligence and genuine psychosis to his work, a combination that made Gable swallow unconsciously when he thought about it.

He picked up the jar containing the head of a Viet Cong from the table and set it on the mantel in front of the mirror. The head wobbled slightly in the yellow fluid and nudged against the glass, the slitted eyes staring up at Gable. It gave him a sense of comfort to be able to pick up the jar and move it wherever he wanted, although he wasn't sure why. He looked out the window at the fall colors in the trees and the glitter of the sunset on the bay, and he wanted to wedge a revolver in the mouth of Johnny Remeta and blow the back of his head off.

His mood was broken by the sound of his wife dropping something in the bedroom.

'Dear, would you come in, please? I can't bend over to get my cane,' she called.

He went into her bedroom and picked it up for her, then had to help her out of bed. She had not dressed that day and was still in her nightgown, and she smelled like Vicks VapoRub and sour milk. Her hand clung to his wrist after she was on her feet and in her slippers.

'Let's have dinner out on the terrace. It's such a lovely evening. I'll order from the restaurant and have them bring it down,' she said.

'That'll be fine, Cora.'

'Would you do a favor for me?' she asked, smiling wistfully. She wore no makeup, but there were gin roses in her cheeks and a merry light in her eyes. He nodded, then shivered at the prospect of what she might ask.

'Would you rub my feet? They ache terribly when the season changes,' she said.

But he knew what that meant. At first it would be her feet, then her back and neck, and at some point she would touch him on the cheek and let her fingers trail down his sternum and come to rest on his thigh. A visceral sensation washed through him and made his scalp tighten against the bone.

'I'm going through the accounts now. Can I fix you another drink and join you later on the terrace?' he said.

That was smart, he thought. She couldn't expect him to perform romantically on the terrace.

But when he looked at her face, the pinched mouth, the eyes that were suddenly masked, he knew she had seen through him.

'I'll call the restaurant now. But do fix me a drink, and bring my medicine from the cabinet, would you, please? I hate to be a bother. I am a bother, aren't I?' she said.

He hated the tone in her voice. She was the cloying victim and martyr now, a role she was a master at. Her entire personality was a snake pit of neurotic aberrations. He never knew which one was going to slither out on the floor.

He took a bottle of vodka out of the icebox and placed it on a silver tray with a Gibson glass and a jar of tiny pearl onions and a demitasse spoon and set the tray out on the terrace. In the distance he could see a boat with a red sail disappearing over the horizon, and he wanted to be on the boat, the salt breeze in his face, a new life waiting for him somewhere in the Caribbean.

He just had to be patient. Every quart of gin or vodka she drank was like lighting a Chinese firecracker in her heart. She probably had over nine million in her portfolio at Piper, Jaffray. Even after he paid the tax on the capital gains, he could begin construction on his quarter horse track in New Mexico and still be able to live on a ranch in the high desert country and keep a cabin cruiser on the Texas coast.

Not bad for a working-class kid who actually walked a night beat in the Irish Channel.

He went back into the den and picked up his whiskey and ice and sipped from it. Through the window he heard Cora on the remote phone, calling the restaurant for a delivery. He just didn't know if he could bear another evening at home with her. He pulled open a side drawer on his cherrywood desk and removed an address book and thumbed through the names inside. He had entered only the initials beside the telephone numbers of the Mexican, Puerto Rican, and black girls who one way or another had come under his sway. There were over three dozen sets of initials in the book.

Some might consider him profligate, he thought. But so what? Long ago he had learned that most people admired the pagan virtues rather than the Christian ones, particularly in their leaders, no matter what they said. Libido and power and success and creativity were interchangeable characteristics of the human personality. Ask any woman whether she preferred a lover who radiated a quiet sense of power and confidence or one who was self-effacing and pliant. If he was lucky, Cora would drink herself unconscious and he could make a call and meet a woman at a motel in Grand Isle. Why not? He could be back in three hours.

But the quickening of his heart already told him why not.

In his mind's eye he saw himself on an empty stretch of highway, in the dark, the walls of sugarcane twelve feet high on each side of him. Then a tire went flat or a fan belt broke, and while he was jacking up the car or staring down at a steaming radiator a car pulled in behind him, the high beams on, but the driver remained behind the wheel, faceless, letting him burn with apprehension in the headlights' glare.

A film of perspiration had formed on his forehead and he drank from his whiskey. But the ice had melted and the whiskey tasted as though it had been aged inside oily wood. Why was his heart beating so rapidly? Was he a coward, afraid to go down the road because of this kid Remeta?

No. He was just using his judgment. Remeta was a cop killer. The odds were good that if cornered Remeta would never make the jail. All Jim Gable had to do was wait.

He was hungry. He washed his face and hands and combed his hair in the bathroom mirror and went into the kitchen and opened the icebox. It was virtually empty. He pulled back the sliding door on the terrace and went outside. She lay supine on a reclining chair, her face rosy with vodka, her teeth yellow in the waning light.

'Hungry, dear?' she said.

'Yes.'

'You've always been a hungry little boy, haven't you?'

'I'd appreciate it if you wouldn't talk to me like that, Cora.'

'Well, your dinner will be here shortly. You'll see.'

'Thank you,' he said, and went back inside and slid the glass door shut.

How long had her mother lived? Ninety-six years? Good God! Maybe not even a quart of booze a day could kill genes like that. What a horrible thought. No, he was not going to have thoughts like that.

To hell with Johnny Remeta, he told himself. He called the beeper number of a woman in New Orleans, and a half hour later she called him back. Her nickname was Safety Pin Sue, a mindless, totally dependent addict who took a narcissistic pleasure in her own self-destruction.

'Meet me in Grand Isle tonight,' he said.

'For you, Jim, anywhere, anytime,' she said, her voice warm with crack.

That was more like it, he thought.

He tonged fresh ice into his drink and gazed out the high window at the darkening greenness of the land, the gold light trapped on the bay's horizon, the sailboat that had turned around and was tacking for home. He raised his drink in salute to the evening.

That's when he heard a vehicle under the porte cochere. He opened the middle drawer of his desk and removed a blue-black .38 revolver and let it hang loosely from his hand.

The house puffed with wind when Cora opened the side door onto the drive.

'That smells delicious. Bring it into the kitchen, would you? My purse is on the table,' Cora's voice said.

Jim Gable replaced the revolver in the drawer and closed it and finished his drink. The wind was picking up, and a red leaf tore loose from a maple and plastered itself against the window. For some reason the leaf, its symmetrical perfection arbitrarily terminated by a gust of cold air, made Jim Gable brood upon an old prospect that he had tried to bury on the edges of his conscious-ness for many years. Was it just mortality? No, it was the darkness that lay beyond it and the possibilities the darkness contained.

Don't have those thoughts. They're the products of old wives' tales, he told himself, and turned to the mirror above the mantel and started to comb his hair, then realized he had just combed it.

He heard Cora's stoppered cane scudding softly on the floor behind him.

'This is my husband,' she said. 'Jim, this is the young man who delivered our dinner. I can't find my checkbook. Do you have some cash?'

Gable looked into the mirror and saw his own startled expression and the floating head of the Vietnamese soldier and the reflected face of Johnny Remeta, like three friends gathered together for a photograph. The teeth of the dead Vietnamese were exposed at the corner of his mouth, as though he were trying to smile.

chapter thirty-three

On the following Tuesday the early edition of the *Daily Iberian* said Letty Labiche had been moved from St Gabriel Prison to the Death House at Angola. Belmont Pugh held what he said was his 'last TV news conference on the matter' on the steps of the capitol building. He used the passive voice and told reporters 'the death warrant has been signed and will be carried out tomorrow at midnight. It's out of my hands. But I'll be waiting by the telephone up to the last second.' He turned his face into the sunrise and presented a solemn profile to the camera.

Helen and I went to lunch together and were walking back from the parking lot to the department when a deputy in uniform passed us.

'The old man's looking for you,' he said.

'What's up?'

'Nothing much. Your man Purcel is trying to destroy St Martinville. They use animal darts on people?' he replied.

Inside, I stopped by my mailbox. It was filled with pink message slips. Three of them were from the St Martin Parish Sheriff's Department. Two others were from Dana Magelli. Another simply stated, in capital letters, 'SEE ME!' The sheriff's initials were at the bottom. I walked down to his office and opened the door.

'What's going on?' I asked.

'I don't quite know where to start. Where's your beeper?'

'Wally sat on it. That's not a joke.'

'Dana Magelli called. Remeta got into Jim Gable's house, locked the wife in the garage, and kidnapped Gable.'

'Too bad. What's the deal with Purcel?'

'I knew you'd be torn up over Gable.'

'Come on, skipper. What's Clete done?'

'He's in a bar in St Martinville. Three bikers are already in the hospital.' I started to speak, but he held his hand up. 'He broke a pool cue across a city cop's face. It's not the barroom follies anymore, Dave. He might get his light blown out. Everybody around here, including me, is sick of this guy.'

Helen Soileau and I drove the nine miles to St Martinville in under ten minutes. The square by the old French church and the Evangeline Oak was filled with emergency vehicles, and the feeder streets were blocked to keep out traffic. We parked the cruiser a hundred feet from the bar where Clete was barricaded and walked up to a black police lieutenant with a thin mustache who stood with a bullhorn behind the open door of his vehicle. The windows of the bar were shattered, and the wall above one of them was scorched black and dripping with fire retardant.

I fanned the reek of tear gas out of my face.

'The shell hit the windowsill and started a fire. You're friends with this character?' the lieutenant said.

'Yeah. He's generally harmless,' I said.

'Oh, I can see that,' the lieutenant said. His name was Picard and he was a Vietnam veteran who had gone away to school on the GI Bill and earned a degree in criminal justice. 'I've got an officer in the hospital. The inside of that bar is totally destroyed. He beat those bikers till they cried and got down on their knees. You either get your friend out of there, and I mean in cuffs, or we cool him out.'

'I think we're overreacting to the situation, Loot,' I said.

'Are you hearing anything I say? He has the bartender's shotgun,' Picard replied.

'Bullshit,' Helen said, and pulled the bullhorn from Picard's hand. 'Hey, Clete. It's Helen Soileau. Dave and I are coming in,' she said into the horn, its echo resonating under the bar's colonnade. Then she threw the horn back into Picard's hands.

We pushed open the front door and went inside. Chairs and tables were broken; glass littered the floor; the liquor bottles on the counter behind the bar had been smashed into jagged shells. In one corner, by the pool table, was the unconscious form of a head-shaved and tattooed man dressed in jeans and a leather vest with no shirt underneath.

Clete sat at the end of the bar, grinning, his scalp bleeding on his face, his slacks and tropical shirt stained with tobacco juice and talc, a can of Budweiser by his fingers. A twenty-gauge, single-load shotgun rested against the inside of his thigh, the barrel pointed toward his chest.

'Is there a safety on that thing?' I asked.

'I haven't checked,' he replied.

'What the hell's the matter with you?' Helen said, glass snapping under her shoes.

'It's just been that kind of morning,' he said.

'We need to hook you up,' I said.

'Bad idea, Streak.'

'Beats being dead. That's the itinerary outside,' Helen said.

He touched the corner of his mouth with the ball of

one finger and looked at the wet spot on his skin. His eyes were lighted, his cheeks filled with color.

'The cop I took down with the cue? He tried to rip my head off with a baton,' he said.

Helen removed her handcuffs from the leather case on her belt, her eyes never leaving Clete's, and threw them on the bar.

'Hook yourself up, handsome,' she said.

'Nope,' he said, and smiled at her with his eyes and lifted his beer can to his mouth.

I stepped beyond Clete's angle of vision and made a motion with my head toward the front of the building. Helen walked with me across the broken glass until we were at the door. Clete salted his beer can, the shotgun still resting between his legs, as though the events taking place around him had no application in his life.

'When you hear it start, come running. Tell the locals we swarm him. If one of them draws a weapon, I'm going to stuff it sideways down his throat,' I said.

I walked behind the bar, across the duckboards, and opened a bottle of carbonated water and sat down next to Clete. I glanced at the biker who lay unconscious in the corner.

'You didn't kill him, did you?' I said.

'They were eating reds in the john. It was like beating up on cripples. I don't see the big deal here,' Clete said.

'The big deal is I think you want to go to jail. You're trying to fix it so you won't get bail, either.'

There was a self-amused light in his face. 'Save the psychobabble for meetings,' he said.

'You'll be in lockup. Which means no trip up to the Death House tomorrow night.'

He lowered his head and combed his hair back with his nails.

'I've already been. This weekend. I took Passion. Letty got to have a dinner with some of her relatives,' he said.

The whites of his eyes looked yellow, as though he had jaundice. I waited for him to go on. He picked up his beer can, but it was empty.

'I need some whiskey,' he said.

'Get it yourself.'

He got up and tripped, stumbling with the shotgun against the stool. Unconsciously he started to hand me the gun, then he grinned sleepily and took it with him behind the bar.

'Up on the top shelf. You broke everything down below,' I said.

He dragged a chair onto the duckboards. When he mounted the chair, he propped the shotgun against a tin sink. I leaned over the bar and grabbed the barrel and jerked the shotgun up over the sink. He looked down curiously at me.

'What do you think you're doing, Dave?' he asked.

I broke open the breech, pulled out the twenty-gauge shell, and tossed the shotgun out the front door onto the sidewalk.

Helen came through the door with one city cop and two sheriff's deputies. I went over the top of the bar just as Clete was climbing down from the chair and locked my arms around his rib cage. I could smell the sweat and beer in his clothes and the oily heat in his skin and the blood in his hair. I wrestled with him the length of the duckboards, then we both fell to the floor and the others swarmed over him. Even drunk and dissipated, his strength was enormous. Helen kept her knee across the back of his neck, while the rest of us bent his arms into the center of his back. But I had the feeling that, had he chosen, he could have shaken all five of us off him like an elephant in musth.

Twenty minutes later I sat with him in a holding cell at the city police station. His shirt was ripped down the back, and one shoe was gone, but he looked strangely serene.

Then I said, 'It's not just the execution, is it?'

'No,' he said.

'What is it?'

'I'm a drunk. I have malarial dreams. I still get night visits from a mamasan I killed by accident. What's a guy with my record know about anything?' he answered.

I woke before dawn on Wednesday, the last scheduled day of Letty Labiche's life, and walked down the slope through the trees to help Batist open up the shop. A Lincoln was parked by the boat ramp in the fog, its doors locked.

'Whose car is that up there?' I asked Batist.

'It was here when I come to work,' he said.

I unchained our rental boats and hosed down the dock and started the fire in the barbecue pit. The sunlight broke through the trees and turned the Lincoln the color of an overly ripe plum. Water had begun streaming from the trunk. I touched the water, which felt like it had come from a refrigerator, and smelled my hand. At 8 a.m. I called the department and asked Helen Soileau to run the tag.

She called back ten minutes later.

'It was stolen out of a parking lot in Metairie two days ago,' she said.

'Get ahold of the locksmith, would you, and ask the sheriff if he'd mind coming out to my house,' I said.

'Has this got something to do with Remeta?' she asked.

The sun was hot and bright by the time the sheriff and the locksmith and a tow truck got to the dock. The sheriff and I stood at the trunk of the Lincoln while the locksmith worked on it. Then the sheriff blew his nose and turned his face into the wind.

'I hope we'll be laughing about a string of bigmouth bass,' he said.

The locksmith popped the hatch but didn't raise it.

'Y'all be my guests,' he said, and walked toward his vehicle.

I flipped the hatch up in the air.

Jim Gable rested on his hip inside a clear-plastic wardrobe bag that was pooled at the bottom with water and pieces of melting ice the size of dimes. His ankles and arms were pulled behind him, laced to a strand of piano wire that was looped around his throat. He had inhaled the bag into his mouth, so that he looked like a guppy trying to breathe air at the top of an aquarium.

'Why'd Remeta leave him here?' the sheriff asked.

'To show me up.'

'Gable was one of the cops who killed your mother?'

'He told me I didn't know what was going on. He knew Johnny had cut a deal with somebody.'

'With who?'

When I didn't reply, the sheriff said, 'What a day. A molested and raped girl is going to be executed, and it takes a psychopath to get rid of a bad cop. Does any of that make sense to you?'

I slammed the hatch on the trunk.

'Yeah, if you think of the planet as a big blue mental asylum,' I said.

chapter thirty-four

As a police officer I had learned years ago a basic truth about all aberrant people: They're predictable. Their nemesis is not a lack of intelligence or creativity. Like the moth that wishes to live inside flame, the obsession that drives them is never satiated, the revenge against the world never adequate.

Johnny Remeta called the office at two o'clock that afternoon.

'How'd you like your boy?' he asked.

'You've killed three cops, Johnny. I don't think you're going to make the jail.'

'They all had it coming. Tell me I'm wrong.'

'You've been set up, kid.'

After a beat, he said, 'Alafair wants to be a screen writer. Tell her to write better lines for you.'

'You cut a deal. You thought you were going to pop Gable and have it all,' I said.

'Good try,' he said. But the confidence had slipped in his voice.

'Yeah? The same person who sent you to kill Gable gave orders to the Louisiana State Police to shoot you on sight. There are two Texas Rangers sitting outside my office right now. Why is that? you ask yourself. Because you whacked a couple of people in Houston, and these two Rangers are mean-spirited peckerwoods who can't wait to blow up your shit. You wonder why your mother dumped you? It's no mystery. You're a born loser, kid.'

'You listen –' he said, his voice starting to shake.

'Think I'm lying? Ask yourself how I know all this stuff. I'm just not that smart.'

He began to curse and threaten me, but the transmission was breaking up and his voice sounded like that of a man trying to shout down an electric storm.

I hung up the receiver and looked out the glass partition in my office at the empty corridor, then began filling out some of the endless paperwork that found its way to my basket on an hourly basis.

I tried to keep my head empty the rest of the afternoon, or to occupy myself with any task that kept my mind off the fate of Letty Labiche or the razor wire I had deliberately wrapped around Johnny Remeta's soul. I called the jail in St Martinville and was told Clete Purcel had thrown his food tray in a hack's face and had been moved into an isolation cell.

'Has he been arraigned yet?' I asked.

'Arraigned?' the deputy said. 'We had to Mace and cuff and leg-chain him to do a body search. You want this prick? We'll transfer him to Iberia Prison.'

At 4:30 I went outside and walked through St Peter's Cemetery. My head was thundering, the veins tightening in my scalp. The sky was like a bronze bowl, and dark, broad-winged birds that made no sound drifted across it. I wanted this day to be over; I wanted to look at the rain-worn grave markers of Eighth and Eighteenth Louisiana Infantry who had fought at Shiloh Church; I wanted to stay in a vacuum until Letty Labiche was executed; I wanted to slay my conscience.

I went back into the department and called Connie Deshotel's office in Baton Rouge.

346

'She's taken a few vacation days, Mr Robicheaux. What with the demonstrations and all outside,' the secretary said.

'Is she at Lake Fausse Pointe?'

'I'm sorry. I'm not at liberty to say,' the secretary replied.

'Will you call her for me and ask her to call me?'

There was a long pause.

'Her phone is out of order. I've reported it to the telephone company,' the secretary said.

'How long has it been out of order?'

'I don't know. I don't understand why you're asking me these questions. Is this an emergency?'

I thought about it, then said, 'Thanks for your time.'

I walked down to Helen Soileau's office and opened her door without knocking. She looked up from her paperwork at my face. She was chewing gum and her eyes were bright and focused with a caffeinated intensity on mine. Then one finger pointed at an empty chair by the side of her desk.

A few minutes later she said, 'Go through that again. How'd you know Remeta was working for Connie Deshotel?'

'The last time Alafair saw him he was sunburned. He said he'd been out on Lake Fausse Pointe. That's where Connie's camp is. Connie was Jim Gable's partner at NOPD back in the sixties. When Remeta tried to shake her down, she got him to hit Gable.'

'How?'

'He's a basket case. He's always looking for the womb.'

'You sure of all this, Dave?'

'No. But Johnny went crazy when I convinced him he'd been betrayed.'

'So you set Connie up?' Before I could reply, she picked

up a ballpoint and drew lines on a piece of paper and said, 'You'll never prove she was one of the cops who killed your mother.'

'That's true.'

'Maybe we should just let things play out,' she said. Her eyes drifted back on mine.

I looked out the window. The sky was the color of brass and smoke, and the wind was gusting in the streets.

'A storm is coming in. I have to get out on the lake,' I said.

Helen remained seated in her chair.

'You didn't do Gable. You want to nail Connie Deshotel yourself,' she said.

'The other side always deals the play. You coming or not?'

'Let me be honest with you, bwana. I had a bad night last night. I couldn't get Letty Labiche out of my mind. I guess it's because I was molested myself. So lose the attitude.'

Wally, the dispatcher, stopped us on the way out of the office. He had a pink memo slip in his hand.

'You wasn't in your office. I was fixing to put this in your pigeonhole,' he said to me.

'What is it?'

'A cop in St Martinville said Clete Purcel wants to talk to you. It's suppose to be important,' Wally said.

'I'll take care of it later,' I said.

Wally shrugged and let the memo slip float from his fingers into my box.

Helen and I towed a department outboard on the back of my truck to Loreauville, a few miles up the Teche, then drove through the sugarcane fields to the landing at Lake Fausse Pointe. The wind was blowing hard now, and I could see waves capping out on the lake and red leaves rising in the air against a golden sun.

Helen laced on a life preserver and sat down in the bow of the boat, and I handed her a department-issue cut-down twelve-gauge pump loaded with double-ought buckshot. She kept studying my face, as though she were taking the measure of a man she didn't know.

'You've got to tell me, Dave,' she said.

'What?' I smiled good-naturedly.

'Don't shine me on.'

'If Remeta's there, we call in backup and take him down.'

'That's it?'

'She's the attorney general of Louisiana. What do you think I'm going to do, kill her in cold blood?'

'I know you, Dave. You figure out ways to make things happen.'

'Really?' I said.

'Let's get something straight. I don't like that snooty cunt. I said she was dirty from the get-go. But don't jerk me around.'

I started to say something, then let it go and started the engine. We headed down the canal bordered by cypress and willow and gum trees, then entered the vast lily-dotted expanse of the lake itself.

It was a strange evening. In the east and south the sky was like a black ink wash, but the clouds overhead were suffused with a sulfurous yellow light. In the distance I could see the grassy slope of the levee and the live oaks that shadowed Connie Deshotel's stilt house and the waves from the lake sliding up into the grass and the wildflowers at the foot of her property. An outboard was tied to her dock, straining against its painter, knocking against one of the pilings. Helen sat hunched forward, the barrel of her shotgun tilted away from the spray of water off the bow.

I cut the engine and we drifted on our wake into the

shallows, then I speared the bottom with the boat paddle and the hull snugged onto the bank.

The lights were on inside the house and I could hear music playing on a radio. A shadow crossed a screen window. Helen stepped out into the shallows and waded out to the moored boat and placed her hand on the engine's housing.

'It's still warm,' she said, walking toward me, the twelve-gauge in both hands. She studied the house, the skin twitching slightly below her left eye.

'You want to call for backup?' I asked.

'It doesn't feel right,' she said.

'You call it, Helen.'

She thought about it. 'Fuck it,' she said, and pumped a round into the chamber, then inserted a replacement round into the magazine with her thumb.

But she was wired. She had killed three perpetrators on the job, all three of them in situations in which she had unexpectedly walked into hostile fire.

We walked up the slope in the shadows of the live oaks. The air was cool and tannic with the autumnal smell of flooded woods, the windows of the house gold with the western light. I took out my .45 and we mounted the steps and stood on each side of the door.

'Iberia Sheriff's Department, Ms Deshotel. Please step out on the gallery,' I said.

There was no response. I could hear shower water running in the back. I pulled open the screen, and Helen and I stepped inside, crossed the small living room, and looked in the kitchen and on the back porch. Then Helen moved into the hallway and the back bedroom. I saw her stop and lift the shotgun barrel so that it was pointed toward the ceiling.

'You better come in here, Dave. Watch where you step,' she said.

Johnny Remeta lay on top of a white throw rug in his

Jockey undershorts, his chest, one cheek, and his arm peppered with five entry wounds. A cut-down Remington twelve-gauge was propped in the corner. It was the same pump shotgun he had been carrying when he first visited my dock. He had not gone down all at once. The blood splatter was on the walls, the floor, and the bed sheets, and he had torn one of the curtains on the doors that gave onto a roofed deck.

The doors were open and I could see a redwood table on the deck, and on top of it a green bottle of wine, a platter of sandwiches, a package of filter-tipped cigarettes, Connie's gold-and-leather-encased lighter, and a big box of kitchen matches with a Glock automatic lying across it. The spent shell casings from the Glock were aluminum reloads and glinted on the deck like fat silver teeth.

I heard a faucet squeak in the bathroom, then the sound of the shower water died inside the stall. Helen pushed open the bathroom door and I saw her eyes go up and down the form of someone inside.

'Put a robe on and get out here, ma'am,' she said.

'Don't worry. I heard you long before you started banging around inside. Call in the report for me, please. My phone's out of order,' Connie Deshotel's voice said.

Helen picked up a pink robe off the toilet tank and flung it at Connie.

'Get your ass out here, ma'am,' she said.

A moment later Connie emerged into the bedroom, flattening her hair back wetly on her head with a hairbrush. She wore no makeup, but her face was calm, dispassionate, ruddy from her warm shower.

'I don't know if I can prove this, Dave, but I think you sent this man after me,' she said.

'You talked Remeta into the sack, then wasted him,' I said.

'He tried to rape me, you idiot. I got my gun out of my

bag and shot him through the door. Otherwise I'd be dead.' Then she said 'God!' between her teeth, and started to walk past us, as though we were only incidental elements in her day. Her slippers tracked Remeta's blood across the floor.

Helen pushed her in the chest with her fingers. 'You're tainting a crime scene. You don't do anything until we tell you,' she said.

'Touch my person again and you'll be charged with battery,' Connie said.

'*What?*'

'I'm the chief law officer of Louisiana. Does that register with you at all? A psychopath tried to rape and sodomize me. Do you think I'm going to let you come in here and treat me like a perpetrator? Now, get out of my way.'

Helen's face was bright with anger, a lump of cartilage flexing against her jaw. But no words came out of her mouth.

'Are you deaf as well as stupid? I told you to get out of my way,' Connie said.

Helen held the shotgun at port arms and shoved Connie through the side door onto the deck. 'Sit in that chair, you prissy bitch,' she said, and snipped a cuff on Connie's left wrist and hooked the other end to the handle on a huge earthen pot that was planted with bougainvillea.

'Are you placing me under arrest? I hope you are, because I'm going to ensure you live in penury the rest of your life,' Connie said.

'No, I'm restricting you from a crime scene. You want my job, you can have it,' Helen said.

I could hear lightning popping in the swamp and raindrops striking the tin roof. Helen began punching in numbers on her cell phone, then she hit the phone against the wall.

'I can't get through. I'm going out front,' she said.

I followed her into the living room.

'Take it easy,' I said.

'She's gonna walk.'

'There's no statute of limitations on homicide. We'll get her sooner or later.'

'That's not enough. When they blow somebody apart and take a shower and then get in your face, it's not enough. It's not nearly enough,' she said.

I put my hand on her arm, but she stepped away from me. 'Just let me do my job. Not everybody in this world is a member of the walking wounded,' she said, and flipped the shotgun's barrel up on her shoulder and pushed open the screen door and went out on the front porch, punching in numbers on her cell phone with her thumb.

I went back through the bedroom onto the deck. Connie Deshotel was gazing into the distance, at a heron, perhaps, or at her plans for her future or perhaps at nothing.

'When you and Jim Gable killed my mother, she took back her married name,' I said.

'Excuse me?' Connie said.

'Right before she died she told you her name was Mae Robicheaux. Y'all took her life, Connie, but she took back her soul. She had the kind of courage you and Jim Gable couldn't dream about.'

'If you want to charge me with a crime, that's your prerogative. Otherwise, please shut up.'

'You ever think about what lies beyond the grave?'

'Yes. Worms. Will you unlock this handcuff and keep that ridiculous woman away from me?'

I looked at her eyes, the sun-bleached tips of her wet hair, the healthy glow of her skin. There was no dark aura surrounding the head, no tuberous growth wrapping its tentacles around the spirit, no guilty attempt to avoid the indictment in my stare. She was one of those who could rise early and rested in the morning, fix tea and buttered toast, and light the ovens in Dachau.

I gave it up. I couldn't look at her face any more. Connie Deshotel's eyes had once contained the reflected image of my mother dying on a strip of frozen ground between fields of sugarcane that creaked with ice, whose clattering in the wind was probably the last sound my mother ever heard. Whatever Connie had done or seen that winter day long ago meant nothing to her, and when I looked into the moral vacuity of her eyes I wanted to kill her.

I turned my back to her and leaned on the deck railing and looked out at the rain falling on the lake. Out of the corner of my eye I saw her shake a cigarette out of her pack and place it in her mouth. Then she picked up her cigarette lighter, the one probably given her by Jim Gable, and snapped it dryly several times. She replaced it on the table and leaned forward, her redwood chair creaking under her, and reached for the box of kitchen matches on which rested the Glock automatic she had used to murder Johnny Remeta.

Simultaneously I heard Helen Soileau say, 'Hey, Dave, the St Martin sheriff's office is trying to patch into you. Clete's going cra—'

That was as far as she got. When she reached the door she saw Connie Deshotel's hand lift the Glock to get to the box of kitchen matches.

Connie's unlit filter-tipped cigarette was still hanging from her mouth when Helen blew most of her head off.

epilogue

Johnny Remeta took the fall for Connie Deshotel's death. It wasn't hard to arrange. In fact, Johnny had made it easy. His cut-down Remington was already loaded with double-ought bucks. I fired one round out into the trees, slipped the shotgun under his chest, and let the coroner and the state police and the sheriff's deputies from St Martin Parish come to their own conclusions.

It was dishonest, certainly, but I don't think it was dishonorable. In fact, it probably saved Helen Soileau's career. Besides, the print and electronic media loved the story we had created for them, and who could be so unkind as to disabuse them of their romantic fantasies? Connie Deshotel was much more likable as a blue-collar heroine in death than the self-serving political function-ary she had been in life.

My own role in her death was not one I cared to think about. I wondered why I didn't unlock Connie's handcuff and allow her to walk outside, away from the crime scene, away from any other confrontations with Helen. There was no evidence to disprove her claim that Remeta had tried to assault her. In fact, I believed at the time, as I do now, that she may have told the truth.

Was it natural to turn my back on my mother's murderer, knowing a pistol lay within ten inches of her grasp? Or was I deliberately incautious? Age has brought me few gifts, but one of them has been a degree of humility, at least a sufficient amount so that I no longer feel compelled to take my own inventory and I can surrender that terrible burden to my Higher Power.

It was late when the paramedics and the coroner and the parish deputies and the state troopers finally wrapped up their work at Connie Deshotel's camp on Lake Fausse Point. The sun was below the horizon in the west, and a green aura from the wooded rim of the swamp rose into the sky. I could hear alligators flopping and nutrias screaming back in the flooded trees, and when the moon came up the bass starting hitting the insects in the center of the lake, chaining the lake's surface with water rings.

I had forgotten all about the call from the St Martin Parish Sheriff's Department. I used Helen's cell phone and got a night deputy at the jail on the line.

'Somebody called earlier. A problem with Clete Purcel,' I said.

'Sonofabitch is spreading chaos all over the lockdown unit. You either quiet him down or he's gonna have an accident with a baseball bat.'

'Put him on,' I said.

'Are you nuts?'

'How'd you like him to do six months with you guys?' I asked.

There was a brief pause. 'Hang on,' the deputy replied.

A few moments later I heard a cell door open and the tinkle of waist or leg chains.

'Hello?' Clete said hoarsely.

'You going to tell me what it is now?' I said.

'When I took Passion up to Angola last weekend? For the dinner with Letty and their relatives? She was wearing a raincoat and that bandanna around her neck. There were two gunbulls outside and a matron inside, but nobody with a lot of smarts. Letty and Passion were going in and out of the john. You get my drift?'

'What are you telling me, Clete?'

'On the way back home Passion was like somebody I didn't know. Weirded out. Crying. Looking out the side window into the dark. I told her I'd be there when Letty went to the table. She said she wasn't going back up to the Death House. Just like that. No explanation.'

I could hear him breathing against the phone, his chains tinkling.

'I think they've both made their choice. I think it's time to leave it alone,' I said.

'You've got to give me a better answer than that,' he said.

But I didn't have a better answer. I heard Clete drop the receiver and let it swing on its cord against the wall. Then someone gathered it up and replaced it in the cradle.

It started to rain again after I got home. I listened to no radio or television that night, and at ten minutes after midnight I put on my raincoat and hat and walked down to the bait shop and turned on the string of lights over the dock and the flood lamps that shone on the bayou and every light in every corner of the shop. I fixed coffee and mopped down the floors and cut and trimmed bread for sandwiches and said my rosary on my fingers and listened to the rain beating on the roof until it became the only sound in my head. Then I realized I was not listening to rain anymore but to hail that bounced and smoked on the dock and melted into white string on the flood lamps, and I wanted to stay forever inside the lighted, cool brilliance of the dock and bait shop, and to keep Bootsie and Alafair there with me and let the rest of the world continue in its fashion, its cities and commerce and inhumanity trapped between morning and the blackness of the trees.

But it was I who would not let the world alone. The next day I drove out to the Labiche home and was told by a tall, high-yellow mulatto I had never seen before that Passion was at the nightclub, preparing to open up. He wore a mustache and tasseled, two-tone shoes and dark blue zoot pants with a white stitch in them and a black cowboy snap-button shirt with red flowers on it and a planter's straw hat cocked at an angle on his head.

'How's she feeling?' I said.

'Ax her,' he said.

'Excuse me, but who are you?'

'What do you care, Jack?' he said, and closed the door in my face.

Passion's pickup truck was the only vehicle in the nightclub's parking lot. I went in the side door and saw a woman at the antique piano by the back wall. She was totally absorbed in her music and was not aware that anyone else was in the building. Her powerful arms lifted and expanded in silhouette as she rolled her fingers up and down the yellowed keys. I couldn't identify the piece she was playing, but the style was unmistakable. It was Albert Ammons, Jerry Lee Lewis, and Moon Mulligan; it was out of the barrelhouse South of fifty years ago; it was Memphis and Texas R&B that could break your heart.

The woman at the piano stool wore jeans and an LSU T-shirt. A streak of gold sunlight fell across her neck like a sword, and on her neck was a tattooed red rose inside a cluster of green leaves.

She finished her song, then seemed to realize someone was standing behind her. She stayed very still, her hair lifting on her neck in the breeze from the fan, then closed the top on the piano keys.

'You want something?' she said, without turning around.

'No. Not really,' I replied.

'You figured it out?'

'Like Clete Purcel says, "What do I know?" '

'You think bad of me?'

'No.'

'My sister was brave. A lot braver than me,' she said.

'The dude at your house looks like he's in the life.'

'It's a life, ain't it?'

'I never heard anybody do "Pine Top's Boogie" as well as you. Don't sell yourself short, kiddo,' I said, and squeezed her on the shoulder and walked outside into the sunlight.

This story has only a brief postscript, and it's not a very dramatic one. Yesterday a package wrapped in white butcher paper arrived in the mail. In it were an old scrapbook with a water-faded purple binder and an envelope taped across the binder's surface. The letter read as follows:

Dear Mr Robicheaux,

Enclosed please find an item that evidently belonged to your mother. When the quarters were torn down, a number of such personal belongings were placed in a storage shed by my father, who was kind and thoughtful toward his workers, white and Negro alike, regardless of what his detractors have written about him.

It is not my responsibility to hold on to the discarded memorabilia of people to whom it obviously did not have great import. Frankly, you have proved a great disappointment. You besmirched my husband's name, and it would not surprise me that you are responsible for the rumor that I deliberately admitted a murderer to my home in order to rid myself of my husband. I understand you invested much of your life in drunkenness. Perhaps you should seek help.

Sincerely,
Cora Gable

I flipped through the pages of the scrapbook, stiff with photos and postcards and ticket stubs and sealed locks of hair and pressed flowers that had been glued in place with brush and jar. There was a wedding photo of her and Big Aldous taken in front of the brick cathedral in Abbeville; a menu from the restaurant in the old Jung Hotel in New Orleans, where she and Big Al had their honeymoon; a newspaper article from the *Daily Iberian* about my return from Vietnam; another article about my graduating from the New Orleans Police Academy.

The next ten pages, the only ones remaining in the book, were filled with articles from both the *Times-Picayune* and the *Daily Iberian* about my career. Inside the back of the binder she had pasted a newspaper photograph of me in uniform, leaning on a cane, and below it a photo of me taken in third grade at the Catholic elementary school. She had created a frame around the two pictures by gluing strips of pink ribbon along the borders of the binder.

My mother had been virtually illiterate and was probably not sure of the content of many of the articles she had saved. Nor was she able to make annotations in her scrapbook to indicate what the articles meant to her. But I knew who my mother was. She had said it to her killers before she died. Her name was Mae Robicheaux. And I was her son.

available from

THE ORION PUBLISHING GROUP

All Orion/Phoenix titles are available at your local bookshop or from the following address:

Mail Order Department
Littlehampton Book Services
FREEPOST BR535
Worthing, West Sussex, BN13 3BR
telephone 01903 828503, *facsimile* 01903 828802
e-mail MailOrders@lbsltd.co.uk
(Please ensure that you include full postal address details)

Payment can be made either by credit/debit card (Visa, Mastercard, Access and Switch accepted) or by sending a £ Sterling cheque or postal order made payable to *Littlehampton Book Services*.
DO NOT SEND CASH OR CURRENCY.

Please add the following to cover postage and packing

UK and BFPO:
£1.50 for the first book, and 50p for each additional book to a maximum of £3.50

Overseas and Eire:
£2.50 for the first book plus £1.00 for the second book and 50p for each additional book ordered

---

BLOCK CAPITALS PLEASE

name of cardholder ....

delivery address
(if different from cardholder)

address of cardholder ....

....

....

....

postcode ....   *postcode* ....

☐ I enclose my remittance for £ ....

☐ please debit my Mastercard/Visa/Access/Switch (delete as appropriate)

card number ☐☐☐☐☐☐☐☐☐☐☐☐☐☐☐☐☐

expiry date ☐☐☐☐   Switch issue no. ☐☐

signature ....

prices and availability are subject to change without notice